I0649489

The One-Eyed King
by: Ed Greenwood

Published by Pendelhaven 2022

Copyright © 2022 Pendelhaven

Pendelhaven
121 2^{ieme} Bourbonniere
Lachute, Quebec, Canada
J8H 3W7
www.fateofthenorns.com
www.pendelhaven.com

Based on the Fate of the Norns world created by Andrew Valkauskas

Cover artwork by Yulia Novikova

Editing: Michelle Franklin

ISBN 978-1-988051-21-5

Published in Canada
Printed in the USA

SHETLAND

ORKNEY

RO

ALBA

DUNNOTTAR

ALVALD

STRATHCLYDE

IONA

OASE

ALT CLUT

AILECH

NORTHUMBRIA

HIBERNIA

JORVIK

ATH-CLIATH

THE GREAT ISLES

WESSEX

WINCHESTER

To Andrew, for the chance to play with Vikings.

To Michelle, for much laughter along the way.

And to Jenny, for a lifetime of adventures shared.

Table of Contents

Ath Cliath

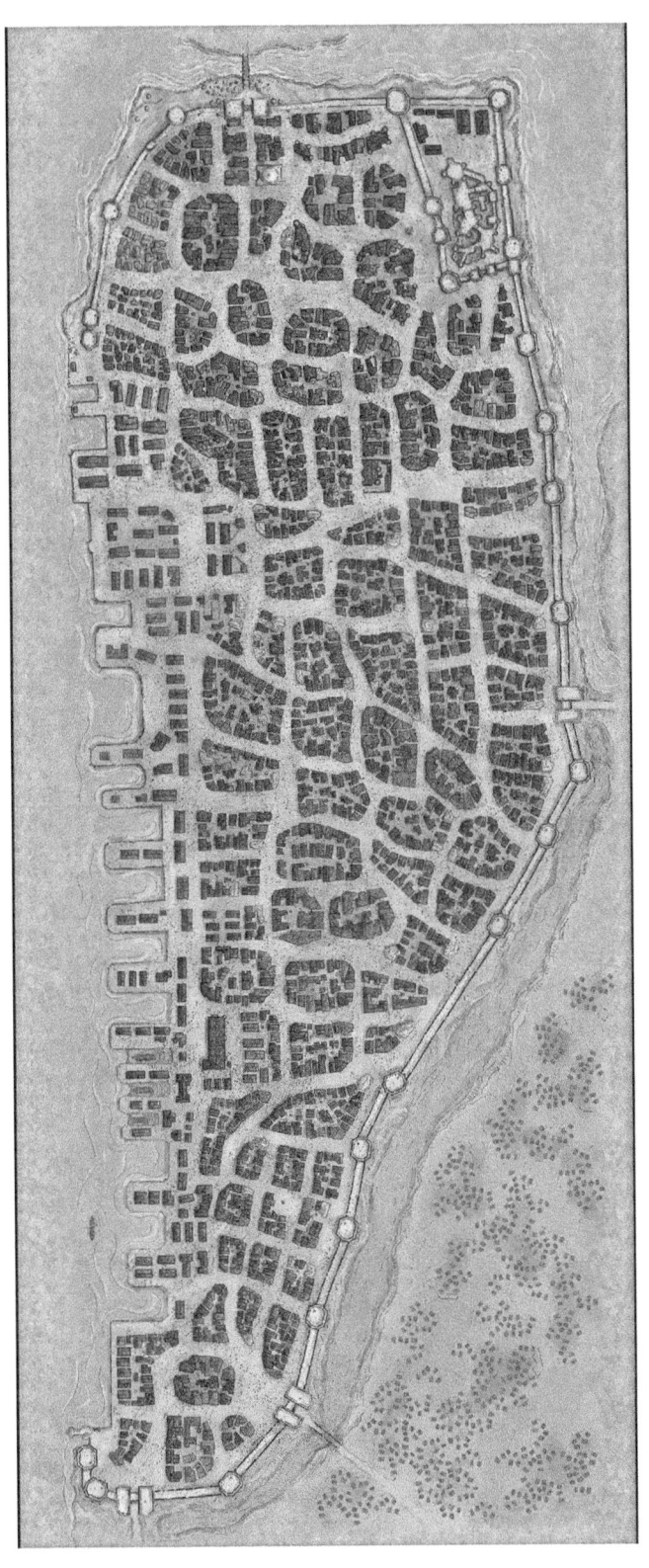

Though she knew not how. Yet.

Would anyone challenge her as she stepped ashore, asking her business in the City of Gold?

"I am come to kill the King," the bluntly honest response, would be a madwoman's utterance, to be sure, but her clan had sent her to do just that, if she could, or work his downfall in some other way, but had not been so mad or foolish as not to provide her with a more palatable tale to cloak herself in.

Oh, there were clans of fools, but the Coriondi were not one of them.

Wherefore, although Mist was but one young woman, and alone—the unexpected blade to take down the richest, most powerful, mightiest king in all the world, and utterly expendable, to boot—they'd prepared her so she could be convincing if need be.

If she felt the need to say she'd been sent to Ath Cliath by her Coriondi elders to see what sort of jewelry was selling well, to report back to the jewelers among them as to how best to sell their work. Atop her own skill and experience, the ways of a huntress, Mist Damhain was now ready—she hoped, after all the wearying peering and querying, all the instruction that had become an endless drone threatening to spill out her ears as fast as it went in—to know this gemstone from that one, all manner of jewels, both gleaming-cut and rough and dull from the deep places.

Ath Cliath was certainly *the* place for gleaming baubles, finery, and far too much coin lavished on such empty luxuries, in this cold and darkening world where food, warm furs, and good boots and sturdy-strong weapons, were what truly mattered.

Ath Cliath, now rising in all of its size and splendour before her as the ship scudded to shore. The City of Gold and Slaves, where the riches of the world were being raked in and heaped up, all a-glitter, under the rule of King Sitric.

The City of the One-Eyed King.

Thus far the favor of the Tuatha De Danann was with her: the wind was blowing from behind Mist, from the open sea, so the overwhelming feast of stenches so large a city could not help but serve up hadn't overwhelmed her. Yet.

There was the dead-fish and rotting seaweed reek that clung to all shores, yes, but thus far, as the strong seabreeze sent the *Storm Swan* up the broad mouth of the Liffey like an eager arrow, not the nose-overwhelming miasma she'd been dreading.

No doubt the stench—and the dread—would come.

#

"The time of dread is upon us all," one of the most wrinkled and dour elders had growled. "The deepening teeth of Fimbulwinter."

So it had. The sun and moon had been devoured, and the world shivered in an ever-colder gloom. Mist's clan, the Coriondi, wanted riches, and especially the necessities of life—food, furs, tools, weapons, and medicines—more widely shared in this dark time, not gathered ever more greedily in just one place by what that same grim elder had called, "This monster of a king who's lost his sanity or fallen under the influence of someone mad, and in his scrabbling for ever-more coins is throwing all the rest of us to the winter wolves."

Mist could see him snarling those words now, if she closed her eyes.

But now was not the time for looking inward at memories. Not with the din rising before her as she rushed to meet the city. The mingled roar of dockworkers shouting, hundreds upon hundreds of folk chattering, wooden wagon wheels rumbling in the cobbles, and the ringing of hammers and heavier things Mist could not see and knew were not of her ken. Yet.

Not that she wanted to tarry in this gilded cesspit, this crowded place of coins and slaves and commerce and luxuries, one moment more than she had to. Even now, the green trees and hills, clean winds and familiar growing things of Hibernia beckoned her back. Stags regarding her through the trees during a hunt, hares in their dozens leaping and running...

Mist closed her eyes and leaned against the rail to keep from staggering at the sudden, intense yearning to be back home, to turn and run from all this to the Coriondi lands she knew and loved, the fields and forests...

And then gulls shrieked, sailors called near at hand and booted feet were hurrying, thudding on the same deck her own thin, worn soles trod. The creaking of wood around her wasn't just the *Storm Swan* now, it was coming from other ships rising and falling in other rhythms, nearby. Which meant they must be close among moored ships now, and about to dock.

Mist opened her eyes again, staring around as the ship slowed, its sails coming down as the sailors scurried, some taking up long fending-poles and heading forward as the *Swan* neared a vacant stretch of dock. Men ashore, waiting to catch the lines the sailors were about to throw, were close enough now that she could see their faces...

And become aware, once again, of the gaze of someone nearer, someone whose eyes had rested on her all too often on the voyage. Mist turned, feigning a casualness she did not feel, to let her own gaze stray across him without meeting his eyes or seeming to pay him any attention.

The darkly handsome Uterni man. Of her age, and seemingly as alone in his journeying as she was. He'd been watching her, had even nodded to her gravely days back and proffered his name—Brandr Fylan—but was he just eyeing her as a woman, or for some more sinister reason? The Uterni were known to support King Sitric. Was he a spy for the One-Eyed King? Did he know her mission, and was on the *Swan* to shadow and thwart her?

Whatever the truth of that, if he did not vanish into Ath Cliath once they docked, she would watch him right back, as closely as his deeds warranted. If she was to stay alive in the richest city in the world, this sprawling den of greedy, grasping coin-thieves, let alone do anything against the King, she was going to have to guard her own back.

And that meant keeping an eye on the likes of Brandr Fylan, especially if they got behind her.

The gulls were circling overhead now, as the ship slowed to a wallow, rising and falling with the waves that lapped against wooden pilings and the docks ahead.

And Ath Cliath smote her, its noise and smells and sheer *size*. Just the doors and windows she could see, and at a glance see also that they were very far from the tallest and grandest the city had to offer, were more than she'd ever seen in all her travels in Hibernia. And the city rose up and up behind the dockside warehouses and hovels, and stretched away into the distance there, and over there, and yonder, too. Mist stared, trying not to gawk and knowing she was failing.

And a part of her noticed that the Uterni had left off staring at her to stare instead at Ath Cliath, rising up before and now around them—and that he was gawking, jaw dropped open and head turning this way and that, trying to take it all in.

And then the *Swan* fetched up against two pilings, shuddered, and yawed back a little, and everyone on deck sidestepped to keep from falling, as the endless forward rise and fall ended at last.

Ropes flew and were made fast. The *Storm Swan* groaned a little as everyone hastened to the dockside rail, a landing-plank was dropped into place with a clatter, and Mist hung back from the initial rush of impatient passengers.

Ath Cliath loomed even larger and grander overhead now, above and all around. Drifting chimney smoke, hundreds of creaking wagons and carts groaning along as many streets and alleys, oxen and people, people everywhere, more folk than Mist had ever seen in one place before. Teeming, streaming armies of them, hastening hither and thither, none of them seeming to notice the *Swan* despite her size and grace.

And why should they? Mist realized, in some bemusement, that the ship she stood on was but one of–twoscore? Threescore? More than that, to be sure, from all the masts she could see– here at the docks.

How was she even going to *find* the King, let alone get anywhere near him, in all of this? Perhaps she was a mad fool, after all.

#

So this was Ath Cliath. Crom take *all*, but it was big!

How was he going to follow the King's gold in all of *this?*

Brandr had felt uneasy since he'd first laid eyes on the beautiful, so-silent Coriondi lass–she was obviously on some stern mission, something far from the everyday, to travel alone and without wares or more than a shoulder-sack. But now, he was feeling something far closer to dismay.

The Uterni, like many of Hibernia's clans, saw King Sitric as clever and cunning, and the vital, essential leader this chilling, darkening world needed, now more than ever before. Ath Cliath was the bright fire, the bustling heart of what was good and energetic and succeeding, as the winter wolves howled and life grew harder. Though Ath Cliath had been great before, it had soared under the ruling hand of Sitric One-Eye, to become the greatest tradesmoot in all the world. The Uterni had supported Sitric all along, and supported him still, but...

Aye, that 'but' was why Brandr Fylan was standing on this deck right now, rather than biding at home. The elders and traders of the Uterni were growing increasingly suspicious of the One-Eyed King. He was awash in gold, and his city with him–and no wonder, with his taxes that doubled the cost of everything that changed hands within reach of the King's tax collectors–but where was all the money King Sitric was making going to?

What was the King of Gold and Slaves up to?

Many clans, not just the Uterni, had swallowed their resentment of a pale-skinned conqueror who knelt to Odin and not the True Gods, because Sitric's success was the one bright beacon in this ever-colder, ever-darker world...but as prices kept rising for useful things, they'd begun to wonder as to his sanity, or secret intentions, or if someone unknown had a hold over him, and Sitric was having to pay them. So a young and expendable clansman had been sent to Ath Cliath to go and look, and see, and report back. Brandr grinned wryly. It had felt like such an honour, to be tasked with this secret mission. Chosen because he was expendable. Not that they'd ever said as much.

But then, does the wolf discuss the preparation of dinner with the sheep?

Passage had to be paid when one boarded ships like the *Swan*, so passengers who could carry what they'd brought were now streaming off the ship, either knowing well where they were headed, or being met by kin or those they traded with. There were open carts heaped with furs to warm folk sitting in them, too, whose carters were hailing those aboard the *Swan*, calling out the names of the inns they were from, and the fine feasts to be had, scented baths, and more.

It all sounded far more expensive than the silver skatt riding in Brandr's boots and moneybelts would run to–though when he'd been given it, it had seemed a fortune to him–and

4

none of the hearth-havens named by the carters offering transport of "esteemed guests" and their baggage to those inns were among three inn names Brandr had been given.

He recalled the brief directions to them all, but wondered if he'd soon get lost trying to find them. Oh, everyone knew Ath Cliath glittered and gleamed and soared, but he hadn't really been ready for all of *this*...

Would he ever be? And just how long would his skatt last?

Long enough?

#

Dun's Hearth, the Fyrefalcon, and Aumaundur's. That much she remembered, but as to where to find them in this huge city...

Mist suspected that asking the way might cost skatt—and she'd been given a store that had seemed wildly large and generous, but that she now suspected might be all too little—and, worse, might be handing herself to someone who'd lead her astray and then rob her. Perhaps if she followed one of these carts to a grander inn—it should be easy, for the streets were so thronged with folk and wagons that the carts could hardly outpace her—and once there, told the inn-folk she'd arranged to meet someone at, say, Dun's Hearth, and ask *them* the way to it...

Yes. That she would do.

Inns were newly come to Hibernia, and rare; in Coriondi lands, as in other clan lands, travelers stayed with kin, or as guests in private homes, sharing tales and giving gifts to pay for the hospitality. These carters had seemed for a moment sent by the gods as timely aid, but their hailings were little different than folk at market calling wares for sale.

Mist listed more closely now to the boasts, and tried to take her measure of the men—men, all—atop their carts giving them.

One she noticed stood silent, beside a more humble conveyance behind the rest, an older man. She liked his face, and as the first of the inn-carts to depart clottered away along the busy street, Mist walked to him and asked, "You provide passage to an inn?"

That earned her a nod and a smile.

"Hallvardr Thorolfsson am I," he said, "and I work for Dun's Hearth, a warm, safe house for those who crave good food and simple hospitality." He seemed to see something in her gaze, and added dryly, "an inn that caters to those who want to save their coins—and to avoid being seen in the brightest company in Ath Cliath."

Dun's Hearth!

"Then I will ride with you, Hallvardr," she replied. "This sack is all I bring."

The carter's smiled widened, and then his eyes looked past Mist's shoulder. "You, too, traveler?"

Mist knew even before she turned who the carter was speaking to, and what his answer would be. It seemed she'd go nowhere in Ath Cliath without Brandr Fylan.

Just whose hound was he?

#

From where he stood, in the shadows of an unlit room looking down on Hallvardr Thorolfsson's cart as it rumbled away over the cobbles, the man with the crooked smile could not hear what was said by the carter to the two slender-luck traders and the two young Hibernians he was taking to Dun's Hearth. Which was why Ake was down there in the street, standing hard by, re-snugging the nearest mooring-lines of the Swan.

5

The carter who was *not* Hallvardr Thorolfsson, yet looked very like him. Interesting.

The smallest of sounds came from the gloom behind him, and the man by the window spun around out of habit—for those who did not fall into the habit of facing those who came stealing up silently were soon too dead to form any habits.

"Mael," a familiar voice murmured, its owner having seen the reaction and deciding prudence would be wise, "it's me."

Mael nodded. The man gliding up to him was missing an ear, which meant it was Runi, whose report he'd been expecting. The only man who knew he was here.

Not that Mael relaxed, or resheathed his dagger.

"The real Hallvardr is enjoying the company of Gloa the Golden, at the Butterhearth," Runi added, in the same almost-whisper.

Mael gave him the full nod of dismissal, and watched him go ere turning back to see the cart turning up a side-street.

He smiled his crooked smile. That was the only sort of smile Mael the Sharp could make, these last six years, thanks to a sword scar that began at the right-hand edge of his mouth and curved up to under his right ear. A keepsake of a fight in which he'd been *just* fast enough.

"Well, well," he said aloud, savoring rising excitement. So much of his service to Sitric Cuaran was distastefully *necessary*, and no more, but this was a mystery to be delved into.

Who was impersonating Hallvardr—obviously with Hallvardr's connivance—and why?

And another thing: a second ship with passengers aboard was nearing its moorings, and the false Hallvardr hadn't waited for it. So it was the four sitting in that cart who must be watched. And Hallvardr, the real and the false, too.

This was what he lived for, the deceptions, the mysteries, the misdirection, the subtle guidings.

And—he hefted his dagger—the not so subtle.

Dark some deeds were, to be sure, but they were the King's will.

And though any king is wise to trust no one at all, Mael intended to be trustworthy. He had no intention of ever betraying Sitric, for the King was doing Odin's work.

And the All-Father was paving the only path that led on through Ragnarok to survival, in this darkening world.

chapter 2

Ath Cliath never slept, but in these darkest night hours, the streets were nigh-empty, most windows shuttered and dark. More than a few of those shutters reverberated to snorings from within.

So it was to their deep rough accompaniment that Hallvardr Thorolfsson stole up to a certain well-greased window at the back of Dun's Hearth. The one farthest from the kitchen doors.

He did not even have to tap on it, for the man who'd impersonated him while he was in Gloa's arms had been watching for him.

The window swung wide. No sooner had his boots touched the floor within than the false Hallvardr handed him his keys, patted his shoulder, and was gone into the night without a word.

Leaving a weary but happy Hallvardr Thorolfsson to close and bar the window, yawn mightily, and make for his bed.

The man who was not Hallvardr Thorolfsson could walk the night as quietly as any cat. He was doing that now, a stealthy dark shadow in the night-gloom. Along this dark alley, then down that one. Clouds had shrouded the moon, so the night was, as the saying went, "a black pit."

Yet that did not seem to slow the impersonator's sure progress.

Nor that of the one-eared man following him.

So silent and deft was that pursuit that the man who was not Hallvardr Thorolfsson knew not that he was being followed, though he stopped to watch and listen a time or two, in good places to look back.

Such precautions merely made his shadower sneer. Runi was among the best at what he did, and taking great care his quarry wouldn't mark him. So his quarry did not.

The impersonator's route led along alleyways ever narrower and darker, and it was in one of these, the lightless shield-width way known as Ylfa's Tongue, that he passed safely, but Runi, creeping close behind him so as to be sure which way the quarry turned at the end of the Tongue, met with misfortune.

A black-cord slip-noose dropped from above as gently as a held breath, settled on the one-eared man's shoulders—and jerked tight and upright, snatching a startled and then frantic and kicking Runi with it.

Struggles that grew wild as he fought vainly to escape the strangle-cord digging deep into his throat...and then faltered in a few final spasms, and fell limp, to hang, swaying slightly, in the lofty darkness.

The gloved hands that had wielded that rope tied it off around a chimney. Hanged men keep.

\#

The false Hallvardr continued, surefooted in the darkness. To stop before a door that bore a distinctive rune, untidily scratched down at boot level where an untutored eye might mistake it for the wear-scars of daily misadventure. He couldn't see it in the darkness, but didn't have to. Nor did he knock.

Just one dirty back door among many, amid the untidy backs of this particular row of lowly backstreets buildings, but the right one.

The man who was not Hallvardr Thorolfsson found the unobtrusive hole in the door alongside the frame with his fingertip, drew his belt-knife and thrust it firmly through the gap. Its tip rang some tiny, high-pitched chimes hanging within.

Almost before he could resheathe his blade an eye-panel high in the door slid open so someone could look out and down at him. Yet no eye he could see appeared, and all stayed dark.

Nevertheless, he said a single soft word.

Whereupon the door opened soundlessly, he slipped inside, and the door closed again. Someone saw.

For someone was watching that door, from a high window not far away. Someone who smiled a crooked smile.

#

The man who was not Hallvardr Thorolfsson followed the silent woman who'd let him in, down dank, worn stone steps into a damp and dripping well-cellar. And through three successive heavy, dark hanging curtains he could barely see by the glow of her shuttered hand-lamp, into a room not much brighter, lit by a candle-end fast sinking behind its scorch-shield.

"Silver?" The voice from the bed was barely more than a whisper.

It did not take the experience of tending many dying to know that this was a deathbed. The old man lying huddled under the furs did not have much time left to him, ere he greeted God at last.

"It's me, Alden," he said, hastening forward. And stopped himself from adding, *I've come in time.*

"Good," said his sick fellow priest. "Belike I'll be gone by morning."

And that would be one more Devout of the White God gathered to the God.

At least this one, sore though his loss would be, hadn't just gone missing. As so many priests of the White God did, in Ath Cliath.

Oswin nodded his thanks to Hrist as she set a stool for him hard by the bed. She nodded back, and retreated to another stool down the room. She was no talker; words escaped her as grudgingly as a miser parted with coins. He sat, leaned close to Alden's failing, rattling breath, and murmured urgently, "So tell me of the missing, Holy Brother. *Our* missing."

This is what he was here to learn. So many priests of the White God had gone missing in Ath Cliath since the coming of Sitric One-Eyed to the throne that he, warrior-priest Oswin Silverlock, had been sent here by his superior to look into their fates. Not that there was much doubt whose hand and will lay behind the disappearances.

The King, who embraced the worship of Odin so fervently that he'd plucked out his own eye in reverence to the one-eyed god, wanted no part of any rise in the faith of the White God in his city. Not that there'd been denunciations, trials, or public executions. Just...priests no longer seen, and the ever-deepening silence.

Most likely the King kept his own hands clean, but suffered others to do dark-work for him. Hardly the first ruler to act so.

Wherefore Oswin Silverlock had come to Ath Cliath not openly as a priest, but as a debt-collector, and had tracked down Hallvardr Thorolfsson, a man of the city who happened to look very like Oswin, and who owed Oswin a favour for past healing.

So it was a return favor Oswin collected, not coin owing. And that favour was the chance to briefly impersonate Hallvardr. Just long enough to ensure two young innocents, on different missions bent but who could both serve to occupy the attention of the One-Eyed King, came safely to lodgings so they could begin their work.

8

Skulking about like a spy sat uneasily with Oswin. He fully intended to reveal his true name, and openly advocate for the White God, once he knew the true situation in the city—if that was the best way to advance the holy cause in this place.

He knew dying Alden here shared his belief that the coming of Fimbulwinter was a sign that all the gods these folk had long worshipped—the Aesir for Sitric and his Vikings, and the Tuatha Dé Danann for the Hibernians whose city this had been until the longships had come sailing up the Liffey one blood-drenched day—had failed them.

If humans everywhere were to survive at all, they *must* turn to the White God, the True God, or at least embrace some of his creed and ways.

Everywhere he went, Oswin tried to turn as many folk as he can to the worship of the White God. He would try here, too. Not if he dared, for he *would* dare.

But find the best way to stay alive and go on doing so, first...

Alden Morgade had lived in Ath Cliath more than sixty summers, and if any man knew the city—outside of Sitric's Court, and all this new glitter-gleam of the last few years—it would be Alden.

"You know most of the names."

"I do. And the likely fates that go with them. But I'd know all that you've learned of the latter. Who's killing our brethren?"

"It's the King's will and command that we die, but he sends his men to slay—a sly, silent one, Mael the Sharp, is his pet serpent—or to take."

"Take?"

"Chained, and sold as choice slaves, in secret auctions."

"So they're slaves here in the city?"

"No. Shipped afar, to wherever their masters need them to toil—and in those various somewheres, worked to death as slaves."

"So if he hates us so, why the secrecy? Why not burnings and public denunciations?"

"Sitric wants no open strife with we of the White God. Strife is bad for trade. Yet he detests the very notion of a challenge to Odin and what he sees as the true gods. The Aesir. So we must die. And oh, it is glorious..."

"Alden?"

"The light! So golden..."

Hrist rose and darted forward, then abruptly stopped, becoming a swaying, intent pillar. Listening and watching Alden, one hand outstretched.

The old priest did not see her. He lifted a feeble hand towards a dark and empty corner of the room. And smiled at something there that Oswin could not see. "Ah, now, I had not thought to see that..."

Oswin quelled the questions rising to his lips.

Alden was sinking fast, and beginning to ramble. His smile broadened as he beheld something else. "Wonderful," he whispered, shaking his head slightly in admiration. "Just... wonderful."

Oswin looked at Hrist, and she looked back at him in silent sadness.

He looked again at Alden, a part of him wanting *so much* to know more about what the old man was seeing. And the rest of him knowing Alden was leaving this world behind, and it would be best if he departed, and let the White God's most steadfast servant in Ath Cliath pass on in peace.

His eyes met those of Hrist once more, and he saw that she emphatically agreed. Without saying a word at all.

It was cold and dark in the alley, and even darker in the alley around the corner ahead. Mael the Sharp snapped out orders harsh and cold, and men hurried. Streaming past him and around the corner, laden with hand-kegs of oil, bulging sacks of dry kindling, and hot hooded night-lanterns.

Mael strode after them, and right behind him came someone cloaked and hooded, whom Mael did not give orders to.

#

The ceiling had a painted-over crack that meandered like an old river, right across it from wall to wall, branching twice. Small wonder; this was an old inn, and old buildings settle.

Brandr lay on his back in bed gazing up at its wanderings by the light of the candle-lamp he really should have blown out, but somehow couldn't bring himself to do so.

The bed that was more comfortable than he'd dared hope it would be, and smelled better, too, thanks to the cedar and rosemary mixed into its straw. And the room around it was well-worn and rather plain, but he liked it. Which was good, considering he could *not* sleep, no matter how hard he tried.

His eyes followed the meandering river across the ceiling one more time.

For his entire journey here, he'd been wondering how he would ever get close enough to the King to learn anything meaningful to report back to the elders. And now that he'd had his first, brief taste of what life is like Ath Cliath, the fears he'd been pushing back had flooded to the fore. His task was going to be *very* hard.

Even someone far less alert and sharp-witted than he liked to think he was should have noticed that spies were everywhere in this city. But who were they spying for?

Even in the streets between the docks and here, he'd been able to feel it. Under the bustle of trade and work, the gleam and glitter, the noise and the crowding...the *tension*.

This city was a cauldron of tension.

Tension that seemed to be building. Folk were waiting for something, and impatiently; so much had been clear, in the talk in the Hearth common room. Matters here were building to something, something that would come soon—but what?

He knew that much, yet in truth he knew almost nothing about Ath Cliath other than it was big, and crowded, and a place of wealth and striving. And where there was coin to be made, and ambition, there was always danger.

So, would Brandr Fylan have time to learn enough just to stay alive in Ath Cliath, before whatever this city around him was rushing towards happened?

#

Mael truly trusted no one at all, but among the men who did the King's darker biddings, under Mael, Stigr and Ulfr could at least be trusted enough to do things competently.

Hook-nosed, heavily scarred Stigr, with his beard of untidy red tufts, could be recognized from afar. Right now, he was where Mael expected him to be, folded into a dark corner of the alley, intently watching, as ordered. Never taking his eyes off the door with the rune scratched on it, even as the first flames licked up from the oil-soaked kindling that had been spread all over the roof, and those who'd swarmed all over the roof laying it, and then lit it, came hastily down.

An owl hooted, improbably, from the other side of the building; Ulfr's signal that no one had yet come out of its front door.

"No one," Stigr muttered in confirmation, as Mael came up to him—and the flames caught everywhere, all at once, rushing up to claw at the stars with a roar.

Sudden heat and light split the darkness, and in it they stood alone, Mael and Stigr and the cloaked and hooded figure. All the rest of the fire-layers were now at their posts, waiting on roofs and around nearby dark alley corners with poisoned spears, ready to hurl at anyone who burst out of the flames.

It was searingly bright now, and the roar was almost deafening, the heat so intense that Mael took a step back.

And another. A shutter cracked in the heat—a shutter on the building next door. Walls everywhere were steaming as long-resident damp was driven out of them, like so many hurrying gray ghosts.

The heat baked Mael's face. He took another step back, and saw Stigr moving, too. The inferno was driving them out of the alley.

Mael smiled his crooked smile. No one was getting out.

He cast a quick glance back over his shoulder to make sure he didn't step into the hooded man with him. And to give warning, if one were needed, that the fire they'd set would soon spread to other buildings, and hand them all a *real* problem.

The hooded man wasn't hesitating, just checking that the stealthy movement he'd just heard from behind him wasn't some foe.

But there was no mistaking that toad-face. It was Ulfr, and the Toad was shaking his head. No one had escaped the front way.

No one would.

The cloaked and hooded figure took a stride to one side, away from them all, raised his right arm, and spoke. Deep and firm, words that sounded like nonsense to Mael. Grand, powerful nonsense. His outstretched fingers drew a rune in the air, that glowed and hung in the night for a long moment ere it flashed—a burst of amber, twisting into emerald green—ere it faded and fell away into nothing.

And at the same moment the galdr's rune flashed, the roaring flames were gone, snuffed out, bringing back the night in an instant.

Blackened timbers creaked, up and down the alley. And Mael gazed at the blackened husk of what had been a building, a very short time ago.

Smoke drifted past, in no particular hurry to be elsewhere.

Mael looked to the galdr, who seemed satisfied with his work. He stood smiling for a long moment, nodding slightly ere he reached up to rearrange his hood, and conceal his face once more. Mael caught a glimpse of a familiar long nose, and an eyepatch. The black one, of course, preferred for runecasting over the showy copper one seen when its wearer sat enthroned.

The hood was back in place now, the face hidden in the dark cowl.

As with a sudden groan that was more like a dying sigh than a complaint, the burnt priest's hovel collapsed into ashen rubble.

CHAPTER 3

Mist came awake blinking. The light was blinding bright.

Straight up and down it shone, like a sword blade catching the sun.

It was the sun.

Coming through a gap in battered old shutters. Unfamiliar shutters; where—? Dun's Hearth. She was in that inn. And outside, rumbling carriage wheels, scores of people talking, some shouting or calling, many clangs...Ath Cliath.

The morning sun was lancing in through the gap to fall full on her face.

Mist sat up. She was alone in her tiny rented room, abed, and the sleeping-furs and blanket beneath were all disarranged as if she'd been thrashing.

Her dreams . . . she remembered nothing.

She'd slept in, and she *never* did that. And the din of bustling Ath Cliath was loud around her; how could she...

By Crom, Morrigan, and Donn, she *must* have been tired!

Her boots were still against the inside of the door where she'd left them, and the bolt still across, so no one had been in while she slept.

At least, not that way...

No. Not by *that* window, not unless they could fly—and open and close window latches soundlessly, from the wrong side. And this room was just too *small* for there to be room for secret ways in. So, no to those dark and fanciful suspicions.

She went to the ewer and basin, bathed hastily, dressed—none of her skatt were missing, another good sign—and left her little closet of a room for the stairs down to the main hearth room.

The warm, welcome smell of boarfry grew stronger with every step along the narrow, meandering hall, and her stomach rumbled loudly before she reached the stair-head.

So beyond a good meal, where to begin, when one has come to the richest city in the world to kill its king?

She'd been given the names of some kinswomen dwelling in Ath Cliath; it would be best to begin by visiting them, for if anyone was watching her, that would seem usual behaviour. And her kin could then, as she was sure they'd been charged to do, report back to her clan that she'd reached the city safely.

If she asked delicately, perhaps they could tell her who to trust in this city if she must run to someone for aid or shelter. Or get medicines, explanations for anything she overheard in the streets, good places to dine or stay if she had to leave the Hearth, and...so on.

More than that, she needed to take her measure of them, decide if she could trust these kin she'd never met, so far as she could recall, before she found herself desperate and running to them. It would be too late to save her neck if she learned then that they were weak reeds, or valued coin and ambition here in Ath Cliath over clan.

Again she wondered why the Coriondi would entrust such a mission to a young and untried huntress, and again thrust away the answer hurriedly. Because she was utterly expendable, and so unlikely a kingslayer that they could deny everything, dismiss her as a madwoman...

No, she would *not* think about that. That way lay dark despair.

So, now, she was here in Ath Cliath at the behest of Aurnia and Síomha and the other elder jewelers of the clan to see what sort of jewelry was selling well—what stones and designs are the most popular—and where. In this haughty, gilded center of wealth and opulence, which shops were the most popular? The most exclusive? In other words, if Coriondi pieces were sent to Ath

Cliath for sale, what would their style have to be to claim top coin? And what city sellers should they be placed with?

If she judged none of them suitable, she'd been instructed to establish herself as a seller, and become her clan's shopfront in the city...and if that was to be her road, she knew enough of the world to know she'd truly need her kin to tell her the unwritten rules and customs, or it would be a road to swift disaster.

Oh, she could mount stones if she had to, and had cut gems of lesser value, but her experience was modest, thus far, that of an assistant. She'd mastered polishing, all right, more than a year of seemingly endless buffing and powdering, and these last few months had helped master jewelers with treatments to alter the hues of stone and of fine metal mountings, too. So she could alter jewelry, do minor repairs, set stones, and act the part of a jeweler. Given her age, no one would expect her to be a master, for veteran jewelers were old and hunched and given to squinting. And she hoped she was none of those things just yet...

The boarfry was good, better than she'd expected, goose eggs enlivened with unfamiliar spices that she liked a lot, and Mist found her heart lifting.

She was excited to be here. Oh, the danger she was in—the perils of Ath Cliath—were foremost in her mind, and seemed insistent to come flooding back there no matter how firmly she sought to push them away, but she was actually *in* the fabled City of Gold, the richest city in the world, this splendid big center of riches and striving. No longer just a name, a legendary, far-off place talked about that she'd never see, she was *here*. It was all around her.

And it was crowded, and noisy, and it stank, but it was alive. With hundreds—thousands—of people, all busy and rushing, all energy and ideas and new ventures. And for all he was feared, its One-Eyed King seemed to encourage it all, not just ride it to ever-more wealth...for if he did not, surely he'd have stamped it out ere now, seized what those who made the most coin owned and hurled them into slavery, or strangled the flood of wealth with too-heavy taxes, driving those who did and earned elsewhere.

There was a saying about the King of Ath Cliath that she'd heard twice or thrice back home, long before she knew she was coming here. One of the skalds had called it "a small new prophecy," so she'd taken care to fix its words in her mind, to guide her, in hopes that before she died she'd see it come true, and know the Gods were with us all.

And that saying ran thus: "When the voice of the One-Eyed King is heard in the house of the hanged man, life will finally take a change for the brighter."

So if she did manage to kill this same King, will she bring all of this wealth and splendor and bustling achievement crashing down?

#

The chamber, deep in Riverfleet Palace, was small and dark, and the ways to it either secret or guarded by locked door after locked door; few of the servants even knew where it was. The last door was narrow and one of a long row of rooms where ledgers and old rolls were stored.

Right now, the small room was lit only by a tankard-lantern, such as warriors were wont to use: a single candle set into a metal drinking-cup. Its flickering light gleamed back at Mael off the King's copper eyepatch as they sat, leaning close over the lone table, the only two occupants of the room.

Mael's murmured report was almost done. "The fire," he added, "spread through a common wall before it was quenched, so much smoke entered the next home, adjoining to the north. A carter's family. All suffocated, we think in their sleep."

The King shrugged. "Regrettable losses."

Mael echoed the words and the shrug.

"And the lives we sought?"

Mael quelled a sigh. "The bones of one man were found in the building that burned."

The King frowned.

"We dug thoroughly," Mael added quickly.

"And?"

"No one else."

The King's frown deepened. "I had not thought," he said calmly, "that those of the White God had magic that powerful."

Mael shrugged again.

"We must be careful," the King added sharply, "and waste no time in eliminating those we can catch asleep or taken with drink."

"As for taking care," Mael responded, "we've intercepted and slain no less than six men hired to end your life in as many days. They're getting more numerous. And fast."

The King's face was as placid as that of a stone statue. "To rule is to be unloved."

Mael nodded. "Yet to be so often targeted by slayers-for-hire means someone—or several someones—are hiring. And kingslayers seldom escape alive, so the price is high. Much gold. The sort of gold-count made and held, these days, only here."

The King nodded unconcernedly. "Some who were wealthy in Ath Cliath before my coming want me gone, and are prepared to do something about it."

Mael nodded.

The King reached for a decanter. "Shatter the blades they send, trace them, and tell me who they are. Slay only those you must; leave retribution to me. Pieces removed from any game board are pieces I can no longer make use of."

"Understood," Mael replied. "There is another thing, a small thing, but you should know. Runi has gone missing."

"One-Ear?"

"The same."

"Turned traitor? Or did someone catch up with him and settle a personal score?"

"The latter, I believe. But we can't afford to assume."

"We can never afford to assume," the King agreed softly.

There had been so many attempts on the life of Sitric Cuaran since he'd seized the throne that the populace had long ago been firmly kept away from him. Citizens had very few opportunities to meet the King face to face, or even speak with him through screens or walls of guards.

These days, royal decrees were announced by the stout and mellifluous Volundr the Voice. Seldom to be seen without cheeses in hand, or a flask of wine surreptitiously vanishing back into a sleeve-sheath. Palace servants told jests about his girth, his pomposity, and the girdles he wore to rein in the floor-ward droop of his belly, but the Voice of the Riverfleet Throne was a capable enough envoy. Who was kept busy lurching between the King and various city guildmasters and Ath Cliath's self-styled "lords," the richest and most powerful merchants.

The King poured for himself. "Anything more?"

It was a clear dismissal.

"No," Mael replied quickly, rising and bowing low. He'd backed only one step towards the door when a tiny chime sounded.

He whirled, one of his blades rising as if by magic into his hand.

The door opened, and from behind it a familiar voice said, "Ronan. Leave to speak. The Rule."

14

Mael drew a second blade as he glided to one side. Ronan stepped around the door and spread empty hands to show he had no weapon ready.

'The Rule' meant something unlawful had occurred—something important and urgent—that the Riverfleet Throne had to know about without delay.

"Speak," the King commanded.

"More than a dozen slaves have died, just before they could be sold at market; someone slipped poison into their drinking-water they were given to drink. So, the Rule..."

Sitric nodded thoughtfully, then dismissed Ronan with a second curt nod.

When he and Mael were alone again, he said, "Leave hunting those who escaped our fire for the moment; trace this poisoner first."

"Of course. No poisons and no poisoning in Ath Cliath except yours, O King. The Rule stands."

"The Rule stands."

#

"God," Hrist gasped, breaking her silence at last, "make me welcome!"

And her head lolled onto Oswin's shoulder, as her last breath rattled out in a long, fading groan.

Oswin held her body upright, to keep her out of the reeking water for long enough to say a last prayer over her.

They'd both known this was coming. Hrist had tarried too long with Alden, not wanting to leave the old priest's side until the God claimed him, despite the fire raging around the very room, embers falling on her head.

She'd been badly burned, even before the floor above had collapsed on her, and Oswin had dragged her desperately out from beneath what would have been her pyre, down into the undercellar of Alden's home.

Which was a wet shared cesspit that underlay three adjoining hovels, and was only partly cleansed by the sea-tides.

Through its filth—Oswin had gagged and spewed from the stench—they'd slogged to the far end of the cess, two buildings away from Alden's pyre, and there stood armpit-deep, shivering in the stink all night.

Oswin said the best prayer he knew, though the disfigured Hrist was past hearing.

In this world, at least.

His prayer done, Oswin grimly let her body sink under the waters of the cesspool.

"Farewell, Hrist," he said softly. "May the God keep you." Then he headed up out of the cesspool by the worn and narrow steps that led into the house above, trying to move quietly so he'd be able to slip out of it without alarming its inhabitants much. Though they'd smell him well enough.

He very much wanted a drink.

#

The best thing about Brandr's cold and drafty room in the Hearth was its balcony. Old and rotting and large enough for two people only if they were on intimate terms, and with a pronounced lean that warned the sane that if two people were going to share the balcony, it would be prudent if they weighed no more than a small child, each, it nevertheless offered both a good view of the inn's front door and the street, and a narrow and rickety outside stair.

He was hunched low on the balcony right now, much to the annoyance of the pigeons who considered it theirs alone, but they'd been annoyed for long enough to cease flapping and wheeling, and find other perches nearby to glare at him from.

The pigeons favoured this balcony and one other because they were the only two balconies shaded by the inn's overhanging thatch, keeping casual drizzle at bay and cloaking anyone on the balconies in gloom where they might pass unnoticed if they kept quiet and still.

Brandr was keeping quiet and still right now, as he watched Mist Damhain depart Dun's Hearth. He smiled wryly as he saw her cautiously peer all around for any signs of a certain person, before hesitantly walking away to join the throngs of the folk hastening here and there along the street.

That certain person is ME.

He was still smiling at that as he turned to go down the outside stair—and someone caught his eye, a stranger. A man, perhaps a laborer or shopkeeper, who'd left off lounging against a wall across the street to sidle purposefully after Mist.

Was he following her? Or just heading in the same direction?

He watched them both, and saw that when Mist crossed to the other side of the street to peer at something in a shop window, the striding stranger threaded between others to cross to where he could get a clear view of what she did.

He was following her.

Brandr dogged the door of his room shut, not that he'd left anything of value there, and started down the steps, sweeping the street with a last long look ere he lost the view afforded by the height of the balcony—and to his shock, momentarily met the eyes of someone else. Ere the man deliberately looked away and took a few steps along the street.

Another man, another stranger. Who had been intently watching Brandr Fylan.

And who'd swung around again, oh-so-casually, now that he was a few paces away and unhurriedly strolling.

He was about to lose sight of Mist—who'd quickened her pace, and was now obviously heading purposefully for some definite destination—around a corner. And the man following her was close behind her, and closing in.

Cursing, Brandr hurried down the balcony stair.

Who was watching him? Why?

And what should he—could he—nay, dared he—do about it?

chapter 4

Ever since the Palace stables had been expanded, this formerly busy passage had been a gloomy backwater, turned into a dead-end opening only into seldom-used storerooms. Its newfound scant usage was a good thing, for the servants who did make use of those chambers would have been startled indeed to learn the hard way how many hardened men with daggers in their hands had keys to their locks, and were wont to hasten quietly through them at all hours.

Two of those men had traversed separate storerooms, to now step out of adjacent doors in nigh-perfect unison.

One had a hooked nose, and a beard of untidy red tufts thanks to the many scars that crossed his face. The other was the man he reported to.

"Well?" Mael asked.

"The priest survived our burning," Stigr growled. "He's two wine-cups heavier in Hrolf's Goblet right now. Shall I silence him? Or have him taken for the slave markets?"

"No," Mael replied softly. "The King has other plans for him. Watch him as closely as you would anyone come to slay the King, and report to me often, but kill him not. That is a royal command."

Stigr nodded, and at Mael's waved hand-sign of dismissal, hastened off down the passage.

Whereupon the door Stigr had arrived through opened again in well-oiled silence, and Ronan stepped out of its darkness.

Mael jerked his head in the direction of the distant and dwindling Stigr. "Watch him, and report back to me. Be seen not. By him or anyone."

"You trust him not."

"I trust no one. Trust is foolishness that twists like a knife in the hands of even doting mothers. Trust is for fools."

Ronan nodded. "And we are not fools." He went.

Mael stood alone in the gloom, watching him go. And after a long moment said bitterly, "From time to time."

#

So this was Aunt Teagan's shop. The innkeeper's directions had been clear, easy to follow, and right.

Mist dared not step back far to enough to get a good overview, so busy was the street traffic—wagons and coaches, not just not carts and people afoot, and all of it hurrying, though she'd seen a dozen-some times how good the folk of Ath Cliath were at dodging to avoid collisions and disputes—so she found a wagon that was being unloaded, close by the shopfronts this side of the street, stood in its lee, and gazed as best she could, sidelong and up close.

White marble pillars with beautiful gilding spiraling up them, to a gleaming arch, deep blue and golden, and within, all warm bright lights and mirrors and sculpted white shoulders displaying furs, furs, and more furs. The dressed pelts of all beasts, an array of hues, more furs than Mist had ever seen in one place in her life before, and all of them splendid garments.

She did not remember Aunt Teagan; if they'd ever seen each other, Mist must have been a babe in arms. But 'Teagan' was a name always spoken fondly among the Coriondi; it belonged to someone bright and pleasant and good-looking, that the men all admired, and the women deemed a success.

She'd been told Teagan made and sold expensive, great-looking luxury 'fur in, fur out' tailored fashionable tunics for men, and gowns for women with fur-turned-to-the-skin inner linings and 'show fur' outer surfaces, for keeping wearers warm while allowing ease of movement. The sort of garments clan chiefs and their immediate families, and the wealthiest of clan elders, wore in upland Hibernia. And no one else could afford.

So of course Ath Cliath was the right place for such an establishment. The City of Gold, where folk could afford what no one else could afford. On the way here, Mist had passed shopfronts a-gleam with golden dishes and bowls, and all manner of eye-catching, splendid things that likely cost more than a Coriondi crofter would make in a year. Each. Not to mention tarts, whose very smell made her mouth water, and told of spices from far, warm lands: saffron and nard.

Mist's mouth welled at the mere memory, though the scent of those tarts was two streets behind her now. She drew a deep breath, squared her shoulders, and went in.

The shop smelled of rose petals and something else floral and faint and as pleasant, something unfamiliar to Mist and presumably from some part of the world distant from Hibernia. "The best from exotic everywhere," as a shopfront she'd passed on the way here had proclaimed. And that was what Ath Cliath was all about, wasn't it?

The bright hopes and wares of all the world, brought together.

For those who could afford it.

Those few.

And on the backs of slaves, too. She'd not passed a slave market yet, but—

Her attention was caught by a strikingly beautiful face. It caught and held the eye, that dark beauty. The face belonged to perhaps the most beautiful woman Mist had ever seen, someone who carried herself tall, as proud and sure of herself as any clan elder, as she strode nearer. Coming out of the shop, clad in tall glossy boots—and how did one make boots *shine* so, and keep them like that?—and a gown that gleamed and glittered all over—were those pearls sewn to it? *Hundreds* of them—and a splendid fur shoulder-cloak, which must have been what she'd just bought. Two stern-faced bodyguards strode before and behind her, giving Mist polite 'give way *now*' looks that she suspected would have been far fiercer had she been a man, or obviously armed, or more shabbily clad.

"Fare you well, Lassairfhina! *Enjoy* the vargr-fur!" called a voice after her, from the depths of the shop—a high, warmly pleasant, liltingly musical voice that sounded to Mist like voices from home. Teagan?

Lassairfhina lifted one elegant hand in an airy, haughty wave of acknowledgement rather than turning or speaking, and swept out into the streets, sparing Mist not a glance.

Mist smiled inwardly, recalling haughty Coriondi women who were far more homely and older and likely poorer than this woman of Ath Cliath, but obviously supped from the same proud well, to paraphrase a line the skalds sang. Folk were folk the world over, it seemed...

Or were they?

Just what she saw on her brief walk through the sleek white wooden mannequins in their furs had likely cost more to make than her entire *clan* could muster by way of ready coin, and that said nothing about how much it would cost the likes of Lassairfhina to buy it, what with merchants in Ath Cliath having to make a living and wanting to make rather more than that, and on top of it all the King's taxes, that doubled—*doubled!*—every price. No clan chief of Hibernia would ever tax so heavily and expect to keep his head...but then, no clan chief would be mad enough to think his clansfolk could pay such taxes even if they wanted to.

Doubled, the price of everything in this glittering city...she could still scarce believe it.

"And how can I help you?" asked a smiling woman whose voice held warmth and kindness, but none of the Coriondi lilt Mist had heard in the farewell call. She was dressed in the most stylish tunic Mist had ever seen—and the only one Mist had ever beheld that was light indoor wear, frankly revealing, and yet at the same time trimmed with fur—and she was *almost* as beautiful as haughty Lassairfhina.

Mist was conscious of feeling like a travel-worn lackpurse from the rural uplands, though all three of the women clustered around the shop's counter—and by Crom if it wasn't a single sheet of dimpled beaten copper, as gleaming and pink-amber as could be!—were giving her smiles that seemed genuinely friendly. But then, how good at feigning did folk in this city have to daily be?

That one was likely Aunt Teagan, but she couldn't be sure...

"I am Mist Damhain," she replied, mustering an answering smile and trying not to sound timid. "I am newly come to Ath Cliath, and seek my kinswoman, Teagan Damhain."

"That," said the oldest, tallest, and to Mist's eye most beautiful of the three, "would be me. Be welcome!"

Mist's heart soared. Her guess had been right. And her aunt seemed delighted to see her.

For Teagan was sailing around from behind the counter with her arms open to embrace Mist. Who fell into them with a surge of emotion that surprised herself, hugging tight and having to fight down suddenly-threatening tears.

In this so-splendid but so *different* city, it felt good to feel at home.

#

Brandr hurried along, wondering if he could lose the man tailing him by sheer speed, but somehow doubting it. And pondering his chances at being deft enough to outpace Mist and *her* shadow, and get ahead of them, without the Damhain huntress noticing him. The sheer haste needed to do that wouldn't catch her eye, for he'd passed and seen youths beyond counting dodging and running amid the throngs of folk walking, not so much playing as rushing about on errands they'd likely been hired to undertake—but his looks would. Being as she was suspicious of him already. And if he got ahead of her, he'd need to keep looking back, or he'd miss when she turned aside or went into some shop or other, and that meant putting his face where she could see it, again and again.

By Crom and Morrigan both, there was more to this shadowing folk than the tavern-tales said, to be sure.

#

"Come in here, where we can talk."

Teagan was leading the way, through two rooms behind the counter into a dimly-lit lounge where she waved Mist to a seat and took another that faced it, close across a low table. From which she caught up two tiny cups and a decanter, poured, handed Mist one, and clinked hers against it, all so smoothly and swiftly that Mist barely had time to catch a breath ere her aunt was asking her about this family member, and that one, and how were the apples this year.

"Fresh from the trees," Teagan added wistfully. "*That's* a taste I can't get here—and can't forget."

"You miss...home? A lot?"

Teagan smiled, and shrugged. "More and more, it seems a dream. The past, that I can never return to, for if I went there now, it would be...changed. *This* is home now, for all its stenches and crowding and unlovely naked ambitions and endless clawing striving." A twinkle rose into her eye. "That you're joining...eagerly?"

"Er, no. Too many worries, too much I know not, and so walk unsure. I'm excited, yes; that's why I agreed."

"To?"

"To come here on behalf of the Coriondi jewelers. The elders asked me to come and see how things stood in Ath Cliath for gems and jewelry. What's selling, and who's selling it."

"Most popular stones? Styles in favour?"

"Yes. Find out, and report back, so our clan's jewelers will know how best to sell here. Who to deal with. If I find no one I think they can trust, they want me to set up shop here, to sell for them."

Teagan frowned and shook her head. "There's wealth and power here that you—that the entire clan—cannot hope to best, or even stand against. There are merchant lords in this city, even if they hold no titles the King acknowledges. And they clawed their way to the top and know how to stay there. They can be ruthless for sport, or when they need to be—and if they judge a new arrival would be stiff competition, they would feel the need to be, all right. You would be more likely accepted as a source of good pieces for their shops, a go-between who brings the stones and work of our clan to the jewelers of Ath Cliath. And in that role you'd avoid the expense of outfitting and running a shop, and being tied to it."

"I see," Mist said, and did, never doubting her aunt spoke truth. "So how does one approach the jewelers here? And which should I seek to deal with?"

Teagan tendered a wry smile. "One approaches with proper respect for their bodyguards. Both the visible and the hidden—for while their doors are open, most jewelry shops in Ath Cliath will hold patrons shopping for gems, who in truth are not patrons at all, but watchers for thieves. Some of them well-armed watchers who can run swiftly, and throw knives or stones to stun even faster. And as I suspect you lack coin enough to hire such at the rates currently holding sway in this city, nor enough familiarity with Ath Cliath to know which ones to trust at any price, that's another good reason not to open your own shop. Yet if you pose no threat, and seem honest, the competition among jewelers here will spur at least one of them to want to gain Coriondi work—at the lowest price they can get away with offering. You'll need to register with the Palace, to sell anything more than once in Ath Cliath, and return there to pay the King's tax on your sales: half of whatever you get. And once you do that, the tax collectors will watch for you. And anyone who rents rooms at an inn but owns a shop can expect to be inspected hard and often, by day and night without warning, to make sure they're neither smugglers nor rod-runners."

"Rod-runners?"

"Those who vanish in the night with wares or gold rods, and are seen and heard of no more. If they make it out of the city, change names and looks, and never return, some of them survive. None do who try to return to Ath Cliath and try the trick a second time. Here, shopkeepers are expected to be citizens, where shop help are not. And those inspections will ruin you, even if trade doesn't, by robbing you of sleep. In Ath Cliath, the sleepy tend to get fleeced, and quickly."

"The more you tell me, the more fear I feel."

Teagan smiled and shrugged. "My apologies, Mist, but better warned and afraid than naïve and then hit hard because one has no armor ready, nor wariness enough."

Mist nodded and murmured the old Hibernian saying. "Where there is coin to be had, there also are wolves."

"And some of them smile," her aunt added the old warning. "Yet if you come to sell good Coriondi splendor and not to compete with them, you might go so far as to trust Asult Ketilsson or Gudmundr Audunarson, who are fair traders and were both farfarers in their younger years,

20

and so have a taste for quality gems and pieces from across the world. Their shops are all lamps and gilding, and glitter like two rows of suns, facing each other across Dunlarr Street. And the Murtaghs, on Westing Street, who were *the* jewelers in this city before the fall of King Niall, and have had to fish new waters and do what they'd never once have stooped to, to cling to good fortune here since. Then there's Aideen O'Cain, on Manylocks Lane, the smallest purse of these four trustworthies, and so perhaps the most ready to chance on a new face and name from Hibernia."

Mist murmured all the names aloud, to try to fix them in her mind, and as her aunt smiled and nodded, she asked, "And what of my cousin, Lasair, who was a better gemcutter than I'll ever be. She came here two summers back..."

Her voice faded as she saw Teagan's eyes turn as hard as two fresh-cut gems for a moment. Then they softened again, and her aunt leaned close to murmur, "In the grave, likely. She went missing in the spring, and I watched the slave markets for a month but saw her not. Something happened to her. Things happen to folk in this city all the time."

That last was like a sword-thrust of cold warning, and Mist drew back involuntarily, took a deep breath, and asked, "So who then can I trust in Ath Cliath if I must run to someone, or need medicine?"

"No one but me." Teagan drained her thus-far-untouched cup in a trice, refilled it, and held the decanter out to pour Mist the same.

Who took the cue and drained hers. Crom and Morrigan, it was like liquid fire!

She frowned at the cup as brief fire raged behind her nose, then grinned and held out her cup. And saw her aunt's grin widen in approval as she poured.

"Too many of the herbalists and healers in this city," Teagan explained, "are peddling expensive addictive drugs with an eye to hooking ever-more clients who want respite from pain and brief physical ecstasy, and are willing to overpay for it, losing their lives to becoming half-asleep addicts."

Mist nodded. "I suspect you have already saved *my* life, by your words here. At the risk of being overbold, what would you deem good places for me to dwell? And daily dine?"

Teagan eyed her in silence, a disquieting twinkle growing behind her eyes, then leaned close again and murmured, "Perhaps it would be best if you shared with me the *real* reason Kailee Damhain allowed her daughter to come to the City of Gilded Greed."

Then she put her head to one side, and regarded Mist with eyes that were suddenly as bright and as sharp as a hawk's.

And Mist stared into that keen and unhooded gaze at a loss for words, not knowing how much to reveal. Could she trust Teagan?

Or had everyone who flourished in Ath Cliath been bought?

Stigr heard the slightest of sounds ahead of him in the dripping darkness. "Ulfr?"

"You were expecting someone *else* down here in the fishstink?"

There was no mistaking that surly voice. Ulfr, right enough.

"No," Stigr made flat reply, not rising to the bait. "I bring orders from Mael."

"Concerning?"

"The priest Silverlock."

"Who swam the cess or called on his gods or some such to survive our cooking-fire, I take it?"

"Aye. It seems the King now has another fate in mind for him, not the pyre. We're to watch him as closely as any enemy of the King, and report what we learn to Mael often, but kill him not. A royal command."

"Is this a Sitric royal command?" Ulfr growled. "Or one more 'royal command' handily whisked out from between Mael's nether cheeks?"

Stigr shrugged and smiled. "I have my suspicions, but..."

Ulfr sighed. "So the Sharp One himself bears some watching."

"Don't we all?"

#

In a place almost as dark, but much drier and better smelling, a door opened. The man stepping through it heard the tinkle of the tiny bell rung by the moving door—and sidestepped, putting hand to knife-hilt. Out of sheer habit, not out of real fear.

For one did not pay one of the best covert dirty-tricks lurkers in Ath Cliath so handsomely up front, just to casually throw him away.

They were both here, the merchant lords who'd hired him. He could tell that by the breathing, the faint scent the woman wore, and the not-so-faint perfume coming from the man. Behind *this* curtain, then, and that one.

He stopped where he was as the woman spoke. She wasted no time or breath on any greeting.

"So what did you learn from Runi, before he died of your...persuasive questioning?"

"That someone used magic to impersonate Hallvardr Thorolfsson—with his connivance—so this someone could meet certain arrivals at the docks and see them safe to their first stops."

"And who were these 'certain arrivals'?"

"Runi knew not. But Mael the Sharp had two of them watched. A young clanswoman of the Coriondi, one Mist Damhain, and a young clansman of the Uterni, Brandr Fylan."

"The one called Mist you will also watch. And keep her alive if you can."

"Above all else I'm at work on?"

"Above all else. For now." And the curtain moved in a way that told him that she'd lifted a hand in a gesture that meant this moot was at an end.

He bowed low and turned away. He knew better than to ask why this young visitor was to be protected. If it became needful for him to know, he might be told.

If the telling became needful.

He hastened. Heading to a refuge where he could sleep, for sleep might soon become more rare and precious than a low price in Ath Cliath, if he was to watch over a bumbling young innocent as well as thwart but not slay the King's covert agents.

"Blunting Mael the Sharp," the woman who'd just dismissed him liked to call it. Aye, he was the Blunter. Though living to see the next sunrise depended, as it always had, on no one noticing and naming him.

#

Ah, *this* must be Daunt's place...

Brandr grinned at the familiar rune scratched low and tiny on the doorframe–right beside the boot of the expressionless man-mountain of a doorguard, who stood like a statue with hands clasped atop the blade of a throwing axe thrust through the broadest black leather belt Brandr had ever seen, so studded with metal buttons as to approach being armour–and slipped past guard and dust-curtain, into a shop that was crammed with cupboards up to the ceiling, behind scarred and stained stout wooden tables. That flanked both sides of a winding path of bare floorboards snaking back to a table-girt blind end. No glitter or splendor here.

"The Offering Hand" said the fading signboard out front, weathered drabness among all the bright lights, gilding, and glitter of neighbouring shopfronts. You had to pass under the board to see "N Daunt" in tiny letters graven into the underside of that board; Brandr only spotted the name because he was looking for it.

And feeling both relief and the first strong throat-catching rush of homesickness he'd felt since setting boot in the overwhelming noise, bustle, and stink of the City of Gold and Slaves.

Neven Daunt was of Brandr's clan, though long a resident of Ath Cliath since retirement from the battlefield. A safe contact here in the city, according to the clan elders, and although the elders of the Uterni might be many things, they were decidedly not fools.

Old, wrinkled, and limping, not to mention battered of features and gruff, Neven Daunt was legendarily fearless, a blunt speaker to kings, and a chider of valkyries to boot.

Brandr had been a child when he'd last seen Daunt–tall, rugged, and at the height of his swordswinging success back then, not an old man lame from battle-wounds–and had adored him. In part because Daunt had been kind to him when it gained him nothing to be so.

These days, according to the elders, Daunt played a large part in keeping grand Ath Cliath functioning by seeing to the needs of its meaner streets–by repairing damaged used items, and assembling odds and ends of fruit and vegetables and smoked meats and fish to sell for very reasonable coin to the less affluent merchants, laborers, and shopkeepers. Those who were just 'hanging on' in their ever-more-expensive home city, yet were the grease that made daily wheels turn, the horn-handed workers who stood–and toiled–between gleaming lords and sullen slaves.

The shop seemed deserted at Brandr's first glance around, but as he strode on, the feeling of being watched grew and grew, and he could not help but notice the shop had been laid out so no one could sidle in and get close enough to hear any converse at the innermost end table, without speakers there seeing their approach.

On the wall above and behind that table hung an oval mirror, so any patron facing it could see back down the table-lined length of the shop to the entrance behind him, and so mark anyone's approach.

And as he'd expected, ere he reached that end table, a grizzled old man shouldered through hanging curtains to stand behind the table, and glare at him across it.

"I know you," he growled.

"And I you, Daunt Of The Bright Blade," Brandr replied, his smile warmer even than he'd intended. "I am Brandr Fylan. I grew."

Daunt let out a wordless grunt that might have been a greeting, agreement, or something else, and then added, "We're all growing towards something. Some of us up, some of us out—" He spread age-spotted, bony hands to indicate immense girth he did not possess "—and some of us down." He gazed at the scarred tabletop before him for a moment, as if in grim regret, then threw up his head like a hawk, and asked, "And you? Are you growing into an adventure, coming here to the City of Gilded Villainy?"

"Drawn to the flame of gold and excitement and being at the bustling heart of high and mighty doings," Brandr smiled back. "Had to see what bathing in gold looked like, ere I set out for darker places and doings—and likely leaner days, the rest of my life."

"Hunh," Daunt grunted scornfully. "Looks ridiculous, is what it looks like. And if you thought folk puffed up like strutting cockerels back home once they had a bauble or two to their name, well, *here* they prance along nigh to bursting, with their preening airs and their florid overreactions to imagined slights—ah, there's a thing, now: best not to bump into anyone in the streets here, lad, lest you find yourself marked for death."

"Truly?"

Daunt shrugged. "Most aren't so daft-headed, but it only takes one…"

Brandr grinned. "I hear you. And if you don't mind, I'd like to ask you a bit about Ath Cliath. Back home, things are small enough and folk few enough that you can see how things work and guess shrewdly enough to suffice about what the gossip doesn't tell you. Here, though…this is all so big and bright and new and *crowded*. I'm fair overwhelmed!"

Daunt's grin at that came swift and wide, and displayed only a few gaps where teeth had gone. "Well, at least you're honest about that, where most who strut these streets aren't. In their need to act coolly, used to wealth and power and style. Honesty is as rare here as gold was, back home. Here, folk look all around not to make sure they'll not be overheard when speaking truth, but gaze everywhere to see who's listening, so they can tailor the right lie to tell."

His grin widened as he saw Brandr glance at the mirror, then oh-so-casually pivot on one worn boot-heel to look in all directions and make sure the two of them were alone in the shop.

"Aye, alone for the moment, lad. My patrons must work for their livings, and there're times of day when they're all doing that. Times that don't last long, mind, so if there's something big and important you ache to know but don't want an audience for your asking, plunge right in, and wait not!"

Brandr stared at the amiable old man, then nodded and did just that. "Right, then. The *taxes* here!"

Daunt chuckled.

"The King must be *bathing* in coins," Brandr went on, "fair *rolling* in it!"

Daunt nodded.

"So where does it all go? What does he *do* with it? Is he just a miser, or chasing expensive hobbies, or has he some big, costly secret project?"

Daunt's smile had gone like a blown-out lamp. He shrugged, eyeing Brandr warningly, and growled, "No one of my acquaintance knows or will tell, but my own guess is the latter—the big secret something." He shot out a wagging forefinger and added firmly, "However, inquiring too closely into such things in Ath Cliath is…unhealthy."

Brandr nodded soberly, then darted glances all around the shop again, leaned in over the counter, and muttered, "I'm being followed. Who might be doing this, and why?"

Daunt shrugged again. "Anyone, lad. The King has spies everywhere, but so do many factions and cabals and interests in the city—for wherever there's wealth and power, there are hidden struggles to go with the public ones, and casualties…and swarming flies."

They exchanged grim nods, both remembering seeing flies buzzing over carrion—but whereas Brandr was recalling dead goats and birds and the shredded kills of night-prowling

24

beasts, he strongly suspected Daunt was seeing dead men, staring sightlessly up at the sky while the flies danced and crawled over eyeballs and face alike.

He put that thought firmly out of his head in time to hear Daunt add, "And there may be times you can slip away from a watcher, but never count on it. In this city, there are just too many eyes, and too many places for them to peer from. So watch your back every moment you're awake, but without seeming to do so—for a spy following you will grow careless if you never seem alert or apt to turn around and look behind you, and so let you spot them and at least act accordingly."

"Conduct myself as if I'm being spied on at every moment?"

"Precisely. Oh, and 'tis time to begin openly and fervently worshipping Odin, as the King does. As an outlander you're already lesser in standing and treatment by the city guards than a citizen; don't compound it by worshipping what Ath Cliath unofficially regards as lesser gods, too."

"So blend in. Which from what little I've seen thus far seems to mean rushing about everywhere, frowning to myself as if I'm thinking deep thoughts and am engaged in matters *very* important—or swagger along unhurriedly, sneering at the very air, as if I'm above all cares and any need to even look at mere mortals, so wealthy and powerful and therefore idle am I."

Daunt smiled thinly. "Mastery of the bedrock-bared basics you have already, I see. So to them I'll add: ask less than you would at home. Here, you can learn much more by watching and listening *without* seeming to do so. No creeping about spying. Just keep your ears open while pretending not to, wherever you go, and be patient. It'll take time to learn anything. If coins grow scarce, come to me and announce where someone can hear that you miss your home, and I'll stand you a meal to talk over old Uterni gossip."

"And being as I've seen no open markets of the sort we see at home, are the best places to do this watching and listening the taverns? There *are* taverns here?"

"Oh, aye. And clean and bright fine eateries where folk go to be seen—and tankards and jacks, as opposed to blown glass goblets, are not to be had, and asking for one gets you sneered at and invited to leave, too. You can tell which is which by how bright and clean the threshold is— and by the fancy-armored doorguards that the brightquaffs have on display outside, and the real taverns lack in favour of hairy-fisted peacekeepers inside. I recommend the Goldgleam, and the Old Odinsword, and the Faerie Lantern down at the seaward end of the city for good drink at fair prices, and acceptable—and talkative—company."

Brandr grinned. These were the most useful words he'd yet heard about Ath Cliath since setting foot on its dirty dockside cobbles.

"And I even more strongly recommend," Daunt growled, "that you avoid Hammaer's Split Axe, and the Grinning Glaistig, and The Skald's Beard; the real dives where men get killed often in brawls, and women don't want to be seen, and anything you drink could well make you sick even before you fall roaring drunk. Men acquire scars if they insist on drinking in such houses. And eyepatches, too."

"I'll not forget," Brandr promised. "May I be so bold as to ask if you recommend any inns, and warn against any, too—"

Daunt's face grew a jovial smile, as its owner suddenly drowned out Brandr's tentative words with a flood of delighted words of his own.

"Ah, but it's good to see you, lad! And *grown* so, if you're the one I remember among so many that were running barefoot and hurling apples about my ears, when last I was back in the old fields of home!" Daunt suddenly sounded both hearty and old, as he came out from between the tables with a lurching gait Brandr didn't recall from his first, almost gliding, appearance.

Brandr shot a look at the mirror and saw that a hard-faced man in a fine cloak, with gold earrings and more gold on his fingers, had entered the shop and was striding down it.

Then Daunt was clapping him on the shoulder and adding heartily, "Well, it's been right good to hear about the old lanes, and the old folk who dwell along them, too, indeed it has!"

Brandr took the hint, patted at Daunt's arm, bowed, and with a broad grin of his own said, "It's been my pleasure, and a delight to see you, after all these years! Be well! Prosper!"

And still wearing that grin, despite half-suspecting it made him look like a lackwit, he waved airily and set off for the shop door, including the new arrival in his smile without really looking at him. He had the brief impression of getting peered at very sharply for an instant by the hard-faced man, and then was past and then passing the doorguard, whom he favoured with the same wide grin, and then he was out and into the busy flow of hastening folk on the street.

He decided to stride as purposefully as every Ath Cliathian seemed to, as if in a hurry to keep important appointments and make gold-rod-heaping deals, and contrived as best he could to glance around without seeming to. Brandr fancied he was getting good at spotting the men following him—so far as he could tell, they were all males, and none of them all that youthful—who seemed, at least here and now, to number three.

At the brisk pace of the local citizenry, dodging creaking handcarts and coffer-and-sack-laden processions of servants with the adroitness of increased experience, The Offering Hand was soon left behind—three blocks, now four, and now lost to view around a corner—and as he increased his pace, he was grimly amused to see out of the corner of his eye, one of his tails forced to huff and puff to get much closer to him, for fear of losing sight of him at a busy streetmoot ahead.

For a wild, silently mirthful moment Brandr toyed with the idea of turning and confronting the man. But no, that would be foolhardy—who knew what the man might do?—and the moment that tail knew Brandr was aware of him and his purpose, he'd been far more careful, or even give way to a replacement, and finding out more about him would become that much harder.

Right. Be not a fool, Brandr Fylan. But there *was* someone he could ask about something—and be heard doing so by all the tails everyone in Ath Cliath might have put on him, to start following Daunt's advice and remake himself into a more desirable resident of Ath Cliath.

Up ahead, a man with the sorriest straggling ruin of a beard Brandr had ever seen was standing on a wagon barking orders to three underlings as they sweated to unload some sacks and carry-chests from the wagon into a shop. A dress shop, by the looks of it, not—thank Crom—a weapons shop or the like. "Fair day, good trader," he called to Stragglebeard, earning startled looks from the sweating unloaders and a suspicious glare from their overseer. "Would you be so good as to tell me where the nearest temple of Odin stands?"

"Stand back, you," one of the men struggling with what looked to be the heaviest of the chests said tersely, coming straight at Brandr when he didn't really need to. The other two watched to see what Brandr's response would be, and he realized they were suspicious of anyone distracting them when they were handling wares. Crom, Morrigan, and Donn, was thievery *that* bad in this city of gold?

He stepped back hastily, almost colliding with the man tailing him who'd been so breathless a street back, pretended not to notice as the men with the chests frowned their ways past him, and hopefully asked Stragglebeard again, "Nearest temple of Odin?"

"Be *off* with you!" the man growled, waving him away. "*Some* of us have *work* to do!"

Brandr nodded, bowed his head as he murmured an apology, took a step back and almost onto the boots of his tail, and then spun around and asked the man who'd been following him, his manner all innocence, "Do *you* know where the nearest temple of Odin All-Father is?"

"Uh...ah...House Of The God's Helm, on Irongate." The man was startled, and trying to turn away so Brandr couldn't get a good look at his face. As if those dirty red downdagger sideburns didn't make him unmistakeable half a block away. "Third moot down this street, turn you left, then look for the helm-shaped roof. Whitestone, tall...you can't miss it."

"My thanks!" Brandr said heartily, ending the man's current misery, and set off briskly in the direction he'd been given.

He strode hard and fast, weaving in and out in the traffic—which was growing even heavier, if that was possible—until he reached the first street-moot. Where he slowed, turned, and gawked all around at the grand buildings like a country shepherd from the back hills of darkest Hibernia.

During his open-mouthed survey, he managed to look back the way he'd come without seeming to dwell on it—and was gratified to see, without seeming to spot them, that all three of his tails were close behind.

Or was it four?

CHAPTER 6

The room was cold, and the roof leaked down the walls when it rained, and on top of that, the floor was uneven and it was none too clean, but Oswin Silverlock had known far worse.

And it had certainly been cheap as lodgings went in Ath Cliath. A lone upper room in a leaning, decaying building in the worst part of the city, reached only up a rickety outside stair.

Oswin had used a name not his own when paying out his coins for the first three months, which seemed to be the norm here unless one paid for a season, or an entire year.

Hard straw over slat-and-rope bed, chamberpot, table, a backless old chair and a rust-mottled symbol of Odin on the cracked, damp-darkened wall...what more did one really need? Well, that rune taken down, for one, and a proper lantern rather than a candle in a cracked dish, for two, but Oswin had left the metal rune where it was, on the wall, and when he headed through the streets now, he walked right past two shops that had lanterns for sale hanging in their windows—black iron and bright pink copper, brand new—and followed his nose to the stink of fish.

He knew better than to buy the salted whitefish, or the massive greybacks hanging from their tails, raw and staring glassily at nothing at all. Not without a keg of ale to wash that salt down, or a good hot cooking-hearth. But there at the back of the shop was what he'd come for, the priciest thing on offer: smoked coldfin, orange where it wasn't sooty black.

Something he loved—and something he could eat in the streets as he trudged home. That and a skin of thrais, the emerald green wine whose making had come from warmer lands but spread to Hibernia with the first Viking traders, and he was good.

He trudged back to his new home—or rather, to almost within sight of it, to another outside stair he'd noticed before renting his room. Oswin mounted the worn old steps as if he owned them and had ascended them every day of his life, until he was rising past a particular roof. He stepped onto its thatch, and clambered along to where he could jump to another, higher roof, and at length another. There he found a sheltered corner he could look down from in relative hiding, though he had to dislodge a handful of sleepy and none too pleased pigeons to do so. In the biting cold, one was too slow. He wrung its neck and thrust it through his belt for later eating, or to trade for something more palatable.

Rinsing the last of the fish smell from his fingers with a little of the wine, Oswin settled himself, sprawled on his chin to keep as low and motionless as possible. He could be seen plainly by someone at his height or higher, a man lying head-down like an arrow on the dark, worn thatch, but his head might well escape the notice of anyone passing below. Patiently, he set himself to watching. Not so much the balconies and windows and rising tiled roofs of the grander buildings of the rest of Ath Cliath, that rose ultimately to gilded domes—real poured gold, some in the city swore, and Oswin believed them—and turrets, and spires in the distance. No, he set himself to gazing at vantage points nearer to hand. The places from which someone could watch the outside stair that connected Oswin Silverlock's rented room to the wider world.

And sure enough, after not all that long a watch, a man—a nondescript labourer or shopkeeper, his face unfamiliar to Oswin—came walking unhurriedly along an alley to where he could casually glance up at Oswin's door and window. He did so, then retreated a few steps to a shadowed alcove where two buildings failed to meet, peered up again to make sure he still had a view of the door and stair and window, then slouched down to sit. Settling down to watch.

Suspicions confirmed. Oswin kept still, lying on the roof and pondering what he should do now.

Given the danger in Ath Cliath to priests of the White God, acting openly might win him a very short life. And his superior must be told of the fate of the fallen priests, not left with silence into which to send later clergy to their own deaths here. So he must soon contrive to slip out of the city unregarded and make that report, then do whatever his superior ordered. Whatever the cost.

King Sitric Cuaran was for Odin—had given up an eye in blot for the god, in the very green and questing flower of his youth—and reportedly had even slain his own brother, merely for turning to the White God. Moreover, he was the grandson of Ivar the Boneless, who hunted and blood-eagled faithful of the God, so long and bloody a tally that Ivar must have fairly staggered under the weight of so much sin.

And from watchers to gate-guards to the crushing taxes, this city was in the grip of the One-Eyed King.

And it did not need a wise man to conclude that openly preaching the way of the White God in a city that was the very roost of the Black Raven would be suicidal folly. Yet to avenge his fellow faithful by violence against the King or the King's agents might, in the end, be little better.

And what damage would he cause if he *did* slay the King, and Ath Cliath—whatever its faults and excesses, one of the last refuges against deepening Fimbulwinter—was then ravaged in the struggle for the throne that was sure to follow?

Yet god rise or god fall, winter freeze all or winter wane, the sin of slavery could not be allowed to continue. What to do?

Aye, what to do?

God was the truth. God should guide him.

Yet it was the way of the White God, more than these cruel and brawling Aesir and Vanir, that mortals should look within themselves and make their ways in the world and uncover the truth for themselves, to find and forge what was right.

Yet rake though he might in his dreams, guidance he'd found none, now that he was here in this city of greed and grasping sin. And the city frankly overwhelmed him, this busy, rich, rushing seat of Odin. Oswin Silverlock was in the place of power of an unfriendly, one-eyed god, under the sway of a one-eyed king, and he felt lost.

So he would pray, and go and report so as to save priests after him, and take counsel with his superior, and be guided by that wiser, holier man.

Yet he would in turn advise that he, Oswin, should be sent back into Ath Cliath with a face and a name not his own, to work against this One-Eyed King's agents—doing violence to them if need be, for they were men who unhesitatingly did violence to others—and freeing slaves whenever he could, and whisper-spreading word of the White God as a better alternative to the Aesir who had led the world into this chill misery.

Yes. His own life would be hard, regardless, but God does not give us easy paths. Only proper ones.

#

Downstairs, Dun's Hearth was a bustling din of chatter and laughter and clinking crockery, the ever-present boarfry smell floating up to Mist freshly strong and pleasant and laced with frying leeks, making her guts rumble despite her mood.

Upstairs, in her dingy, tiny room, Mist let her eyes wander the jagged wandering ways of the cracks in the wall-plaster that were already growing familiar, and felt very alone.

She *liked* Aunt Teagan. A lot. Yet she'd kept from her the deepest secret. The one she wanted to share, with someone she'd just met but that was her closest, kindest friend here in this strange, crowded city.

She told she was in Ath Cliath to gather information on jewelry sales and tastes for Aurnia and Síomha and the other clan elders. And she'd let Aunt Teagan in on part of the secrets; that they'd sent her because they wanted an updated sense of where the King was taking the city, and the moods and doings of the populace from the eyes of someone who doesn't live there, and so wasn't, as Aurnia Sharp-Eyed had put it, "under the influence of all that gold."

She'd said nothing at all about her mission to act against the King, because for all she knew Teagan was his lover or under his thumb, and could be a spy for him.

Oh, she'd wanted to tell. She wasn't a lover of secrets, or deceit; she liked open honesty, and friends. She liked Teagan and wanted to trust her...but dared not.

At least, not yet. Not until she could be sure.

But how, in this unfamiliar city of so many teeming folk, with folk always bustling everywhere, even by night, and who knew how many spying eyes among the crowds—and it only needed *one*—and everyone talking to everyone else, in friendships and with pacts and agreements she knew not and that perhaps went back years, could she ever be sure?

The crack she was eyeing as she pondered wound its way to the ceiling, and Mist stared at the old water stains up there—right above her bed; *wonderful*—darker and darker thoughts racing. How could she ever get close enough to the King to work him any harm?

And if she did, what could she, one lone lass half the weight of some of the guards she'd seen here, and with a shorter reach and much less experience with any blade, *do?* Her very youth and being alone and being unknown here were her armour, aye, but...

It was about then that her mind caught up with her wandering gaze, and she realized that an eye was staring down at her out of the gloom. From the crack where the wall at the head of her bed and the ceiling didn't quite neatly meet.

She couldn't help but let out a startled little shriek.

The eye promptly vanished.

But had that been a smirk she'd glimpsed for an instant, as it did so?

#

Another two slaves had died since the initial report, which made the poisoner's tally sixteen. The King was *not* going to be pleased.

Not that he gave a whit for the fate of a slave, but lost or spoiled goods are lost or spoiled goods, and Sitric Cuaran could not abide needless waste. Moreover, with so many dead, word of it would slip out, could not be prevented from spreading...was spreading already.

Mael knew the King would have preferred that Mael the Sharp had pounced swiftly enough to make things otherwise. Yet trying to trace this poisoner had thus far been more than a little like struggling through river quicksand with the tide coming in.

All he really knew was this: aside from two pairs of slaves, all belonging to the same owner, there were no connections among the dead. So far as he could tell. Which meant the poisonings weren't about hitting at the slaves or their owners, but at the slave-seller.

Or at least, the poison had been given to the slaves as they were being assembled and held for sale, in the seller's care.

Passing on from what he knew or could deduce to mere suspicions...

After listening to the earnest testimony of the desperate-to-impress "clerk of the King" who'd been sent to question the slave-owners and the slave-seller (a man who was no clerk at all, but a junior shadow-hand of the King whose anonymity had been sacrificed to preserve that of Mael, Ulfr, Stigr, and the rest) Mael believed one thing with certainty.

The poisoner was someone who cared not a whit for slaves, their owners, or the seller, but had been experimenting with a poison they'd somehow acquired, to see how strong it was...or even, perhaps, if it was a poison at all.

As for whatever the deadliness was, it was something different than earlier poisons whose work Mael had seen. It brought on lassitude and then sleepiness...and some time later, death came suddenly, with a lone great tremor or body spasm and then a little white foam leaking from the mouth of the dead.

So, sixteen dead in an experiment, to see if a new toy or tool is what was paid for. There were drawbacks to having ambitious, willful folk with great wealth all crowded together within the same city walls...

And how many of those citizens, in this city of racing rumors and secrets sold and spying, spying, always *spying*, knew about the Rule?

The Rule was secret, though half the Palace must know about it by now. The King's first and foremost Rule, the one he personally told every one of his shadow-hands after their blood-oaths of loyalty.

Poisoners were to be hunted down and slain, and their poisons destroyed, as swiftly as possible, with no trials or jailings or word to the public.

The Rule obviously existed to keep the city from dissolving into a cauldron of rivals and foes dealing death to each other, but Sitric was so fierce on this one point, almost as strong as his insistence on "Odin first"—why?

There were no poisonings in Sitric's family past, so far as he knew—and he knew that lore well, at least back to the birth of Ivar the Boneless. Could it be that poison was one of Sitric's fears?

Because the King's magic, as a galdr of power and achievement, could do many things, but staving off the effects of poisons wasn't one of them?

Well, now...

#

Brandr was back in his room at the Hearth, eating more of the boarfry that seemed to be every midday and evening meal, for as long as the inn kitchen held out. It was hearty enough, if a bit salty—and the ale he was washing it down with, from the cheaper of the two hearth room kegs, was watery enough that no one would dared have serve it in Hibernia save to goats and pigs.

But he wanted to dine alone, so he could think. He knew full well there was a watcher overlooking his tiny shuttered window, another in the inn foreroom downstairs, and yet another loitering somewhere on the street outside, watching the inn door. For all he knew, there was a spy outside on his rotting balcony, though he knew the watcher staring at his window could just as easily survey the balcony—not to mention the Hearth's kitchen door, that opened onto the alley. Endless money bought endless eyes.

So this was how the King ruled. By seeing all, and knowing all, and being ready.

And through fear.

Well, Sitric had built something stable enough, Brandr had to grant him that. Ath Cliath had been a rich and bustling merchant haven before the One-Eyed King had come and taken it by the sword, but he'd built it into something stronger yet. A haven against the cold, *the* place to come and buy what one wanted—and needed.

If, of course, one had coin enough. By Crom and Morrigan, but things were expensive in Ath Cliath!

Everything cost dear. In large part because half the price of everything goes to the King. So was Sitric just a miser, or was he paying someone hidden to keep him on the throne? Or work magic for him? Or indulge some private obsession? There were clan chiefs like that, who chased pretty shes married to others, or the biggest stags, or elusive monsters for their heads as trophies. Power did things to minds.

So what was Sitric up to?

"Hey?" Brandr asked his cracked wall. It declined to answer.

Well, how to find out? Follow the gold. Seeing what the King spent might mean getting the right post in the royal household—a long job, particularly with the King's suspicion so heavy on him, personally—or for all he knew, every last new arrival in Ath Cliath—as to run to at least three everpresent watchers. Did they seek rest while Brandr Fylan was snoring? Somehow he doubted all eyes would turn away in the hours of darkness when skulking was easiest.

So back to the gold. Follow the gold. To begin with, trace the tax payments collected on behalf of the King. But how?

The royal tax collectors were everywhere in Ath Cliath, always in trios or more, always with an escort of at least two soldiers. They wore distinctive badges—on both shoulders, gilded brooches graven with the badge of the city: a sheaf of barley above three horizontal rods, with a fish swimming horizontally below the rods. That wasn't much different than the tax-takers Brandr had seen traveling Hibernia on their mules, with their intricately knotted "takings" satchels.

If he shadowed one of these trios, he'd surely be seen doing so. But what if he didn't begin his shadowing until near dusk, when their working day was drawing to an end? No need to pursue a particular trio to their final destination, just be out in the streets with dusk drawing down, shopping for himself. Then, when he saw some of the King's tax-takers, get close enough for just long enough to see what that destination is.

And then come back the next nigh-dusk, *not* following any tax collectors, to see if other trios of the King's takers converged on that same spot. And then?

Become a roofer or cesspool-emptier, to have some pretext for tarrying near wherever it was? Wouldn't the King's guards—and spies—be watching for anyone getting too interested in where the tax collections go?

Hmm. Well, the outlander Brandr Fylan was clearly under suspicion already.

So he might as well begin earning that suspicion, and getting to his task. The sooner results were gained, the less likely Ath Cliath's cursedly high prices would leave his swiftly dwindling purse utterly empty.

He did *not* fancy a life of crime, just to feed himself, in this city.

It was all too apt to be a short and painful one.

ChAPTER 7

Wagons were *LOUD.*

It had taken Oswin Silverlock an uncomfortable scramble on his belly in yard-mud, and then the better part of a day of squirming and stretching and sewing in his room, to improvise a harness of belts, but—thanks to the favour of the White God of course—it worked very well. He'd managed two small miracles.

First, he'd managed to strap himself securely and closely to the underside of a stout merchant's wagon of his choosing departing Ath Cliath. And secondly, he'd managed to do so unseen.

He hoped.

Yet the favour of the God and Oswin's up-sleeve store of miracles seemed to have run out at the same time. Right now.

As the wagon rumbled slowly—Teeth of the God, how slowly!—out of the city in the company of eleven other wagons, all of them empty of all but weathercloak-leathers and idle ropes and straps used to protect cargoes, Oswin was being driven swiftly mad—and deaf; it was a hard-run race between them, that unfortunately both could win—by the incessant creaking of the wagon's greased axles. The nearest of which—KouerrrRRRRAWW, Kuerraww—was all too close to his head.

Teeth clenched and eyes screwed shut against street-grit, Oswin silently shouted every prayer he knew, one after another, in a fierce and endless chant, numbed by the wagon's jarring because he had to keep his left fist braced hard against one of its crossbeams to make sure the knife strapped to that forearm stayed in its sheath, in case he was too weak and numb to unbuckle himself later, and needed to cut himself free.

KouerrrRRRRAWW, Kuerraww, KEEREEErauwww...

Holy Hand of the God, would this *never* end?

And then it did, for a moment at least, as the wagon ground to a stop with a last eardrum-lancing creak. They were at the gates, and he heard the low muttering of bored voices as the gate-guards collected the exit tax that had to be paid, and poked half-heartedly with their spears at the leathers. One eager-beard bent down to peer at the underside of a wagon, but thankfully it was three wagons before Oswin's, and he saw not the tensely motionless priest in dark and dirty homespun tucked up between distant crossbeams.

A moment later, they were moving again, and Oswin was breathing in the stink of the dung the oxen of seemingly all the wagons ahead of his had dumped during the brief halt, as he literally passed over it with about a handspan to spare, and the sounds of the wheels was changing as cobbles and grit gave way to softer mud mixed with many small stones.

KouerrrRRRRAWW, Kuerraww...

They were out into the surrounding countryside, and a far more evil smell was rising now, as the wagons got closer to the midden-hills of Ath Cliath's wastes. Another innovation of the One-Eyed King, Oswin had heard; before his coming, the river had taken what was in every chamberpot, though much of it had returned each high tide. Now the reek of the river had become the stink out here, two hills away from the city.

Which meant that no merchant would camp outside the gates and trundle handcarts in to evade the king's taxes anymore—nor tarry this close to the city. They'd press on to the first ford, where the oxen could drink.

And Oswin could free himself, if he could manage it without the traders seeing him, and part ways with his creaking conveyance to become a man bathing in the stream. Which he needed to be not just as an act, but because he was now covered with axle-grease.

Which, by the smell of it, was rancid boar fat.

So now he stank. And was heading for the pains of needing badly to relieve himself. *KouerrrRRRRAWW, Kuerraww, KEEREEErauwww...*

Oswin smiled wryly at the road-mud passing by under his nose, and reflected on how many folk thought priests lived a soft life of idleness, all eating and dining well between mumbling a few memorized prayers.

He would have given a lot to be one of those priests. A pity they were almost certainly mythical.

#

Mist found herself standing backed up against the door of her room, her heart pounding, She was panting, terror clawing its icy way down her spine, as she stared at the crack where the watching human eye had been.

She'd just had to get herself out from under where it could gaze.

It *had* been human, she was certain.

And a man's eye, she was sure of that, too—though in truth, it could be the eye of a beast or a monster, and a she to boot, for all the proof Mist had, or chance to get at a proper look at it.

Whatever it had been—still was, and likely still above her now, and who knew how thick this old and cracked ceiling was?—she was still so frightened that she couldn't stop shivering.

Watching eyes could be *everywhere* in this city around her. She *hated* that feeling.

She'd always hated being the blundering innocent, the newborn sheep surrounded by wolves.

And she was that right now, more than she'd ever been in the green familiar countryside of home.

Where she wanted to be right now, back home, far from this nasty, deadly city, so big and dirty and scurrying, for all its gilded splendours.

She wanted to turn and tear open the door her shoulder blades were touching, fling it wide and run, run, run clear out of the city. Aye, flee Ath Cliath right now, and leave it behind forever.

Yet she would not do that.

She would *not* go home in failure.

So what to do?

What to do?

She drummed against the door with her fists, still her with her back to it, and thought hard—until her racing thoughts chanced upon how easy it would be to slip a sharp dagger through the door and into her, and she sprang away from it in fresh throat-strangling terror and raced across the room, breathing hard anew, to beat the heels of her clenched hands against the wall with a rising growl of exasperation until she hit upon an idea.

She was being hunted—so she would become the hunted thing.

She would slip away from the inn and start sleeping on rooftops, wrapped around warm chimneys. She would buy and cache food she could eat cold, in her hands and on the run. She would become a lurking watcher, keeping to the shadows and moving by night.

Not give up her room, not yet. Not until she knew this would work.

She'd need a good hiding-place to huddle in during the daytime—and what if all such were already taken by skulkers already here in Ath Cliath, who lacked coin enough to live any other way, but didn't want to leave?

34

So she would have to see if she could do this. See if there was a window or roof-gable or corner or something where she could hide from prying eyes—including Aunt Teagan's—at Teagan's home and shop.

But if they were watching her right now, then they'd watch her searching, and see whatever she saw, and so her hiding place would be no hiding place at all!

So what to *do?*

Well, lead her spies a merry faerie dance! Yes! Travel wildly all over the city, looking for hiding places without seeming to do so, doubling back on where she'd been, rushing here and there...anything to exasperate a watcher, until they grew weary of her madness, or lost sight of her. And it was time to broaden the handful of shops she knew, and find good places to buy food and clothes and tools...

Mist Damhain drew a deep breath, pulled on her boots, squared her shoulders, marched across the room and flung open her door.

And set off. Ath Cliath, do your worst!

#

The chairs were hard and cold, but that was to be expected. Gilding and polished marble please the eye, not the spine or backside.

The four people sitting on those chairs were among the most powerful 'old coin' merchants of the city, rich and established years before the coming of the one-eyed Norseman. Wherefore they were unaccustomed to being kept waiting.

Yet they'd expected the wait, as a means of showing them their powerlessness when matched against the King, and so were coldly amused rather than exasperated. Boredom was not something that afflicted any of them; to prosper in the new Ath Cliath, the City of Gold and Slaves, or even to hang on to what they had, as Hibernians among all these pushy new Northmen and outland slavers, one needed shrewd and busy wits, and the four had those. They slept little, and when awake, were always thinking, their thoughts racing. They'd been rivals, but over the years had grown to respect each other, so it had not been hard to make covert common cause against the King Sitric the One-Eyed. Over time, they'd become friends.

Indeed, as much as any of them dared trust anyone in the world, they trusted each other.

The one who first drew the hidden eyes that watched them in that coldly impressive hall was the woman.

Coldly, darkly beautiful Lecora O'Hart, shapely beauty clad in perfectly-tailored purpleweave so dark as to be night black. Her long dark hair fell free, her skin was white and soft and perfect, so striking she caught most gazes and awoke awe—until one saw that her dark eyes were like two drawn daggers.

Men, the other three, and she dominated them without seeming to try.

Handsome, hawklike Ardgal Loughnane, black brows and piercing brown eyes beneath a tall flame of upthrust red hair, long legs in hose, tunic richly trimmed. A gorget set with gems at his throat, massy rings of gold on slender fingers. A half-smile that revealed nothing, eyes as fierce as Lecora's.

Cairbre Dathaill, an elegant wit. Mouth quirked in irony when silent, as it was now. Lithe, gliding, dancing-eyed. Emerald-painted fingernails to match the flash of his eyes, black lace at wrist and throat, a doublet slit to display three layers of rich fabrics, one goldweave. Restless, but with the discipline to fall into statue-like watchful immobility, seeing and hearing all. Playing statue right now, patient and amused, mockery drawn and ready.

Torloch Dargan, burly and broad-shouldered, a-gleam from chased metal plates sewn here and there in his stylish jerkin, and a gold torc at his throat as thick as a fat sausage. Solid rather than fat, himself, a sleepy lion whose half-lidded eyes missed nothing.

They looked rich and dangerous, commanders, sharks who glided through life devouring lesser fish, and that's just what they were.

Except here in their home city, now that King Sitric reigned and gathered all the gold to himself, and had somehow cozened everyone wealthy in seemingly all the world to rush here to trade, and make him still richer. Sitric's folk lorded it above mere Hibernians.

Wherefore this quartet of old-coin prosperity had many times demanded audience with King Sitric to discuss matters of trade and civic regulations in vain, ignored as serenely and coldly as they were wont to ignore the eager trade-with-me pitches of obvious swindlers and gold-hungry innocents.

Until today. The result of their sixty-sixth request—but the first in which their polite letter of supplication had mentioned their increasing concerns over preachings in the streets from priests of the White God.

That had got their audience nigh-instantly granted, by hastening royal messenger.

They'd been kept waiting, of course, in a high-vaulted hall that had been full of grand tables and comfortable chairs in King Niall's time, but now stood empty.

As empty as Sitric's compassion.

Not that they'd been trusted to wait alone. Even had they not known the tapestries in this hall concealed spyholes that undoubtedly all sported peering eyes, they sat under the impassive gazes of door-guards in gleaming gilded armour, helmed men a head taller than all of the four—who were all tall folk unaccustomed to looking up at anyone. These silent pairs of sentinels looked to be twice the brawn and weight of Dargan, the biggest of the four.

So the merchants sat in silent, smiling thought, saying and gesturing nothing that any spy could have interpreted in any wise. Just waiting.

For what suddenly happened, without herald or ceremony. A door opened in smooth and freshly oiled silence, and King Sitric Cuaran strode into the room.

A tall and impressive figure in a sweeping dark robe with upswept horned shoulders, wearing a high-spired crown none of the merchants had ever seen before that added the height of two heads to his real one. Eyepatch a-gleam with jewels, face smilingly unreadable.

He came to a stop and stood tall and terrible, backlit by the bright golden glow of many reflected torches flooding through the doorway behind him.

Might and wealth personified.

The four merchants would have been more impressed had they not recognized the ploy as one they'd made use of themselves, a time or six before in their lives. They were gazing upon a man striking a pose, who knew full well how impressive he looked.

Nevertheless, they hid their smiles. They knew well how this game was played.

"Good citizens, you requested audience, and I am here. Speak."

The slightest mocking stress on the word 'good.'

Ardgal Loughnane rose from his seat and held forth a rolled-up scroll, bound with a cloth-of-gold ribbon.

The King held up one hand in a firm 'Halt!' gesture, and repeated more firmly, "Speak."

Ardgal sat, his scroll undelivered.

"Great King," the Lady Lecora said gently, "we all have our gods, who guide us. And 'tis the nature of all to resist and mistrust change, though to prosper and flourish one must embrace and ride it. Your reign has transformed our city, bringing many new ideas that have advanced us all, and we speak out against none, for we are not gods to see swiftly what is good and bad, nor to stamp out or champion ideas if we did. So we accepted the entrance of priests of this new faith of

36

the White God, and their preachings of one true god, though we embraced not such nonsense. If one feasts on dishes from all over the world, one is likely to taste food one finds horrid and never to be sampled again—yet the rich variety gained is worth such unpleasantnesses. So we welcome not these preachings of but one god—but have begun to notice the sudden disappearances of the preachers. One after another, all abrupt vanishings. Others have noticed, too, and they have begun to ask: is the Riverfleet Throne silencing these deluded holy men?"

The King's face did not change. "Safety and order in Ath Cliath—the same order that lets us all trade and prosper, secure within these walls—is my first duty, before all others," he replied, his tone as gentle as hers.

The four had their spies and agents in the shadows, even as the King had his, so they all knew the truth, though it hung in the air between them unsaid.

Priests of the White God who'd gone missing in Ath Cliath were killed by Sitric's agents if they fought, or enslaved and worked to death as slaves if they did not—sold to masters who would ship them out of the city to toil elsewhere. King Sitric wanted no open strife with the clergy of the White God, but detested the very notion of a challenge to Odin and the *true* gods—the Aesir. He'd never say as much to his four guests, Celts of Hibernia who worshipped gods like Crom, Morrigan, and Donn.

"This we both grant and celebrate," Torloch Dargan growled in his deep voice.

Ardgal rose again from his chair and again proffered the scroll—but the door-guards stirred and started forward, faces hard and hands going to weapons.

Even as King Sitric, his face suddenly even harder, waved Ardgal back and commanded coldly, "Read it to me."

Ardgal smoothly backed to his chair, and read aloud:

To King Sitric Cuaran, Lord of Ath Cliath, King of Hibernia, King of Jorvik, Jarl of Jutland, Head of House Ivar, these:
We, independent merchants of the city of Ath Cliath, all,
Do hereby request and beseech you, as master of law and order in the city under your hand, and relied upon by citizens high and low to uphold law and order,
And deeply appreciating all you have done for trade and enrichment of all, and trusting that you are dedicated to maintaining good trading conditions and the greatest possible market access for all,
Do allow the freedom to worship all gods, including preachings both public and private, so long as no citizen is coerced into reverence to a deity and in a manner they do not themselves embrace, within Ath Cliath and such ships, barges, and encampments as may be within reach of Ath Cliath's lawkeepers and soldiery, and concerned with commerce in the city and located in or near the city for that purpose,
And granting that it be understood that no citizen may harm another citizen, nor trammel any citizen's freedom, in the name of the worship of any god,
And humbly requesting that the Riverfleet Throne publicly acknowledge that all citizens of Ath Cliath are equal before the law, and that all visitors, for purposes of trade and otherwise, be treated equally, not held in greater or lesser regard because of the deities they venerate, renounce or shun, or worship differently than others,
And that this be the King's justice, day upon day, until the end of all days
We have caused our names and trading seals to be here affixed:
Lecora O'Hart
Ardgal Loughnane
Cairbre Dathaill

Torloch Dargan
Biorach Mag Sharain
Eithne O'Birn
Druian O'Tarpaigh
Rian O'Cathail
Drystan O'Scollain
Aeducan O'Limhain

...

And Ardgal read out the rest of the names, fifty-two in all, then tried again to hand the scroll to the King. Who waved it away as if he wanted to dash it savagely to the floor, with the curt words, "I have heard, and shall consider. Prosper, loyal citizens of Ath Cliath. Prosper."

And he turned, tall and terrible, strode away, and was gone as quickly as he'd come, through a door that locked behind him with an audible click-clack and rattle, even if they had dared follow.

The four merchants looked at each other, then as one silently arose and departed the hall. Leaving the petition lying on the floor.

CHAPTER 8

A tiny bell chimed. Mael regarded it impassively for an instant ere whirling away to stride to the darkest corner of the room and there slide open an oiled and soundless panel with his foot.

Affording him a view of a length of brightly-lit passage far below, and the head of a man traversing it. Ulfr.

Mael closed the panel again and calmly returned to his work—only on the far side of the table, so he could face the door when it opened. He didn't bother to turn the lists he'd been examining around. He could read upside down as readily as the usual way.

Ulfr knocked softly, then entered without awaiting a reply.

Mael nodded greeting and cocked his head in wordless question in the same unbroken movement.

"Oswin Silverlock," Ulfr said flatly. "Gone without trace. I've checked with all of our eyes I could reach unseen and in haste. No one's seen him. If he's still in the city, he's in hiding or *very* well disguised. We're watching all the known White God devout in case he meets with any of them."

"Your hunch?"

"He's fled Ath Cliath."

"Fangs of Nidhogg!" Mael cursed. "Well, then, I'll need you to—"

Another tiny bell chimed, three along from the one that had knelled earlier. Mael broke off speaking to sigh deeply and spin away from the table.

"Later," he flung over his shoulder curtly at Ulfr, strode to the wall, did something swift and deft to it that Ulfr couldn't see through the Sharp One's body, swung part of the wall open to reveal darkness, stepped into it, and closed the wall again behind him.

A secret door Ulfr had never known was there. Well, well.

He'd already lofted his eyebrows, but he let them fall again as he turned away to retrace his way here. Without saying a word. Or moving a muscle of his face.

There would be watchers. There always were.

#

Mael strode surefooted in the darkness, his well-worn boots nigh soundless on the soft dark rug that had been laid down in the passage to bring as much silence as possible. When he reached the door he wanted and swung it wide, two bells chimed a sing-song fanfare of warning in the room he was entering, a small chamber entirely hung with rich blue tapestries, and containing only a small table with a lamp flanked with two stools.

King Sitric Cuaran stood there awaiting him. Mael could see in an instant that he was angry.

"I met with the merchants Lecora, Ardgal, Cairbre, and Torloch in the Empty Chamber," the King said flatly, without greeting or pleasantries. "Ardgal tried to give me a petition. Twice. Have one of the crones we trust test it for poison. If there is poison, have Ardgal torn or cut apart in the streets. In front of one of the other three."

"And if there is not?"

"Have him butchered in front of at least one of his fellow schemers—all of them, if you can catch them together—regardless. And have poison loudly claimed. It's time to thin the ranks of the serpents underfoot in my city, and sew fear anew among the survivors. Be brutal."

It got cold in a hurry in Ath Cliath, if the wind was blowing from the sea as the sun lowered. As she hurried along the alley, Mist told herself that was why she was shivering.

Herself knew better.

She could still see bloody teeth scattered on the cobbles of a city street, and the man who'd lost them clutching a jaw that hung broken and awry, dripping gore. Not far from where another man was sprawled on the cobbles with his brains showing through a split skull, hair all red and matted...

She winced, gorge rising at the mere memory, and resolved fiercely to stay well away from the Skald's Beard forevermore.

Not that she'd been drinking at that notorious tavern, merely hastening past it, but she never wanted to pass it again. Not if the brawls it spewed out onto the street were all like *that*.

Nor did she want to return the Hearth, with its ever-present spies. Not tonight. Not unless her new hideaway on Aunt Teagan's roof was too bitter cold.

And it shouldn't be. She'd found a corner, earlier in the day, in what should be the lee of the prevailing winds, where the roof of Aunt Teagan's attic ended and overhung a lower roof of the next floor down. It was easily reached up the uneven blocks of this back corner of walls, too.

Up she went, weary but smiling. Earlier in her whirlwind tour of shops she'd procured what she wanted, and so had left in her roof-nook a sack holding two new blankets, a cloak in case it rained, a hand-cloth, a skin of water, and a small metal coffer into which she'd jammed a handwheel of cheese, a sausage, and a heel of garlic-drenched bread. All the comforts a traveling lass should need, seeing as there was a gutter not far across the roof she could relieve herself down, if she—

Movement, in her private little corner of roof!

A man, rising and whirling at the small sounds of her own progress across the roof-thatch, her opened sack in his hands.

Their eyes met. His belonged to one of those who'd been following and spying on her.

And they were hard and unfriendly, above a scowl that was shifting into a sneer.

As he advanced.

Mist's heart pounded. She dared not retreat, not with a four-floors fall onto hard cobbles at her back.

And she didn't want to. Fury rose like a sudden dark wave in her, warm and snarling and nigh choking, and she sprinted to meet him, sidestepping at the last moment to get upslope of him, then duck low as he grabbed for her, and shove hard.

He staggered back and went down on his behind in the crackling thatch, hands like talons clutching her and dragging her down with him.

Rank sweat, and breath like rancid fish, as he tugged her close and then *bit* at her ear! Mist strained her head back, and discovered almost too late that she was offering him her throat to grab. She twisted away desperately and got backhanded bruisingly across the throat as her reward, a blow that left her husking for air and unable to shriek.

Oh, she tried, but all that came out was a croak, as he shoved up, hard, and sent her over heavily on her back and sliding. Down the thatch, head first.

Panic stabbed her innards with icy claws, and then the man was atop her and clawing at her eyes. She brought her knee up, hard, and he *wuffed* in astonished pain and collapsed atop her like a sack of dead hares she'd had to carry once, a dead weight. She kneed him again, rolling on her shoulder as she did so, and kicking, to get half out from under him and spill him down the

40

roof. If she could roll him off but not get grabbed...

One roll she managed, and when he clutched at her she slapped his hands away with all her snarling might, but that left him free to dig his fingers into the thatch and halt his sliding roll.

He clawed his way right back up the roof at her, grimacing in pain but otherwise showing no sign of the damage she hoped—she *knew*—her knee had done. One of his dirty hands came at her throat again, and this time she offered it, not to let him throttle her, but to have the chance, inside his arms, to punch him in *his* throat as hard as she knew how to punch.

He shuddered and recoiled—ah, she *must* have hurt him!—and his hands fell away from her throat. Mist scoot-shuffled up the thatch to where she could drive one booted foot into his gut and kick or at least shove him back—

But he squirmed and twisted around her boot like a sly eel and heaved himself up from the roof in a great pounce that brought him down on her arm and shoulder, all of his weight crashing down, pinning her.

Mist struggled, but it was like trying to lift a castle atop her. She flailed and kicked helplessly, while he grimly crawled farther atop her, clawing his way like a cat across her until he was entirely atop her, heavy and stinking and breathing hotly into her face. She twisted her head away to keep his foul mouth from kissing her, but he was spitting into her eyes, and through their suddenly stinging, swimming gaze she saw with still-mute horror that he was closing both of his dirty, hairy hands around one of hers, just above the wrist, and tugging...

He's trying to break my wrist!

Mist knew that in another moment he would, and then she'd be helpless to stop him shoving her off the roof. She was going to die here, die on this rooftop in this unfamiliar, unfriendly city without anyone from home even knowing—

He got a good grip and grinned nastily at her, their noses almost touching. And now it seemed he did want a kiss, was opening his foul maw to—

Crash his face down against hers, suddenly limp and heavy.

There was suddenly something wet and sticky in her hair. And spattered across her forehead.

"*Sorry*, Mist. I'm usually tidier than that."

It was Aunt Teagan, towering over her and the man whose brains were now all over her and the fireplace poker in her aunt's hand.

Which she set neatly on the roof ere calmly rolling the dead man off Mist and to one side, to make very sure that she wasn't at all tangled with him before she turned him as if he was a mere doll or bundle of clothes before shoving him into a roll that left the thatch crackling—and the roof suddenly bereft of dirty-handed men.

The thud sounded wet and heavy and very, very final.

"My, my, but thieves are getting clumsier and clumsier in the city, these days," Aunt Teagan remarked, almost cheerfully. "Can't even climb around on my rooftop without falling to their deaths."

Then her strong but gentle hands were helping Mist up, and Mist was trying to sob but managing only a sort of dry husking whimper.

"Come," Teagan said gently, and led her by the hand to an open window well along the roof from the corner.

The way she'd obviously reached the roof. Mist clambered head-first through it and tumbled thankfully down a stepstool to one of the cleanest attic floors she'd ever seen.

Teagan disappeared for a moment, then came back with the poker and Mist's sack, and said briskly, "We can do better than the *roof*, lass."

She closed the window and firmly dogged it shut—there was a stout metal bar hung with bells that got fitted onto the dogs last, to prevent them being easily or soundlessly turned by anyone smashing the window from the outside—then led the way through the gloom of old storage chests and broken furniture to a well light was streaming up from, and down the stairs it held to the floor below.

There she flung open the second door on the right and tossed Mist's sack into the room beyond. Mist followed it and found that it was lying on a neatly-made-up bed.

"Behold the room," her aunt said in dry tones, "where you've been staying, as my guest, all this time."

When Mist stared at her open-mouthed, she winked and added, "Bide here for a moment. I'll be back with something warming. Chamberpot's under the bed if you need it."

Mist sat still, trying to make something more than a whisper or a hoarse squeak come out of her mouth. She was managing words by the time her aunt reappeared with two cups of steaming hearth-broth to sip.

The best meal Mist had ever tasted.

They sat on the bed sipping and silently eyeing each other, for what seemed like a long time.

Or perhaps Mist just wanted it to never end.

She realised her cup was almost empty, and tried to make it last, shaking her head slightly. She shuddered only once.

He was gone, he was dead, he couldn't come clutching her ever again.

"Care to talk about your…roof-dancing partner?" Teagan asked gently, then. "Or anything?"

"Not particularly," Mist told her. And managed a wry smile, to soften her reply.

Teagan nodded, unsmiling, and sipped more broth.

Silence fell. And stretched.

Their eyes met. And held.

Mist knew she was expected to say something, but gave her aunt only silence.

After a few long breaths more, Teagan lifted her mug and transferred her gaze from Mist to it.

"The young are always full of hope and dreams. And rage," she told it. And sipped. "They haven't been crushed yet." Another sip. "They always intend to change the world, but if they find a place to call their own in the world as it is, and that place has rewards, they stop being young and knowing they can and will change it, and start being older. And knowing they can't. All they can do is ride the changes that come to the world anyway. As they do nothing."

Their eyes met, and Mist shuddered deeply.

Sometimes, truth cuts like a knife.

#

Dusk had fallen by the time the four merchants reached the lamplit front steps of Lecora O'Hart's grand mansion.

Its tall paneled doors began to swing open; the servants had been watching for her.

"Come in," Lecora bade Ardgal, Cairbre, and Torloch, turning to face for as they reached out to touch her hands in farewell. "A good meal awaits us, and better wine, and—"

Her face changed as she saw what was coming for them.

Masked men, racing out of the deepening night, from every street and alley mouth, a silently sprinting army with drawn daggers in their hands.

"Beware!" Lecora cried, hiking her skirts to draw the daggers that rode in hiding high on

42

her thighs. Her three partners whirled, saw their doom, and snatched out their own belt-knives, swearing.

"Into the house!" she hissed at them, backing up the foremost step without looking. "*Hurry!*"

But there was no time left to do that.

Like a swarming tide of dark leather, the masked men broke over Ardgal, Cairbre, and Torloch, bearing down their struggling arms by sheer weight and numbers and then leaping atop them to slam them to the cobbles. Where Cairbre and Torloch were briskly clubbed into numb-armed helplessness and then senselessness with viciously-plied dagger hilts, clubbing like so many war hammers—but Ardgal they sank their blades into, driving deep.

Then they tugged on their hilts to forcibly spread-eagle him, their daggers slicing great long gashes down all his limbs, the blades catching on his joints after they'd pulled his limbs wide.

Ardgal shrieked, an endless high raw screaming that made Lecora weep as she watched.

Watched helplessly, for six blades were at her throat, and cruel hard hands encircled her upper arms. More masked men reached her, and now hands were clasped around her ankles, too.

She watched as a burly masked man drew an axe from where it had been slung down his back, whirled it lovingly overhead, and then brought it down like a woodsman splitting firewood. Chopping at Ardgal Loughnane's joints, fresh dark blood fountaining as his body spasmed.

It took a surprisingly short time to dismember him alive.

If he was still alive. With all that blood, and the masked men swarming to take turns burying their daggers in his torso, it was impossible to tell.

Lecora heard the gasps and shrieks—and retchings, too—of her servants and guards behind her, and knew without turning that they were keeping still because of the daggers at her own throat.

Ardgal had stopped screaming. Now his last gurgles died away, and in the sudden silence the owner of one of the blades menacing Lecora murmured in her ear, "To try to use poison in Ath Cliath, against the King's Rule, is always a fatal mistake."

#

The broth was all gone, but Teagan and Mist were still talking.

"You came here for more than gems," Mist's aunt said gravely, as they stared into each other's eyes.

Mist sighed, then looked away, shaking her head.

"Not that much trust between us? Even now?"

Mist knew her face was flaming. She looked up at Teagan through fresh tears and hissed, "What you know not, you cannot be made to say!"

Teagan almost smiled. "What little I know not," she murmured, then set down her cup and put her arms around Mist.

"Be careful," she whispered in Mist's ear, as they embraced. "Oh, be careful. The King is a superb dancer."

"What?" Mist asked, genuinely bewildered. What did *dancing* have to do with—?

"Taking a city is a matter of swords. Or starvation. Keeping it, however, is far harder, for the keeper is now the target, pinned to his throne. And there he must sit, as all who do not wish him well ready their slings and arrows for him. Trusting in his armor—the mailed fist of might—or in his dancing, the weaving webs of mutual benefit and manipulating foes into endless 'the times are not right to strike' moments. The good dancers can last a long time."

CHAPTER 9

Mael had never liked the masks. Somehow they made it harder to keep one's balance in the dark, as well as cutting down on what one could see out of the corners of one's eyes. Yet Mael had not lasted this long by putting foolish comfort and preference above prudence.

Or the King's will.

It was very late, now, or early, and the city around them was dark as they hastened back to the palace—Mael, Ulfr, Stigr and all the masked rest, trotting easily, daggers sheathed now.

The only nearby source of light and noise was the Skald's Beard, and they stayed wide of it, taking a side-alley and two streets that added some time to their journey but kept them out of sight of that tavern—for the patrons still on their feet there at this time of night were too drunk to know fear, and a King's shadowhand slashed or skull-cracked in a senseless brawl was still slashed or skull-cracked in the cold and sober morning, whatever fate had been meted out to the drunkard who had so served him. The King's long-ago quiet back-chambers decision still held: ignore the place, leaving it a vent for rage and disputes and general discontent, rather than quelling its tumult with a heavy hand and driving its roistering into hiding—and more ire towards the Riverfleet Throne.

The King's shadowhands were amid a stretch of warehouses now, guarded within and truly dark without, nothing astir in these wider streets but scurrying rats.

Which meant that eyes to mark them were few, and they could slow enough to regain their wind.

Stigr used his to ask curiously, "So what was this poison, that it was so obvious a crone knew it in a trice?"

Mael shrugged. "The King has a way of giving orders that makes what he wants done, as opposed to what he says, perfectly clear. I wasted no time hunting crones. The King wanted Loughnane slain as a warning to all, his three fellow schemers in particular, so we slew Loughnane. Don't take your ease; the moment I've reported the deed done, we'll be storming Loughnane's house and confiscating everything. So, we'll be needing wagons. Your task."

"We will?" Stigr grinned. "And how do you know *that?*"

"As I *said*, the King has a way of giving orders..."

#

"I am sent here to work against the King, or even do away with him if I can," Mist found herself admitting to Teagan, at last.

Her aunt merely nodded; it was obvious she knew as much already.

"B-but I'm *scared*," Mist blurted out. "This—" She waved a wild hand to indicate the city outside the walls, and all around them. "—is all so new, so *big*, so *beyond me*. What can I do, one lass from the clan farms and fields, against all the King's warriors, and spies, and—and gold?"

Teagan shrugged. "And *that* is why he still sits on the Riverfleet Throne. Others have reached this same thinking before you."

"But I am my mother's daughter," Mist said fiercely. "I'll *not* run home like a frightened hare, having done nothing. Can you get me into the Palace?"

Teagan smiled. "I can take you there right now. And get us both inside by...secret ways. Yet if we get caught, you must be prepared to act as if the King wants you in his bed, and that's why we're there. And act convincingly, for our lives will depend on it."

Mist stared at her. "*That* will work?"

Teagan's smile acquired a twinkle. "It has before."

Mist lifted an eyebrow. Teagan's smile didn't change.

After a moment, Mist shrugged. "Whatever I need do. But surely if the King welcomes any strange lass into his arms, one of them before this would have come with a knife. Or poison. Or both."

"You'll not get as far as the King. Far from it. But there are courtiers aplenty in Riverfleet Palace, and some of them are men who won't say no. But we're not trying for that; we're finding our pretext for going in. And being found in the halls there, and challenged. We can say we were turned away, and are seeking a way out."

Mist let out a loud sigh of exasperation, resignation, and—why not, by the gods? She lifted her chin, and told her aunt fiercely, "I'll chance it."

"Then come. *No* weapons. Not even the smallest knife. And, Mist Damhain, *try* not to get us both killed this night."

Mist managed a wry grin. "I can but try."

#

Aha. *That* door.

The stone arch half a block away was certainly nondescript enough, and lacked guard, placard, or hanging lantern. Brandr turned away before some stray eye could catch him watching it, strode a few doors down, then pretended to find something of interest in a shop window.

He found himself gazing at jeweled hairnets. Well, why not? You could buy everything else done up with gold or gems in Ath Cliath, why not hairnets?

He half-turned back in the direction of the arch, head bent as if peering at something at that end of the shop window but looking up sidewise from under his brows.

Yes! He could now see the connection he was looking for, up along the roofline. Where the sun was still bright, though dusk was upon the city and the light was getting dim down here at street level, in the shadows.

Although the door he'd tailed the tax-takers to seemed to belong to a building at last four along the streetfront row away from any of the outposts of the Palace—courtiers' offices and the like, that spread out from the grand rising bulk of the Palace into the city like reaching fingers, or better, talons—the roof of that building was joined, along with all the rest along yon street-front, to the spired stone pile on the end that *had* to be a courtiers' den. And where there was one continuous roof, there was likely a continuous attic, or linked attics…and for that matter, perhaps even linked cellars.

So he'd found where at least four trios of tax collectors, and their soldier escorts, went when their "taking" day was done. Yes, there was another threesome, approaching the same door, and now looking oh-so-casually but warily down the surrounding streets to see who might be watching. Brandr turned away and started striding, making for home ere night came. He'd go shopping along the street where that door was on the morrow, and look more closely. It'd be guarded, surely…

He'd turned a corner and was a block away and about to cross another street when he heard the first ragged shouts and screams.

Not coming from where the tax-takers had headed, but from the distance, far down the street he was crossing.

And headed his way.

Then the shoulder-to-shoulder hastening foot traffic that he'd come to know was normal in Ath Cliath erupted into darting, ducking aside, frightened folk—like fish he'd seen trying to escape a closing net in a cold Hibernian river once—and he saw apples dropped, bouncing, and rolling underfoot. Men tripping and staggering, then sprinting. What was—?

And then he saw the flash of blades.

Not fighting, nor yet determined hacking. What he was seeing was dirty, unshaven men in work-stained smocks running like the wind, waving swords and knives and at least one ornate, gilded table leg that had been torn away from the rest of its table at anyone in their way or who looked like wanting to dispute passage with them.

"Slave break!" someone bellowed in astonished fear, a bare breath before Brandr reached the same conclusion. So escaped slaves were not a common occurrence in Ath Cliath...

He ducked under a fat merchant's arm, around two frightened and exclaiming women clutching richly bagged wares, both of them dressed in clothes the richest man in his clan might have strained to afford, and got himself to the nearest alleymouth.

In time to whirl and watch that armed human tide burst past.

He counted, as best he could. Someone had freed—and armed—at least twoscore slaves!

And then he saw gilded helms. Soldiers of the King, armored and with spears in hand, pushing through the street crowd that was rushing the other way to get away from the slaves. Brandr heard them curse as frantic citizens slammed into them repeatedly, knocking them off balance and slowing them and forcing them to point their spears at the sky time and again.

Then they were through, shouting at the onrushing slaves and bringing their spears down—and then they were snarling and shuddering in the heart of a whirling storm of desperate swords and knives as the slaves swept over them and past...and sagging to the cobbles, butchered before they could make a stand.

The slaves swept on, and Brandr followed slowly, keeping close to the front walls of shops and pretending to just be headed in the same direction, not chasing the ragged running men nor paying them overmuch attention. He wanted to see Ath Cliath's response. The slaves were running wildly, but if they knew the city at all, surely they'd be making for a gate to get out, and there'd be gate-guards...

There were, and more soldiers, and the cobbles before the gate became a bloody battlefield where a few in royal livery fell, but far more slaves, ere the few survivors fled, seeking an easier gate, or a place to hide, or perhaps a drowning death in the river.

Brandr was far from Dun's Hearth, and decided, with full night coming on and lantern-bearing bands of soldiers converging from everywhere he looked, that heading for his room at the inn would be prudent. He didn't want anyone who served the King to notice him, and mayhap remember his face.

Aye, head for home—or such a home as it was. No doubt the usual spies would be waiting.

#

The young Hibernian did not notice the two men struggling under the weight of a barrow piled high with bulging grain-sacks as he turned to head for the inn.

And little wonder. They kept their heads down, faces hidden in cowls, but from time to time the older, leaner one gazed at the blood and bodies on the cobbles by the gate, and his face was sad.

That face belonged to Oswin Silverlock. He, the man with him, and a handful of other faithful of the White God had worked to free the slaves and arm them—and it had been a mistake and a sin.

He felt sick, knowing they would likely all die and that he was powerless to stop the bloodshed. This was not the first time that he'd disagreed with the wisdom of orders given him by his superiors, and no doubt it would not be the last.

He mouthed a silent prayer to God to forgive us all, and put his shoulder into making the barrow creak on its way. It was easy for a priest who'd never set foot in Ath Cliath to order that slaves be freed, to work against the sin of slavery, and to shake King Sitric's rule and slave-sale-tax profits.

But how did it help anyone, if it caused violence and death?

#

Mael tore off his mask thankfully and nodded at the guards waiting inside the unobtrusive door the King's shadowhands usually used, the one closest to their armory. Stigr and the rest strode with him, jesting and chattering now.

"*Properly* clean your blades, mind!" Mael barked. "Nobles are sour enough that his blood'll likely eat at your steel worse than other mens' gore!"

The shadowhands around him were still chuckling at that as they turned the corner and burst into the armory, glad that, unlike Mael the Sharp, they didn't have to report to the King ere they headed out again to plunder Ardgal Loughnane's mansion—

And came to a sudden astonished, silent halt.

A tall and terrible figure stood waiting for them, in the heart of the room.

A man they knew.

The King, crowned and armored and night-cloaked, as if the city was at war.

As they stared at him, the Lord of Ath Cliath coldly snapped out a few names, and added the words, "You will hasten and find these citizens, and protect them—*right now.*"

"O-of course, my king," Mael replied. "Protected against who?"

"The slaves now running amok in the streets," the King replied bleakly. When the jaws of Mael and the other shadowhands dropped open, he added contemptuously, "You think you hounds are my only eyes and ears?"

Then he strode past them and out of the room, flinging back over his shoulder: "*Hide your faces!*"

Mael and Stigr exchanged glances, then they and the rest hastened to the shelves and racks around the room, to snatch down their full masks, and the hoods that went with them, and extra weapons.

"Helms and soldiers' jerkins with the royal badge!" Mael bellowed. "And big war axes, all! I'll explain on the way!"

Then he turned and added in a growl to Stigr, "This *doesn't* mean you get out of procuring the wagons, mind!"

"Never doubted it," Stigr grinned, as Mael led the rush back out into the dark back passages of the Palace.

None of the hurrying shadowhands noticed two pairs of eyes silently watching them through the open doorway of a dark robing room.

#

When Mist stirred to speak, her aunt laid a firm finger across her lips. They waited in silence for what seemed to Mist a very long time ere Teagan removed it, and breathed, "Yes?" in the very ghost of a whisper, with no hiss to the 's' at all.

Mist sought to match that way of speaking as she whispered, "I counted eleven, and saw

47

all their faces."

"The sharp-featured one, who commands, is Mael the Sharp," Teagan murmured back. "The one with the hooked nose and the scar is Stigr; the toad-faced one is Ulfr. The tallest, thinnest one is…"

#

Heartsick, Oswin had left his fellow to deal with the barrow, and turned to hasten after the last few fleeing slaves. He could at least witness their deaths, and pray for them.

They were well ahead of him, out of sight, but easy to trace by the shouts of soldiers and betimes the clang of swords and knives.

He caught up to them as they reached another heavily-guarded gate—and again, couldn't get out. They raged and milled about as Oswin stole into an alleymouth and horns began to blow.

The King's warriors were coming from all directions. Among them were full-helmed, darting men with huge war-axes, who rushed right past the cornered slaves and smashed down the doors of houses the slaves had their backs to, then withdrew, some of them into Oswin's alley.

He scarce had time to slump down and play the sleeping drunkard ere the axemen were in the darkness with him and turning to yell, "In! Get inside!"

And the slaves poured into the homes whose doors were shattered. Shrieks and angry yells promptly arose within them, followed by the clash and clang of blades swung in earnest. Followed by a thunderous charge of heavy-booted soldiers of Ath Cliath, racing to the succour of citizens whose homes had been invaded by the desperate miscreants.

Oswin, slumped uncomfortably against a rough stone wall, could hear those very words declaimed in his head, and had to quell his urge to shake it and despair aloud. He settled for wincing, as he heard the first unmistakeable sound of the house-trapped slaves dying. It sounded like they were fighting hard to take the King's soldiers with them, in what skalds now liked to call "a pitched battle." The nearest house to Oswin fairly shook—and then the casements of one of its upper windows abruptly burst open to pour two struggling men out and down, down to the cobbles, head-first. One was a King's soldier, the other a dirty, ragged man who had two blades through him, but his hands locked around the royal warrior's throat.

They bounced once, together, then lay still, blood slowly seeping out from where they lay.

Oswin closed his eyes tightly against that sight, and listened to the last few raw dying screams.

"There are more!" one of the axemen standing over him snarled suddenly. "Hear you?"

And sure enough, from the far distance came fresh shouts and the clash of arms. That set the axemen running again, heading for that new battle, and in a trice Oswin had the alley to himself again.

He peered through slitted eyes, then feigned a drunkard's groaning spasm so he could look back behind himself, down the alley. The moment he was certain he was alone, he sprang up and started running after the axemen.

After half a block he already knew, heart sinking, where he and the King's axemen were heading. Right past the Skald's Beard.

Where, sure enough, a few pantingly sprinting moments later, he found that the drinkers inside that tavern had seen the fleeing slaves outside, blearily judged them ideal targets to pound to the cobbles with their fists. Gleefully, they'd sallied forth to do just that, and had already bludgeoned senseless half a dozen of the slowest, wounded slaves.

By now, the noise and tumult had brought many citizens into the streets, angry and spoiling for trouble. Carts and tavern stools were being hurled, men were brawling with their fists, and half-asleep faces at windows were hurling insults or shouting boisterous encouragement—and even wagers.

Only one house was ablaze, but even as Oswin spotted the leaping flames, he saw them all suddenly die away into darkness, going out as if by themselves. "A miracle!" he whispered to the night sky. "God, thank you for turning not your face from us, even here in this den of Odin-worshippers!"

#

Despite his breathlessness from sprinting here with heavy axe and helm and all, Mael cursed. Trust these *idiots* here in the mean streets to set a fire or three!

"By morn, half the city could be burnt—and the King will have all our hides for it!"

And then a string of oaths died half-finished in his mouth as the merry flames abruptly darkened, sank, and died. Mael looked around wildly for the cause; that *had* to be magic at work, and the King would want to know *yesterday* if anyone was working magic in his city—

Then the swirl of a cloak caught his eye, down a dark alley, and he relaxed, smiling grimly. He knew that tall cloaked and hooded figure as it turned away, and its stride confirmed it.

He hastened after the King, just in case any overzealous soldiers saw that departing figure and thought to strike first and ascertain identity second.

Mael knew without looking that Stigr and the rest of the shadowhands were following him. The streets weren't safe this night; the King needed an escort.

Yet it seemed the Lord of Ath Cliath was in a hurry right now, and was not exhausted from hewing down doors and fighting in the streets, nor wearing and carrying unaccustomed weight. Try as he might, Mael could never quite catch up to the hooded figure with cloak streaming in its wake, and soon enough, he and the other covert agents of the King found themselves following their master into the Palace through their usual back door.

#

Mist winced at the thought. If they'd been just a few breaths slower...

The axemen were doffing their helms to reveal masked faces as they hastened in through the door she and Aunt Teagan had just used to get out of the Palace. Undetected, she hoped.

Teagan lifted her head and sniffed the air. "Storm coming," she murmured softly.

Mist was making use of this chance to name and count each shadowhand crowding through the narrow door. "Eleven," she said at last. But they were led by another, a twelfth," she whispered aloud.

"Behold the King," Teagan whispered back, wryly.

Mist stared at her. And then shivered.

ChAPTER 10

The chatter in Dun's Hearth was loud and excited. The news was all over the city.

Oswin clutched a cup of hot broth—all his stomach seemed to want this morn, though the morning fry smelled inviting enough—and kept his head down, as tongues wagged all around him in the common room.

An *army* of slaves had escaped in the night, armed to the teeth, and murdered scores of citizens before the King had personally led his soldiers to try to recapture them all. Yet it seemed they were crazed, inflamed by foul magic of the White God, and had to be killed to stop them slaughtering everyone they could, heedless of their own safety! Yes, the King protected the city from what could have been—would have been—far, far worse!

The gods themselves seemed angered by what had befallen, for the sky was darkening for a storm; longtime residents of the city were eyeing it and muttering, "Bad one coming, by the looks of it," and similar, as they ducked back in from morning errands to dine.

The young Hibernian, Brandr Fylan, was sitting alone at a corner table, looking as exhausted as Oswin felt, but likely not as heartsick.

The priest's heart plunged to new depths as new arrivals pushed into the room.

"I was *there*, I tell you!" one was growling loudly. "I saw it all!"

Oswin knew him. Ulfr, one of King Sitric's covert dirty-workers, and he thought two of the men with him were also shadowhands. One of that pair caught his eye, and he hastily put his head into his cup and drank deep, despite the nigh-scalding heat.

So the King had ordered them to spread word of his heroics—and of the lurking peril that endangered this fair city, had he?

Oswin had already been weary and heartsick. He had not thought anything else that could strike his ears this morn would leave him aghast, but...something had, and this was it.

He needed something stronger than this excellent broth, and he needed it *now*.

He had caused *so* many deaths, and achieved nothing for the men he'd thought he was bringing freedom to. And the King of Ath Cliath was swiftly and deftly turning it all to his own advantage.

Orders or no, he, Oswin Silverlock, had made a fool's blunder. Worse, he had sinned.

The strong drink he'd signaled for came, and he drained it in one gasping gulp and asked for another ere the man who'd brought it could turn away.

He asked for two, so that when that man returned, Oswin could swiftly drain another jack, and still have one in hand. To at least taste, as it too went down.

#

It had been a hard trot through the streets, but Mael surprised himself as he hurried to the King; it seemed a breathless man could still yawn.

Stifling another, he sidestepped into the room where Sitric was sipping mulled wine and going over the latest import and export reports. The King looked his wordless question.

Mael bowed. "We've found the priest Oswin Silverlock. In the Dun's Hearth inn. Half drunk. Should we take him?"

The King surprised him by saying firmly, "*No*. Nor Brandr Fylan or Mist Damhain—who was in these halls last night, I'm told, and I'd like to know how *that* happened."

Mael frowned. "How indeed?"

The King half-smiled. "Find out. But unless they menace me directly, I want none of those three harmed, or taken, or even trammeled in their doings. Any damage they do is just what I want, to provide the populace—the merchants of this city who were wealthy and powerful before I came, in particular—with vivid examples of just what my oh-so-oppressive rule is protecting them from."

#

Teagan looked in on Mist, in the little bedchamber under the attic. The young Warrior Queen of the Damhain was asleep, face down in the bedclothes, but judging by her movements and muffled, incoherent exclamations, deep in a nightmare.

Teagan sighed and headed down to the kitchen. Cooking was her way of comforting herself.

There was excited chatter in the streets outside, and heavily armed patrols of soldiers were everywhere. Including in the alley, where each one in turn examined the bloodstain where the man who'd failed to fly after being rolled off her roof had landed, and long since been taken away.

And then, each and every patrol, straightened up to glare suspiciously up at the roof and then at every one of her back windows, as if royal-spy-murderers lurked eagerly behind each one of them.

She decided to keep her shop closed and shuttered today. The city was in an uproar.

#

The morning frying was abating, for most who lodged at Dun's Hearth were long since up and about their business—shop-work or warehouse strongchest- and cask-hauling, for most of them—but a few rooms held renters who'd gone back to bed, and were now snoring.

Brandr Fylan, for one, and the priest Oswin Silverlock, for another.

Mael yawned again. All this trotting across the city wasn't making him any younger.

There, and about time, too!

It was Haddr Three Fingers, and his arrival meant that a certain nigh asleep on his feet Mael the Sharp, and a just-as-tired Stigr, were relieved.

Haddr could now keep watch over the Hibernian or the White God worshipper, and there was a backup outside in case either left the inn, and Haddr followed to see where they went and what they did.

Well, it was a living.

The wind was rising as Mael and Stigr headed for the Palace, and their waiting sleeping-chambers. The sky was getting dark fast, which meant the coming storm would be a bad one.

It was.

They were still two streets from the Palace when it hit, a gray cloak or curtain advancing through the sky sweeping over them and suddenly becoming a driving downpour that drenched to the skin even before they could get out a curse.

They cursed anyway, and with feeling, as they trudged the last weary—and now soaked—strides to their door and inside, where they found their part of the Palace dark and cold. They squelched their ways to their rooms, half-deafened by great peals of thunder now rolling over Ath Cliath.

"Odin's angry," Stigr growled, an instant before lightning blinded them both.

"Thor, too," Mael replied, as more lightning stabbed down. "This'll give the slavers the excuse they need, in the wake of the slave-break, not to open their markets today."

Stigr grunted and shoved his door open to hurry and light a fire against the chill, even before he got his dripping-wet things off.

Mael did the same, to the thunderous accompaniment of rain hammering relentlessly on the Palace roof. There'd be flooding by the river, if it kept up like this.

And the worst of it all was, this could be the displeasure of any god one cared to name. No doubt those dolts of the White God would blame it on King Sitric's evil rule and the slavery he allowed, whereas the most devout of Odin would blame it on the One-Eyed King not exterminating the White God-lovers everywhere he ruled, and beyond.

All Mael knew for certain was, if this kept up, and the King sent him out as often as usual, he'd catch his death of cold.

Best send many more down to Niflheim before him, if that was his fate.

#

The rain hammered on every roof in all the city, hard and relentlessly, its din stretching on and on. In the Skald's Beard, the ceiling wept as all that drumming water found leaks and poured—not dripped—down through the roof-beams and old, rotten attic flooring, then down the upright timbers of two floors beneath to fall like mill-spouts in half a dozen places across the taproom, spraying surroundings with the force of its ongoing arrival, drenching the tables and causing much wearily disbelieving profanity.

A few patrons staggered blearily to their feet to unsteadily assault servers, holding them personally responsible, as the deluge continued to splash on the tables—and on the snoring slumped forms of a few drunkards who'd already passed out.

The servers fended off the clumsy, heavy-fisted attacks with ease, and half-rushed, half-dragged persistent belligerents to the doors, and heaved them out into the wet.

The street was now its own shallow but raging river; the waters dark with what was being washed off walls and cobbles.

And so it was all across the city, as the storm raged on.

#

Forkundr Redbeard staggered into the gloomy room wet and cursing, and brought a lot of the storm with him.

The four men already around the table winced and shielded their drinking-jacks against the rain until he got the door slammed again, and his drenched cloak off.

"Have you ever seen the like?" he greeted them, by way of not apologizing for his tardiness. "How many of the worst city hovels'll be washed away down to the sea before it's done, I wonder?"

"Odin's judgment, that's what it is!" Borekr Ketilsson growled into his drink, as if he expected it to agree with him. "Odin's frown upon us all."

"Aye, but for what?" Eylir Grimsson barked. "The King'll say, sure, that it's divine displeasure because he's been too slow to conquer and sweep away all who cleave to other gods—like the White God!"

The long-nosed, nasal-voiced man who'd been warming his hands at the lone lit lantern in the room, at the center of the table, spoke up as sourly as usual. "Ah, but if he starts butchering and burning the priests of the White God, it'll be the beginning of the end for him, for all his piled-high gold and bright power! Ath Cliath flourishes when it's a trading-floor for all, not for a

52

favoured few who keep slaves to do their work for them! No slaves toil in *my* shop!"

Forkundr snorted as he dropped heavily into the last vacant chair. "As if you'd ever had enough skatt all at once to rub together and buy even *one* slave, Falki, to say nothing of gold rods!"

"Bah! I'm an *honest* trader, *friend*, and if that leaves me a stride behind and a coin short of others in this grand new City of Gold and Slaves that Sitric the Snake is building, so be it! *I* can face Odin clear-hearted at my dying day, where our so-proud King and so many of those who fawn over him and count their new jewels will be joining him in torment in Niflheim!"

Forkundr shrugged and drained the flask he'd produced from somewhere in one long pull. He and Falki Longbeak had no deep love for each other, but they hated King Sitric Cuaran more than they detested each other.

"Were you followed here, Fork?" asked the last man at the table, in the gravel-laced deep warhorn voice for which he was known across Ath Cliath. Grimkell the Throat he was to one and all, now that his mother was dead. A skald who crafted eulogies and hero-praises for fees, he'd been composing an unflattering Saga of Sitric for as long as anyone could remember; it now ran to more than a hundred verses, and Grimkell could win arguments by merely threatening to recite it.

"No," Forkundr said shortly. "Not in this. I did see one of the King's sneak-rats, but he made the mistake of following me across the timbers where they're re-roofing the Sword Stream, and I turned on him with a timber and shoved him into its flow. Last seen shouting feebly for help, a good way downriver."

There was a general roar of coarse mirth at this. "First bath he's probably had in years," someone suggested inevitably, and Forkundr was toasted by those who had flasks with them that still had something in them.

"So," Grimkell growled, leaning forward until his nose and beard with both in peril from the lantern and lowering his voice to a rumble akin to a vargr purring—if that was the right word for the contented sound vargr made after they'd eaten enough raw red meat to be sated. "We're agreed, and blood-sworn: Sitric Cuaran must be removed—from the Riverfleet Throne and likely from the ranks of the living. Time to start talking about how we'll manage this *small* task."

There were cynical chuckles. Every one of them—shopkeepers and lesser merchants, all— were Norse and worshipped the Aesir, and they'd all supported Sitric or sailed in his warships, to fetch up here in Ath Cliath and flourish because of his rule. But they all thought the gold and his ambition had led him astray almost from the moment he'd put on the crown.

It was time, and past time, that he be removed.

Aye, but how?

#

In the howling heart of the deluge, the huge and expensive draft horses were snorting, bucking, and betimes kicking their displeasure at being out amid stabbing lightnings, street-shaking rolls of thunder, and the driving, hammering, *biting* downpour. Yet they were well-drained, and the drovers were smart enough to use gently voices rather than their whips, so the large and well-fitted wagons creaked through the nigh-deserted streets at a plodding pace. The drovers huddled beneath layers of seal-skins, heads bowed against the blinding, driving rain so they could see—and sat on the foreledges to keep low for fear of the lightning.

When at last they reached the mansion of the slain Ardgal Loughnane, they thankfully drew up, sprang down, threw their skins over the heads of the horses to calm them, and splashed up grand steps that were awash in spray like the decks of a ship in stormy seas.

Fearful servants opened the doors only a crack at their hammerings, cudgels ready in hand, but relaxed when the foremost and burliest drover pulled back his hood and they saw the lionine face of Torloch Dargan.

He growled a generous offer to serve under his roof to the servants, was answered by fearful nods, and the men who'd come with him streamed inside and started emptying the contents of the house out into the wagons. Torloch turned, drew his sword, and stood watch.

He was damned if Sitric One-Eyed would order the murder of a leading merchant of the city and then plunder the man's worldly goods ere half Ath Cliath knew he was dead.

He and Lecora would get to Ardgal's coin and fine things before the King's thieves could. If Sitric Cuaran could kill citizens and take their goods untrammeled, no one was safe.

Greed ruled that Odin-lover. Oh, it was strong in most merchants, but in that one it had become madness.

And madness must be stamped out, not allowed to spread.

#

Oswin came awake very suddenly, shivering. He was wet with sweat, yet cold as ice.

And clear-headed, as alert as if roused for battle.

He could see it just as clearly now, awake in, yes, the middle of the night, as he'd beheld it in his dream.

The vision that could only have come from the White God.

That showed him what he must do.

Clarity, that's all he asked from God—and God had given it to him.

"Thank you," he hissed, through chattering teeth, as he stumbled to the waiting ewer of wash-water, and emptied it over his head to dash the sweat away.

Arrghh. He kept that heartfelt pain-shout silent, for he'd known just how icy the water would be. It hadn't disappointed. Ill things rarely did.

Reaching for a towel, Oswin heard the rain hammering on the window-shutters with renewed force. He shrugged and left off bothering about the towel.

Wet as he was, he started tugging on his clothes. They stuck to him and made it a clumsy struggle, of course.

Just like the life of every worshipper of the True God.

#

The storm was building to an even greater height. Wildness not seen in Ath Cliath in years—generations. Lightnings were stabbing at the tallest towers again and again, the air alive with their crackling fury. The air smelled of blood and hot iron and scorched stone.

Again and again, the bright bolts split the sky. Striking the towers repeatedly—and a certain smithy on Hightide Street, thanks to its great stores of metal.

The House of Six Smiths was deserted at this time of night and in this weather, for the six forgemasters who owned it knew what befell in their forge-floor when lightnings struck from the sky.

What they feared to be too close to was happening right now. Blue-white and blinding bolts that had struck the roof howled down any path and into the big room where a prentice—long since fled—would in better weather have been keeping the forge-fire stoked.

Time and again, lightnings snarled, crackled, and played eerily across the anvil, and along the bench where the forge-hammers and tongs lay in neat array. Crash and flash, crash and crackling washes of Thor's Fury across everything, then crash and flash again.

And amid this blinding chaos a door abruptly opened.

Its opening sounded an alarm, a stout pull-cord attached to the door-edge setting several hanging skillets—old, cracked, and rusting, but still good for making noise—to clanging together. Yet for once their din would go unheeded, for the lightnings had been ringing that alarm often and enthusiastically for some time now.

A dark figure stood just beyond the threshold, peering through the doorway, awaiting a lull.

And when it came, that intruder darted forward, snatched up one of the hammers, hefted it, nodded as he turned in feverish haste, and raced back through the door, pulling it shut behind him.

Whereupon a great crack of thunder heralded the coming of the largest, fiercest white lightning bolt yet. It rent the roof of the smithy asunder, stabbed down with a deafening, blinding roar—and split the already-battered anvil.

Outside in the downpour, the fading flash of that same titanic bolt lit up the face of the hammer-thief as he strode determinedly away down the street. Strode without hindrance, for there were no soldiers of the King out on patrol in this storm.

It was Oswin Silverlock.

#

A naked man sat alone in a small room behind three successive locked doors. He was without lamp or lantern, but thanks to the lightnings that betimes came clawing down the chimney to rage around the room, and the rest of the time flashed and snarled their furies all about the Palace, it was not dark.

Not that the Lord of Ath Cliath needed to see the runes, to know them.

Sitric Cuaran was a galdr of long accomplishment, though it was his custom to speak or trace ruins in the air and unleash their power to smite and burn and slay, not cast rune-graven tiles on a bare round tabletop and seek to divine Odin's will from how the runes fell.

But this storm was a great opportunity, both in the respite it gave from every last servant, citizen, and courtier seeking the King's attention for just a pestering moment, and in the risen power so easily harnessed as it seethed and swirled about the city.

And it was timely, for these latest challenges to the Riverfleet Throne were so weak that he could easily swat them away—and yet unusual, and so intriguing. He wanted to understand them ere he destroyed them.

So he'd done off his crown and robes and all, to sit here with nothing between him and runes, no enchantments on ring or blade to mask what the runes might tell him.

What Odin might want him to know.

"For I am nothing without the Allfather," he murmured to the gloom, "and I am his hand in this darkening world of false gods and their mischiefs."

He gathered all the runes in both hands, closed his eyes as he shook what he'd grasped, and tossed them all gently into the air.

"So guide me, Odin."

The crack of lightning that came then blinded him, plunged the room into darkness, and hurled him over backwards to bang his head on the floor. The last thing he heard, as darkness claimed him, was the *klack klack* of rune-tiles striking the walls of the room—hard—and rebounding.

chapter jj

His head was on fire, and pounding.

As if it was the anvil, and a smith Sitric could not see was striking it again and again with his hammer, shaping metal that glowed just the right hue as it was hit, and hit, and *hit* again...

Head ringing to clang of that energetically-wielded hammer, Sitric came awake before he could see who the smith was—someone tall and broad-shouldered and long-bearded, who wore a war-helm—or what was being forged.

Sitric's right hand was clenched into a claw, and throbbed with pain.

He found it obeyed him not, and he had to use the fingers of his other hand, with some effort, to pry his right hand open.

And when he did, he discovered in his palm what he'd apparently been clutching all night: a lone rune-tile.

Its face was blank. Ginungagap. The Void.

The soul. His soul. Perhaps also a signal of a greater destiny for him, in the eyes of the Norns.

It—*any* rune—had several meanings; galdr or not, the gods might hint at which meaning applied to him...or they might not.

We forge our own destinies, one of the skalds had said, centuries ago. An annoyingly trite maxim.

Right, then, Sitric grandson of Ivar, what shall your destiny be?

Conqueror, richest king in the world, builder of gleaming heights of civilization never attained before; he'd thought he'd won himself more in the way of destiny than any man needed, or could expect in a life...but it seemed Odin wasn't finished with him yet.

Or was this the work of other gods? Did they think him so much a pawn and mortal hand of Odin that they wanted their opportunities with him?

Or was that his pride speaking? Granting himself an importance gods would sneer at—or worse, deem good reason for his humbling?

But why should he not be proud of what he'd done? Far more than most mortals, and he had years left yet.

Or did he?

Dung of Nidhogg, it was enough to make a man's brains churn...

He bathed in the warmed and scented water piped and pumped to his close-room, ignored what his dressers had left out for him, and chose his own garments.

Fine, kingly robes. Flame orange for today, yes. For he was the cleansing flame of change, and would ever be...

The Void rune. What did it mean?

His oblivion, perhaps before the day was out? Or was he to bring oblivion to others?

Bah. Brain-churn, indeed.

Sitric chose his tallest, grandest crown, seated it carefully on his head so that it came to just *there* on his brow, inspected himself in a looking-glass taller than he was, and nodded.

Imperious enough. Time to go and conquer things.

The storm had finally moved on, leaving the city drenched and dripping. Bright sunlight greeted him through tall windows as he strode through the Palace.

Courtiers bowed and then scattered, like so many rabbits sent scurrying by a wolf.

Sitric came into a sun-dappled room of many archways in the walls and little furniture to clutter its broad expanse of floor, and there sat down at the lone place prepared for him at a grand
56

new table that displayed the kingdoms all around Ath Cliath in colored tiles inlaid into its high-polished surface.

With Ath Cliath at the very center, of course.

Hot broth was set before him, and a domed platter of slices of cheese, fresh boarfry, and sea-bream, with an array of sauces in little dishes flanking them like so many oversized pearls.

And then decanters of morning wines and ale, with chased silver cups to drink them from. Followed by small side-platters of fruit skillfully carved into the shapes of various sorts of open flowers.

He nodded, and hovering servants fled out every archway, leaving only one standing in a distant arch with his back to the King, awaiting a clap of Sitric's hands as a summons.

As this was to be a repast of private enjoyment, the table lacked the usual platter of messages and court notes for his urgent attention.

Which was a good thing, for although Sitric enjoyed the cut and thrust of wits and words that made up the daily battles of any royal court, there were times when he hungered for the heft of a sword or a good axe in his hand. Conquering was certainly easier than ruling.

He was on his second cup of ale and his third plate of slices when an anxious-looking courtier, splendidly dressed, came hastening through another arch.

Sitric's sunny mood darkened. Dalkr was no dandy; for him to be dressed in such finery this early of a day meant that he was not the bearer of good news.

And his urgency and manner…

Quelling an inward sigh, Sitric extended a wordless hand in a 'speak' command as Dalkr came trotting up.

"Lord and King," was the almost stammered response, "I bring ill news. During the night, despite the fierce weather, someone unknown—or several someones—armed with hammers or the like smashed the splendid statue of Odin you erected before the Palace gates. It's shattered beyond repair, I fear, mere rubble on its plinth."

Suddenly there were anxious faces at every archway, watching. Waiting for his response.

Sitric's self-control nearly slipped. He knew his face had gone cold with fury, and before he could restrain himself, he'd crushed the cup he was drinking from effortlessly in one hand, ale running over his fingers.

Yet he managed to thank Dalkr politely and nod to him in dismissal.

"Every act has a price," he murmured to himself, the words coming out as slow and emphatic as leisurely-laid stones. "And I shall see that this one is paid."

#

The deft and silent servants who'd brought Cairbre Dathaill and Torloch Dargan to this place nodded and withdrew, leaving the two merchant lords facing Lecora O'Hart at what seemed to be more or less the center of this vast, damp cellar of many broad stone pillars. Water dripped in the distance, slowly but steadily, and there was a faint reek of mildew.

Too damp to store wares, and so empty. Cairbre surveyed the pillars marching away in all directions, turning on one elegantly booted heel to do so, and commented, "Luxury."

Lecora shrugged. "Good sightlines, to see anyone spying on us. Words echo and carry, mind, so kindly mutter."

Torloch nodded heavily. "Sitric teaches us prudence. And rage. So, how shall we avenge Ardgal's death?"

Lecora shrugged again, the slightest shift of shapely black-leather-clad shoulders. "Poison, of course; how else?"

Cairbre's smile was no more than a brief wry twist of his lips. "If we are to be treated as poisoners, why not *be* poisoners?"

"The King's Rule and his savagery at enforcing it," Lecora replied, "tells me he has not the galdr's rune to protect himself against poison."

It was Torloch's turn to almost smile. "So," he said grimly, "poison it shall be."

He and Lecora both looked to Cairbre, who was rumored to trade in poisons, among the medicines and perfumes his ships brought from afar.

And who now stirred into striding, two paces one way and then back again, jaw set in thought. "It sits ill with me to use such means, but against this snake anything needful must be done."

Lecora and Torloch both nodded.

"And as it happens," Cairbre added, "certain of my suppliers have recently shown me exotic venoms from hot jungles in far southern lands that can be dissolved in wine or ale and yet retain their efficacy."

Lecora nodded as if this was not news to her at all. And given the reach and ranks of her spies all over the city, it might not have been. "So, how to get it into the King's wine, and his alone?"

"There, I believe I can be of help," Torloch said. "A favour is owed..."

#

Warm and full of good food, Mist sat in Aunt Teagan's kitchen, enjoying the smells and the flickering lamplight.

To her surprise, she felt a certain contentment over and beyond the pleasant feeling of mere comfort. She and her aunt had been cooking together, and then eating, and talking all the while, and at some point now lost to her—if she'd ever noticed it at all—Mist had gradually reached the conclusion that no matter what Sitric might be up to, he shouldn't be slain, because Ath Cliath needed to survive as the hope of Hibernia and possibly all humankind in deepening Fimbulwinter, and he seemed to be the key to the city staying strong.

But his murderous agents, now...

#

It was a disconcerting day for folk in Ath Cliath. The King's soldiers were suddenly everywhere in the city, asking everyone questions about their whereabouts the previous night.

"Did you know Ardgal Loughnane?"

And regardless of the reply, this was followed by a fierce, snarling into faces, "Oh? When were you last at his house?"

And always suddenly and loudly, "Do you revere Odin?"

Citizen or visitor, those being questioned were frightened. Most denied knowing Loughnane, but claimed to revere Odin, even if they didn't. Even the drunkards at the Skald's Beard were compelled to make surly reply.

Many gave replies that neither pleased nor satisfied the soldiers, and were dragged away for firm questioning. When citizens demanded to know what was going on, the soldiers refused to say. A generous handful of folk suspected this sudden aggression might have something to do with a statue reduced to rubble at the Palace gates, but those who said so got no confirmation from the soldiers—just harsh hands laid upon them, with haste and enthusiasm, to rush them away from the sun and freedom, no matter their protests.

58

"Did *you* know Ardgal Loughnane?"

The question was barked so loudly it was almost a shout.

"Well, did you? *DID YOU?*"

An inarticulate cacophony of protests, denials, and cursing was the response, but overriding it a louder, deeper, rougher voice: "*Don't* give me that! I'm not stupid! When did you last see him? *When were you last at his house?*"

Oswin Silverlock came awake to this symphony beneath his window, the angrily insistent voices prodding him up from his bed and into full wakefulness as his feet struck the cold hard floor. He staggered to the window and thrust open the shutters, but took care to stand back, not lean out where he might be seen and perhaps ordered down—for they certainly sounded like soldiers.

He dared the briefest of peeks.

They were.

Silently he mouthed the strongest, crudest curse he knew, then sagged against the wall beside the window to listen.

When the soldiers had finished bullying the citizens outside the Hearth and moved on down the street with a few of them in unhappy custody to question the next nearest folk, Oswin closed his shutters again and went back to bed, smiling coldly as he recalled what he'd done with the hammer when the last shards of the statue were rocking and settling at his feet: hurl it high, to crash down on the Palace roof, unnoticed by anyone in the lightning-laced thunders of the storm at his height.

So was this the next storm, building to its own height?

#

Mael was in a hurry. He barely noticed the workers struggling with pickaxes and prybars to lift the plinth at the gate—but he *did* notice. The towering statue of brooding Odin had cast a substantial shadow, and that shadow was no more. Two full carts of rubble heralded how busy the workers had been—and how little recognizable was left of Odin Triumphant.

History, now, and almost gone from Ath Cliath without a trace.

To be replaced by a bigger, better Odin just as fast as Mael could help bring that about.

Hence his haste. On a royal mission to seek the sculptor Markvard Stonecleaver of Westsheaf Lane. A stonecarver known to be a devout worshipper of Odin, and skilled, and to be able to work fast.

Markvard was to be brought before the King and offered however much gold it would take to get him to drop all else and make a statue of Odin bigger and grander than the destroyed Odin Triumphant—and as fast as possible.

"Push the King," Sitric had said with glacial calm, "and the King pushes back."

#

Brandr was awake but still weary; last night, the fury of the storm had awakened him repeatedly. He'd eaten a morning meal in the common room rendered unpleasant by his questioning at the hands of the King's soldiers, though they'd put their queries to him with less than half the aggression he'd heard them employing in the street outside.

Brandr suspected this was because the innkeeper had already endured their questions, and had told them that no one had left the Hearth during the night.

A flat lie, he suspected even more strongly, but it had prevented all guests still abed from being dragged from their slumbers and barked at. The sort of trouble no innkeeper wants, even without a tyrannical King being involved.

They were gone now, out into the street to ruin the days of other folk, and Brandr found himself alone in the common room with the keeper.

Who looked as exhausted as Brandr felt, and proved it by sinking into the chair across from Brandr with a sigh and a groan, and pouring himself a jack of strong wine larger than the cup of steaming broth he'd already been nursing.

Brandr gave the man a smile between jack and cup, then told the ceiling softly, "Once there was an innkeeper who was beyond weary from toil, who'd fallen asleep in his night doorguard chair and so saw and heard no one at all arriving or departing until he awakened in the chill dawntime—and wanting no trouble with the King, soldiers, or trade at his inn, he said only that no one came or went."

Brandr added to this a very direct look across the table at the innkeeper, who calmly drained his jack of wine and said flatly, "No keeper of my acquaintance would behave so, oh no."

And added the briefest of winks, his weathered face otherwise even more deadpan than usual.

"Of course. I find myself mistaken," Brandr said with a smile, found his feet, and headed for the stairs.

It would be most prudent to keep to his room for now, what with all of these soldiers striding everywhere and pestering everyone.

About halfway up the worn treads, it occurred to him that whatever dark deeds and intrigues King Sitric was involved in or even hatching, he shouldn't be slain, forced from his throne, or even weakened in the eyes of the wider world.

As that world needed Ath Cliath just now. Needed this gilded city not just to survive, but to flourish, as the hope of Hibernia and possibly all humankind in the face of cold, dark, deepening Fimbulwinter. For all folk might fear or hate him, the King's harsh but attentive rule seemed vital to the city staying strong. So it followed that all Brandr Fylan should do was ascertain if the King was secretly paying anyone with all the gathered taxes—and is therefore beholden to someone.

Someone aside from Odin, that is.

Perhaps Sitric Cuaran was merely a religious fanatic who poured money into temples and priests to further their work. Hmm.

He must find out, then depart the city to report—and thereafter stay away from it, for its allure was strong.

Ath Cliath was money, and power, and energy; the feeling of getting things done. All of which called to him, and by Crom and all, he wanted them—but he must renounce them, or he wouldn't be Brandr Fylan anymore. He'd be someone else.

Someone he was not at all sure he'd like.

#

As they talked on, Mist was forced to agree with Aunt Teagan that any effort on her part to eliminate the ruthless, agile slayers King Sitric employed as his covert agents, his—what had Teagan called them? *Shadowhands*—was doomed.

She'd likely not even take down one of them before she lost her own life, let alone more than a dozen. So to cross blades with any of them would just be throwing her life away.

So how, then...?

Poison.

Teagan gave her a look across the kitchen table, and with a start, Mist realized she'd inadvertently said that word aloud.

"Not an honourable weapon," her aunt said calmly, "but fitting to take down serpents and other vermin. The question is: if you remove Sitric Cuaran, does the greatness he's brought to this city perish with him? Ath Cliath is a heap of gold and gems and other riches the like of which this world has never seen all gathered in one place, and it will be fought over. Will it be shattered and ruined in the struggle? Or survive? And if the Riverfleet Throne survives, will the bottom warming it belong to someone as ruthless, sly, and coldly nasty as the One-Eyed King—or someone worse?"

"But...but such questions could be raised against any change in rulership," Mist pointed out, "to ensure that no ruler was ever removed. Ideally, we would have a shining replacement king—or queen!—waiting in our back bedchamber, and many militarily-strong, rich, well-respected citizens pledged to back our new choice, so that as Sitric's corpse was carried out one door, they would step in through another and be in place before any other seeker after power could get ready—but with this King, or any king who employs spies and shadowhands as this one does, such preparations just aren't possible. So removing them is a must. Oh, he'll rebuild them, I know, but doing so will keep him busy so he hasn't the time and enthusiasm for worse mischief—and in the meantime, prudence born of fear will keep his ruling excesses to a minimum."

Teagan was nodding and smiling. "You see the endless dance clearly enough. And you know the danger to you—and to me, and to all of our clan—in trying this. Something I know the clan accepts, or they'd not have sent you. Something *I* accept, know you. So, though it cost us our lives—and it probably will, and the losing of them is unlikely to be quick or at all pleasant—we go forward with this, yes?"

"Yes," Mist said firmly. "If we can see a way to do so. How to get poison? And how to, ah, deliver it so it doesn't slaughter palace servants or innocents, but just the King's pet slayers?"

Teagan reached out across the table and took Mist's hand. "Come."

Her aunt led her to the stairs, and up.

"You have poison upstairs?"

"Any house holds many poisons, not least in its cookpots, but no. Nothing practical. We're headed for one end of my attic. To a spot where I can be sure no one can get close enough to eavesdrop without my hearing them approach. Not as comfortable a place to plot as my kitchen, but safer. We must be prudent before all else, now."

Mist nodded, and they climbed the stairs, put their heads close together, and began to whisper in the gloom.

chapter 12

Grimkell the Throat sat idly harping in a high window, seemingly alone and bored. Or preoccupied. If there were any spies watching, they could not see the widely-separated sequence of men who climbed the stairs within, to stand by the door well away from the skald in the window to murmur to him.

And Grimkell murmured back without ever turning to look at them, or act as if he was other than alone with thoughts of new songs and chants and sagas.

"So?" he muttered now.

And Falki Longbeak muttered, "We create another slave-break, all over the city this time; every pen and market, and every chained work-gang freed. All at once. As a diversion, while we set afire all of Cuaran's private holdings—the houses and shops he collects rents from, all over the city. When he rushes his soldiers to deal with the fires, we storm and loot the Palace. Give him so many distractions all at once that he lacks soldiers enough to hurl at them all—but in all the scurrying about they'll be targets for the best of us with bows and spears and hurled axes, stationed in high windows all over the city. The King himself will be too hard to get to, but if we can reduce his court to just him and a few serving-maids, he'll just be one man against us all; we can shut him up in the Palace to starve, and run the city without him!"

"You believe too many sagas, you do," Grimkell murmured, "but setting aside that too-neat victory you hand us at the end, there are ideas here we can work with. Far more practical than all the hiring of mercenaries and pirates I've been hearing from those who climbed my stairs earlier."

Falki nodded. "A beginning, nothing more. I haven't figured out how to make the soldiery loyal not to Sitric, but someone new—or how to stop them from choosing one of their own to take the throne, if Sitric falls. We lack coin to pay enough pirates and mercenaries to eliminate the soldiers—and if we do, who protects us against *them?* As I said, just a beginning, half thought through. I must go; there are deliveries I must oversee."

"Of course," the skald said, by way of farewell. "We build from sound beginnings—and pray to Odin that we are given the time to go slowly, and build wisely. A luxury afforded to few. And fewer still are wise enough to make use of it."

#

"Guide me, Lord of All," Oswin whispered, staring intently at the cross he'd taken from around his own neck and laid on the floor before where he knelt.

It was crudely fashioned, by his own hand, for that was best. One gave one's life and self to the White God, utterly. Which was both easy, and hard.

Easy because it gave a purpose for life that one could trust in, and *know* was good and for the best. And hard because God's guidance was not always clear.

He was praying for guidance now. The vision, and the sheer energy of the storm, had made him *so* sure of what he was doing as he smashed the statue.

Ah, but now...

Now he thought his destruction of the statue had been a mistake, a misreading of God's intentions as to what he was to do. He'd taken the vision as literal, when it was metaphorical.

The way to proceed against King Sitric and what Ath Cliath was becoming under his rule was *not* to defy, nor to preach and proselytize. It was to change daily life, to change the beliefs of people high and low not about the gods or tenets of faith, but about the world around them and how they should live in it. Change attitudes, change the way things are done in society. Sitric has been doing this for his own selfish ends; he, Oswin, shall do it to better all humankind in this darkening world, this Fimbulwinter. He shall stay in the city and persist at it, by talking to folk, by helping them in small ways, by showing them new ways of doing things—the small things of daily life. It shall be his life's work.

It is very likely to be so, Oswin reflected wryly, as he got up off his knees, kissed the cross, and settled it back upon his chest. For there was a very good chance he'd get killed doing it.

#

Brandr came down the stairs in the wake of two other guests with bulging sacks on their shoulders. The laden pair hastened through the common room and out the front door onto the busy street.

That left the innkeeper, nodding farewell to them, alone in the common room, though the clang and clatter of washing-up and cooking was coming from the kitchens.

Brandr hastened to his side. The innkeeper raised an inquiring brow, and Brandr asked hesitantly, "I'm not of this city; I know not who to ask what, at the Palace. Can you tell me: who there should I ask about where tax payments go—once they're in the Royal Treasury, that is. How are they spent?"

The innkeeper's gaze was discouraging. As were the gruff words that came out of him. "No one. If you value your neck, don't ask such questions."

Brandr opened his mouth to ask if there were public records anywhere to save him asking anyone, but the innkeeper waved him away and strode out into the street to greet four merchants with coffers and sacks strapped to a cart, who'd stopped to peer up at the Hearth's signboard with frowns of indecision. Possible paying guests.

Fair enough, and Brandr did not want to make an enemy of the master of Dun's Hearth. Yet knowing not what best to do next, he sat down at one of the empty tables in the common room to wait for the innkeeper to be free again.

Soon enough the old man was, and in good humor, too, for the four merchants had paid well for two adjacent rooms and the rent of a thrice-locked storage room for the wares that would be following them. After showing them to their chambers and setting the maids to bringing them baths and hot water to bathe in, the innkeeper returned, nodded to Brandr but held up a hand forestalling any queries, and passed out again into the street.

Where he stood peering down it, awaiting somewhere.

Not quite enough time had passed for Brandr to grow restless when the old man spotted whoever he'd been watching for. He turned, caught Brandr's gaze, and beckoned him as imperiously as any clan elder.

Brandr hastened to join him.

"Lad, I've a suggestion, if you can behave well enough not to run afoul of yon lady's bodyguards—or the woman herself. Look yon. The one in black, coming this way with four bodyguards and a scribe."

Brandr turned, looked, and within the promised ring of watchful bodyguards, beheld a tall and stunningly beautiful woman in an elegant gown of black, but booted like a warrior. Shapely, slender, moving with idle grace, purposefully yet not seeming in haste, dominating the street without seeming to notice, or care. Coldly detached, with dark eyes that seemed to stab Brandr when they met his gaze for a moment. A long fall of black unbound hair, skin as white as new-fallen snow...

"W-who is she?" he almost begged the innkeeper.

Who smiled wryly, as if he'd seen others react like Brandr before. "Behold Lecora O'Hart, one of the wealthiest and most successful traders in the city. Runs many endeavours, sponsors more, suffers no fools, and gets richer by the season. Nigh as powerful as the King, in her own way, and she'd not flourish as she does if she understood not coin and the making of it better than most. So why not ask her if she knows how the large amounts of tax she pays get spent?"

"I—I will. *Thank* you," Brandr blurted out, and hastened across the street, spreading his arms to show he was unarmed as the bodyguards stiffened watchfully at his approach, and shifted to block his way to the lady merchant, clapping hands to sword-hilts.

Golden sword-hilts.

"No closer," one rapped out sternly, but Brandr was in full flight. Swords hissed out.

"I—I mean no harm," he said hastily, eyeing what suddenly seemed to be a vigorous forest of sharp and deadly points rising to menace him.

The scribe was peering everywhere, shooting searching glances in all directions at once.

"I—seek you something?" Brandr asked her.

"She is looking," the woman in black said coldly, neither slowing nor hastening her pace, "for the snatch-thieves or other ruffians we judge you to be posing as a distraction for. I'd keep back, if I were you. The flesh of young fools stands up to war-steel not well at all."

"Ah, uh, perhaps so," Brandr heard himself stammering, "That is—I, uh, Lady O'Hart? May I ask you a question? It won't take long!"

There were blades at his throat now, smoothly staying there as the lady in black proceeded down the street and Brandr sidestepped hastily to keep up with her.

"I am a busy trader," came the calm reply, "and on my way to transact business right now. I find myself *not* in the mood to stop and talk with strangers."

"Well, would there be a better time? It's only the one question! I've been told you're, ah, wealthy and successful, and might know."

"Know what?"

"Know where all the taxes the King takes from you—from us all—*go!* As in, what does he spend it all on?"

The lady in black stopped abruptly and spun to face Brandr, her bodyguard's blades melting away as she stepped forward, eyes flashing.

"Let us discuss your availability for a meeting," she murmured, the coldness gone in an instant. She was staring into his eyes as if she could see everything about him if she gazed long and hard enough. Brandr found himself suddenly even more at a loss for words.

"I—I'm at your disposal," he managed to gulp out.

"As a rural clansman, newly come to the city, your trading is not yet spun up to a frantic pace, and your social whirl likewise," she said gently. "So, your name? Residence, here in the city?"

"Uh—ah—Brandr Fylan, and I'm staying—" He waved wildly down the street, momentarily startled by how far they'd come, and some how knowing the innkeeper was standing, gently smiling, by the inn's open door. "—at Dun's Hearth, here on this very street."

The Lady O'Hart almost smiled. "I know it. And I may be available to speak with you this evening, or more likely on the morrow. I'll send men to call for you at the Hearth, to escort you to where we'll meet."

Brandr stared at her for a moment of pleased disbelief, then launched into stammering out his thanks. He was still at it as she gave him an airy wave of farewell that was almost a salute, one warrior to another, and strode on, her scribe right behind her. The bodyguards smoothly closed ranks around her again, blades sliding back into scabbards, the rearmost pair contriving to walk backwards with smooth grace so they could keep watching Brandr suspiciously.

All the way out of sight.

#

This was the grandest house—mansion—Mist had yet seen in Ath Cliath. Oh, she'd laid eyes on grander buildings aplenty, but none of them had struck her as definitely a private residence. This one was, but its stones soared into spires and balconies and arches, and its entrance was a broad, steep flight of stone steps curving up from the street, flanked on both sides by a languid, fearless pack of huge, menacingly staring sculpted stone vargr.

A beautiful lantern—unlit in daylight hours—hung in the stone arch before the tall black door, which swung aside as easily and silently as if it was floating when Aunt Teagan pulled the cord that set bells deep in the house to tolling.

To reveal a woman who stood tall and stern in a long black dress, her hair white with age. She wore large dangling earrings fashioned out of what looked like scraps of armor plate, or perhaps snapped-off shards of old but rust-free swords, and Mist judged her two decades older than Aunt Teagan. Or older.

"Teagan," she said, in a voice rough from disuse, that somehow also sounded warmly welcoming.

"Mist Damhain," Aunt Teagan said by way of reply. "My trusted kinswoman."

There had been the slightest emphasis on 'trusted.'

The old woman nodded and said directly to Mist. "I am Embla, and this is Agata." And as she spoke that name, as if heeding it as a cue, a second old woman who looked very much like Embla but a trifle taller glided into view out of an inner archway, grave and serene in her own black gown.

"You are here to see Mother," Agata said, and did not make of those words a question. "Come."

And she led the way.

Mist noticed that the front door had two massive timbers that pivoted to drop into massive metal brackets to bar the door against a battering ram, and that Embla was dropping them soundlessly into place. The grand mansion was a fortress.

Mist looked all about—or as much as she could, without seeming to do so—and was startled, though she tried not to show it, to see that as the two sisters escorted them back through the house to a grand staircase, Agata walking ahead of them and Embla behind, both had drawn daggers from beneath their gowns and were holding them ready.

The stair swept its broad and curving way to a gallery looking down into the hall it had ascended from, and they turned on that gallery to take another flight. The house was silent around them, as if deserted. Yet at the same time, it felt watchful. Was there magic at work here?

Then Mist realized what was behind her unease. When Embla had shut that soundless front door, she had shut out Ath Cliath entirely; not a sound of the bustling city around them reached into this soaring old stone house.

Soaring indeed; they'd climbed a narrower, steeper flight from the gallery to another floor, and there walked a little way to a narrower, enclosed stair that was steeper yet.

And took them to yet another flight; it seemed they were climbing into the sky, though the floor they reached now seemed as spaciously silent a labyrinth as those below.

Their guard of sisters led them along a passage that took several turns and offered yet more ascending stairs that Agata and Embla ignored, to deliver them at last at an arch-topped door of wood crossed with broad iron bands nailed in place as if a treasure vault or prison lay beyond.

Agata knocked with the pommel of her dagger, then opened the door without waiting for a response, and waved Mist and Teagan to enter within.

They found themselves in a dim, lofty-ceilinged room hung with a labyrinth of tapestries. There was an old smell. Teagan shouldered through one gap, then another, and then came to an uncertain halt, not knowing the way on through the hangings, which were becoming more diaphanous and less heavy of weave as one proceeded.

Agata came gliding among the tapestries, having taken another way, to show them on, and they proceeded what seemed a very long way until abruptly they were passing the last tapestry, and gazing upon an old crone, who sat facing them on a bed that smelled of her as if it was a throne.

She was black-gowned and imperious, but far more wrinkled than the two sisters, and had lost most of her hair.

"Greetings, Mor," Teagan said softly, as humble as if addressing a clan matriarch.

"You, I know," the crone said bluntly to Teagan, "but you"—disconcertingly sharp black eyes turned to Mist—"I do not know. Yet you would not be here if whatever this is did not concern you. So, speak. What do you want of old Mor?"

Teagan kept silent, so Mist said softly, "I stand in need of...procuring some poison."

"Procure, is it?" Mor's voice was like smoke, or a lash, holding no quaver of age. "What fancy words the young do use! *Buy* is the blunter one you should have employed. *What* poison? Do you know poisons?"

Mist lifted her chin, met those hard eyes squarely, and said, "I do not. Yet I do know that I need the poison to be something without a smell or a strong stain, that when cloth is soaked in it, will bring death—beginning with a swift collapse, or slumber—when breathed in, when that cloth is over the nose and mouth."

Mor's smile was like a flourished sword. "Ah. I like young women who know what they want. That certainty of purpose earns them a small chance of making something of themselves, before they become old and their bodies fail them, as mine has. The best death-draught for your purpose is qeltreth."

Silence fell.

"Qeltreth? I have never heard of it," Mist admitted, feeling as if she was failing some sort of test.

"I would have been very much surprised if you had. Being as I know of a handcount of living women—not more—who even know its name. Fewer still can make it."

"You can?"

"Of course. From crushed bees, and the distillate of the right wildflowers, and other things I shall not name. It is made neither swiftly, nor easily. Which is why a dose enough to kill three grown men, if one is fortunate and they are not, will cost you five thousand skatt."

Five thousand—?

Mist doubted she'd ever earn as much as that, from one end of her life to the other.

"I...am sorry to have troubled you," she said sadly. "I have far too few skatt to even sicken one man, it seems." She looked at Teagan. "We should go."

Teagan stirred, as if about to say something reluctantly, or needed time to choose the right words to say.

And then the bitter disappointment inside Mist made her blurt out bitterly, "I don't even know how many lives I need to end. However many sneak-serpents the King of Ath Cliath

66

commands."

There were two faint gasps from behind her. Mist whirled around. The gasps had come from Agata and Embla, who were standing close behind Teagan and Mist, respectively, daggers raised and ready.

They had been eager gasps, of pleased approval.

"That," Mor said flatly, "was a very foolish thing to do. I could send word to the King right now, and end your life that swiftly. Yet I will not. Instead, I will give you as much as you need without taking a thing in payment. Not one coin."

It was suddenly very quiet in the room.

"If you can rid this city of those cruel vipers," the old woman went on, her voice sounding much younger now that it was afire with enthusiasm, "it will be worth the price of many doses, and much more. Oh, the King will get himself other serpents—but it will take him some time to get ones as deft at dark-work, to drive home his malice deftly upon us all, as these seasoned ones are. And while he's doing that, we can push for change. Not to change the King, but to change small things for the small folk, to turn us to a better path, a road upward. The mighty will always have their feuds and their grand plans, but let there be hope for all. Room for all to breathe. So take all the vials you need, with my blessing. We have all suffered at the hands of those snakes. And other parts of them, too."

chapter 13

"Cozy," was all Cairbre Dathaill said, as he squeezed into the closet that was already crowded, Lecora O'Hart and Torloch Dargan standing shoulder to shoulder among many mops and buckets.

"Not a chamber the King's shadowhands might expect three mighty merchant lords to meet in," Lecora murmured.

"Not one *this* mighty merchant lord wants to meet in again," Torloch grunted, moving his foot so the bucket that boot was standing in grated in tiny circles along the floor.

"*Stop* that," Lecora reproved, in a whisper. "No unnecessary noise."

Torloch's answering grunt deepened into a growl. He turned to Cairbre. "Well?"

Cairbre touched one end of the jeweled torc he wore—he didn't have to do more than that to tell his fellow lords that it could be unscrewed, to reveal something hidden within—and smiled triumphantly. "Larr-serpent venom. Likely the only such in Hibernia. Nineteen rods a vial."

Lecora arched an eyebrow at that, and turned her head to look at Torloch, their noses almost touching. His face displayed neither smile nor any hint of triumph.

"The favour I sought to call in has turned to dust and ashes," he said grimly. "The, ah, individual at the Palace who owed me was caught in some minor deceit, nothing to do with us, and the King had him casually executed. That hope of getting into the palace is literally...dead."

The three traded silent glances for a time, ere Cairbre voiced the obvious. "So we must send an agent into the Palace to poison Sitric's wine. But who?"

Silence returned, and hung between them in the tiny room for a long time before Lecora whispered, "Me. Ardgal was my friend."

Torloch stirred, his broad shoulders shoving all of them into sidestepping motion. "We've lost him already. Not you, too."

Cairbre nodded. "Lady, you are the hand that guides us, our sword in all battles. Without you, Torloch and I and all the others are little more than so many independent grumblers—and Cuaran will take us down one by one, while the rest of us snarl and hesitate and in the end do nothing but die when he deems it our turn. And if you do this, you *will* be going to your death."

Torloch nodded too. "What price Ath Cliath," he asked the lady lord, "if you are too dead to dwell in it?"

Lecora shrugged. "And if I want not to go on living in *this* Ath Cliath, the one ruined by Sitric One-Eyed?"

"But if he takes you, and sets to work on you..."

"You have nothing to fear that you should not fear already. If he tortures me or fills my mind with spells and I babble all, I can't betray you—for he already knows we three work together."

"Lady, I think you are wrong to do this," Cairbre said gently, "but I cannot stand in your way. I am too in love with you for that, and admire you for this decision, even if it is a mistake."

"I, too," Torloch rumbled, "think you should not do this, but cannot find it in me to stand against you. So let us plan, and plan anew, until we have covered everything and given you the very best chance we can to succeed *and* get back out again alive."

Cairbre nodded. "And to begin with, how can you even hope to reach our King, now that he's grown so suspicious, and the slaves have risen once, and would-be slayers have sought his life time and time again?"

Lecora smiled thinly. "Oh, I can always reach Sitric Cuaran. Leave *that* to me."

The two men in the closet with her merely nodded. They knew that Lecora O'Hart had betimes shared beds with King Sitric Cuaran, and with King Niall Glundub before him, and so knew her way around the Palace.

And through the One-Eyed King's most intimate defenses.

#

The betraying floorboard creaked.

Grimkell the Throat and Falki Longbeak broke off murmuring of possible plots against the One-Eyed King across the table, and casually dropped hands to the hilts of their blades, patting the coins and contracts spread out between them that were there to make this look like a business meeting between busy traders.

The outer door squealed ever so slightly.

As someone sought to open and close it stealthily.

Then there came the faintest of nearer footfalls in the passage outside, ere the door they were both staring at inched open in well-oiled silence, and a man scuttled in.

He was bent double and shooting hawklike glances in all directions as he came, the very skald's caricature of a sneak-thief.

Excited of eye and manner, Forkundr Redbeard straightened up and hissed in a whisper possibly audible two streets away, "The one eye sees not!"

"For there is still no sun," Grimkell chanted wearily. "Aye, Fork, what news?"

Forkundr peered suspiciously all around the room, even under the table, then burst out "Magnus the Small, of the Battle Wolves, is here in Ath Cliath!"

Falki shrugged, but Grimkell frowned and leaned forward.

"And you know this how?"

"A man who knows him saw, and told someone else, and the rumors are racing. This same man knows most of the King's shadowhands by sight, and when this Magnus stepped off a ship, a shadowhand watching the docks *ran* to get another shadowhand to set watch on him, then ran on to the Palace, to tell the King!"

"Who was not expecting him, then," Grimkell said softly. "And where did the seithkarl go? And what did the King do?"

"The King sent shadowhands swarming out of the Palace like an army. What seithkarl?"

"Magnus the Small," Grimkell explained patiently. "Where did he go? What did he do?"

"Went to the home of Vigmarr Bent-Neck, was let in, and hasn't set boot outside its walls since."

"Third in wealth among the city's slave-traders," Grimkell said. "Perhaps second, by now."

It was Falki's turn to frown. "What can be happening?"

Grimkell took up his drinking-horn from the table, and asked it, "Aye, what indeed?"

#

"Still shut in with Bent-Neck," Mael reported, "and not even a maid sent shopping has left that house. High walls around it, with only three gates, and we're watching them all, plus a man in an attic to make sure there's no signalling, or message-birds coming or going. So far, *nothing.*"

The King frowned. "What can he mean, by coming here?"

Mael shrugged. "What do the runes say?"

Sitric's glare was as sudden as it was cold.

"The runes," he hissed, obviously upset, "have told me nothing. The Allfather is silent."

The two men stared at each other grimly, knowing what this could mean.

Sitric Cuaran might stand lower in Odin's favour than Magnus the Small.

#

The tap on Brandr's door was soft yet somehow peremptory.

He pulled on his boots and put hand to dagger-hilt ere approaching it and asking, without opening it, "Yes?"

"You wanted to speak with a certain lady," a man replied, low and calm. "Come with us now, and so find her."

Brandr drew in a deep breath, shot the bolt, and flung the door wide.

The passage was full of handsome dark-clad men in expensive boots, wearing swords and daggers and 'Oh, I always look this bored' expressions.

"Brandr Fylan?" the one right in front of Brandr asked, and when Brandr nodded, he turned on his heel and marched down the passage, flinging a single word in his wake: "Come."

Brandr closed and locked his door and then hastened to catch up, the other men falling into step around him.

He'd never had an escort before, and part of him felt grand and important. But that part was busy warring with another part of him that feared he was surrounded by jailers, marching him to his execution.

They took the alley door out of the Hearth, and headed for the darkest, dirtiest cross-alley, that Brandr had avoided until now. No one bothered them, and even the rats scurried out of their way, as they strode purposefully along, Brandr in a protective ring of expressionless men.

They turned a corner into an even worse alley, where the cobbles underfoot were shattered and uneven beneath all the refuse and suspiciously-crimson puddles.

"Drunkard's Walk," the only man of them all who'd talked to Brandr offered unexpectedly. Well, well, that name was notorious enough that he'd heard it several times, and had some idea as to why it enjoyed such a fell reputation. But if there were any dismembered bodies strewn along it just now, he missed catching sight of them.

Another corner, and then another where men stepped out of dark doorways in menacing union and then froze at the smiles that greeted them, and the number of smiling men surrounding Brandr, and retreated as abruptly and quietly as they'd appeared.

And then another corner and they were out onto a wider street, walking faster now. A shutter crashed to the cobbles, up ahead, and Brandr saw ladders and men up repairing a roof that needed it. Another shutter was detached and flung down; already cracked, it shattered into many skittering shards of wood that heavy-booted workmen kicked aside as they walked the replacement shutters out of a cart to hand up.

Amid the hammerings, a new signboard was going up above the front door. Brandr peered, curious—and just in time to see "The Skald's Beard" for the last time before it was covered by a brighter, newer sign that read "The House Of The Hanged Man."

"Well, well," said one of Brandr's hitherto silent escorts, from close behind him. "No more Skald's Beard. About time."

"What a name to choose, though! Hanged Man?" said another.

"Heh. Old Lugh Blackjaws hanged himself when the Palace hit him with a tax bill that would have cost him the place—so it's by way of being a mocking tribute to him," explained a third.

"So who owns it now?"

"The King, of course. Who else?"

At the end of that block, they turned a corner into a wide street where many wagons were rumbling out of warehouses, under the eyes of watchful guards who gave Brandr's group hard and suspicious stares that the handsome men serenely ignored.

They strode along for three blocks of his, the warehouses growing older and sootier but grander in size and stonework, ere Brandr's escorts abruptly turned left and tramped through a wide wagon door into the cool dimness of a lofty unlit warehouse that was eerily silent. Casks and crates were stacked neatly everywhere, loft-ladders were in place and there were even labels made of hide scraps pinned in place with stones and horseshoes in a neat row along a railing, and the reek of candle-lamps just blown out hung heavy in the air.

It was as if a sweating warehouse crew had hastily stepped into hiding at their approach, and might leap out with yells at any moment.

But wherever Brandr looked, there was no one.

His escort led him deep into this maze of neatly-stacked cargoes, to the heart of a vast and cavernous space, where something that had been motionless in the darkness suddenly moved, startling him.

Brandr only just had time to see that it was a lone woman in a long dark coat, turning to face him, before his escort abruptly spun around and strode back the way they'd come, leaving him standing alone.

Then they spun around again and stood in a neat row a dozen paces away, eyeing him. Each man had one gloved hand on dagger-hilt, ready to snatch and throw.

"Lady O'Hart," Brandr greeted the darkly beautiful woman facing him, and bowed.

"Brandr Fylan," she replied, and took a step closer. "I've thought about what you asked me, and made some arrangements. If you come with me, right now, I can get you into the Palace— to see certain clerks who handle the city tax takings. *But.*"

She strolled closer. She was wearing the most beautiful boots Brandr had ever seen. He'd known there would be a 'but,' and waited patiently to hear what it was.

That seemed to please her; she smiled at his silence, then asked bluntly, "Why do you want to know where the taxes we pay go? Do you know the danger you're courting?"

Brandr nodded. What he was going to do next might be the last mistake he'd ever make, or might be the best thing to do right now. He knew not.

So he drew in a deep breath, met Lady Lecora O'Hart's gaze squarely, and told her, pitching his voice low so that she and not the line of her armed men standing behind him, "I am of Clan Uterni. Whose elders and traders grow more and more suspicious of the One-Eyed King. All know he has taken in more gold than most of us will ever see, but where does it all go? Ath Cliath impresses us all, as the lone bright beacon in a world growing ever more dark and cold— yet the prices of needful things keep rising, and my elders have begun to openly doubt Sitric Cuaran's sanity. Or does he have dark intentions? Or serves he some master, someone who has a hold over him, and is paying them? So the elders sent me—young, expendable, no one of note or standing—here, to learn what I can and report back."

Her face was unreadable, so he added, "And that is the whole truth of it."

"And how do you, a young stranger, a backcountry Hibernian not of the city with, as you say, no standing, intend to compel the King's tax collectors to tell you anything? Or the King, for that matter, from whom they take their orders?"

Brandr shrugged. "I can but try. I asked the elders what you ask me now, and they told me to use this tale: that they, the elders of the Uterni, had heard from several mouths that the King of Ath Cliath has been sending wagons of silver skatt out to their clan lands, and secretly burying the coins. At first, they thought the tales mere drunkards' fancy, but the talk has persisted, with new sightings—so could they be true? Where *does* the money go?"

Lecora shook her head. "They've spun that tale up out of nothing at all. So far as anyone has been able to find out, the King buries no riches anywhere that isn't right under his hand, or eye. He will know they're lying."

"But will he? Won't he think *someone* has been burying wagonloads of skatt out in the country, to spur the tales, and want the silver—and want to know more about who's doing it? And perhaps even want to talk to me?"

A smile slowly rose onto Lady O'Hart's face, and grew across it. "There's hope for Hibernia yet," she murmured.

Brandr found himself warm with unexpected excitement, even pride.

"Come," Lecora added briskly, and strode past him out of the warehouse, her bodyguards closing in around her. Brandr hurried to accompany her.

To the Palace.

\#

Full night had fallen, and it was dark in the alleys they were taking, but Teagan walked without hesitation, a silent shadow in the night. Heading for a modest door in a little courtyard at the rear of the Palace, amid the wings where food was delivered, laundry and cooking were done, and servants dwelt. A secret way in that she knew of old. That should not be guarded.

Walking hip to hip with Aunt Teagan, passing the dark stone walls of uncounted scores of buildings as they went, Mist could guess how her aunt knew of a secret way into the Palace—but if Teagan wasn't going to say more about that, Mist certainly wasn't going to ask her.

They'd reached the most dangerous part of their journey yet, the spot where homes and shops ended and the Palace walls loomed. There was a lanternlit spot far to their right around the great curve of stone—a wagon-gate—but Teagan turned to the left, felt her way along the wall to a certain stone that she caressed as if was a lover, nodded, and did something to the stone that Mist could not see. With the faintest of grating sounds, it opened, and Teagan reached back, took firm hold of Mist's arm, and hauled her into the darkness.

It was dank, smelled of wet stone and mildew, and utterly dark the moment Teagan pulled the wall shut again. Her hip moved against Mist's as she turned—they were within the thickness of the wall, in a sharply diagonal passage so cramped that a big man with shield and spear would have grated and struck sparks with every movement—and did something else that made the inside of the wall, at the far end of the passage, open and let them out into the night again.

On the inside of the wall, in a courtyard where wings of the Palace that never slept emitted faint clatters of work and the mutters of muted converse on either side, ahead.

Teagan had told Mist earlier that half not getting caught was to stride in an unhurried, relaxed, but confident manner, as if you had every right to be where you were, knew where you were going, and were bored, *not* apprehensive.

And she was walking like that now, straight out across the courtyard, heading for halfway along the wing to their left. Mist kept right behind her, trying not to look up at the rising towers and balconies of the grander parts of the Palace that loomed up ahead and above, dark and terrible against the sky.

Before she could begin to wonder if someone was watching from one of those balconies or tall windows, and would send guards to accost them the moment they set foot inside the Palace itself, Teagan reached a certain spot along the wall, in a dark stretch where there were no windows, did something, and made a door that looked like solid stone between two wall-buttresses swing inwards.

72

More darkness, and again Teagan reached out and towed Mist inside to join her in the thickness of this new wall, then closed the outside door, turned, took two steps to the other end of the unseen diagonal passage they were in, and opened an inner door—to stare, in the dim light of distant lamps, into the startled face of an armored guard. Who left off yawning and looking bored in a twisted instant to gape at them, a shout of alarm rising in his throat.

Doomed.

chapter 14

Teagan lunged forward like a swordsman before the sentinel could utter more than a gasp of indrawn breath, and embraced him, pinning his arms to his sides and locking her mouth on his. As she kept on lunging, bearing him over backwards to the ground.

Mist was astonished to see her arms moving on the man's shoulders and back as if she was ardent—and when she had to break off kissing the man to breathe, she said exultantly, "I win the wager! He's right where Sitric said he would be! Ah, but the young guards *are* sweeter!"

And between thumb and one finger she deftly opened a vial at her belt, dipped her forefinger into it, and slipped that digit into the guard's mouth as she purred and fondled him, and with her other hand guided one of his hands down into her bodice.

For a moment, he growled in wordless pleasure—and then the growl trailed off into a rattle and he slumped.

Teagan waved at Mist to peer up and down the passage, to make sure no one had seen them—but it was deserted.

Mist squatted to whisper, "No one." And then heard herself asking, "Is he dead?"

"No," Teagan replied, emptying the rest of the vial into the guard's slack mouth. A golden syrup. "Mead mixed with something that makes you fall asleep *very* swiftly."

Mist gave her a stern look, which made her grin like a young lass up to mischief, and murmur, "It's called laatha. Potent, and unwise to mix with drink; it clouds the mind. With luck, when he wakes, his memories will be so mixed with the vivid nightmares he's about to have that he'll remember only that he met with women, and nothing more."

The secret door they'd used opened into a little alcove, and the two of them propped the guarded into a sitting position in it, and flitted away down the passage. No longer two shadows, but servant women of the Palace—Teagan pulled a towel from her house out of her bodice and carried it before her as if it was wrapped around something she had to take somewhere—on dutiful business bent.

They heard folk, but saw no one. Aside from the kitchens, the Palace was quiet in these wee hours, and Teagan knew the way to where they were heading, and was easily able to avoid the few servants who were awake and working, along their route.

The Palace was *big*. Mist had tried to memorize where they turned, in case she had to flee back along the way they'd come, but in doing so had long since lost track of how far they'd come, beyond "a good long way, by Crom!" ere some sort of excitement erupted, ahead; they heard doors banging open, and excited voices calling to each other to come and see.

The tones were of awe and wonder, not fury or fear, but Teagan laid hand on the nearest closed door, opened it, and strode into the darkness, Mist darting after her and then running into her as her aunt stopped dead.

Teagan restored her balance with one strong arm, drew the door closed, and murmured, "Still and silent, now. Listen."

There came the falls of running feet outside the door; they'd quit the passage just in time. Doors opened and voices demanded to know what the matter was.

"A Valkyrie!" a man explained excitedly. "Riding the sky on her steed—circling low over the Palace! Right up *there!*"

"Has someone died in battle?" a woman demanded to know, but no one replied; there were excited squeals from farther off, and "A Valkyrie?"

"A Valkyrie!"

The Palace was astir, as servants rushed to where they knew windows and balconies with good views could be found.

"The King must be told!" someone cried.

"A Valkyrie?" Mist whispered.

"Ah," Teagan smiled. "My hired diversion. Right on time."

"You hire *Valkyries?*"

When Aunt Teagan snorted with mirth, she sounded just like Mist's father. "No, but I can hire a seithkona to craft an illusion of one. One of my friends and trusted clients, by the name of Lassairfhina. She does good Valkyries, and as the King reveres Odin, it will certainly interest him."

Mist remembered the stunningly beautiful woman who'd been leaving Teagan's shop when she'd first found and entered it. Well, well. It seemed even bustling, crowded, sprawling Ath Cliath could be a small world, from time to time.

Would those times prove too often?

Teagan touched Mist's elbow as a signal and abruptly turned down a side-passage, into deeper gloom. Lamps here were few, far between, and half-shuttered to boot; there was just enough light to make out walls, doors, and the occasional sidetable. Teagan was walking more warily now, slowing and taking greater care not to make a sound.

Abruptly Mist began to recognize doorways and tapestries from their earlier visit; they were near their goal, the armory given over to the shadowhands. It should be...

Yes, and seemingly unguarded and deserted. Teagan held up a hand, and Mist halted obediently; her aunt turned, pointed at her, and then at the floor where she stood.

Stay here; that was clear enough.

Before she could finish nodding, Teagan was gone—through the door into the armory. It seemed a very long time before she returned, but couldn't really have been all that long, by the number of breaths Mist had drawn.

"Robing rooms and all are clear," her aunt murmured into her ear. "You go in and apply the poison; not too much, so nothing's soaked enough to stay wet for long, and *don't move* anything you don't have to, so you can put everything back just as you found it. I'll stand guard out here to delay anyone approaching."

Heart pounding, Mist stepped inside the armory, and went to the racks and the shelves where the masks lay, each in its own recess. In case she somehow spilled Mor's poison, she wanted to be where even spillage could do some harm to the King's dark agents.

And then, suddenly, she found herself calm. Almost serene.

With unhurried care and no fumbling at all, she used vial after vial, sprinkling not too much of the deadly draughts on every last mask; what she had left over she applied to the bottom edges of each hood, where a wearer would grasp them to pull them on, and so get the death on their fingers.

When she was done, she stepped back, surveyed the room to make sure she'd left no trace and everything looked in the same place as when she'd found it, then rejoined Aunt Teagan.

Who smiled and led the way back the way they'd come.

Mist hardly dared hope they'd manage to slink away from the Palace entirely unseen, but they did.

Or at least, she *hoped* they had.

The guard they'd left sitting in the alcove that held their secret way out was gone—alcove bare and no sign of him.

Mist's heart froze as she watched Aunt Teagan look around wildly.

Yet all was still. No guards, no sign of alarm. Teagan opened the wall and they rushed into it gratefully. Only a few steps more to be out on the streets, and safely away in the night.

Unless, of course, they ran into a patrol…

#

Brandr was tired and frustrated when he stepped back out into the streets, but his heart rose a trifle when the now-familiar escort of handsome but expressionless men strolled out of doorways and alley mouths to ring him about. They'd walked with him for almost a block when the two closest men on his left drifted apart, and he saw the Lady O'Hart had been walking on their far side. She sidestepped smoothly to join him.

"We'll see you safely back to the inn," she greeted him. "So, tell me, how did your time with the royal tax clerks go?"

Brandr's bitterness welled up. "They would tell me nothing. I must speak to the King—and they all but told me my queries would be futile, and were likely to irk the King enough that I'd be made a slave on the spot."

"I am not surprised," Lecora replied. "So you have your answer."

"I do?"

"If neither the King nor his tax clerks will say where the money goes, then they are hiding something, are they not? Tell your elders so."

Brandr frowned and nodded. They'd gone another block ere he asked hesitantly, "May I ask you something? Two things?"

"Of course. And I hope to give you better answers than those of the Palace did."

Brandr managed a smile. "Who was that sleeping guard, and why did you have me carry him to the wine cellar?"

"I know not his name, but our moving of him helped cover up someone else's mischief. And your other question?"

"Where did you go, all the time I was getting nowhere with the clerks?"

Lecora smiled. "I was seeking better wine than that cellar holds."

Then, much to Brandr's astonishment, they were slowing, and Dun's Hearth was before them.

Whereupon he discovered *real* astonishment—as the Lady Lecora O'Hart put her arms around him and kissed him.

Startled, he stiffened awkwardly, but when she made no move to pull away, he responded, tasting her warm salt-sweetness—though he couldn't help but see, past the glorious fall of her hair, a row of expressionless stares. Belonging to her bodyguard, standing close, on all sides. Their hands were on their sword-hilts.

Then Lecora let go of his lips and drew back. Was that sadness in her eyes, just for a moment?

She disengaged from him gently, took a step back, and regarded him unsmilingly. "I hope we shall see each other again, Brandr Fylan. Guard yourself well. This is a dangerous city."

And she turned on her heel and strode away, her bodyguard falling into formation around her with casual ease, pair after pair of them staring Brandr down as they turned to join the rearguard.

Brandr stood where he was and watched them all walk off down the street, purposeful and in graceful unison. Not looking back.

Only after they were out of sight did he turn and enter Dun's Hearth.

Under the amused eye of the innkeeper, who'd been leaning against the doorway watching, all the while.

"Aim high, you do," he said gruffly. "Man of danger."

Brandr's face felt hot; he knew he must be blushing a deep red.

But it seemed astonishment was not done with him yet. The innkeeper took firm hold of his elbow and steered him across the common room to a back corner table—where a covered platter was waiting.

As Brandr sat, blinking in surprise, the innkeeper unhooded the platter to reveal a cloud of steam and a hot meal beneath it.

Then began to pour warm mulled wine, to go with it.

Brandr's stomach growled loudly, announcing to the world how hungry he was even before he realized it.

The innkeeper set the wine and its decanter before him, then took the platter-cover and headed for the kitchens.

"Idiot," he said to Brandr, by way of farewell. "Trying to make love on an empty stomach."

#

The King looked up from the latest written tallies on the table before him. "Well?"

Mael the Sharp bent near and murmured, "Magnus the Small has not stirred from the house of Vigmarr Bent-Neck. Nor have Lecora, Cairbre, and Torloch attempted to communicate with him. Or he with them."

Sitric Cuaran nodded. "Keep watch on them all. Nothing more. Yet."

Mael bowed and glided away. Only after the door had closed behind him did Sitric pull a cord nigh the arm of his chair that caused a gong to sound elsewhere, and a Palace steward to enter, bow, and silently await the King's commands.

They were not long in coming. Sitric reached the end of a column of figures smaller than last month's takings, but not alarmingly so, and said without looking up, "Summon Volundr the Voice to me. Have him come without delay."

"Your Majesty," the steward replied gravely, and departed as deftly and silently as he'd come.

Sitric set aside the parchment of figures and picked up the one that had been awaiting beneath it.

There were times when having a pompous buffoon as an envoy could be useful. They were rare, but they did come along. And this was one of them.

The man was a fat, sneering windbag as well as an insufferable ass. Which made him nigh-perfect for insulting or bullying citizens a king wanted insulted or bullied.

Which was what Sitric wanted to do just now.

Goad the three wealthiest surviving merchant lords of Ath Cliath to see if they'd do anything sufficiently rash.

Giving him their behaviour to cloak his tyranny. If he started arresting or executing citizens and seizing their wealth and property without warning or pretext, it'd not be long before the populace would begin to flee the city as fast as wagons and ships and even their own calloused feet could take them, leaving him lord of nothing.

Yet in his increasingly sad experience of human nature, everyone was up to something. And if you nudged them, would do or say something that could be used as full justification for whatever you wanted to do to them. Brutally.

A door was flung open with a flourish, to bang off the gilded, many-leaping-vargr bumper that kept it from marking the wall, and rebounded with a shudder.

The King did not look up from the tally he was scrutinizing.

A self-important throat-clearing followed.

The King continued his study of the figures.

"You sent for me, Lord King of Ath Cliath?" The question was mellifluous, as grandly inflected as any skald milking a line on a stage.

At last Sitric Cuaran looked up, his face grim and unfriendly, the eyepatch giving him a sinister appearance. Only after Volundr had begun to visibly quail did the King summon a wide and obviously insincere smile to his face.

And then let its beaming splendor drop right back off again, to say briskly and unsmilingly rather than affably, "Ah, Volundr! I did indeed. I have a task for the Voice of the King. I need you to go to three citizens and personally deliver to them a royal summons: to attend me here in the Palace just as soon as they are able. You need not do it politely."

"Your desire is my command!"

"Indeed. And to answer the question you are currently struggling to frame, these are three so-called merchant lords—Lecora O'Hart, Cairbre Dathaill, and Torloch Dargan—who dearly want me dead. You may make it clear to them that their King is aware that they've been plotting my death, and is not afraid of them. Be cold, be condescending, be superior. It is past time to let them see how futile their schemings and strivings are."

"It shall be my *pleasure*, O King."

"No doubt," Sitric Cuaran said dryly, giving Volundr a genuine smile for the first time— and then a nod of dismissal.

As he bent his attention to the tallies once more, his rotund and sidewhiskered envoy backed away, bowing his way back out of the room, declaiming grandly as he drew the door closed again, "It is past time to let them see how futile their schemings and strivings are."

The man was echoing his words to fix the phrase in memory, Sitric knew. He nodded at the just-closed door and added calmly, "Then they'll either give up, or become desperate and do something rash. So executing them will be a pleasure rather than a drudge-duty."

#

The scarred and disfigured woman banged open the kitchen door at the rear of Ath Cliath's largest temple of Odin with her ample behind. Only her gnarled arms and misshapen fingers could be seen, for she always hid the rest of her under a cowled robe when out of doors.

Grunting under the weight of the basket of peelings, leek trimmings, and other kitchen refuse, the cook of the House Of The God's Helm shuffled across cobbles slippery with grease and marked with many old stains to the parked an unattended wagon that would depart with them at dusk, dumped her basket in—and froze. There was a fresh stain on the cobble right in front of her, of a peculiar shape.

Setting down her basket, she lurched to the closest-to-the-wall end of the wagon, and squatted as if to relieve herself, peering up and down the alley as she spat.

Seeing no one, she straightened up again and muttered, "Aye?"

"Can a seithkona alter what runes turn up when someone wyrds?"

The murmur came from the far side of the wagon, from under a cleaner and better-sewn cowl than her own, that belonged to a plain black robe concealing someone whose voice the cook knew: Lecora O'Hart.

"Yes," the cook breathed back, "though the cost is great. Not just the disfavour of the gods, but the curse of the Norns themselves. *The* curse. The Norns like it not when mortals meddle thus."

"So what, then, would make a seithkona meddle so?"

"A need that outweighs the Curse. I had such a need."

"Had?"

"And so am under the Curse. Or I'd not be able to hide and work in *this* house." The cook nodded at the temple behind her, knowing that the Lady Lecora couldn't see her doing so—but didn't need to.

"Would you meddle again?"

"Why not? I am damned, and doomed, and cannot escape."

"So can you affect the runes when a powerful galdr wyrds for guidance?"

"As powerful as the King?"

"Why, yes. As it happens," Lecora said, and leaned around the end of the wagon to add a thin-lipped smile.

The cook lifted her own cowl just high enough to let the Lady see her matching but bitterer one.

"Why, yes, as it happens," she echoed. "But to steer him awry, or make him doubt his own powers or sanity?"

"Yes," Lecora replied.

chapter 15

It was almost as if all of these insolent, sneeringly handsome young men *delighted* in leading the Voice of the Riverfleet Throne astray!

Direction after glib and airy direction they'd given Volundr the Voice turned out to be wrong, or out of date: Cairbre Dathaill had *just* moved on, from The Hawksroost club on Fleshers' Lane to Fleinn's Fortunate Flagon, the tavern on Stormgate High, and thence from the sweets shop Glenna's Choice Jewels Upon The Tongue to the fashionable eatery Old Oraldr's Oxroast on the Boughmarket.

Wherefore Volundr was hot, short of wind, and darkly furious by the time bursts of laughter coming from the back room of the Kraken's Coils club lifted his hopes.

He lurched and shouldered past younglings who had sharp elbows indeed to get a look at the source of the mirth—and almost let out a huge sigh of relief.

Almost, for suddenly many bright young eyes set in grinning faces were watching him. Waiting to see what the Voice of the King was doing here, who would grieve as the result of his visit—and, doubtless, what sport could be made of it.

And there, at the heart of it all, was Cairbre Dathaill, gleaming in a bright new cloth-of-gold cloak over garments as red as a waterfall of rubies, a handsome, well-dressed wit at the heart of an attentive crowd of young and well-dressed wits—busy being drawlingly witty.

For a moment, dark rage nigh choked the King's envoy.

A moment in which Cairbre greeted him with, "Volundr the Voice! Come straight and hot from the Palace like a vengeful vargyr! What news?"

Volundr drew himself up. For this audience, lofty elder statesman, to be sure. "News for you, as it happens, Cairbre Dathaill," he announced loudly—and was gratified when all the chatter died to tense silence in an instant.

"If it were up to me," he went on, "this would be done more privately, but the King desires urgency. In the form of a royal summons, to appear before him in the Palace as speedily as your legs can take you there."

"My legs? Oh, so this is not an arrest?"

Volundr put on his best pitying smile, and gestured behind himself without looking. If he did, he knew someone would be aping or mocking him in some way, to raise a titter. "Do you see any soldiers? No, I come alone. To tell you that the King is well aware that you and certain *friends*"—Volundr let his gaze wander slowly around the arc of attentive young dandies, and made it frosty with disapproval, which for some reason made one honey-haired youngling he didn't know repress a snigger, Allfather smite him!—"have been *scheming* to bring about his death."

The Kraken's Coils was deathly still now, right out to its threshold, so the faint din of the street outside could be heard.

Volundr hooked his thumbs into his belt, squared his shoulders, stared into Cairbre's eyes with a gaze that promised death, took one slow, doom-of-the-conqueror step forward to stand alone in the clear stretch of floor, and added crisply, "That's treason, foolhead, in case you're unfamiliar with the term. Yet the King stands unafraid of you and your plots, and desires to discuss them with you."

"Well, now. I'd best dash home and change into something suitable for being slave-branded, then," Cairbre said easily.

"Oh, no," Volundr replied silkily. "No rushing to snatch up poisons and other weapons—or to try a coward's escape, more likely." He put on a grim smile and added, "The King means *right now*."

And he turned on his heel and strutted for the door without waiting for a reply, or looking back.

It seemed a very long walk through the silent club, and he was almost at the door when he heard one young voice from the rear room murmur, "I can almost pluck one of his tailfeathers from here. Should I, I wonder?"

"And have him fart all his innards into our faces as you burst him like a bladder, and let out all that hot air? No *thanks*," said someone else, and Volundr the Voice marched stiff-backed and scarlet out of the Kraken's Coils to the fanfare of a great rolling roar of mirth.

At least all the guffaws and shouted obscenities were laced with a clear edge of fear.

The One-Eyed King might not be loved, but he *was* feared.

Which was better.

#

Mist had fallen in love with Teagan's kitchen. The hanging herbs, the cozy nooks with lamps just where they were needed, and handy cutting-platters set on the running countertops in each one; it felt like a safe, relaxing refuge. That came with the mingled scents of lavender, leeks, and whatever was cooking.

"How will we know if what we did has succeeded?" Mist asked, stirring the pot hanging over the hearthfire.

Her aunt shrugged, then said softly, "It might be wisest if you quietly left Ath Cliath now. And went home and reported, then disappeared to somewhere you'd not likely be looked for in."

Their gazes met.

"I don't want to be wise," Mist said. "I like it here. At the center of things. Danger and crowding and smells and all, it's where things are HAPPENING."

Teagan smiled broadly. "Of course."

"Of course, what? Because I'm young and foolish and want to be in on things?"

"Of course, because you're Mist Damhain."

#

"Ah, but what does it mean? That's what *I* want to know! Is the All-father turning his face from Ath Cliath?"

Volundr strode past, pretending not to hear, but he was listening intently as he came to an abrupt halt to let two sweating men wrestling a heavy cask trot past.

The talkers were a Hibernian sea-trader and two shopkeepers, one of them a burly dark-skinned woman unloading wooden four-bottle carry-cases from the trader's wagon. But talking about what? What were they trying to divine the meaning of?

"Is Odin losing his grip on us? Was the Fury Thor wresting dominance from the All-Father?"

The trader shrugged. "Fimbulwinter, remember? *I'd* say he's already lost it, but I know you Aesir-worshippers see things differently—or want to. But think on that. The world getting darker and colder, no proper bright days any more..."

An assistant bustled out of the shop to take some of the carry-cases, and asked what Volundr was tarrying to hear and wondering how much longer he could do so without being noticed.

"Hey, now, what's this about Thor?"

"Well, he's god of storms, and The Fury That Shattered Odin was the worst storm to hit us in *years*—and shattered Odin's statue, too."

"Hunh. I thought some madman with a hammer did that."

"One did. We call him Thor. Har-har!"

"*That*, friend, is *not* funny."

Which was when Volundr noticed the trader's eye had fallen on him. He made haste to lurch on, not looking back.

The Fury That Shattered Odin, now, was it?

How much talk like this was there, across the city?

The King must be told, of course, but would be less than pleased to hear it, of course. Nevertheless, Ath Cliath stood or fell on the shoulders of its king. Before he'd conquered it, there were no gold rods, no sea of riches and bustling commerce. Just Hibernia's busiest port, which wasn't saying much; fish hauled in and beer guzzled and a little wool out.

Or so he'd heard. This, around him, these tall buildings and forests of banners and signboards—all Sitric Cuaran's doing, every last one of them. His own life, and that of everyone who worked at the Palace, too. "We owe it all to our King," he muttered to himself, striding grandly along, the Voice of the Riverfleet Throne cleaving the street crowds with disdainful, practised ease.

He barely even noticed the patrol of soldiers who'd quietly fallen in behind him, and their silent glares of menace that were now parting the crowd for him.

All he knew was that after his exhausting search for Cairbre Dathaill and his humiliating departure from the Kraken's Coils, his journey to the grand home of Torloch Dargan was swift, direct, and easy.

Though once there, not even the grim soldiers at his back could produce Torloch. The merchant's steward was an old, much-scarred retired Hibernian warrior who looked down the broad steps of the house he kept in order as if hungry for the tiniest excuse to charge down them and rend the King's soldiers limb from limb with bored ease, ere returning to retirement. And flatly informed the King's Voice that if he wanted to talk to Torloch—and talk to Torloch he must, for no one in *this* house would take a message to him—he must repair to those of Torloch's warehouses that could be found along Darvyre's Way, where Torloch now was.

And where he was, unlike certain folk the steward could lay eyes on right now, *working*.

And with that, the old steward turned his back on them, marched through the tall metal-shod front doors of the grand house, and shut them with a boom.

It was not true that Torloch Dargan had a 'Begone' banner that could flutter down to impart its message to unwanted guests, but to Volundr, it certainly felt as if one had dropped to unroll in front of his nose. Seething, he turned in the direction of Darvyre's Way.

Why couldn't these self-styled merchant "lords" of the city be like the King? Stay where they were supposed to be, and let others do their bidding for them?

What else were riches and power good for?

His ire at crazed, contrarian Hibernian merchant lords raged all the way across Woolwagon Way and down Coppergates Street into Darvyre's Way, and along it to the huge new warehouses adorned with the red stag's head of Dargan.

Wagons were drawn up in front of one shed, where many men were hastening to and fro, so Volundr marched up to them, prepared to loftily demand the whereabouts and surrender unto him of the citizen Torloch Dargan.

Only to find the man himself unloading casks larger than Volundr from the wagon alone and grunt-walking them into the warehouse like a strongman at an Odin-feast, while his workers did other tasks, like stacking and tallying.

Volundr the Voice planted himself, squared his shoulders, drew in a deep breath, and demanded, "Torloch Dargan?"

The cask that was swung past him growled, "I was the last time I looked. What business would you want to be having with me?"

"The King's business," Volundr said crisply.

"The King makes all business transacted in Ath Cliath his business. Could you be a bit more specific?"

"Treason," Volundr snapped. "Is that specific enough for you?"

"No," Torloch replied shortly, lifting another cask. "I have better things to do."

"The King," Volundr said heavily, "believes otherwise. He is well aware of the plots you've been weaving with the Lady O'Hart, Cairbre Dathaill—and, I believe, the, ah, *unfortunate* Ardgal Loughnane—and desires you to know that he fears them not, but does desire to discuss them with you as soon as you can get yourself to the Palace."

"Does he, now? These casks won't unload themselves."

Volundr sidestepped to where he was out of the way of Torloch's journeys between wagon and warehouse, but could meet the laden merchant's gaze whenever he was carrying a cask, caught Torloch's eyes, and added with a grim smile, "The King means *right now*."

Torloch shrugged. "When these casks are done."

"I'll tell him you said that."

"Good. Please do." And Torloch went back for the next cask.

#

Brandr blinked at the now-familiar ceiling cracks. He was in his room in Dun's Hearth. Well, of course.

The innkeeper had fed him, after...

The memories came flooding back, confused at first, but he sat up, muzzy-headed, and stared at his feet, trying to puzzle out how long he might have slept.

He failed. No, he knew not how long he'd been asleep. Not without talking to the innkeeper, or a fellow guest, and that would recall getting dressed, and departing this room, and he was just too busy yawning to do that yet.

One of the most vivid memories came back to him then. Lady Lecora O'Hart's lips on his. Brandr shook his head in bemused disbelief.

That one could use her charms as a weapon.

Did use her charms as a weapon.

But what did she want *him* for? He, Brandr Fylan, young Hibernian clansman? Expendable fodder?

That *would* be the Ath Cliathian way, and she was very much of Ath Cliath. One of the elegant, deadly dark gliding sharks among so many smaller fish.

So here he was again: what to do? What use was he, here in this city?

"Tell your elders so," she had told him, all but ordering him to get out of Ath Cliath. And yet...he wanted to stay, now, in this dirty, crowded, bustling, ridiculously expensive place.

Here he felt alive. Important things happened here...and were going to happen.

Soon.

Ath Cliath was rushing towards big and important things happening.

So, until then? What to do?

"Bah!" Brandr told the ceiling, as he fell back onto the bed—and used the momentum to spring back up again, to his feet this time, and reel into the nearest wall, cursing softly, as he sought to clear his head, find his balance and his strength, and remember where the chamberpot was.

In sudden exasperation, he forced himself to hasten, bumping into the walls and blundering into the end of the bed as he fought to dress swiftly.

A battle fought and won, and he was out and heading downstairs, suddenly famished.

Food, food, *food*. Yes, *that* was what to do next.

One man was dining alone in the common room: Oswin Silverlock, the priest of the White God.

Who looked up at the sound of Brandr's tread on the stairs, saw and recognized and smiled, then waved at Brandr to come and sit, joining him.

Well, why not?

A maid bustled out of the kitchens, bringing inviting smells with her, to see what Brandr wanted. A choice he would miss once he was back home, for places other than Ath Cliath had certain handy, cheap viands for given times and places. The stew was hot and ready in the cauldron, so he settled for that and mulled wine to wash it down with.

"So," Brandr asked, trying to make it clear by the manner of his asking that he was friendly and curious, not hostile or a spy, "what is a holy man of the White God doing here, in a city under Odin's hand?"

Oswin shrugged. "Seeking to change the city, for one."

"Change it how? And how does one man change a city? Short of becoming its king at the head of a marauding army, that is."

Oswin smiled thinly. "That's not my way. The way of the sword is for those good at hefting one and remembering which is its sharp end. I am not one of those."

"So what way, then?"

"A way you could help me with, or yon maid, or the nearest carter in the streets, if he has a pleasant disposition. Change the lives of the working folk in Ath Cliath. The cooks and laborers and crafters and shopkeepers, not the rich."

"By showering them all with gold, or their own slaves to do their work for them, or some such?"

"By convincing them to work together and cook together—and divide the spoils—rather than buying and selling so much in their daily lives, for buying and selling enriches only the king. And getting them to pay attention to what the King does, so as to see what might lie ahead for their city, and decide if they want to be a part of it—or leave, and not be part of it, if the King leads Ath Cliath into war, or more slavery."

Brandr blinked. "Most folk mistrust places they know not, and prefer to stay close by home."

Oswin nodded. "Don't I know it. I did not say this convincing would be easy. But as one newly come to Ath Cliath, who has known other places and other ways, can you not see my thinking? Why not go beyond Sitric One-Eyed's reach, and flourish there? Trust not in kings to rule you for the best, but assume they'll rule you for their own betterment, and watch what they do rather than trust them."

Brandr nodded. "My thinking runs along similar lines. Tell me, do you know where all the taxes collected for the King go? Oh, some for his courtiers and the Palace and fine wine and new crowns and all, but what happens to all the rest of it?"

Oswin shook his head. "I know not. And I don't believe anyone outside of the Palace—and a very few folk at the Palace—do. Which makes one wonder, does it not? Perhaps King Sitric's just gold-mad, a miser who must have ever more. Yet he doesn't strike me that way. To me, he seems more one who gathers wealth for some great—or at least very expensive—purpose. I don't think it's to assemble an army for some great war...or if it is, he's doing that elsewhere and in secret.

84

And I think we must uncover what that purpose is, and as soon as we can. In case the One-Eye King is a great evil we must stop at all costs, ere he achieves what he wants done."

Brandr stared at Oswin, aghast. "But how?"

Oswin smiled. "We are neither of us spies, are we? Yet I fear we must become so."

"Just like that?"

"I did not say it would be easy. If changing ourselves was easy, more would do it, and their lives with the changes, and profit much thereby. As would, perhaps, the world."

"So, where to start?"

Oswin shrugged. "After this meal they're bringing to you now? I think we must get to know the citizens of Ath Cliath better. Perhaps we can find one of those who knows what the King does with all his gold."

"Before it's too late?"

The priest's smile was thinner this time. "As the skalds say: before it's too late."

chapter 16

"The Lady O'Hart," the owner of the eye peering out at him through the little sliding window informed Volundr coldly, "is *not* at home."

Volundr the Voice drew himself up and asked just as coldly, "And when is she expected to return?"

"I know not," was the reply. "I am her servant. *Not* her keeper."

Volundr was still trying to think of a suitably nasty reply when a company of identically dark-clad handsome young men, wearing matching swords, daggers, expensive boots, and slightly wearily bored expressions came striding down the street.

They mounted the steps, thrusting Volundr firmly aside. He fought for his balance and snarled, "*Do* you mind?"

"Not at all," said the nearest man. "I'll do it again, if you'd like. These steps belong to the Lady Lecora O'Hart, not to the likes of you."

"*I*," Volundr snarled, "am the Voice of the *King!*"

"You're the best he can do? Is it an affliction, or a derangement? Should Ath Cliath be looking for a new king?"

"You *mock* me, lout! And mock the *King!*"

"I do nothing of the sort. You delude yourself. Be off with you—the Lady O'Hart has returned after a night of important meetings, and desires her bed."

"She is with you?"

"She is," a woman's voice came flatly from the midst of the company of men—and they parted as if a spell had been cast, to reveal a tall, darkly beautiful woman in black, booted as they were. She had long, unbound hair, and eyes that stabbed at Volundr like two blue-black daggerpoints. "Well?"

"Lady, I am Volundr, Voice of the Riverfleet Thro—"

"I know who you are. Why do you seek me?"

"I am charged by King Sitric Cuaran—"

"I know who he is, too. We're doing well."

"*Charged* by the King to inform you that he is fully aware of the plots you and Dathaill and Dargan—and until he was properly chastised, the traitor Ardgal Loughnane—have been hatching against him. He desires you to know that he fears you not, and wishes to discuss your treason with you just as soon as you can get yourself to the Palace. In short, you are bidden."

Volundr turned to rake the handsome young bodyguards with a look of scorn and added, "*Alone.*"

The Lady O'Hart yawned. "Really? I thought those days were over, between Sitric and me."

"Your fellow conspirators are summoned, too," Volundr snapped.

"I see."

She *did* look tired.

Volundr smiled grimly. "The King means *right now.*"

"Of course he does, faithful cockerel," Lecora murmured. "He hasn't learned yet that his impatience earns no frantic haste among those who work for a living. Now run along and tell him I said that."

Volundr, who'd been just about to threaten her that he would tell the King her every insolent word, found himself opening and shutting his mouth wordlessly, with nothing at all in his head to say.

The Lady O'Hart swept past him and into her home, her bodyguards gleefully crowding Volundr off the step into a hastily-stumbling descent down the lower steps to the street.

He lost his footing at the bottom and crashed down hard to the cobbles, dashing the wind out of himself.

When he found it again and sat up with a snarled curse or two, it was to find two bodyguards standing over him, arms folded.

They were not—quite—smiling.

#

The King looked up as the secret door opened and Mael the Sharp drifted silently into the room.

"This is becoming a habit," the Lord of Ath Cliath remarked. "What news?"

"Magnus the Small has departed the city, taking ship as suddenly and quietly as he came. At no time during his visit did he so much as inform the Palace of his presence."

Sitric shrugged.

"A snub?" Mael suggested gently.

Sitric shrugged again, then set down the parchment he'd been reading and said calmly, "Have one of the lesser Palace envoys summon Vigmarr Bent-Neck for an audience with the King. Polite but urgent, so he hasn't time to concoct any flowery tales he hasn't thought up already."

Mael bowed. "Of course. You suspect?"

The King spread his hands. "Nothing, until I hear and see *how* Vigmarr lies to me. Perhaps Magnus was covertly trying to get a good bulk price from Old Bent-Neck for a lot of slaves, and seeing how swiftly they could be had. For a war, or something else fatal."

He and Mael traded grim looks at *that* thought.

Neither of them had to voice the questions that hung in both their minds right then.

A war on whom? And why not tell a King sitting in a palace mere streets away, unless you don't want that king to know?

"I'll put the others to watching everyone who sets boot outside Bent-Neck's house, to see where they go and who they talk to," Mael said quietly. "Before your envoy reaches him."

The King nodded.

As Mael bowed his way out, he saw that the King was juggling some small things in his palm.

Runes. He'd wager a flask of very good wine on it.

#

Volundr the Voice nursed his aches and pains—a hip, an elbow, and a knee, to say nothing of his pride—all the way back to the Palace. Black rage seethed in him, ire at how he'd been bested at each of his meetings with the miscreant traitors. Roiled and sickened his stomach, but found not satisfying eruption, no way of venting.

He muttered curses under his breath with each painful, lurching step. Those three, those insolent three. They should have been fearful, cowed by the King's name and the thought of their own impending dooms—but no.

Robbed of his rightful satisfaction thrice. Was he losing his touch?

He was the Voice of the King, but this day it had seemed that meant nothing, commanded no respect, made him a despised laughingstock.

Folk should quail, citizens of Ath Cliath should turn pale and give way at his approach.

Had he, invisibly and without noticing, become a step too old? So his bluster—aye, admit it, he *did* bluster, and why should he not?—carried no brawn any longer, and folk sniggered rather than knowing fear.

What, then? Was it time to retire? To leave Ath Cliath with all the gold he could fist, and go to his sweetheart in the distant green hills of far Hibernia?

Ah, Aoife. Aoife O'Drum, mighty of shoulder and buxom of build, a wife to marry and settle down with on a big successful farm where they could rear many sons and daughters. Aoife, the real treasure. The treasure gleaming gilded Ath Cliath could not afford him, for all its riches and bustle.

The Palace loomed, ahead. He should have been striding gleefully triumphant over having been sneering and high-handed to three rich and powerful 'old coin' merchants of the city, the self-styled Lords of Ath Cliath. Putting them in their places was what had made this job so, well, *fun*. He'd report to the King and then retire to the morning feasting hall for a celebratory drink.

Well, he needed that drink, all right. And still needed to report to the King.

Frown of Odin, but things were turning sour.

In this darkening world of ever-deepening cold. King Cuaran had kept it all at bay, with all the riches and the bustling commerce, the furs and gold and slaves…but for how much longer?

And how much longer could he, Volundr, dance the dance?

Bah, what was *wrong* with him? Insolent puffed-up lordlings being insolent; that should be no surprise. Why, then, was he so grim?

Aoife…aye, to get away from all of this, and be with her.

He was three strides from the new statue of Odin when its neck suddenly cracked—and its head plunged from its shoulders, to shatter in thousands of stone shards at his feet.

Volundr staggered back, aghast, amid their bouncing and rolling wrack, as the guards flanking the grand Palace gates sprang from their posts to charge at him, as if it was his fault.

The one on his left was faster, and reached him first.

Or would have done, if the rest of the statue hadn't abruptly toppled, felling him like a broken child's doll.

Volundr sprang back with a shriek, slipped on the still-moving rubble underfoot, and fell. Heavily, losing his wind yet again, then cracking his head on the unyielding cobbles.

The last thing he saw was the second guard looming over him, wearing a scowl like a stormfront, spear in hand.

#

"S-someone tampered with the painted clay temporary statue Markvard Stonecleaver put up before the gates while he carves the real one," a white and shivering with fear Palace servant whose name Sitric did not know and whose sniveling face he cared not if he ever beheld again.

"I understand," he said curtly. "*Go.*"

And the terrified man almost fell in his scurrying haste to begone.

Sitric sighed heavily, and let the rising anger drain out of him with his breath. He might have laughed, had he been there to see fat Volundr fall. Might.

He stood abruptly, letting tallies and missives flap in his wake, suddenly tired of the accounting and the scrivening.

Where were those traitors? He felt like swinging a sword, lopping off heads and slashing open throats and ribs…

Conquering, *that* was living. Ruling felt more like being in a cage. A cage that got smaller and smaller when your back was turned, until you lacked even space enough to pace or prowl.

Sitric strode across the room, snatched up his runes, murmured a prayer to Odin, then cast them down on the table to scatter like so many rattling dead men's fingerbones.

The one that turned up right in front of him, rolling to show its face at the last, when the others had grown still, was the arrow. Tiwaz. Discipline.

Odin's will was clear.

Sitric gathered the runes gently back together, and let the restlessness, the need for violence, fade. He would be the gently-smiling, glacially calm Lord of Ath Cliath again, the man who saw and anticipated all, and so walked a step ahead of foes and rivals.

He would be the one all in the city feared.

The One-Eyed King.

Where *were* those traitors?

#

"They're saying," Forkundr Redbeard said excitedly, leaning forward over the table, "that Magnus the Small has left the city. Sailed back out without a word to the Palace or striding the streets, like a thief in the night!"

Borekr Ketilsson spat out some gristle, and pinned it to the table with his knife and then lifted it for a narrow-eyed inspection to be sure it didn't hold wasn't some morsel of meat he was missing. "Well, isn't that what he is? A thief in the night?"

Eylir Grimsson snorted. "Practising at being envoy? Blunt insults to the fore?"

"*Honesty* to the fore, more like. But you know what this means, yes?"

"Yes," Grimkell's deep voice said simply, and no more.

It was left to Falki Longbeak to voice the obvious. "So no one else is going to take One-Eye off the Riverfleet Throne for us. We have to get to work on removing him ourselves. *Now*."

"Yes, but we need a plan. A good one. Or it'll be our necks we're dooming, not his. He has his spies and soldiers and rich traders beholden to him and all. We have…the five of us, with our anger and these tankards and no scheme to get from here to a new king."

"Men die when kings fall," Grimkell told the table in his deep rough growl. "There's always a brawl for any empty throne, and blood spilled. Our plan must take us not just to Sitric's fall, but beyond it to who'll succeed him."

"You?" Eylir joked.

"*No*," the gravel-voiced skald said flatly. "I *know* I'd be a bad throne-warmer. The trouble is, too many folk don't."

"Well enough. Who, then?"

"Someone who doesn't want the throne, but has wits and wiles enough not to become a welcome-mat under the boots of any bully with an army or an alliance of the mighty. Ath Cliath is the richest, brightest city in the world—and that draws all the greedy and unscrupulous to—"

"Yes, yes, I'm not a puling babe who knows naught of the world. We need names of successors, and ways to take down Cuaran. Who is a galdr, and favoured of Odin, and has been successful enough to make a lot of folk who detest him keep their jaws shut and their patience to the fore, so they go on letting him warm the throne. He's a *success*, damn him."

"I see him as being in the right place at the right time and not being such an idiot as to mess it all up in a spectacular fashion. He's more the slow creep into greater and greater oppression, until none of us can breathe and he *has* to be removed. But yes, we have to do this right, or we'll pay the price and he might even slip out of whatever noose we've tightened on him."

"So start thinking. Of something else beyond poison, which is what everyone thinks of, and he's most on guard against."

"Toppling a Palace tower on him? Tough to survive that."

"Or some other building that's not full of soldiers loyal to him and on watch for intruders. Lure him to a building we can work on."

"How? He's a *galdr*, by the Norns! The runes will warn him of anything we get up to that requires a lot of work and preparation."

"So can we spread madness? To have others lash out, at times and places Cuaran won't expect?"

"How? Skalds can sing of spells and toppling towers and floods and great serpents boiling up out of the sea because they *make it up*. We have to come up with something real, and it has to work the first time, because if we bring down the war hammer and he escapes it, we'll never get him that way again; he'll be on his guard and even getting at him will become nigh-impossible. He has gold enough right now to become a recluse who rules through a score of petty tyrants who all serve him."

"Yes, but he likes the cut-and-thrust, to be close to the people, likes to summon citizens and browbeat them in person. We must use that against him."

"Now I'm hearing wisdom. Use a man's nature against him. Say on."

"This isn't a saga, and I'm not a skald. I can't think of clever schemes to slay a man. Where I came from, you walked up to a man, challenged him with axe in hand, and sought to kill him. None of this sly-work."

"I still like toppling a tower onto him."

"*Now* who's playing the skald? Buildings don't just fall down, you know."

"Oh, yes, they do, just not all of a sudden with a king standing under them. Those sort of buildings need help."

"So we'd have to lure him into our prepared-to-collapse building, by putting something deep in there he'd want to see for himself."

"A sign of Odin?"

"The gods *are* real, Fork. They're not going to sit idle while we or any other deceitful mortal uses their names and signs falsely."

"What about a spell to make Cuaran's runes explode in his face? He's a galdr, he works with them all the time."

"What *about* such a spell? Do you know one? Or how to craft one? And do you think the Norns will stand idle and let you create one, and sew mistrust of wyrding and keeping runes by in the minds of everyone? Use your *head*."

"And if we don't use our heads wisely, the King will use them. Cutting them off the rest of us, for a start."

"Would something to drink help us think of something, d'you think?"

"No, it'll just get us headaches and loose-tongued, to endanger us while wasting an evening," Grimkell said flatly. "We've walked that road a time or three before."

"So what, then? Do we set traps for the man's snakes, to kill them off until he stands alone?"

"That has some merit, but it won't be easy. Not only are they far more experienced at traps and ambushes and nasty knife-work than any of us, our pacing has to be just right. Too abruptly, and everyone else with a grievance against One-Eye will rise against him. Too slowly, and he'll replace the shadowhands we lop off, and the dance will be endless."

"Unless we could kill them all at once, somehow."

"How?"

"Collapse the Palace on their heads?"

"And just how are you—not we, *you*, because the rest of us aren't such idiots as to try it—going to get into the Palace for months of work cutting this pillar and that buttress, so it can be made to fall down all at once, to command rather than in the first high wind or at random, without being seen and stopped? Fatally?"

"Hoy, we're just spinning up ideas, not working out all the details!"

"Details, he calls them!"

"Well, wait a moment, how does the King keep from being poisoned?"

"Magic?"

"On every morsel the man eats? That's a *lot* of magic!"

"Well, he's spending all those taxes on *some*thing!"

"Yes, but if the Palace was full of runecasters or seithkona, we'd have heard about it ere now. Servants *talk*."

"The King has food tasters?"

"Well, there you go, then: poison all of his tasters."

"And how do we do *that?* That's just as hard as poisoning the King, only as many times harder as he has tasters. And we have to get them all at once, or the game fails and they'll be on guard against poison. And if we just poison the food, it'll be cooks and maids and the like who'll sicken and fall on their faces, not the King! We *have* to find a way to get at the man!"

"I can't think of a way to get at him, that's the trouble."

"Me, neither."

"And that," Grimkell growled, "is why the One-Eyed King is still on the Riverfleet Throne."

And silence fell.

chapter 17

"I...I'm here to see the King," Vigmarr Bent-Neck said sullenly. "He summoned me."

The guards said not a word, but eyed him coldly as the gates swung open with a deep and somehow mocking groan.

"Hmph. Needs oil," one guard said to the other, ignoring Vigmarr as he hesitantly stepped between them.

And walked on, alone, into the Riverfleet Palace. A hulking man, large and soft-footed, twisting his body at every stride so his left flank was foremost, his spine and shoulders twisted and his head lower than his shoulders and set to one side. Unlovely, yet gentle. An odd man, many said, to deal in slaves.

And odd men are suspicious.

So much the King's face said—silently—as Vigmarr was ushered into his presence, and the door shut quietly behind him.

Silence fell. And stretched, giving Bent-Neck ample time to regard the two hulking and impassive warriors, in full war-harness, who stood behind the shoulders of the One-Eyed King, hands resting on axe-heads and faces coldly unreadable. Their eyes were fixed on the slave-dealer, and their gazes were unfriendly.

There would be other royal defenders behind him, Vigmarr knew, hidden behind walls or tapestries, ready to hurl means of slaying in an instant. There always were.

He denied the Lord of Ath Cliath the satisfaction of seeing fear, or the restlessness borne of nervousness or guilt, but merely stood like a stone, waiting. Patiently.

Competent kings were busier than slave-dealers. Both men knew who would stir first.

"So, Vigmarr Hrafnkelsson," the King said quietly, without greetings or pleasantries, "word has reached me that you've had a visitor. Word that came not from you nor from him, which surprises me. I expected that such an important personage as Magnus the Small would come to Ath Cliath openly, not steal in and out again like a thief in the night. Such conduct raises suspicions. And he came to you, and stayed under your roof, so that suspicion lingers. Clinging to you."

"As is the way of suspicion," Vigmarr replied calmly. "Which is why it is better banished from all of our lives. The lives of kings especially."

"Would that were possible," said Sitric. "Yet kings who try that tend to live short lives, that end violently. Regrettably, treason flourishes wherever suspicion withers."

"So the skalds say, and wise old crones too, for that matter. Yet I say to you, King Sitric Cuaran, that you have no need to be suspicious of me. I, and my fellow slave-traders, flourish under your rule; we desire it to continue forever."

The King smiled. "And yet, I would hear from you—in full and frankly, holding nothing back—why Magnus visited you, and what passed between you while he was here."

Vigmarr nodded. "I am unsurprised. Yet it was a private matter. And that is all I prefer to say."

"Vigmarr Hrafnkelsson," Sitric Cuaran said icily, "I am your *King*." And he paused and waited.

When Vigmarr gave him only silence, he added, "I can have the truth dragged out of you. Painlessly or otherwise."

Vigmarr regarded him expressionlessly. "So you can kill me getting me to talk, or the Battle Wolves will kill me for talking. Not nice choices. Vigmarr is only as good as Vigmarr's word, and it has been given. So I will keep it, and so, keep silent. Though I will tell you, Sitric

Cuaran, that Magnus and I discussed nothing that concerns you or Ath Cliath."

"And if I believe you not?"

"Then you know me not, and are a fool besides. Kings need men like me: men of their word. The only sort that can be trusted, in the murky worlds of kings and courts and intrigues and diplomacy."

"I grant that as truth, yet another truth is that all men lie—including you. And I ask myself: why would a seithkarl so trusted by Hildolfr the Battle Wolf come in secrecy to a slave dealer, and stay overnight? What could he possibly want from such a man? Slaves, obviously, and for slaves one comes to the market and bids, like all others. Why meet privately? Why would a seller of slaves grant such a meeting, which can only be intended to press him for more favourable terms? Why, to buy slaves in bulk, without all men knowing. And why would Hildolfr, a commander of mercenaries, need slaves in bulk? To open a new mine or build a new fortress, perhaps. But a king must see deeper, and farther ahead, and prepare for the worst. And the worst is war."

The One-Eyed King stopped speaking, hard cold gaze locked with the calm eyes of the slaver, waiting for Vigmarr to fill the deepening silence. But the man before him did not even stir.

So Sitric added softly, "Why keep your meeting secret from the King of Ath Cliath? When the war might involve Ath Cliath. In short, I must prepare for an attack on my city from Hildolfr. Even a child can follow the inevitable chain of thoughts here, Vigmarr. Yet all you give me is that I would be a fool not to trust you. Whereas I cannot escape the conclusion that I'd be a fool *to* trust you."

The slave-dealer nodded, his lowered head bobbing eerily below his shoulders. "Fairly spoken, my King. If I had not given my promise to Magnus that what passed between us would remain secret, I would tell you all. But I *did* give my word—and if I break my word, I am nothing. Before the gods, not just before kings and all men. I would be left broken, less than a man, not just a man ruined, whose livelihood would lie in tatters because no man would trust me henceforth. You can mistreat me, and harm yourselves in the eyes of all merchants, and dim the bright success of Ath Cliath that you have built—for it has been built because they trusted you, and so came and traded, despite your taxes, for they deem Ath Cliath their best trading-floor. Yet if they see how you treat an honest merchant..."

"But what if they believe that Vigmarr Bent-Neck is *not* honest? That he did treason?"

The slave-dealer smiled sadly. "Yet another truth is that all men lie—including you," he said, in perfect mimicry of Sitric Cuaran's speech. And added in his own voice, "Something the good citizens of Ath Cliath have decided for themselves, already. If you spread rumors of what I've done or said, it matters not how silent you've rendered me—many will think you're lying, even if you are not."

The King went red.

"And before you make the threat," Vigmarr added calmly, " I know that the best axe to your hand at this moment is to threaten to deny me from trading in the new slave market, when you open it. Mere days from now, yes? That would end my slaveselling in Ath Cliath, to be sure. Yet it would also drive me into the arms of your foes, who would buy slaves to work harm upon you. And I would trade with them, if they trusted me and allowed me to keep my word."

The One-Eyed King sat silent, his face dark.

"I and all slavers in this city and the wider world who send slaves to our markets know you've built the new market so that all trading is done under your hand and eye, and so all fees are paid to you, rather than to those of us who own the older pens and auction halls. And we grumble, just to ourselves, but acquiesce—because, when all is said and done, we trust that what you build and control will work best for all. In the long run, we'll all prosper. But, my King, if you shatter that trust..."

"Do you threaten me, slaver?" Sitric's voice was soft, barely more than a whisper.

"No, my King, for I am no fool—and no traitor. I threaten not. I inform, and leave it to the wisest of kings I've ever known in my life to make the right decision."

Silence fell again, deep and dark. The King of Ath Cliath sat like a statue. Stone-faced and brooding.

The slaver stood regarding him, as calm as ever. Far calmer than the two glaring warriors behind the king.

Who stirred, after what seemed an eternity, to say quietly, "Odin take you, Vigmarr Hrafnkelsson, if you are betraying me or Ath Cliath. Yet candor is rare enough, and kings should value it, just as you say. So I am inclined to trust you."

He stood up, and the warriors behind him relaxed, moving slightly for the first time since Vigmarr had laid eyes on them. And it seemed to the slaver that there was movement behind the tapestries, accompanied by the slightest of sighs. Of relief?

Sitric Cuaran walked slowly forward until his nose nigh touched Vigmarr's.

"Don't," he added softly, "make me regret this trust. Or Odin shall surely make you regret it, with a thousand torments. Or more."

And he turned on his heel and strode out of the room. The two warriors followed.

After a moment, Vigmarr Bent-Neck gave the tapestries a solemn salute, then turned and left.

His back, between his shoulder blades, felt naked and imminent danger all the way home.

#

Truly, Odin smiled on this city.

And all because of one man. Its One-Eyed King.

Dainn would be meeting him soon. *So* soon. His hero, the mortal most favoured by the All-Father.

The priests who'd sent Dainn forth as the newest priest of Odin had told him Sitric Cuaran was the most favoured of the Mightiest of Gods, and bade him take himself in all haste to Ath Cliath, to assist King Sitric in every way he could.

So here he was, Dainn Gulbrandson, priest of Odin, newly arrived in Ath Cliath. The newest and least of the All-Father's holy servants—but then, as he'd been told repeatedly and earnestly, by holy men steeped in years who should know, every devout hand, however small or inexperienced, could make a difference. *Did* make a difference.

And that was *so* needed, now, with the world growing darker and colder.

Not that it didn't have its bright moments, and bright spots. He was looking at one of them right now.

Tall and impressive the dressed stone front of the new slave market soared up into the sky before him, grand despite the din of hammers and chisels and the workers' rubble and untidiness all around.

Balcony after balcony; he let his eyes climb the ascending column of them. Vantage points for favoured buyers to stand and watch arriving slaves, once it was up and running.

During the opening ceremony, they'd be crowded with dignitaries. And he'd be standing on the lowest, largest, and most splendid balcony, just *there*, beside the King himself. The mere thought made Dainn's heart soar.

"How could I not," he murmured aloud, "be in admiring awe of a king so swiftly successful, so rich and powerful, and so devoted to Odin?"

King Sitric Cuaran would consecrate the new slave market to Odin in a solemn ceremony,

94

opening it for business—and the eyes of the city would be on not just the King of Ath Cliath, but on Dainn Gulbrandson, as he conferred the purifying blessings of the All-Father on the builders and this magnificent stone hall they'd raised. The world would see the depths of his devotion.

The Fangtooth had been only too happy to have someone take charge of that part of the proceedings. Oh, he'd been pleased to take the gold the priests had sent, too—heavy, it had been; Dainn's back and arms could still feel the ache of its weight—but if Dainn was good at one thing, it was judging folk, and the slaver was clearly one of those who flourished in back rooms and murmuring across tables, not out in the full sun under the eyes of hundreds.

Not that Fengr Fangtooth would have to do that, ever again, soon. He'd not have to do anything at all he didn't want to do, so long as he obeyed the King of Ath Cliath. The urbane, neatly-bearded slaver was the owner of this big new slave market, and what Dainn had brought from the priests of Odin to pave his approval of giving Dainn a free hand in shaping the ceremony had likely all but covered the coins the Fangtooth had contributed to its raising. For the slaver had combined funds with some bakers, tavernmasters, landlords, and tavernmasters to have enough coin to build the place—and two of the bakers, in lieu of coin, had contributed the land under Dainn's boots that stretched away for much of a long city block with the tall new slavemarket hall atop it.

As he admired the soaring stonework, Dainn knew he was wearing a broad, beaming smile, but why not? This was going to be *golden*.

The priests had told him the words that had to be said, but had left the rest of the ceremony to him. So he would plan things, starting here and now, and a big part of it would be putting himself at the King's side at every moment.

"Golden," he said aloud, and turned away, happily planning.

It did not take long for a worker who'd been sitting among the heaped timbers and stones and coils of rope nearby to rise and casually drift after him.

Borekr Ketilsson smiled thinly, in the shadows in the lee of heaped building stones where he was standing beside the unrolled plans for the market's south face, and transferred his attention from watching the workers hasten to finish the topmost balcony to watching the King's shadowhand stroll after the young priest.

Of *course* the shadowhands were suspicious of this young lad come out of nowhere, who gloated aloud about Odin's favour and staying close to the King. Fanatics were like daggers with hilts as sharp as their blades; prudent men never turned their backs for an instant.

Grimkell, Fork, and the rest must hear of this. A gloatingly ambitious young priest of Odin was something new in the mix, a stone to shatter placid waters and create many ripples.

The King must die, but schemes must be thought through until they were both precise and solid. If matters went awry, and the market itself suffered—what if a wounded and furious Sitric ordered it torn down?—than Borekr's investment would suffer with it.

And he was not a man who had coins enough to toss some here and others there, and care not if they bore no fruit. His savings were at risk.

He turned his head back to the plans, so if the shadowhand glanced back, it would seem as if Borekr Ketilsson wasn't staring after him. Yet he kept his gaze, under lowered brows, on the dwindling figure of the shadowhand, still on the young priest's trail.

And the moment he was certain the shadowhand was out of sight, Borekr turned and *ran* in the other direction.

#

Brandr stiffened. Who could be knocking on his door?

Not the innkeeper, not so softly. This was an unfamiliar knocking.

He felt for the knife at his belt as he approached the door, and murmured, "Yes?"

"Young Fylan, I think you should take a walk with me."

Brandr relaxed. He knew that rough voice.

Its owner gave him a sour look from under white-bristling brows. "Not starving, I see," he grunted.

Brandr grinned by way of reply, and the veteran trader turned on his heel and strode away without another word. Brandr hurried to close the door of his room and hasten after the man.

Cathal Faolain was one of the most successful merchants among the Uterni. Known for being terse and surly, yet year after year bringing home more silver and larger cargoes than any two fawning, widely-smiling younger traders. He'd almost certainly been sent by the clan elders to see how Brandr was getting on with his mission.

Faolain led the way without a backward glance or any attempt at stealth, down one street and along another, then into a courtyard where stairs ascended the outside of a crumbling old house to a flat part of its roof, stone sealed with pitch underfoot in a small walkout where an arched window proved to be also a door. On all sides, the gently-sloping tiles of the rest of the roof fell away, streaked with bird-dung. The breeze was brisk.

Obviously a place Faolain had been before—and just as obviously, chosen because no one could overhear what was said up here unless they were sharing the small flat area.

"Well?"

Brandr met the hard old eyes and swallowed. This was not going to go well.

"I..." He drew in a deep breath, lifted his chin, and said firmly, "I've thoroughly considered the situation, and decided not to...send a certain man into the arms of Odin."

Faolain stiffened, face going dark, but all he said was, "Why?"

"I don't see any way to reach the man. He's well guarded—he has his spies and bodyguards—and almost never goes out in public, these days. Why throw my own life away in a wild attempt that must surely fail? I *am* still seeking ways to fulfill the task."

"Well, *that's* a relief." Faolain's sarcasm was heavy with disgust. "Nice to hear your wits and will haven't been *entirely* lost in the flurry of spending all your Uterni coins wenching and carousing."

"I am *not* wenching or carousing," Brandr replied. "I *am* thinking of the consequences of, ah, the sudden murder of a particular person without the right strong hands ready at hand to seize the crown. Wild war everywhere helps no one, Uterni or not."

"So you need an army to help you, is that it?"

Brandr shook his head. "I need to see a way to do it cleanly. A sure path to success, and a strong successor who'll not be worse than...the incumbent. Otherwise, this city of coins and success may become a battlefield for years to come, and the Uterni and all suffer for it."

"I," Faolain told a nearby patch of roof-tiles, "have a little time on my hands. And am not least among the bowmen of the Uterni. Arrows fly where I intend them to. Can you arrange a sure path for *my* success?"

Brandr shrugged. "This morning I would have had to say no, but word is spreading across the city that there'll be a ceremony when the new slave market is ready for trade, to open it."

Faolain's smile was that of a smug wolf. "Opened by the King."

Brandr nodded.

"I just need as long as it takes a calm man to breathe, with a breeze no stronger than this, and a clear flight for an arrow," the veteran trader told him. "Find me a place to bend my bow that's no further from the King than yonder red roof is from us. We must scheme, for this slaying *must* be done."

ChAPTER 18

"Were you followed here?" Grimkell's voice was sharp.

"I'm *not* a dullard," Borekr told him.

"No man thinks he is," Eylir informed the table, "and you're more excited than I've ever seen you. A *child* could smell your eagerness coming off you—let alone one of Cuaran's shadowhands."

"And you rushed from one of us to the next," Forkundr Redbeard growled. "Leading those shadowhands right to us!"

Well, of *course* they were all alarmed. They'd never seen Borekr Ketilsson excited before. Come to think of it, Borekr couldn't remember the last time he'd felt excited.

"Well, if I have," he snarled, "*listen* to me, then we can be gone again, just as hastily as we assembled, hey?"

"That will *not*," Falki snapped, "save us."

"Will you *listen?*"

Grimkell held up an imperious hand, and silence fell in an instant. During which the skald frowned and pointed—and Forkundr and Falki scurried to obey, making a swift round of their gloomy meeting-place to peer out every window and door.

Finding everywhere they looked bereft of lurking shadowhands, they shook their heads and returned to their seats at the table, to lean forward over the lone lit lantern like the others.

"We'll listen," Grimkell told Borekr. "Speak."

"Well, then, I was at the new market, and overheard something of great interest. There's a new priest of Odin in town, a shining-eyed lad fairly bursting with his own importance and love of the god and of the King Odin smiles upon. He's the sort who babbles to himself."

"And what did he babble?"

"The beginnings of his half-hatched plans for the ceremony that will open the market for trading, once it's ready."

"The King will be part of this, I take it? With all of his shadowhands and a good number of soldiers on hand glaring at everyone who so much as lifts a hand?"

"Yes, but hear me: it seems the King, with this preening young dolt at his side, will be standing on the lowest balcony!"

"Be still, my beating heart! Oh, but the glories of architecture always smite me! Borekr, *why should we care?*"

"Well, if you'll *shut it* for a moment, Fork, I'll tell you! First you need to remember that, as an investor in this bright new establishment, I have access to the place—if timbers must be cut or other, ah, *rearrangements* made. And then you need to know that the south face of the hall has a *column* of balconies running up it, one on each floor, so important buyers can survey the slaves being brought for auction."

"I begin to see."

"*Yes!* There's no need to topple a tower on the King, when the ceremony will have him standing on the lowest balcony. What if that balcony is, ah, *fixed?* So it comes crashing down, One-Eyed King and all?"

Eylir sighed. "Fall some three man-heights? Four? If Odin smiles upon Cuaran, he'll easily survive that unscathed! And from all we've seen, the All-Father *does* smile on One-Eye! He'll probably *walk* away, sneering!"

"Ah, but don't you see? There're balconies all the way up! *Directly above* Sitric's crowned head! What if the one above breaks free and comes down on the King's head? *And* the one above that? That'd do him, sure!"

"Hoy, now!" Borekr's excitement was spreading around the table.

Grimkell winced. "It's a long, long chance, but..."

"But what better one will we have, hey? And if we leave the balcony he's standing on untouched, and they're watching for anyone tampering with it—or just giving it the hard-eye over and over again—they'll find nothing wrong with it!"

"It is worth," Forkundr Redbeard said firmly, "the try."

He was staring at Grimkell the Throat as if in challenge, but the skald was nodding slowly. And looking at Borekr with approval.

"Well done. I think you have something."

The common roar of approval was under all their breaths, but it was enthusiastic nonetheless.

#

Sitric Cuaran looked up sharply.

The junior envoy standing before him was literally trembling with fear.

Quelling a frown, the King waved at him to speak.

"M-my King," the man stammered, "I bear to you the words of Lady Lecora O'Hart, Lord Cairbre Dathaill, and Lord Torloch Dargan, who gave them to me and bade me deliver them *just* as they delivered them, with not a one changed. May I?"

The King's assenting gesture was patient.

"W-well, then," the envoy—Oraldr, that was his name—rallied, "Please tell the King, with the greatest respect, that we answered his summons, as conveyed to us so eloquently by Volunder the Voice, and attended the Palace with alacrity. Only to find his Royal Highness unavailable. Meeting, we were told, behind closed doors with someone else. So, suspecting that enthusiasm had this once overridden competence in the mind of the inestimable Volundr, leading him to make some trifling error as regards day and time of our requested audience, we have returned to our various unfolding threads of pressing daily business, but will be happy to attend the Palace again, forthwith, if a new summons should reach us."

Oraldr ran out of words and fairly cowered, obviously expecting a furious outburst from his king, but Sitric Cuaran merely gave him a wintry smile, waved a hand, and said, "Go yourself, without delay, to the lady and the two lords, and convey to them politely that I *do* require their presence here before me, at their earliest convenience. And that if I must come look for them myself, I shall do so at *my* convenience. Politely, remember."

The envoy nodded and rushed off, almost colliding with a young man in plain robes who was being ushered into the chamber by two grim guards who gave their King the slight nods that indicated this personage had been thoroughly searched and questioned.

"And who might you be?" the King inquired, finding himself inclined to cut short any awkward pleasantries.

The young man bowed low. "Dainn Gulbrandson am I, newly consecrated to Odin, and sent here to Ath Cliath by the priests who trained and ordained me to officiate at your consecration of the new slave market. So I have hastened here to the Palace to present myself to my King."

Sitric Cuaran's brows rose, then fell again, as the young man, obviously unable to hold his tongue in his eagerness and hero-worship, burst out in paeans of praise of Sitric's kingship and reverence of Odin, and of Odin's greatness and of how inspiring both were to him, personally.

The flood of swift words raced on, so fawning that Sitric was at first irritated, then amused, then—though he showed this not, he trusted—somewhat (inwardly) moved by the young man's obvious hero-worship and fervent dedication to Odin. And it was pleasant, in these deepening days of being hated and feared and envied on all sides, to have someone adoring him.

Out of the stream of verbiage he gathered that Gulbrandson had been charged by the priests who'd sent him to plan and conduct the ceremony, and that market owner Fengr Fangtooth had agreed to this after receiving a bribe from those same priests, delivered to him by the young priest—who would doubtless be horrified to hear that payment described as a "bribe."

At last it seemed Gulbrandson was running down. Into the faltering flow Sitric inserted a warm smile and the command, "Go and think through your ideas for the ceremony, write them out in coherent detail, and return on the morrow to offer them for my approval."

As eagerly as he'd said and done everything in the royal presence, Dainn bowed low, stammered his agreement and thanks, backed away with many additional bows, and then hurried off.

Hem-weighted to keep it from swirling wildly, a tapestry moved slightly, as out from hiding behind it glided Mael the Sharp.

Who promptly nodded his head in the direction of the departed priest.

"Of course," Sitric told him, then watched his senior shadowhand depart in swift, lithe silence.

"And on and on the rats run," he murmured to himself. "Can I yet make them dance, I wonder?"

#

Ake Hill-of-Wit was in a dark mood. "Look yonder," he growled. "It'll rain soon. Let's make this short."

The uppermost floor of the new slave market was a maze of boards, posts, sawhorses, and gaps in floor and roof; the cold river breezes blew through with no hindrance at all.

Yet with no buildings this high nearby, and the banging and chain-rattling and occasional shouts or curses of the workers three and four floors below, it was clear no spy could see or hear them. And that was very necessary, just now, with the King's shadowhands poking and prying everywhere.

"Agreed," Fengr Fangtooth said, and waved at Dagr Fire-Nose. "You called this moot; why?"

Dagr looked at Julfr Blacktooth, beside him, then at Fengr. "It's Vigmarr. The King questioning him, that is."

"*Threatening* him," Julfr growled.

"Aye," Ake agreed. "That's what it was, plain and simple. We—with him—are the foremost slave-dealers of the city. The engines of Cuaran's success and wealth. And yet. And *yet*."

"Indeed. Scant gratitude he shows us," Julfr agreed. "I know kings don't feel they're kinging it if they aren't slapping *someone* around, but why us?"

"And from what I've heard about what he put Vigmarr through, it was more than a warning slap," Fengr said heavily. "So I'm not opposed to meeting, Dagr, and want to hear you out. So..."

They were rivals, day to day, and not disposed to be overly friendly to each other, but they'd long since learned to work together, if uneasily. And they could read each other's faces, and voices; they were all concerned.

Dagr sighed heavily, then launched himself. "This, then: is the King turning against us? And if he is, what do we do? What *should* we do?"

"Get us a new king," Julfr growled. "I'm no lover of this one."

"Easily *said*, but dangerous to attempt," Fengr warned. "Not just because of his shadowhands, but because the city'll erupt. Everyone and their old crone of an aunt grabbing for the throne, knives in the streets, perhaps open war as kings decide they want Ath Cliath's gold... but we all know this. And Sitric One-Eye has always been his own man, not biddable by any bribe or—"

"Has always been *Odin's* man," Dagr rumbled. "I don't like fanatics. They always do just as they please, but do it afire with divine righteousness. Don't even have the base honesty to say they're serving themselves first, always have to cloak it in serving a god and so being *right* in what they do—when we all know it's filling their purses and exalting themselves for their own gain, just like all the rest of it. Bah!"

"I don't think any of us like holycloaks," Ake replied, "either the ordained ones or the self-serving sorts like Cuaran, but let's keep this away from bellyaching and on the practical. As in, what do we *do* about One-Eye? Bearing in mind that we're making a lot of gold, and any move against him can only harm our takings, and where we stand right now, atop the heap. Many would give much to be where we are."

Fengr started to pace, scowling. "Well, now. Are we all firm and hard that Cuaran must go?"

"I am," Julfr grunted, "but you knew that already. Hear me, Fengr. This King already takes huge taxes on each slave-sale, cutting our profits to a seventh of what they could be, or more! What if he takes it into his head to start approving or disapproving of individual sales? We could starve!"

"But would he ever do such a thing?" Dagr shook his head. "That would be madness!"

Julfr snorted. "Madness? Hah! He's a *king!*"

"And all kings are mad, or on the barking brink of it, hey?" Fengr's smile was mirthless. "We can't risk war and all the gold we *do* make for something someone *might* do—or we'll never stop butchering those who could become foes, and possibly do something to cross us! That way *does* lie madness: ours!"

"What he did to Vigmarr was hounding," Ake said heavily. "Any trader *must* be free to meet with any other trader, and who I guest under my roof is *my* affair. What if Sitric One-Eye takes it into his head to hound the rest of us, treating us all like foes or criminals? Then he'd get our slaves, and our gold, and call it his kingly right to do so! Or a commandment of Odin's!"

"And no one would dare to stand against him," Dagr said grimly. "So, then, is it time to remove him?"

"Months back," Fengr said slowly, "I invited the King to open the new slave market, as is only fitting. I've heard nothing to tell me his acceptance of my invitation has been shaken. So that'll be one time soon he'll be within reach—though seen by many, and no doubt guarded heavily."

"Seen by many is good if we're removing him," Julfr pointed out. "We want it known he's gone, not wild rumor having him slain a dozen times over, but rising to walk through Odin's favour, or escaped unharmed because we slew some hapless dupe he got up to look like him, or not dead at all but working some trickery to make his would-be successors stick their necks out to be hewn through when he rushes out of hiding to pounce and make warnings of us all. Rotting on some spike is not the goal I have in mind for my head."

Dagr shrugged. "Me, neither, but it's what we all risk, or anyone risks, who raises a hand against a king. So, again, I ask: do we take down this King?"

Rain suddenly started to fall, in big loud drops that in a handful of moments built to a wet roar.

Fengr looked at Ake, and shrugged. "So, not short enough, after all."

"I didn't think it would be," the Hill of Wit said gloomily. "Removing kings never is."

#

"It's the waiting that gnaws at the soul," Teagan said softly, as Mist strode frowningly across the kitchen for the eighty-third time. Or was it the eighty-fourth? "Come and bake bread and stop *pacing*, girl."

"They're cruel, evil men, and deserve to die," Mist burst out, "so I do not feel that I did a bad thing, yet will we even know they've died? Ever? Or will the Palace hush it all up? Keep it all secret?"

Teagan shrugged and spread her arms to indicate her inability to be an oracle.

"What we need," Mist said, fiercely, "is a crisis. A situation where the King will feel the need to use all of his shadowhands—in public, so they'll need to be hooded." She looked at Teagan across the bread dough and added, "And lacking a crisis, we must *make* one."

"Mist Damhain, Maker of Crises," Teagan said softly, but did not smile, and her voice held no hint of mockery. "How?"

Mist stared at her for a moment, looking almost trapped, and then a sudden flame kindled in her eyes.

"The talk in the streets is that the new slave market is almost ready," she said eagerly. "Won't the King want to have something to do with its opening? To tell all the citizenry 'I did this for you, you have me to thank for the riches we all share'?"

Teagan smiled. "He will indeed. And I'm sure the owners of the new hall have invited him to open it."

"Well, then," Mist said softly, "an attack on the King then would do it."

"*If* expected ahead of time. If not, the shadowhands would most likely be scattered among the onlookers, disguised as ordinary citizens, not massed and hooded."

"A rumored attack, then," Mist concluded. "Which is something we might accomplish—the rumors, that is—where a real attack would be beyond us, or something feeble and futile."

"And fatal," Teagan told the dough she was kneading. "So, we start rumors?"

"We start rumors."

"Disguised," Teagan said firmly, "or that, too, is likely to prove fatal. The King has more spies than just his shadowhands."

Mist nodded.

"Leave the disguises to me," Teagan added. "A matter of making ourselves look uglier. And we blame outlanders of some sort, no one of the city. That'll be more readily believed. Not Hibernians, of course. Norse rivals of King Cuaran."

"Are there such?"

"Oh, yes. Every rich and successful man has rivals, if not outright foes. And Sitric murdered his brother Sicfrith; some of his own kin have never forgiven him for that."

"Why did he do that?"

"It's said Sicfrith had turned to the White God, and Sitric, who sacrificed his own eye to Odin, was enraged when Sicfrith told him—and butchered him on the spot."

Mist shuddered. "And now he sits on a throne, and holds the lives of thousands in his hands."

"Including ours."

Mist winced. "I wish you hadn't reminded me of that."

"Dear, none of us can go through life forgetting or looking away from the unpleasant, and chasing only what we love and enjoy and revel in."

"Mmm. Is that how kings go wrong, do you think? Chasing what they love and setting aside all else?"

"It's how all humans go wrong, and gods, too. If we neglect the hard tasks, the nasty work, what we don't welcome—or worse yet, deny it and leave it undone—the path of our life takes wrong turning after wrong turning. Until we've not only lost ourselves, and know not where we're going, but we can't avoid the sharp thorns or swordpoints or unyielding stone walls of what we've tried to avoid. And then we crash."

"Clever words," Mist sighed. "Aunt, you should have been a sage, or a skald."

"I've been both those things, and more besides. I prefer making bread. What's *your* vice, Mist Damhain?"

Mist stared back at Teagan. Her aunt was not smiling.

"I...I don't know."

"*Yet,*" Teagan said, threw her dough into the air, then caught it without her gaze ever leaving Mist's.

chapter 19

It was a cold morning, and the river-mist still clung to Dainn's robes as a fine dew as he was ushered into the presence of the King. Who sat reading and occasionally scribbling on a succession of documents an impassive servant was handing him. A mug of hot broth steamed unregarded at the royal elbow.

Sitric Cuaran looked up.

"Ah, Dainn Gulbrandson. You have your plans written out for me?"

The priest knelt, extending a parchment. "I do, Dread King."

"Oh, hopefully not 'dread' yet," the King replied cheerfully, gesturing to the servant. Who smoothly took Dainn's writings from the priest's hand and held them before the King.

Who read them more rapidly than Dainn had ever seen anyone read before, then nodded. "I see the what, written down here, but tell me the why. What's your intention, Priest of the All-Father?"

"I plan to assemble many devout of Odin to attend the ceremony, all in holy vestments and chanting Odin's praise upon you, and your works, in unison. To show the world Odin supports you, and you do His work."

"And?"

"And," Dainn added, emboldened, "this will be a great opportunity to denounce the White God and declare that Ath Cliath is *the* city of Odin."

The One-Eyed King's lone remaining eye narrowed in thought.

And then he slowly nodded his approval, a smile rising onto his face.

A ruthless smile.

#

In a familiar vast, damp cellar of many broad stone pillars where water dripped in the distance, slowly but steadily, and the stink of mildew was faint but persistent, the Lady Lecora O'Hart arrived, preceded and followed by two impassive mountains: bodyguards who were impassive, dark-armored, and bristling with scabbarded and sheathed blades.

A lantern was unhooded just long enough to show her the man who held it: Lord Cairbre Dathaill, standing waiting for her. Then the darkness reclaimed him.

"Why need we meet here and now?" Lecora asked calmly.

Wordlessly Cairbre stepped aside and unhooded his lantern again. This time its small round beam fell upon a staring, terrified face. A dead face. The neck of the man it belonged to was bent at a sickening angle.

"And who," Lecora asked, unruffled, "is this? Was this?"

"An envoy of the King who wanted me—and you, and Torloch—to hasten to the Palace to urgently meet with the King. A pity he fell down some steps before he could deliver that message." Cairbre's smile was like that of a smug wolf.

Lecora sighed and shook her head. "Sitric isn't going to believe in any accidents, when it comes to his envoys."

"Assuredly not. Not after I've killed six or seven of them. He may even have to start delivering his messages himself."

"And coming out of the Palace and within our reach," Lecora murmured.

"Or the reach of others," Cairbre purred. "Sitric Cuaran has a *lot* of enemies, just lately."

The door that most eyes would have assumed was just part of the wall opened in sudden oiled silence, and Mael the Sharp strode into the small, gloomy back room of the Palace.

The chief feature of the chamber was a small table with four chairs drawn up around it. In one sat the senior shadowhand Stigr, and in another, the senior shadowhand Ulfr.

Mael bore a parchment, and cast it down on the table. "Read," he commanded.

Ulfr was faster, but Stigr's hands were closer. The hook-nosed, bearded, and much-scarred shadowhand took in the document at a glance and promptly passed it across to his toad-faced fellow hand.

Who perused it just as quickly, and let it fall onto the table.

Mael sat down, and nodded in the direction of Dainn Gulbrandson's written plans for his ceremony. "I mistrust this young hothead of a priest," he said grimly, "and mistrust this ceremony he's planning even more. Citizens everywhere, all of them too close to the King—and every one of them could have darts to hurl, or a handbow, or some other fell weapon."

"*I* mistrust," Stigr said coldly, "the workers finishing the market hall. New faces among them, yesterday, and *all* of them busy on the balconies above the lowest one where this priest and the King are to stand. What is so wrong with those balconies, all of a sudden, that wasn't wrong before?"

Mael stiffened. "Watch them," he snapped, "as if you're a hungry hawk."

"Of course," Stigr replied.

"Shall I watch the annoying young priest?" Ulfr asked.

"Raudr and Sirikr already are, and Naddr's been sent to hear if he's who he says he is, from the priests this Dainn says sent him here," Mael replied. "The King shares your suspicions."

"And he's to be allowed to recruit openly?" Ulfr snapped. "It's going to be a madhouse!"

"More of a madhouse than Ath Cliath is already," Mael replied with a mirthless smile. "But worry not; your task is to watch everyone he chooses."

Ulfr's store of vile oaths was impressive. Both Stigr and Mael sat back to enjoy it.

It was a tavern of Cathal Faolain's choosing that Brandr did not know, far across most of the city from Dun's Hearth, and the two of them were tucked into a back corner that shielded them from most eyes but let them hear every word uttered in its dark and labyrinthine taproom.

And just now, those words were loud and rising louder with excitement. Word that had spread across Ath Cliath like the rays of the rising sun. It seemed a young priest of Odin was recruiting 'devout of Odin' to take part in a ceremony to open the new slave market hall, with the King. Those he recruited would receive vestments and pay! A gold rod each!

"Gold?" one man bellowed in disbelief. "What dreamer's empty nonsense is this?"

"No, *truth!*" another insisted. "A blood-pact of Odin! To be paid ere sunset on the day of the ceremony!"

"To those still alive," a cynic muttered.

Brandr and Cathal Faolain exchanged glances, and nodded in unison.

"Go and get yourself recruited," Faolain muttered. "Our chances have just improved."

The Green Lady wasn't one of the noisier taverns in the city, but its common room was lively right now, full of excited talk. Talk of gold.

Gold for all! Or at least, a gold rod for anyone who could get themselves recruited to put on a silly robe and chant the praises of Odin upon the King at the opening of the new slave market hall.

"Devout of Odin? What does that even *mean?*"

"The One-Eyed King is a cold-hearted, cruel tyrant who delights in harming the lowly and weak," another man muttered, "but for a gold rod I'll say Odin kisses his brow—Jotun-dung, kisses his *behind*—a dozen times any day!"

"Are they recruiting women? Surely a woman can be a devout worshipper of the All-Father!" a woman cried, rapping her drinking-horn on her table.

At their favourite table, along the back wall nigh the cooking-hearth, Eylir Grimsson and Forkundr Redbeard exchanged glances.

"Thanks to this beard, I'm too well-known," Forkundr muttered, "but go and get yourself recruited, so you can be standing right there. With a poisoned weapon."

"They'll never allow anyone with a weapon to get close to the King," Eylir hissed.

Forkundr lifted a hand. "Now lift yours."

Eylir frowned in puzzlement, but did so.

"Regard your smallest finger," Forkundr growled, pointing at it. "Nail long and untrimmed. Cut it to a point. *That's* your weapon, when poisoned."

Eylir smiled slowly. Then he drained his tankard and pushed himself up from the table. "I go to find this enthusiastic fool of a priest."

"Aren't they all?"

#

So a young priest of Odin, newly come to Ath Cliath, would be in charge of a ceremony in which King Sitric Cuaran opened a new slave market hall for business. And was recruiting "devout of Odin" to wear vestments and chant Odin's praises upon the King and the new hall.

Oswin Silverlock climbed the stairs to his rented inn room with a heavy heart. Cuaran was the One-Eyed because he'd sacrificed the other to the All-Father; it was no secret he exalted Odin, and held all veneration of non-Aesir in contempt. Would this ceremony not be a perfect opportunity to denounce other faiths, or even command that Ath Cliath be purged of them, holy folk and all?

Should he get out now?

Was that mere prudence, or had he let fear overmaster him—or would the White God regard fleeing the city to be turning his back on god and vows?

He was willing to die, if it came to that, though torment would as surely break him as it did any man. But if his death was no more than throwing his life away, in a futile gesture, how did *that* help the White God? How did that further the faith?

He needed answers. Answers he could trust. And that meant...

Stepping into his rented room, he closed and barred the door, drew off his boots, laid down on the bed, closed his eyes, and devoted himself to praying.

Earnest, eyes shut, wholehearted praying. Crying out to the god, albeit silently.

And returning again and again to the same plea.

Guide me. Send me a sign.

More than ever, he needed the White God to tell him what to do. Was his entire mission here a mistake? Or had he taken a wrong step, and was going about it wrong?

He thought he saw a glimmer of white light, deep in his mind, around a corner he could not turn, but there. Only for a moment, but there. Without a doubt.

He poured his heart into one last entreaty, and then opened his eyes and stared at the ceiling, exhausted.

Would a sign come?

Or should he stride forth, seeking it?

Well, that certainly offered wider horizons than this little room, to be sure. He sat up, reaching for his boots again, and—

From somewhere outside, not far away, there arose a mighty *crash*.

Rending wood, then shouting, then a loud sobbing that sounded like a woman, but was so full-throated that it must be a wounded beast.

Oswin stamped on his boots and rushed out the door, not even bothering to close it in his haste to get, and *see*.

The common room of the Hearth was nigh-deserted, the open front door and the few folk left in the room all peering out it telling him why. Something had befallen in the street outside.

Then he was outside and seeing for himself. A cart and a wagon had collided in the street, and the cart was but splayed and splintered boards, with the carter down and dazed, whimpering and bent over a broken arm. His mule was a motionless, bleeding heap, but half atop it lay the wagon's ox, thrashing in pain; it was the source of the sobbing Oswin had heard.

Tears were streaming down the wagon drover's grim face as he drew a half-axe from his belt and picked his way as close as he dared, mindful of lashing hooves. Setting himself, he shook his head in grief—and brought his blade down.

Twice, thrice, and the sobbing stopped.

And then he turned and drove the half-axe deep into the mangled front of his wagon, lurched free of the dead beasts, and stalked over to the carter.

Before Oswin or any of the crowd that was crowding close to watch could stop him, he took the carter by the throat, hauled the man to his feet, and gave him a shove that sent him staggering.

The man was still back on unsteady heels when the charging drover reached him, landing a full-weight punch to the carter's broken arm.

The man shrieked and fell over backwards, with the drover pouncing on him, hauling him upright again—and this time, bringing his other hand into the fray. He clamped the carter's head between both of his hairy hands, jerked viciously—and his victim fell limply and heavily to the cobbles, neck broken.

Roars arose from the crowd, of anger or blood-lust or approval, but Oswin did not join in the chorus.

He stood still, staring at the dead man and the panting, still-furious drover.

Here was his sign.

Just as the drover had slain the carter, without mercy, he, Oswin Silverlock, must eliminate Dainn Gulbrandson.

For the good of the city. For the White God. For those who did not kneel to Odin, everywhere.

But how? Well, the ceremony would be a good opportunity, for the priest would surely be there, and no doubt preening in public, if he knew anything about zealous young clerics...

#

Orrusti wasn't known as the Old Stump for nothing.

He sat in the same place day after day, at the front of his crammed, littered used-sundries shop, surrounded by the most valuable swords and tools in his inventory, with a half-barrel beside him as his trading table, wearing an apron that bulged with nails and hasps, hooks and bits of fine chain. All for sale, if the right bargain could be struck. And the Old Stump was all about bargains.

And an increasing number of citizens of Ath Cliath knew that, and were prepared to overlook Orrusti's stout and bristling shaggy looks and his loud wheezing and personal cloud of tiny flies and his everpresent and pungent flatulence because of those bargains and the low taxes that went with the Old Stump's low prices. Wherefore business was brisk, and the Old Stump flourished, and Ath Cliathians were able to acquire gently and not-so-gently used and useful items that made their lives easier.

"And making our lives easier is what it's all about, no?" as Orrusti was wont to say.

A shadow fell across him, but Orrusti didn't look up. He knew who it was, and that this silent arrival belonged to a group of men who preferred not to be seen.

"I am in need," the man said quietly, "of some oak veneer. This wide—" A piece of scrap wood landed nigh Orrusti's filthy-booted feet. "—and this long." A cut-down walking-stick landed with a clatter across the scrap. "Precisely. Fourteen of them. Immediately, if not sooner."

"Immediate," Orrusti rumbled unconcernedly, "costs more. Sooner costs *much* more."

"I know this, and so does my purse."

"Sundown," Orrusti replied. "Back door."

"Sundown," the man replied. "Back door." And the shadow moved away.

Orrusti didn't strike the rusty pot that served him as a gong to summon his errand-lads until his newest client was quite gone out of sight.

There are shadows, and then there are shadows.

#

"Misgivings?" Teagan asked. "Because of the means?"

Mist shook her head. "No. I worry about the chaos that might follow what we've done, when it happens, but not the poison."

"No?"

"No. Oh, I'll grant that poison is an evil weapon, and it sickened me to stoop to it, but the cause is just. And more than that: warriors who are strong, or berserk, use those, ah, skills without hesitation to win battles and so, murder others. I am weaker, and smaller, and know not the ways of sword and axe and bow; why should I not use what I can? How is that more evil than what they do, daily?"

Teagan smiled. "You see the world as a sage, and give tongue like one, too."

Mist sighed. "Is that what I should become, if by some gods-gifted miracle I survive this?"

Teagan shrugged. "You must find your own path, and choose it. I point out paths, and no more. Folk who decide the lives of others for them, *they* are the cruel ones."

Mist nodded slowly, then looked up at her aunt.

"But when it comes to the shadowhands, we're deciding their lives. We're taking them away."

Teagan shrugged again. "And how is that more evil than what they do, daily?"

#

"So, Devout of Odin, how do you feel? More holy?"

Brandr sighed and shook his head. "More like a fool than I've felt in many a year," he told Faolain, unfolding the bundle of old homespun to reveal what was inside it. White robes.

"My, but *those'll* show blood," the veteran trader said dryly, passing a flask to Brandr. "Best bundle them up again."

Brandr obeyed, then took a swig from the flask. Its contents were unfamiliar, but wonderful—and fiery. When he'd mastered his coughing and wiped his watering eyes and could speak again, he firmly passed the flask back ere his reluctance to ever part with it could grow strong, and asked, "How will you get close enough to…"

He mimed an arrow slicing through the air.

Cathal Faolain shrugged. "I know not, yet. Three buildings offer good places for an archer, two more give poorer ones. I'll have to see how strongly they're populated with the King's soldiers and shadowhands, then make my choice."

"You'll have to slay them."

"Of course. *That* will be a pleasure, King there to pincushion or not. Not to mention a civic service to the fair folk of Ath Cliath."

#

"The support beams are nigh cut right through! Only wood to *just* over the thickness of my thumb remains! And the two balconies above are the same! They can support two men at once, no more!"

Stigr nodded impassively. "Calm yourself, Krokr. We expected this, remember?"

"Yes, but should we not move now? To accost and slay the workers responsible, and put the rest to replacing the beams while we stand over them, glowering and snarling?"

"And warn the traitors behind these traitors that we've uncovered their scheme, and give them time to come up with other perils to the King? No, not yet. We wait another day, perhaps two, depending on how quickly the work goes. *Then* we pounce."

"All right, but…but how can you be so *calm?*"

"Years of this, Krokr. Years that leave a man dead, or broken, or calm. I chose calm."

#

"Absolutely *not!* I choose my own Devout of Odin!"

"I did not make a request, priest. You will assemble your selections in the Palace for a rehearsal, and courtiers shall interview each of them. While we listen, and watch, and go and learn more of this one and that, as the needs arise. And there may be some we detain, and you shall go forth and choose alternatives for those unfortunates."

Dainn Gulbrandson eyed the man with the sword scar that began at the edge of his mouth and curved up to under his right ear, then burst out in exasperation. "Who *are* you?"

Mael the Sharp smiled thinly. "My name is unimportant. And you are unlikely to live long enough to have need of it."

CHAPTER 20

"No hammering, this morning; Odin-blesséd peace!"

"They're all done bar the sweeping up and washing, now. The place opens tomorrow; all the proclamations are being posted on inn and tavern doors across the city right now."

"Proclamations? I thought there was going to be a big ceremony, with warhorns and the King and all! Was rather looking forward to it, in hopes of free ale, and cakes, and all of that."

"There is going to be a big ceremony. That's what the proclamations are about, you dolt!"

"Oh. *Will* there be ale?"

"The King and Palace don't confide in *me*, Lofarr. You'll just have to go, and see, now won't you?"

#

"*Now* can we pounce?"

"Calm yourself, Krokr. Have you seen the beams?"

"Yes, and they're all now whole, so I know you had them replaced—but I don't know how this was accomplished without my seeing it. No new workers, none of the old ones gone...highly suspicious."

"That's how things are supposed to be done. So smoothly that someone who's watching closely sees nothing."

"How did you do it?"

Stigr's smile fell back off his scarred face. "Later, Krokr. We have the morrow to get through, first."

"But—"

"But silence, and attention elsewhere, is what we need right now, from every loyal and competent shadowhand."

Krokr opened his mouth to say more, saw Stigr's expression, and wisely closed it again and nodded, instead.

Stigr's stony face grew a brief but beaming smile—ere it fell back into cold and stony disapproval, and he turned away.

#

There was a sharp rap on Brandr's door. Cathal Faolain promptly went to the floor beside the bed, and dragged Brandr's heap of laundry over himself.

"Yes?" Brandr asked cautiously, nigh the door.

"Messenger from the Palace!" came the officious reply. When Brandr opened the door, a lone young man in a splendid uniform was standing in the passage.

"Brandr Fylan? You're summoned to attend the Palace, as fast as you can get yourself there, for a rehearsal, Devout of Odin. Bring the robe you were lent."

And without waiting for a reply or acknowledgement, the messenger turned on his heel and strode away.

Brandr closed the door and turned to Faolain, lifting his eyebrows mutely in a 'Well, well' signal.

Faolain shot bolt upright, a soiled tunic still draped over his head, and put out a hand to grab Brandr's arm.

"You're *not* going. Stay right here." And he hauled the tunic off his head and hastened out.

Brandr sighed and gathered up his laundry again.

He'd barely straightened up and sat down on the edge of his bed when his door opened again, to admit the returning Faolain.

"Where did you go?" Brandr asked curiously.

"I greatly fear," Faolain replied, "that the Palace is now short one messenger. Dangerous occupation, that; murderous alley snatchpurses are *everywhere* in the city, these days."

"But—but—"

"With luck, Flower of House Fylan, you were far from the last of the Devout he was sent to summon, so a lot of you won't show up for this rehearsal, not just one Brandr Fylan."

"But why not attend?"

"If I was a shadowhand of the King, or a clever, ruthless king like Sitric Cuaran, I'd want to weed out all potential foes and troublemakers from my ceremonies, not leave the selection entirely to some young zealot of a priest newly arrived from the wilds of nowhere. Who's to say that Odin-lover isn't a spy or alley-dagger for some rival king? Or would-be usurper?"

Brandr shuddered. "What a dark mind you have."

"It's the sort of dark mind you'd better acquire in a hurry, lad, if you want to grow any older. Try to get it by tomorrow, hmm?"

#

Mist spun around, almost dropping the bowl she was wiping dry. "Tomorrow? We've barely had time to *start* spreading rumors!"

Teagan smiled mirthlessly. "Undoubtedly the short notice is to deny the King's foes time enough to plan anything. And there will be other opportunities, if this one fails."

"So do we go and attend, or stay safely home?"

"Oh, go and attend, of *course*. Get a good look at your target, so you'll know him later. Take your measure of his bodyguards, and see if you can spot the shadowhands. No, there's no need to hide and cower—and no point, either. There is no 'stay safely' in Ath Cliath any more, if there ever was."

#

Lady Lecora O'Hart smiled. "Of *course* Sitric wants me to attend his little public flourish. And you and Torloch, too. He needs scapegoats on the scene to implicate and arrest."

Cairbre frowned. "So, do we go?"

"Of course. With all of our bodyguards. But we keep well back. That way, if something goes awry and there is tumult, we can eliminate as many shadowhands and inconvenient courtiers as possible ere melting away—but if nothing goes wrong, we'll be so far away that Sitric will have to turn his entire ritual on its head to even reach us."

"I have a bad feeling about this ceremony. He's planning something."

"He always is. But then, so am I. And according to my hired eyes, so are others, too. Sitric may have a surprise or three tomorrow. Unwelcome ones."

"And if he ends the day in triumph?"

Lecora shrugged. "We're playing a long game, remember?"

"Invitations delivered to every ship in port, as you commanded, O King. With your precise wording. By their faces, most of them knew at once that their attendance was expected."

The One-Eyed King nodded. "And which outland captains did you speak with?"

"Rokr Much-Sailing, Freyr the Easterner, and Hrimnir Seal-Killer. And I recognized the banners of two ships Hamall boarded: Ingvarr Left-Handed, and Gautarr the Ever-Oppressed."

"And where is Hamall, that he's come not back to report this himself?"

The most junior Palace messenger frowned. "I-I know not, Your Majesty. I've not seen him since then."

It was King Sitric's turn to frown. "That's...unfortunate."

He waved a hand in dismissal, and the messenger fled, fear clear on his face.

The King turned to the tapestries. "Another one gone missing, Mael. Our enemies are getting just a little too bold for my liking. I think we'll make tomorrow's proceedings a learning experience for them."

Mael nodded. "Fleinn's command have arrived in the city, and been fed and sent to bed. They'll be ready by dawn tomorrow."

Sitric Cuaran smiled. "I've missed swinging swords and watching foes flee. Mark well anyone you see hurl a stone or draw a blade against any in my livery tomorrow. Highborn or wealthy, I think they'll make fine slaves for the inaugural auction. A lesson for everyone else."

Mael bowed. "Your will guides me, O King."

"Oh, don't *you* start. I always feel it's mockery, coming from you."

"*Never*, my King. Those whose crowns truly fit are all too few in this world. I am honoured to serve one of them."

And Mael bowed again and was gone, even before the One-Eyed King could lift a hand to dismiss him. Sitric stared at the door the Sharp One had vanished through, thoughtfully, then rose from his chair and strolled across the room to where he could look out over the roofs and turrets of the central city.

"There's going to be trouble tomorrow," he murmured aloud. And smiled.

"And I'm going to enjoy it."

#

Forkundr Redbeard didn't even wait for the servant to quite get out of the room ere he demanded, "What's this about you being sick, Fang?"

Fengr Fangtooth pointed at the door his man was still vanishing through, and gestured firmly at Forkundr to close it. The Redbeard did, spun around, and growled, "Well?"

"It's the only way I can avoid being *right there* when...you know."

"And if the King survives, he'll be looking for men to blame. I think you'll be on his list anyway. Eating bad eels or whatever, it still looks suspicious when the owner isn't there."

"Yes, but he'll have to send his soldiers to find and take me. If I'm standing handy, some hothead might gut me before I even have time to protest."

#

"No," the voice from the other side of the wall growled, "plundering the Palace would *not* be a bright idea. Stick to our agreement, and you *might* live to see tomorrow night."

Neven Daunt smiled thinly. "It was just a thought."

"One best discarded. I can clear your way to the armory, but keep your people quiet, or the guards the King will leave behind will hear and pounce. And the way to the warehouse they've put the slaves in until the bright new hall is open, that'll be clear, too."

"The streets of Ath Cliath are going to be lively tomorrow."

"Not for the first time, nor the last," the unseen man replied—and something small and metallic popped through the hole in the wall and clinked to the ground.

Daunt looked down. Two keys, joined by a leather thong.

"The larger, cruder one is for the warehouse," the voice added. "The smaller, the armory. Give them to the river as soon as you can, once you've used them. I go. Pray that you never hear from me again."

"My thanks," Daunt replied, scooping up the keys. Thrusting them into the safe-pouch inside his jerkin, he strolled away without a backward glance.

He had to admit to himself that he was a trifle curious as to why a senior shadowhand was working against the king he was sworn to serve, but he knew better than to betray to anyone at all that he'd recognized the voice that spoke to him through this wall and others.

He was doomed anyway, but it would be nice to elude death long enough to see Sitric Cuaran taken down, or at least humbled.

#

The three tall, burly men had the look of warriors, but had given the master of the inn to understand they were slave buyers. They kept to themselves, and that included touring a nearby mansion that was for sale; after looking it over with the keeper of the keys, they told him to await them at the front door while they took another look at the bedchambers.

"There's a tension in the city," one of them said softly, watching the sun sink low through the tall and splendid windows of the largest bedchamber. "Its folk are expecting trouble on the morrow."

"Aye, but I'll be very surprised if Cuaran dies. Hence our orders."

"I won't forget who must die," the third muttered. "The shadowhand who reached out to our King first, and then as many of Cuaran's other shadowhands as we can manage."

"You recall their faces?"

"I know the six I'm to look for."

Each of them, with the aid of a seithkona who had scores to settle, had fixed the faces of six men in their minds. One man, the shadowhand who *must* die, they all shared in their sixcount, but the others were all different.

The trio were here because Constantine of Alba did not deem the time right to make war on the One-Eyed King of Ath Cliath—but did want to know more of what was about to unfold in Ath Cliath. And help certain matters along, if possible. If Sitric Cuaran's most capable agents could be slain, that time could come soon.

"Ah!" one of the three said then, and did something to the wall that made a hidden door swing open. He was almost disappointed to find no one lurking behind it, listening—and more than enough dust and cobwebs to tell him that no one had been, moments earlier.

"Well, well," said another, gazing into the revealed secret passage. "It seems this house will not do at all. Shall we look at another?"

"No," said the third shortly. "I'm for bed. It's going to be a full day tomorrow."

"Fangtooth is shamming sick," Forkundr Redbeard said heavily. "He doesn't want to be anywhere near when those balconies fall."

"Prudent of him," Eylir Grimsson commented, looking up from the dagger he was sharpening.

Falki Longbeak eyed it sourly. "You'll ruin that little toy if you don't leave off shaving down its cutting edge. It'll be naught more than a needle."

"Go rut with a camel," Eylir replied pleasantly.

Borekr snorted. "He'll have to find one, first. And though they say you can get *anything* in Ath Cliath, I'm not so sure a live camel is to be found."

"Who said anything about a live one?" Eylir asked, holding his dagger up to inspect it.

"Is this your only news, Fork?" Grimkell rasped.

"No. Three men arrived in the city this evening, veteran soldiers who've known command rank by the looks of them. One of them I know: Cenhelm Halshaw. He serves King Constantine of Alba–closely."

There was a stir around the table.

"That *is* news," Grimkell admitted. "None of you have seen any signs of other warriors, in the city already, that these could rally? Who've perhaps come in alone, or in pairs or trios, this last month or so?"

But none of them had.

The skald nodded. "So these are here to see what befalls tomorrow. And perhaps take advantage of any swords-out to covertly slay someone, or meet with a spy for Alba who lives in the city."

"I wonder what other kings have sent watchers?" Eylir asked his dagger, holding it up to the light again.

Borekr shrugged. "All of them. This *is* Ath Cliath."

Eylir shook his head. "It's a local failing to think all coin, and important business, and everyone who sets fashions and spurs great events, comes here or dwells here or gets sponsors here. I was talking with a far-traveled trader once, and he said the merchants of every city think as much. Sometimes, all you see is all there is to see."

"True," Grimkell agreed, "but we have to think and prepare as if there are conspiracies behind our backs, and deeper meanings, and secrets in plenty that turn and twist unfolding events. That way, we may be disappointed from time to time, but we'll never get caught with our breeches down."

"That should be Sitric Cuaran's motto," Borekr grinned. "Never Caught With Breeches Down."

Falki shook his head. "Ho, wouldn't *that* be tempting the gods? Why, if I was Odin and saw that, I'd slap the mortal using it to his knees *so* fast..."

Eylir shrugged. "If Odin was inclined to slap the One-Eyed King down, he'd have done it years ago; Cuaran's certainly given Him provocation enough. But no, He seems to smile on our king. Time and again Sitric takes this or that bold risk, and it pays off. I doubt any of us would share his shining luck, if we tried it."

"You sound like you want to rush to Fangtooth's sickbed, and share it," Falki grunted.

Eylir gave him a glare. "Found that camel yet?"

The master of Dun's Hearth looked up from the tankards he was wiping as a dozen grim-faced men in matching cloaks shouldered through the front door. "Yes, sirs? Rooms for the night?"

"No," the foremost of the arrivals growled, parting his cloak to reveal royal livery. Some of his fellows, behind him, did the same. Soldiers, all of them, in full armor crisscrossed by belts and baldrics bearing heavy weaponry. "We're here on royal business, so no insolence or obstruction, or—" He drew a finger across his own throat meaningfully, sneered, and added, "Now, which rooms—*quietly*, mind—are occupied by the outlanders Brandr Fylan, Oswin Silverlock, and Mist Damhain?"

The innkeeper frowned. "I…"

Steel sang as two of the soldiers drew their swords in slow menace, wearing cruel smiles as they did so.

"You're going to lose a finger for each of those three, if you hesitate an *instant* longer in answering me," their leader told the innkeeper. "And then your nose. A man looks *odd* without a nose."

"Urrkh," added one of the soldiers at the rear. Urgently.

Then he toppled heavily, elbowing the man beside him. Who turned angrily—in time to get a dagger hilt-deep in one eye. All around, other soldiers were collapsing, slamming into their fellows and sending them staggering forward.

And whirling, swords up.

Three tall, burly men stood over eight fallen soldiers of the King. The newcomers had bloody blades and daggers in their hands, and eager gleams in their eyes.

"I thought Ath Cliath *welcomed* outlanders," one of them said lightly. "Sitric Cuaran can hardly go on amassing gold hand over fist if the wider world stops coming to his doors to trade, now can he?"

"Who," snarled the leader of the soldiers, paling in rage and fear, "are you?"

"Just concerned citizens," came the mocking reply—arriving only a moment before a dagger, hurtling end over end. The soldier struck it aside at the last instant, spitting out a curse, but the man who'd hurled it came charging in his wake, snatching out another dagger—and when his sword swept the King's soldier's blade aside, that dagger swept up under the soldier's chin, going in hilt-deep.

He fell at the same moment as another soldier, and with that, the last two surviving soldiers whirled and ran, fleeing across the Hearth common-room.

A hurled tankard rang off the head of one of them, but he never slowed. He had to claw at the alley door to get it open, though, and it was the last thing he ever did—aside from topple sideways to the floor, his neck half hewn through.

The last soldier died gurgling, trying too late to plea for his life, as two blades slid into his throat from different angles.

His slayers let him sag, then calmly started wiping their swords clean on the dead mens' cloaks. While the third of the newcomers plucked up the thrown tankard, took it back to the innkeeper, and asked, "Have you a cart or a wagon we could borrow for a short time? We've twelve heaps of refuse here that properly belong at the Palace gates."

"Y-yes," the master of the Hearth replied. "And…thank you."

The newcomers all gave him smiles, and one of them added, "Our *pleasure*."

One of his fellows was already dropping the seldom-used squared timber into its cradles, to bar the Hearth's front door. "Just until morning," he said. "The vermin seem active tonight."

"We're here for the ceremony tomorrow," explained the third of the newcomers. "I *do* hope it won't get out of hand."

ChapTER 21

It was a bright, breezy forenoon; the wind was coming upriver from the sea, bringing with it the tang of salt and the faint smell of rotting dead fish and seaweed.

More than half the folk of Ath Cliath seemed to be crowded around the new slave market hall, and along the streets flanking it and leading away from it. Spears and gilded helms were massed among them, and in a solid wall all around the walls of the new building.

On the lowest and largest of the splendid stacked balconies that ascended the front of the hall, just over the wide—and closed—entry doors, stood King Sitric Cuaran of Ath Cliath, in a tall and gleaming gold crown, wearing a wise and wintry smile and flanked by courtiers. The balconies above were deserted except for a royal soldier each, stiffly at attention and bearing grounded spears.

The rooftops all around were crowded with more soldiers, who'd kept mere citizens off these high vantage points. More soldiers, in a wide oval ring, clutched their spears horizontally to form a barrier, keeping open an expanse of street cobbles in front of the hall—and in this space, facing the King with his arms raised grandly, stood a young priest of Odin in spotless robes.

Dainn Gulbrandson's voice might not last much longer; a rasping quality had already crept into it from the unaccustomed full-throated bellowing he'd had to employ to cut through the incessant *chattering* of the crowd. Yet he still had a few words to say, and they were important ones.

"Odin the All-Blesséd All-Father smiles upon this city, its great King, and what we do here today! Hear now his words of praise!"

That was the signal the Devout of Odin inside the hall had been waiting for, and they strode out onto all of the balconies in their white robes, crowding to the front railings to begin the chat Dainn would now lead.

As the priest of Odin smiling up at them threw up his arms, open to embrace the sky, and drew breath to begin words that Odin would surely have approved of had the King of the Aesir had a chance to review them, there came the briefest of low groans, from wood in torment, ere the sharp cracking and splintering sounds that heralded the balconies breaking off—and plummeting.

Screams rent the air, then were drowned out by the mighty crashings.

#

Neven Daunt hunched his shoulders to keep as low as possible so he'd not be seen, a lone old, limping man in the heart of a ring of walking women. Shopkeepers, crafters, fishwives—the backbone of Ath Cliath, the working women who kept home and hearth and did the daily work, unheralded and ignored in the halls of power. Tall and thin, short and fat, lovely and unlovely, they shared a hatred of the Palace and its soldiers and courtiers, the tax collectors most of all, and of the King who sent them forth to collect such stiff taxes.

"What does he *do* with it all?" they demanded, nigh-daily, ere falling to their individual grumblings as they worked. And any who stood against him, or spoke against him, ended up in slave-chains. So they were united in one thing: they detested, *hated* the One-Eyed King. Almost more than they feared him. Yet these few, these forty-one, were daring to do more today.

With the King away from the Palace to open the new slaving hall, they'd left their hearths and counters and workbenches to form a human ring around the man who'd recruited them, old

Neven Daunt, accompany him to the armory, and ferry weapons out of it to a certain warehouse. Wherefore they carried leather shoulder-satchels and carry-bags, woven baskets in slings, and simple hides and blankets to wrap around swords and axes to make bundles. And they walked without haste, but purposefully, to the Palace.

There it was now, the back gate that should be open to let them in.

They hesitated, not quite daring to put hand to latch amid the iron bars, so Neven reached between two ample hips and undid it.

And they were inside. A rippling murmur of surprise and apprehension, then silence but for the occasional scuff of boot or slipper, as they walked across an inner yard, to a squat stone building with a black iron-girt door covered with bands of metal and great fist-sized bolts.

Neven opened this door, too, sliding its massive bolt-latch. *Claaack.*

The door swung wide, offering a view of stony gloom—and a guard in full armor frowning at them, who a moment ago had been lounging in boredom and was now rather alarmed.

"Halt!" he barked. "Who are you, and what're you doing here?"

The women regarded him uncertainly, wavering.

"Be off with you!" he roared, putting hand to the hilt of his sword. "Get you gone! This is the Royal Armoury; you can't be here!"

And he drew his sword. One woman stepped back, and stumbled over the feet of the woman behind her, who had not retreated.

The guard brandished his blade. "Begone, washerwomen!"

Suddenly a tall, sturdily-built woman rushed at him. He whirled to sword her—and the women now side-on to him parted like waves cloven by an onrushing ship, and from between them darted an old man with a sword in his hand.

The guard whirled back, hacking—but his own movement drove his throat onto the edge of the old man's sword.

He slashed, frantically, but his own blood was spraying out, not welling, and the limping, lurching old man was dodging, and parrying like an expert swordsman, and...the world was darkening, going away...

Neven Daunt plucked a ring of keys from the belt of the dead guard, fitted the largest one into the lock of the door behind the sprawled man, and told the women gruffly, "swords and daggers are best, but these handaxes will serve, too..."

And the women calmly formed a line and strode past him as if they plundered armouries every day.

#

Crash crash CRASH, bur-DOOM.

The balconies slammed down, each one shattering the one beneath and adding it to the plunge, as white-robed bodies hurtled into space, tumbling down to splattered death on the unyielding cobbles below.

Unyielding except where they shattered, bouncing up in shards from their ear-splitting sunderings as stonework struck them and cracked. Soldiers were crushed to a red slush amid all the yelling and shrieking, and tumbling stone shards laid open the young priest of Odin like a boar readied for the spit.

Everyone seemed to be shouting, a great tumult of fear and disgust and...delight?

And unharmed in the blood-drenched heart of it all stood the King.

Though he'd plummeted to the street with the balcony he'd been standing on, he'd done so upright, the balconies above bouncing off air above his head as if he stood under an unseen

116

dome of shields. He landed lightly, more bouncing stones and plunging bodies also avoiding him, and strode clear.

An arrow sought him then, racing from a window to...glide to a halt in midair right in front of Sitric Cuaran's face.

"Odin smiles upon him! Look, the King is protected by the All-Father!" someone cried, and others took up that shout.

"Fools," someone closer to Brandr in the crush of the crowd hissed, "he *is* a galdr. He shielded himself before he came out of his Palace, and no wonder. *He's* no fool."

Another arrow was loosed by the same unseen archer, leaping lightning-swift, but it, too, was stopped by something unseen.

A third came speeding—not at the King, this time, but to sprout in the throat of a toad-faced man whom very few there knew to be Ulfr of the shadowhands, who'd been hastening to the King's side. The shaft plucked the man off his feet and hurled him back, dying, as the King peered up at the window the arrows were coming from.

Brandr was looking up there, too, and got a glimpse of Cathal Faolain, teeth bared and hacking with a sword, but momentarily driven back against the window frame by the sheer weight of charging soldiers. And then Brandr was shoving and striking folk aside in his determined haste to get to that building and find a way inside and up to the room behind that open window. All around him now was a tumult of fleeing, screaming citizens and rushing soldiers. There were trampled bodies underfoot, and spears were being leveled to spit citizens and force a way through them, and the air was full of hurled stones.

Then warhorns rang out, from the Palace and from off to the west, somewhere in the city. And the western ones were an all-too-familiar three-note descending fanfare that meant...

"Slave break!" soldiers started shouting, on all sides. "*Slave break!*"

Brandr saw a doorway and made for it, clawing men aside who wouldn't get out of the way, but risked a glance back before he plunged into the building where Faolain was likely already dying, and saw the One-Eyed King calmly issuing orders that sent officers rushing their soldiers off westwards, to the slave break, and one officer waving his arms imperiously as he rallied his gold-helms around the King.

And as Brandr raced into the gloom of the building and up a stair that had dead soldiers sprawled on its steps, he heard Sitric Cuaran's magically-amplified voice echoing off the buildings all around.

The King calmly proclaimed the slave market open for business, as firm and eloquent as if no violence had befallen and his citizens were all kneeling in reverent silence before him.

And then Brandr was up the stair and racing along a passage to the next flight up, a passage that had a window overlooking the front of the new slave market hall. As he tore past and turned to mount the second stair, he had a glimpse of the King's back; King Cuaran had turned and was heading back to the Palace, soldiers all around him with their spears outthrust in all directions to keep folk at bay.

And the air was dark with thrown things as people began to pelt the soldiers with stones and anything else they could snatch up and throw, including dead bodies.

And then Brandr was pounding up steps, growing winded, and there were soldiers at the top cursing and reeling and bleeding, falling back from a room where there was shouting and the skirl and clang of steel. Was he in time?

His dagger was out and plunging into the back of a neck, then opening a throat from behind, and he shoved that second man away and snatched the man's sword out of a failing hand and burst into the room beyond.

And Cathal Faolain was grinning at him through clenched teeth, drenched in blood but still on his feet, with dead and dying soldiers heaped in a carpet of royal livery and bright fresh blood underfoot.

"Ah, but it's a good day to be alive!" the trader snarled. "For a little longer, at least! Come, youngling, let's hew our way back to the inn; this is thirsty work, all this soldier-slaying!"

"But...but they'll mark our faces, and come for us," Brandr stammered.

"Not if we don't leave a one of them alive," Faolain grinned, lurching forward. A spasm of pain creased his face, and he faltered and spat out blood.

A *lot* of blood.

"Getting old and slow," he gasped, when he was done and could straighten up again. "A few years back, lad, and none of them would've touched me!"

And then he pitched to the floor, crashing down on his face.

And lay still.

Brandr clawed him over on his back, but Faolain's eyes were already going dull. And amid all the soldier's blood on him, dark wet blood was welling out, low on the trader's side, where a sword had sliced deeper than just his belt.

"Make the clan *proud*," the trader managed to say fiercely, clutching at Brandr with fingers that had iron in their grip for a few fading moments.

And then he was staring at nothing at all, forever, and sagging limp and heavy, and Brandr was rising with a sob bursting up out of his throat that became a wordless shout. A yell of wordless anguish that took him across the room like a dark storm wind to hack open the face of a soldier who was still alive, and then out to the stair-head again to find and fell another, and another.

Brandr rushed back down the stairs swording everyone who still looked alive, hacking and shouting like a madman, until there were no more soldiers alive to look back at him.

Which was a good thing, because he was nigh done. He had to lean against the wall to catch his breath before he went back out into the street.

Panting, he wiped sword and dagger clean, dropped the blade, and found a better one still scabbarded on the sprawled body of a soldier who was beyond needing it. Taking it for his own and putting his dagger away, he squared his shoulders and strode out of the open door as if the house was his own and he owned the street beyond it, too.

Halfway across the blood-and-body-drenched cobbles in front of the slaving hall, a soldier glared at him, and lowered his spear to menace Brandr with its point.

The Flower of the Fylans matched him frown for frown.

"What're you *doing*, fool?" he snapped, and pointed imperiously in the direction of the now-distant King, still in the heart of a storm of hurled stones and shouting, furious citizens. "Did you, or did you not, hear the orders? *Defend the King!*"

The soldier stared back at him for a long moment, then nodded and turned away. Brandr let him take two strides ere bounding after him and cutting his throat from behind.

"Defend the King, my *arse*," he snarled, as he let the man fall, spear clattering, and set off after the procession of soldiers around the distant Sitric Cuaran. There should be other soldiers he could kill, ere they reached the Palace.

Cathal Faolain was worth at least seventy gold-helms. And Brandr Fylan intended to exact that price, ere the sun set.

#

When Neven Daunt flung down the chain that had secured all of their linked manacle-chains to the stout post that held this end of the warehouse roof up, the slaves peered through the gloom at him in suspicious disbelief.

"Want a chance at freedom?" he asked, and pointed at the weapons the women had laid out on the warehouse floor in a neat row. "The nearest city gate is *that* way."

And he stepped well back, grinned, waved, and fled the warehouse.

Behind him, the rattle of chains built into a sudden roar.

#

Crash crash CRASH, bur-DOOM.

Mist shrieked, despite herself, as the balconies fell, each crashing into the one beneath and shattering it ere it broke off and joined the general plunge of wreckage down the front of the bright new hall. Devout of Odin were flung clear, as loose-limbed and helpless as the rag dolls she'd played with as a babe. Mist looked away from the first of their wet, splattering landings, and found herself gazing at Teagan beside her.

Her aunt was devouring every detail of the unfolding horror, an avid light in her eyes, head thrust forward and mouth parted in anticipation.

Mist saw that eagerness slide into disappointment, and looked back at the death and stone-shard-bouncing destruction to see why.

And beheld King Sitric Cuaran, upright and unscathed, striding calmly out of the chaos, with arrows gliding to a halt in midair rather than strike him, and hurtling stone shards bouncing aside.

"His galdr magic," Teagan whispered in disgust. "Is there *no* way to be rid of the man?"

They watched the King's soldiers—those that hadn't been crushed under the balconies—rallying and lowering their spears to menace citizens they deemed too close.

"Come," Teagan said firmly, taking Mist by the arm. "This is no longer a safe place to be. They'll start looking for anyone to blame, next. We go. *Now.*"

And she dragged Mist back and away from the scene, ducking and shouldering and elbowing her way through the tightly-packed crowd of shouting, shrieking, or just gawking people. Mist let herself be towed; her aunt ducked down the first side-street, where folk were fewer, and started to *really* stride, moving so briskly it was just short of a trot.

At the first street-moot, Teagan turned right. They were now facing the way they had been to watch the ceremony, and heading back uptown, in the direction of the Hearth and Teagan's house. The crowds were lighter here, though at every cross-street there was a flood of folk trying to get away from the market hall—and the streets behind it, in the direction of the Palace. By the shouts and screams and clang of steel behind those fleeing folk, there was fighting in those streets.

"The King retreats to the Palace," Teagan observed dryly, "and his citizens demonstrate their displeasure in him. Probably by throwing whatever they can in his direction."

And she towed Mist along faster again, setting a brisk pace for several blocks.

"W-what will happen now?" Mist dared to ask, the moment they slowed again.

Teagan shook her head grimly. "That depends on how furious—or afraid—King Sitric feels. I do hope he's lost a respectable count of soldiers and shadowhands today, even though the more he's lost, the more he'll rage. And punish Ath Cliath. I think we'll shutter all the windows, bar all the doors, and bide inside tonight and tomorrow."

"Aunt," Mist whispered, drawing close to Teagan's ear, "what would you be doing right now, if I wasn't here?"

Her aunt looked at her, and that eager fire was back in her eyes. "I'd have my bow out and be trying to take down every last shadowhand I could spot. And any soldier who saw me doing it.

Sitric Cuaran may be able to cloak himself in magic and so stay alive, but he'll find it harder to play tyrant over an entire city if he stands alone."

chapter 22

He'd not needed the knife he'd brought; someone else's murder attempt had done his work for him.

Those balconies hadn't fallen by accident. They'd been prepared, so the weight of all the Odin-worshippers crowding onto them would make them break off.

And they'd claimed not the king they'd almost certainly been intended for, but dozens of Devout and scores of soldiers—and one Dainn Gulbrandson, Priest of Odin.

It was tempting to think the White God had done his work for him, but no. Such indiscriminate, wide-swath murder was not the Gods' way.

This was someone else's evil.

"And isn't that what my life must be dedicated to fighting against?" Oswin Silverlock muttered, under his breath. "Someone else's evil?"

So he was trudging along streets distant indeed from the new slave market and its fresh blood and death, heading home.

And 'home' here in Ath Cliath meant his rented room at Dun's Hearth. Though perhaps it would be prudent to relocate elsewhere, in case today's disaster got used as a pretext for rounding up and executing—or selling into slavery; this *was* Ath Cliath, after all—all convenient scapegoats.

Yes, perhaps it'd be wisest to—

Shouts ahead, and a scream, and crashings. More screams. What *now?*

He kept walking, towards the din, too the street-moot ahead, and there beheld, coming along the cross-street and now flooding across his intended route—a stream of folk, mainly men, clad in filthy and torn clothes, some of them wearing little better than rags, and a few with rusted manacle-cuffs still on wrists and ankles. Racing along waving swords and axes and daggers, cleaving viciously through anyone who stood in their way.

Slaves! Another slave break! *That* was what those horn calls must have meant!

As Oswin watched, he saw a few gilded helms and spears overwhelmed and trampled down, as a few soldiers unwisely tried to make a stand against the ragged human tide.

My, but the city was devouring royal soldiers today! That would save the King some gold come next payroll—but then again, the more lightly he was guarded, the more his foes might find the courage to try to take his life.

Yes, Sitric Cuaran would be looking for scapegoats.

If he had the time.

And then Oswin Silverlock caught sight of something that left him wondering. Far down the cross-street, just ahead of the foremost running slaves, an old man stepped out of a doorway and pointed insistently and repeatedly, directing the fleeing escapees off to the right.

Oswin wished he knew this city better; he couldn't tell if the man was sending them to the nearest city gate, or turning them aside so they'd blunder through more of Ath Cliath, and do more damage but end up far more likely to all get recaptured, or more likely butchered by the King's soldiers.

Which was it? Or was the man a slaver, trying to guide escaped slaves into a private trap, to be retaken and not lost as sales?

By the God, it was enough to make a man's head hurt!

And kings had to deal with these sorts of thoughts every day. No wonder they were so cruel, capricious, and seemingly mad.

Oswin had never wanted to be a king, or hold any sort of power, but now he *really* didn't want to have to wield any sort of authority. Perhaps he could be a gardener on a grand estate, or a cook in a wealthy man's kitchen...

Anything to stay far away from the slave pens, or a crown, or soldiering for a king.

The slaves were all gone out of sight now; he could track them only by the ever-fainter shouts and screams, in the distance.

Oswin Silverlock stopped, drew in a deep breath, found the tall buildings he'd been using as landmarks, and then set off walking again.

Heading for the Hearth, hurrying now, to try to get there, settle his bill, and get gone before any soldiers could show up looking for him.

Cruel, capricious, and seemingly mad, aye.

He'd gone another three blocks before he found himself short of wind, and realized he was praying aloud, under his breath, in an unending, almost frantic stream.

#

"Well," Forkundr Redbeard growled darkly, "that went about as well as I'd expected."

"So he *is* favoured of Odin," Falki said disgustedly.

"Perhaps, but what *I* saw was more a powerful galdr who expected trouble and prepared for it," Grimkell rasped. "And I trust all of you saw that one of his senior shadowhands went down."

"And a *lot* of gold-helms," Eylir put in. "Enough to put holes in any cordon around the Palace, if he tried to assemble one right now."

Borekr nodded. "A good two score right there under the balconies, but a lot more as they fought their way back to the Palace, through the streets. *That* was what lifted my heart: that the people hate the King and his soldiers enough to dare to throw stones at them, in broad daylight."

"And flowerpots."

"And stone benches from a mansion balcony, that I saw. And they were solid, too; soldiers went down, maimed and *dead*."

"Yet when all is said and done," Forkundr said firmly, "all we accomplished against the King was to warn him, so he'll take proper precautions from now on. I didn't see a scratch on him."

"Well, we'll just have to think up some other way of taking him down."

"Such as?"

"Drop something bigger than a few balconies on his head. Like his entire Palace."

"Easily *said*, but how?"

"We'll need fire, brought together with something that'll explode. A *lot* of it."

"I predict," Eylir told the ceiling, "that the planning ahead of us is going to take ale. A *lot* of it."

"That's fitting. For when kings take killing," Grimkell the Throat said in a deep voice of doom, laced with his gravel tones, "they take a lot of it."

#

Ah! The shop with green awnings. He was almost at the Hearth, now. Just another three blocks...

And then Oswin Silverlock froze, his heart skipping a beat.

Out of the usual throngs of people ahead—the street traffic was as heavy as always here, as if no horn calls had sounded and nothing at all out of the ordinary had happened in the city

122

today—came two gold-helm soldiers, spears in hand. And then two more. Another six, then four more. Spreading out across the street in a line as they advanced on him. Royal soldiers, their eyes definitely on him, and they didn't look friendly.

Oswin looked around wildly, but saw no place to run to.

Oh, *no*.

He was going to die here, on this street, his life a waste...

Got to get away, run and hide, call down the wrath of the God, do *something*...

In desperation, he slapped his head with both hands and a wild flourish, like a tavern-table actor comically signalling that he'd forgotten something, then turned on his heel to stride back the way he'd come. Almost immediately, he heard imperious shouts from behind him, bidding him "*Halt*! Hands *away* from your sides! Turn around, priest, and get on your knees!"

So they knew who he was. They'd been looking for him.

Doomed, to be sure.

Nonetheless, Oswin pretended not to hear, and quickened his pace.

"You heard me, man! Halt *now*, or it'll go ill with you!"

Stammering out prayers so fast his tongue began to stumble over all-too-familiar words, Oswin almost broke into a run, but then saw and heard a spear hiss and then grate along the cobbles right beside him, its point striking sparks.

He hesitated, then with a sob of fear stopped, spread his arms wide, turned, and sagged to his knees.

Where he beheld a curious sight.

The soldiers were coming for him, right enough, stern and scowling and now in an orderly street-wide line.

Yet behind them, out of an alley they'd just passed, were streaming silent, handsome dark-clad men in matching cloaks and expensive boots, all drawing swords and daggers as they came. They all seemed to be smiling sardonically.

And then, striding in their midst, Oswin saw a lone woman. Tall, eye-catchingly beautiful, and clad as all the men were. Her dark-eyed gaze was as sharp as any dagger, and stabbed at him out of a face as white as snow, framed by a long free fall of raven-dark hair.

He could have sworn she winked at him.

And then, from behind where Oswin knelt awaiting death, spear-points already lowering and turning towards him, he heard a voice drawl, "Ah, *here* we are. This is going to be... satisfying."

There was a coldly mocking tone in that voice that chilled Oswin and made him jerk around swiftly, afraid more soldiers had somehow appeared behind him.

But he saw no spears, gilded helms, or royal livery. Instead, he beheld a handsome, imperious dandy of a man in a goldweave doublet, with lace at wrist and throat, leading another force of bodyguards—for that's what they were, he realized, these men and those surrounding the winking woman—out of an alley mouth, into the street.

Before he could say a word or scramble to his feet, they were past him, and advancing on the line of King's soldiers—and so were the woman's guards, converging with the line of gold-helms caught between them.

And as he watched, dumbfounded, the bodyguards effortlessly and ruthlessly butchered the royal soldiers, catching and parrying the spears as their fellows darted in to thrust swordtips into throats and faces and then slash sidelong at the next soldier, sending the line into swift, surrounded-on-all-sides disarray and then...oblivion.

As the last gilded helm clanged and bounced on the cobbles, a few ragged shouts of approval rang from windows, up and down the street.

They seemed to chase Oswin as he bolted, pelting headlong down a narrow but handy alleyway, afraid these deadly bodyguards would now look to eliminate all witnesses.

Oh, God, forgive me! When did I become so craven?

#

There were four—no, five—soldiers, walking together and glowering at the people on the street they were hastening through, but Brandr didn't hesitate.

He strolled up to them unconcernedly, sword held ready behind his back, and the moment he was close enough, ducked low when the rearmost soldier glanced back, drove the pommel of his sword hard into the back of the man's knee, and when the man shouted in pain and crumpled, bounded up to sword the next startled, whirling around soldier across the throat. Blood sprayed, but Brandr was already chopping aside the spear in the next man's hands and charging into him, shoulder against chest, driving the man back into his fellows. Who stumbled, but shoved themselves away, dropping their spears, to drag out swords and daggers with deft, practised speed.

And suddenly Brandr had eye-gouged the man he'd charged and that man was falling with a shriek, but leaving the cobbles clear for him to see that the man he'd first felled was up and snarlingly armed, and so were the last two, spreading wide with swords out to catch him between them.

And closing in, carefully, positioning themselves so he couldn't possibly defend himself against all three of them, or break free of their tightening ring.

So this was it. He was going to die here, with Faolain's price unpaid. Well, *partly* paid; by his count, he'd downed twenty-seven goldhelms.

He rushed the man whose knee he'd first struck, hacking in a flurry with both sword and dagger, not trying to strike home but rather to parry and so get past and around behind the man, but the man sidestepped with ease and veteran skill, and—

Toppled, eyes bulging in sudden, astonished pain.

There was a knife standing slim and terrible out of the man's ear that hadn't been there a moment earlier.

Brandr wanted to stare at it, but didn't dare spend the time. He leaped over the falling body and slashed desperately behind him, his steel clanging off the sword reaching for him, to land awkwardly, hop aside, and whirl to face those last two…

Last one.

The other was down, throat slashed open by a tall, burly man who was smiling with delight. Beside him, another two tall and burly men were calmly sidestepping to catch the last royal soldier between them, just as the trio of soldiers had done to Brandr.

With a curse, the man tried to flee in a sudden whirl and scramble—but one of the burly men caught up a fallen spear and cast it at the running soldier's ankles, and he stumbled, reeled, and fell. They pounced on him while he was still trying to roll to his feet, stabbing his neck and throat ruthlessly with their daggers, pinning him to the cobbles as his lifeblood flooded out.

"Grand day, isn't it?" one of his burly saviors said to Brandr then, and added a grin. As they wiped their blades clean, resheathed them, and walked away.

After a moment, Brandr decided that enough citizens were staring open-mouthed at the trio; he didn't have to, any longer. He saluted them, cleaned his own steel on the bodies, slid them back into sheath and scabbard, and went on his way.

Vowing to stick to lone soldiers, or pairs at most, from now on.

Ah, fair Muirenn, her eyes so big and smilingly dark, and her lips so red and soft and warmly welcoming...

Not to mention her...her...

Volundr the Voice shook his head, vividly remembering his one and only fleeting caress of shockingly firm ivory curves.

Ohhhhh....he drained the mead in his jack in one fiery-sweet pull, sighed out the wondrous pain of riding out its fire, and reached to refill it.

Soon he'd leave the service of King Sitric, and depart crowded, stinking Ath Cliath for Muirenn's fair farm, far out in the rolling hills of Hibernia, and marry his sweetheart.

Muirenn, who'd waited for him so long. Muirenn, who would give him many laughing, playing sons and daughters, and be waiting for him in her broad bed every night when he blew out the last lamp...

Oh, bliss.

Just a few more seasons of welcoming King Sitric's gold rods into his purse, and he'd be wealthy enough to buy out all of Muirenn's neighbours, so their enlarged farm would take in Wyrm Lake and all three of the hilltop woods one could see from her front window...

Volundr smiled, nodded, and took another swig of mead. It was going to be *wonderful*. Oh, yes. From the—

"*You!* Useless windbag! *Come!* We have need of whatever brawn you can muster, fat-guts!"

Volundr stiffened, whirled around, and drew breath for the most dismissive, oath-laden tirade he could muster.

And then stopped, his mouth open but not a sound coming out.

His summoner was Mael the Sharp, and the head of the King's shadowhands didn't look in any mood to be crossed.

Volundr found his voice. "H-how can I serve?"

"You heard that a heap of murdered soldiers was found this morning at the Palace gates?"

Volundr hadn't, but decided that now wasn't a good time to say so.

That judgment was aided by the fact that Mael was grabbing him by the arm and marching him out of the room. Volundr only just had time to drain his jack again and toss it at the nearest table, before they were out in the passage. He missed.

"Well, there's a fresh lot of them," Mael went on, uncaring, as Volundr choked and gagged and reeled in his iron-strong grip, "and the King's been seen returning to the Palace— still a good way off, and being pelted with stones and chamberpot-dung and the All-Father knows what else by the *good* citizens of Ath Cliath. And we know he's heard the horn calls about the slave break. So he's not going to be in any too good a mood. Wherefore we *don't* want him discovering more of his soldiers, freshly butchered, in the way of his getting through his own gates—now, do we?"

"N-no-*no!*" Volundr managed, clawing in his mind for his customary professional eloquence but finding nothing much.

"And most of the Palace garrison and my command and a lot of the servants are out there in the city, busy with their duties to make the slave market opening ceremony unfold smoothly, though I'm hearing that it very much *didn't*, so I find myself short of sheer strength of numbers and brawn to shift dead men into carts fast enough to get them *out* of the royal way. Which is where Volundr the Voice's loyalty and heroics come in. I'm told some of the soldiers are in small enough pieces that even a fat-guts like you should be able to lift them."

Suddenly Volundr regretted that second jack of mead. Not to mention the first. As his stomach decided to lift like a breaching whale—and then turn over and crash down again. Down, down, *down*...

"Oh, *stop* that," Mael snarled. "We're short of mop-maids, too."

#

The master of Dun's Hearth recoiled in startled fear. Where had the man *come* from?

He'd been watching the street so attentively, expecting trouble, *ready* for it—and now a dagger was almost under his chin, and the grinning face of the man holding it was *so* close...

"*You*," the man said, "are on our list."

"Our?" he asked, backing away. That wickedly-sharp point followed, inexorably.

"No King reigns for long without the support of the truly loyal. 'Shadowhands,' your like calls us, as you cower. Wise of you. Not that it's any help at all, once we've marked you as a traitor. You've only been allowed to go on living this long because we knew where to find the man Fylan, and the priest Silverlock, and the woman Damhain—though she seems to have gone missing. So suppose you begin your begging and pleading by telling me where she's gone."

They'd been retreating from the front door of the inn through all of these softly menacing words, back into the dark and deserted common room.

"I—I know not, truly. She still has her room, she just hasn't been back for a night or so..."

"Guaire Ó hIarlatha, your death can be swift and merciful, or it can be slow and painful. Earless and fingerless you can be, for a start. It's the truth I'm after, not lies and evasions. And retreating from me will only bring you up against a wall, sooner rather than later. Now I'll ask again..."

They were in the kitchen now, backing through the flaps of hide into the warm den of hanging onions and the aromatic, simmering pot of potato and leek soup.

"...where has the lass Mist Damhain gone to? And who's she been meeting with, spending time with? Hey?"

Past the broth...

"No, Guaire, not that way. *No* closer to your cleaver, thank you very much. I can kill you at any moment, mind, but I'd prefer to let you live long enough to tell me what I want to know. The King's had his eye on you for years, did you know that? No? Well, he has, and—"

The side of the stew-pot was hot enough to make the innkeeper's calloused palm sizzle, but that was a small price to pay to slap it hard into the face of his tormentor.

Where it drenched him thoroughly and blindingly ere breaking his nose.

He barely had time to howl before the nearest boning knife took him under the chin, and then the master of Dun's Hearth had hold of an empty, unused sauce-cauldron, and was battering the man's head to the floor and on and on for a good bit longer than that, until only softness met the little pot's hard, blackened bottom.

"I *said* I didn't know," the innkeeper told the dead man on his kitchen floor softly. "And that was the truth. Not that the King cares."

He stepped back, gulped in a deep breath, and added, "And that's the problem. Our King cares about entirely the wrong things."

Chapter 23

"I am gratified at your presence, Neven Daunt," said the voice from the other side of the wall. "So few folk in this city are still reliable, these days."

"You have another little task for me, I take it?"

"You take it correctly."

"I remain at your service."

"And you see matters clearly, too. Even more gratifying. You waste none of my time crossing words against mine like sword-blades, or hinting and threatening. You have *no* idea how weary I get of such behaviour."

"You've taught me the inadvisability of having ideas," Daunt replied, leaning against the wall. He might as well take his ease, seeing as the owner of the voice was so talkative, just now.

And as the King seemed to have survived entirely unscathed, the 'little task' ahead was likely to be neither small nor safe.

Which meant he might never have the chance to lounge against a wall, ever again.

#

Locked. Brandr shoved against the broad, iron-strapped front door of the Hearth, and found no give to it at all. Barred, too.

With a sigh—my, but weren't the gods smiling on him this day? Or perhaps it was Odin smiling on his foes, and he was merely within reach, to take harm—he went to the end of the block, and along, and up the alley. It was a slim chance he'd find the kitchen door of the Hearth open, but it was that or seek a hidden place to rest, and he was suddenly weary. All the sword-swinging and slaying, no doubt. Gods, killing was so hideously *easy*.

He was three trudging steps away when the door he was heading for swung open, and the master of the Hearth peered out. Warily and over his shoulder; he was dragging something heavy and had obviously unfastened the door one-handed and rammed it with his behind to get it open. He stiffened at the sight of Brandr, but by then the Flower of House Fylan had seen what was being dragged; the body of a man whose head was too battered for him to still be alive.

Brandr swung the door wide and murmured, "Let me take his feet. If you don't have to drag him, it'll leave less of a trail in case anyone comes looking."

The master of the Hearth looked back at Brandr and said quietly, "Thank you."

"If we carry him to the back of yonder stables, I'll drag him from there on down the alley to the end of the block," Brandr offered. "Where, as it happens, someone else's corpse is already lying. Perhaps I can make it look like they killed each other, or died in the same brawl."

"And if someone sees you?"

Brandr laughed mirthlessly. "Between the new slave market hall and here," he replies, "I've killed forty-one of the King's goldhelms. After they killed a friend of mine. A *lot* of people saw me doing it. Which reminds me; for your safety and mine, I'm going to have to find new lodgings. So what do I owe you?"

The innkeeper let go of the dead man, stepped forward, and hugged Brander almost fiercely. "*Nothing*," he muttered. "Not a skatt. I am honoured to have had you under my roof."

"My purse thanks you," Brandr told him dryly. "I don't know if I can get the One-Eyed King off his throne, but I can certainly thin the ranks of his soldiers. And his shadowhands, too. And I'm far from the only one doing it. Three men saved my life a few streets away, when I took on too many goldhelms."

"I think I've met them," the master said with a smile. And then leaned close and muttered, "Seek Ualgarg's Casks and Kegs, on Winespill Street. Tell them Guaire sent you, and you're looking for a 'bed unseen.'"

Brandr stared at him, then nodded. "I'll do that." And he started dragging the dead man along the alley.

The innkeeper waved farewell and went back into the Hearth.

He'd scarcely closed and bolted the kitchen door when there came a summons at his front door. An insistent knocking.

He went, lifted aside the bar, and cracked open the door on its stout latch-chain.

Four royal soldiers stood outside, grim and weary and more than a little battered; one was missing his gilded helm, and three had lost their spears.

"We seek a man, innkeeper," the oldest, shortest soldier told him, consulting a note and then thrusting it back into his belt pouch. "A Hibernian by the name of Brandr Fylan."

The master of the Hearth shook his head. "I've been shut up tight since the horns cried the slave break. That name is known to me; he was staying here, but it's my belief that the Brandr Fylan who came to Ath Cliath died earlier today."

#

"For men dedicated to ridding Ath Cliath of this mad King, in favour of a Norseman less greedy and less Odin-ridden," Eylir told the table dryly, "we're peerless at flapping our jaws at secret meetings."

"That," Grimkell the Throat said grimly, "will do. Folk should always be able to laugh at themselves, but I draw the line at mocking our purpose. We're perilously close to being ineffectual as it is."

"Ho!" Borekr Ketilsson spoke up. "Speak for yourself! I'm not close to being ineffectual, I've mastered being ineffectual."

"Aye," Forkundr Redbeard growled. "You *roll* in it."

"Hound jokes?" Falki Longbeak asked wearily. "Again? You need new material."

"Enough!" Grimkell said firmly, slamming his fist down on the table.

"Ssshh," Eylir reproved the skald.

Grimkell gave him a glare and snapped, "We're met to come up with new ideas to get at we-all-know-who. Some way of breaking through all of his soldiers, and shadowhands, and magic. *Remember?* Now, any ideas?"

"Tell me," Falki asked, "just how good is a galdr at working his magic if he hasn't had any sleep for, say, three days?"

Forkundr shrugged, a moment faster than Eylir and Borekr. "If we knew better how galdr magic worked..." he offered glumly.

"I know a seithkona I can ask about that."

"Eye, we *all* know seithkonas."

"A seithkona who for years went adventuring with a galdr," Eylir elaborated patiently. "And so, should know."

"Good," Grimkell said swiftly. "Go you and ask her, Eye—after we're done here. So let us for now assume there is some value in keeping the King sleepless, even if it mars not his magic but just makes him forgetful or impatient or angry. *How* do you propose to keep the king awake?"

"Frequent horn calls, for many different emergencies," Falki said promptly. "Since

128

buying the effects of an adventurer last month, I own the right sort of horn."

"Oh? What did this adventurer die of?"

"Old age, in his bed. Not under any curse, nor the disfavour of any god, so far as I know."

"They'll be hot to hunt down anyone making spurious horn calls, that's for sure," Grimkell told his drinking-jack. "I hope you own a hiding place and the retained ability to run like the storm winds, as well as a horn. And unless you're blowing that horn in the Palace, the King will likely be able to ignore it—and after you've kept him sleepless for the first night, the ability to sleep through it, too."

"Oh, horn calls are just one means," Falki said. "They won't suffice on their own."

"So name us some other means."

"An infestation of rats in the royal wing of the Palace."

"And how're you going to manage *that?*"

"I've been paying the street lads I use as rat-catchers in my warehouses double for live rats for three months, now; I've amassed quite a collection."

"Are they eating each other, or are you feeding them?"

"They are, because I am, but very little."

"Well, that's very interesting, but I highly doubt you're doing it in the Palace, still less in the royal wing. Being as you still have a head on your shoulders to spout nonsense at us."

"Unlike certain sarcastic defeatists in this room," Falki replied sweetly, "I've also secured a contract to supply the Palace with certain date-and-almond-paste sweets. My deliveries are to the south kitchens of the Palace, which are a stone's throw—trust me, I've tested this—from the royal wing. So I can get close enough to the King. That's where I can blow my horn and get his full attention, too."

"The *first* time. I suspect you'll be fleeing madly, with soldiers seeking to seize a horn hard on your heels, shortly thereafter."

"Quite likely, but a lot of those soldiers are likely to trip and fall, on all the loosed and hungry rats underfoot."

Grimkell drained his drinking-jack, and felt the prompt need to refill it again. "Well, you've certainly outlined clearly how you're going to *entertain* Sitric Cuaran. I'm not so sure rats galore and fire warnings, army sighted alerts, and slave break alarms are going to rob him of much sleep—unless we can wound him enough to leave him in lasting pain. Unless, of course, galdr magic can quell pain or heal wounds."

"If there's one thing a life spent trading has made me heartily sick of," Eylir Grimsson told the table, as if he was hoping it would grow a mouth and venture a supporting opinion, "it's men who waste wind saying, 'That won't work, and I'll tell you why.' Tell us what *will* work. And pass the mead, if that's what you're drinking."

"It seems to me," Borekr said flatly, "that without knowing the pertinent details of what galdr magic can and can't do—and more, what the galdr named Sitric Cuaran can and can't do—we lack the basic competence to forge any useful plans against the King."

"And it seems to *me*," Falki told the far wall, as he strolled in its direction, "that we lack basic competence, period."

An awkward silence fell, for although Forkundr Redbeard had bristled, thrusting his jaw forward and glaring at Falki, he opened his mouth and then shut it again without saying a word. And when he looked to Grimkell, the skald was nodding grimly, as were Borekr and Eylir.

"So is this all futility, then? Risking our necks for naught but certain failure?" he asked at last, heavily rather than furiously.

"No," Grimkell rasped. "For have we not all known idiot kings before, by reputation if not direct rule? And have not even the gods blundered? Show me a man who claims to have been always wise and all-seeing and right, nigh from the cradle, and I'll show you a liar. We do the best we can."

"And hope," Eylir said quietly, "it is enough to bring down a king."

Silence fell again, until he broke it by saying, "Well? Let's hear some more foolish plans, then! If the One-Eyed King is so brilliant and cunning and powerful in magic, foolheaded errantry may be the very scheming that catches him unawares—and succeeds, where the prudent way he's prepared for, so it can't help but fails. Surely one of you has some hare-brained scheme to catapult cats with poisoned claws over the Palace walls, or some such!"

"Not cats!" Falki said quickly. "They'll eat my rats!"

#

"I must be bolder," Oswin Silverlock hissed aloud. "Braver! What sort of servant of the God am I, to run like a scared rabbit? I came here on a holy mission, and must not waver from it." He winced. "More than I already have."

He squared his shoulders and started to stride along confidently. "Not throw my life away, no, for how does *that* serve the God? But I must act, not hide and cower. And not do violence to envoys or soldiers, other than to resist *their* violence, because they are merely following orders. It is the King himself who is evil—and his shadowhands, who willfully break the laws of Ath Cliath and of human decency and moral standards, to do the king's will. And—who knows?—perhaps their own wills, criminal side-activities, to line their own purses and eliminate creditors, and…but no, I suspect that, as it seems many citizens here suspect that, but of proof, I have none. I must not speculate, and damn them for what I surmise they're up to. So let us believe the best about them, that they do nothing for personal gain. Yet still they are evil, serving an evil king by doing things they must know are evil and unlawful, and doing them willingly. So they I *will* act against!"

And having thus fiercely resolved, the priest of the White God shook his head in disbelief. For shop-women he had come to trust had pointed out a handful of men to him as shadowhands of the King, and there ahead of him, walking away from him along the cross-street he'd just come to, was one of them! Strolling with a nonchalance that seemed at first glance to be false.

In short, the man was up to something.

Well, now…

Oswin Silverlock began to follow him, doing his best to seem that he just happened to be heading the same way. In case the man looked back to make sure he wasn't being followed.

Yet, through block after block, and several turnings onto other streets, the shadowhand did not. Perhaps the King's dark agents were so confident that the city was theirs, and none would dare challenge them, that they'd lost all fear, and then all prudence.

Oswin walked faster, to draw nearer.

The White God would be his shield, for he was doing the God's will.

#

"Leek and potato, of course," Teagan said merrily. "The very best soup for times when one is upset and must devour time uncomforted, for in making it, there's lots to do. Peel, you."

And she handed Mist the small, hook-bladed peeling knife, and pointed her to the straw-covered bin in the darkest corner of the pantry that was home to the small mountain of potatoes.

"Now there are those," Teagan added serenely, "who prefer to call such soups potato and leek, but such folk haven't consumed *my* soup. Mine is definitely leek and potato."

130

Mist grinned, and came back to her aunt with a lot of potatoes bundled heavily in her apron. "This many?"

"More," Teagan replied, eyeing them. "We'll be using the *big* cauldron." She pointed at it with the wooden spoon in her hand, then set it down to pour mead for herself and Mist. "There's no need to go parched while cooking. Drink—but no bleeding on the potatoes, mind."

"I'll *not*," Mist replied, nettled, "get *that* drunk."

"Oh, I believe you, but the warning must be given, for I have in my time encountered such promises before, given by weaker souls than you, and encountered their lamentable breaking, and—"

As if that word had been a cue, there came a faint but unmistakeable crash, from several floors above them in the house.

Teagan froze, and flung up a hand for silence, and Mist gave it to her.

Then Teagan became a brief whirlwind, racing to close a door here, and latch a door there, and pluck down knives and cleavers and pots to arrange them in hiding under bowls and dough and a heap of unwashed leaks, all over the kitchen.

She was just finishing, and wiping her hands clean and dry on her apron, when a man loomed up in the open, doorless archway that connected the kitchen to the back hall.

Teagan picked up her mead, and took a sip. "I don't recall expecting to welcome any *invited* guests into my home tonight—so who are you, sir?"

The man smiled crookedly. It was the only sort of smile he could muster, given the scar that ran down one side of his face and across one end of his mouth.

"You do not need to know my name," he sneered.

"Ah, but I do," Teagan replied softly, "for the dead-carters get *so* upset when tombstones must be left blank. You're a shadowhand of the King, are you not?"

The man's smile lessened. "That I am. How did you know?"

"My mind is a rather large warehouse, but it retains some secrets. Just as yours seems unable to relinquish your name."

"There is only one name that matters," the shadowhand replied silkily, "and that is: Mist Damhain." His cold, unsmiling eyes shifted to Mist. "That would be you, would it not?"

"And if it is?"

"I have come here to slay the King's foe, the outlander Mist Damhain," came the cold reply, "and find my patience for fencing with words to have just run out. So, *die*, as they say!"

And a knife spun out of his sleeve so fast that Teagan's flung cleaver only *just* intercepted it, as Mist ducked away.

With her other hand, Teagan flung her mead into the man's face, and charged right after it, slamming into him before his own charge could clear the kitchen table and reach the side of it where Mist was swiftly retreating.

The shadowhand's free hand came out from behind his hip with a wicked knife in it, but Teagan had already plucked up a bowl from the table and flung it, hard. It shattered, and by his stifled shriek, so did some of his fingers, the knife clattering to the floor.

With a snarl of rage he flung his other arm around her neck and tried to jerk, hard, to break her neck, but Teagan had already dropped down his front, punching him hard in the groin, to wrap herself around his ankles and twist.

There wasn't room for him to topple over, but his overbalanced body tried, succeeding in slamming the side of his head hard against the table-edge.

He rebounded off it, dazed, but clawed out two knives from sheaths on his person and flung them, and the rolling Teagan grunted in pain as one struck home.

Mist flung a bowl into his face then, then two of the largest potatoes, and then a cleaver, but although it laid open his forehead bloodily, he swayed back, plucked it out of the air, and came for her, hacking viciously down at Teagan as he passed.

She screamed in pain, and Mist screamed in fear and rage, and the shadowhand laughed—and from somewhere close by in the house came an almighty *crash*.

Biding inside at home did not seem to be a winning strategy this night.

chapter 24

It was taking Brandr a long time to cross Ath Cliath in the deepening night; royal soldiers seemed to be everywhere. Large groups, with lanterns, on vigilant patrol. Too large to challenge and have much hope of survival, so it behooved him to stay hidden from them, taking refuge wherever he could and journeying on only when they'd passed and were safely elsewhere.

It would have helped immensely, he thought more than once, if it hadn't been so damned dark—and if he'd had the slightest idea where Winespill Street was.

The King's tax collectors knew, of course, and so of course could anyone who outranked them at the Palace, as there'd be a map they could consult at will. Come to think of it, he'd never seen a map of the city for sale anywhere, in any of the shops he'd poked around or shopfronts he'd peered at from the street.

Well, now, *could* mere citizens—or worse, outlanders such as, ahem, Brandr Fylan—get city maps? Perhaps for many gold rods, in back rooms, as something of great business, or security, value? Hmm; how to find out? Ask the master of the Hearth, or Neven Daunt, for if it *was* a matter of security, then merely asking the wrong person would get him followed. Or worse.

It hadn't taken Faolain's death to make Brandr heartily dislike what Ath Cliath was, under the rule of King Sitric Cuaran, but the more he saw of it, the more he detested what he saw.

There was an underlying cruelty to this city, not just the vargr-devour-vargr savagery of gold is king, and humans can be bought and sold as slaves, and elbows-out merchants doing each other dirty daily, but a malice towards anyone who knelt not to Odin, and who revered not the One-Eyed King almost as much. Citizens—and outlanders who visited longer than briefly, and paid attention to more than buying or selling—knew fear, if only at the backs of their minds, and that fear never left them. There was a feeling of being watched, of malice...

Not just on the part of the King's soldiers, and not just at the grasping hands of the tax collectors, and not just thanks to the watchful and dagger-wielding shadowhands. The King might have only one eye, and might bide in the Palace much of the time, but he had spies everywhere, and took an interest in what they saw, and reached out to strike down, or claw to himself, folk in Ath Cliath who stood too tall and spoke too freely and fawned on Sitric Cuaran and his deeds and projects insufficiently.

And it seemed beyond one man to change this, even if that man was a towering warrior-hero and not an expendable youngling of a Hibernian clan neither numerous nor well-known in Ath Cliath.

But he was going to try to change it. Murdering the One-Eyed King might be more than he could accomplish, might even have disastrous consequences—Brandr shuddered at the mere thought of armies burning and swording their ways across Hibernia, slaughtering thousands to avenge one slain king, or locked in a vicious struggle to succeed a dead Sitric Cuaran on the Riverfleet Throne—but if he shake Sitric's confidence, so his grip on the crown changed forever in its nature, that would be something. To have the principal occupant of the Palace fear the people dwelling in the many buildings outside his high walls, as well as all of them fearing him, that would be an achievement of lasting worth. That fear might make a lesser man more of a tyrant, but to be honest, *could* Sitric Cuaran be more of a tyrant, given his obvious intelligence and foresight? A brute could easily be a worse butcher, but Sitric was no brute.

And, Brandr reminded himself as he clambered up a drainpipe to a roof shallowly pitched enough to give him so cover from an approaching patrol of soldiers, and sprawled himself across its lowest slates, causing sleepy gulls to give him dirty looks as they shifted aside to make room, the One-Eyed King was up to something.

He wasn't taxing so stiffly out of mere greed, unless all the wiser citizens' opinions and gossip Brandr had overheard was mistaken. No, Sitric Cuaran wanted wealth—*lots* of wealth—for some secret purpose or project. And it wasn't glorifying Odin with gigantic temples, or those temples would already be soaring above Ath Cliath's tallest roofs.

So what *was* Sitric Cuaran up to?

And was uncovering that secret worth more to Clan Uterni than assassinating a one-eyed king?

Likely, for bringing word back to the clan elders about what King Sitric was up to *was* his root mission, not teaching Sitric fear and respect, or relieving him of his life. Brandr's clan needed to know the truth about Ath Cliath's ruler, so they could plan and look ahead.

Not deal with the chaos of a king assassinated and the struggle for the throne that would inevitably follow. Perhaps killing soldiers and courtiers and shadowhands would be silencing mouths that could tell Brandr more about the King's secret schemes...but then, perhaps slaying minion after minion until the King stood almost alone might let Brandr and others glimpse the schemes that Sitric kept so hidden right now.

Decisions, decisions, all with consequences that in many cases were hard to see beforehand.

Brandr grinned wryly, startling a half-asleep gull that was eyeing him from close at hand, as the thought struck him that making so many decisions with half-seen or unintended consequences bound to them was quite likely the life of King Sitric Cuaran, or any ruler of like reach and importance.

Below him, the patrol passed obliviously, several of the soldiers arguing so vociferously over who had been the real foes of the King at the ceremony to open the slaving hall that the officer leading them snarled at them to leave off and be silent.

They heeded long enough to get about seven shopfronts away ere their voices rose again, and the patrol leader barked at them in real fury.

Brandr decided not to raise blade against those particular goldhelms if he encountered them again and recognized them. They were sewing more dissent in the ranks than his slayings could.

And although this particular roof wasn't ideal for sleeping on—what he needed was a smoother roof with a shallower pitch, not overlooked by any nearby windows and with some sort of barrier to keep a snoring Brandr Fylan from rolling off the edge to a messy death on hard cobbles below—the weather wasn't cold enough now to kill him, if he spent the nights sleeping on rooftops.

Which might very well be how he'd have to spend this one, intrepid undercover agent of the Uterni or not.

A gull pecked at him experimentally, and Brandr pounced, wringing its neck and tossing it over the roof-edge in one movement.

The rest of the gulls eyed him with new respect.

#

The shadowhand hesitated for a moment, cleaver raised. His head was tilted to try to hear what sound, if any, would follow that distant crash.

Nothing.

He waited.

Still nothing.

So he shrugged—and came for Mist, hacking viciously.

Who'd not been idle during the brief pause. She'd sidestepped across the end of the table to its other side, to try to draw this slayer away from Teagan, and while doing so had snatched up a carving fork and its matching knife.

Now she grimly parried with these, trying no attack of her own, and managed to fend off the first flurry of chops from the man's heavy, swiftly-swung weapon. No slicing edge reached her, but the sheer force of steel striking steel numbed her hands, and she retreated.

The shadowhand came around the table after her, growing an unpleasant grin and slowing his attack to fence with her, obviously having fun.

Mist kicked a kitchen stool out from under the table and into his way, but he sprang over it without even looking down, his grin widening—then snatched up one of Teagan's upturned bowls and scaled it at Mist.

She ducked, and it glanced off her shoulder—as the pot that had been under that bowl came at her hard, slamming into her forehead and then her shoulder ere it clanged to the floor. Mist reeled back, wincing, and the shadowhand charged.

Mist went right on retreating, back around the table and along it to where she'd first parried the cleaver, wondering how long the man would chase her ere he vaulted the table or ducked under it or some such, but he seemed to be still enjoying toying with her; grin still in place, he followed her again around the kitchen table.

As she reached the table's end, he launched another charge—but slipped in what must be Teagan's blood underfoot, and Mist was able to get out of reach, even when he leaned across the corner of the table for a great full-arm slash with the cleaver.

Which was when Aunt Teagan rose unsteadily up from the floor behind the man, drenched in blood from a great cleft in her shoulder, with the pot that had just clanged to the floor in her hand. She swung it as hard as she could—and dented it across the back of the shadowhand's head.

Her wound robbed the blow of much of its force, but he staggered sideways, dazed and slack-jawed, for a moment—and then shook his head to clear it, spun away from his pursuit of Mist to face Teagan, and charged her with a snarl.

Teagan stood her ground, the dented pot her only weapon. The shadowhand growled into her face as the bloody cleaver in his hand swung back for a killing blow—but into the kitchen like a vengeful wind came Oswin Silverlock, festooned with the splintered shards of Teagan's oldest and most rotted window-shutter. He slammed into the shadowhand, punching and clawing.

The arm that bore the cleaver was borne back against the table by the priest's full weight, as Oswin tried to punch the shadowhand's throat and at the same time claw at the man's face, with far more enthusiasm than skill. Yet by luck a finger caught one of the man's eyes, forcing tears and a roar of frantic pain—as Mist launched herself across the table and drove first her fork, and then her carving knife, through the man's cleaver-arm.

The cleaver clattered to the tabletop as the man's roar became a shriek—and then he was twisting like an eel to try to snatch out another of his many knives and stab the priest still clawing at him, and a reeling, bleeding Teagan was snatching up another of her put-ready-for-this-fray bowls, this one metal, and slamming it down over his head like a war-helm, momentarily blinding him.

Lost in the bowl, the shadowhand got his dagger out and stabbed blindly—taking Oswin right through the palm of his hand.

The resulting wail momentarily deafened them all, and then Oswin was reeling back, sobbing like a baby, and Teagan was driving home the boning-knife that had been put ready under that bowl, hilt-deep into the shadowhand's back—and Mist was driving the carving fork into the man's throat with one hand, and slashing the throat open above the long tines of the fork with the carving knife in her other hand.

Blood spurted, blinding her, and the shadowhand's shriek became wet and bubbling, but he was twisting free of them all and staggering around in a turn to face them, one hand racing to his throat to try vainly to quell the loss of his lifeblood, and the other darting to some of the many still-sheathed daggers strapped up and down his body, to pluck and throw.

Through his own pain and tears, Oswin saw the peril—and launched himself at the man, lowering his head and ramming into the shadowhand's gut.

They went over together, crashing heavily to the floor with the priest on top. His weight bent back the shadowhand's wrist and drove a dagger the royal agent had just drawn deep into the man's own chest—and all struggling suddenly stopped.

The man under Oswin sagged limply.

As Mist rolled off the table to do some staggering of her own, that ended with her standing over the shadowhand long enough to be sure he was dead.

And then rushing to see to Aunt Teagan, binding her shoulder with an apron and then a tablecloth. When she was settled, pale but trying to smile, Mist turned to the whimpering, blood-drenched priest who'd saved them both. He was rocking in pain, bent over his hand with tears streaming down his face.

"Hands hurt *so* much," Teagan murmured, as tenderly as any mother trying to comfort her child, and Oswin clenched his teeth and through them asked, "Is he dead?"

"He's dead," Mist said grimly, "and I don't know how to bury a man I can't carry, in a city of hard cobbles."

"Wrap him up in a blanket so he can't be recognized," the priest gasped, "and rope him to me, and I'll tow him through the streets as a burial. And give him to the river, once I can do it unwatched."

"Tow him? Can you stand?"

"I *must*," Oswin replied, and forced himself to his feet, to stand gasping and shuddering and looking down at his now-bound hand in disbelief. He tried to move the fingers, winced at the pain this caused, and then wiped sweat from his face so he could blink and properly see Teagan and Mist, and tell them, "I can." Then he looked at Teagan and added tentatively, "Ah, my apologies for your window-shutter, lady."

That sent Teagan to laughing, and she clutched at her shoulder and moaned in pain, but waved away his fumbling attempt to pray over her, and said to Mist, "Towels and old clothes and cleaning rags in the rooms through *that* door, and there's rope at the back of the pantry, at the end of the row of crocks. Bind up yon corpse as he suggests and set him on his way towing—before I come to my senses and try to think of some saner alternative that inevitably won't work. Sir, you have saved our lives, and we stand in your debt. If there's anything we can do…"

Oswin gave her a lopsided smile. "Pray for me, Lady, to whatever gods you hold dear. Oh, but this hurts."

"As to that," Teagan told him, "I can give you something that will help for a little while."

And she clambered to her feet, hissing in pain and wincing twice or thrice, and got out a decanter that she put to his lips.

And the priest drank deeply, ended spluttering and blinking at her, then gasped, "That's the best wine I've ever tasted."

Teagan smiled. "Good. Have more."

And Oswin did, and they soon sent him on his way into the night dragging the dead man rather unsteadily, but with a grim, determined smile on his face.

"I have done some good," he said aloud, into the night, then said it again. And it became a chant that took him right past a patrol of soldiers, who eyed him closely but said not a word, and halfway down the sprawling length of Ath Cliath ere lack of lantern-wielding patrols coincided with a stretch of river with a dock hard by but no dock just below the railing a weary Oswin Silverlock was leaning on, and no building walling him off from the waters.

Gratefully he did off the rope, rolled the corpse over until that so-heavy body passed under the lowest railing, and gave it to the river with a splash.

"May all of our problems leave us so cleanly," he muttered, watching the dead man bob to the surface and start to drift. Out to sea.

And then he started the long trudge back to the house where he'd killed a man, because the thought struck him that the Hearth was no longer safe, and he had no other place to go.

#

It had been some years since he'd needed to sneak into the Palace unseen, but the covert way in Neven Daunt had learned years back from Lady Lecora O'Hart still worked. Which either meant he was walking right into a trap, or the overconfident incompetence of whomever was responsible for Palace security was staggering.

Daunt hoped it was the latter. Being as he was here to carry out his little task for the voice from the other side of the wall, and if he succeeded, there would be a trail of dead men on the polished royal floors ere dawn.

The shadowhand traitor wanted him to eliminate three courtiers, beginning with the Keeper of the Vaults. And if he survived this night's work, and made it safely out into the city again, he was to start assassinating tax collectors, armed with a copy of the Palace payroll the traitor had given him, so he knew who they all were—by name, at least.

He'd be paid fifty gold rods per courtier, and twenty per tax collector, which was rather more than honest trading netted him in any span of a few nights, this past year. He hadn't told the voice from the far side of the wall that he'd grown to detest the rule of the One-Eyed King so much he'd have done the killings for free. One lowered one's market value in a trice that way.

And he was, before all else, a seasoned professional. Which is why he was striding unconcernedly along Palace corridors as if he had every right to be there, and was frankly bored or tired thanks to the late hour, and yawning for either reason—not skulking and lurking like a nervous intruder who doesn't want to be seen.

That relaxed, weary confidence took him straight past a maid busy with a mop, who didn't even look up, and then a hurrying manservant laden with freshly laundered linens. Daunt turned a corner, saw the door he was seeking, and headed for it.

Only to find it locked.

Out of habit, he sighed in not-so-feigned exasperation and turned to face the corridor, to make sure no one was watching ere he set to work with the fine collection of lockpicks that lived between the inner and outer metal facings of his belt buckle.

And found himself staring into the eyes of a cruelly smiling man who was gliding silently up to him with a drawn dagger in hand. A stride or two ahead of a second dagger-wielding, sneering man, who was walking in a wide, soundless arc to come at Daunt from the side.

"Well, well. You've just made your last, fatal mistake, I'm thinking," said the nearest shadowhand.

"And that," Daunt replied lightly, his own dagger seeming to leap into his hand, "just goes to show how badly you can be mistaken. You see, that fatal mistake is yours."

And they charged at each other, eagerly, daggers flashing.

Both of them were smiling coldly.

And both of them plucked and threw a second dagger as they came.

chapter 25

Neven Daunt ducked, snake-swift, and the shadowhand's hurled dagger *thunked* off the locked door behind him.

"Who is it?" called the Keeper of the Vaults, from the room beyond that door.

But by then, Daunt was too busy to think of a clever reply.

He found himself preoccupied with trying to stay alive, in a frantic but silent struggle that had begun with his catching hold of the shadowhand's dagger wrist and forcibly swinging the man around to where he could watch the second shadowhand's approach.

Yet during that swing, his foe's free hand dipped to snatch out yet another dagger—the King's nastywork agents seemed to wear large personal arsenals at all times, he'd come to notice—so Daunt kept on swinging him, so as to bring them both against the nearest wall, hard.

Hard enough, he hoped, to crack some shadowhand knuckles against unyielding stone. But the man was fast—younger and faster than he was—and had earlier eluded his own thrown dagger with almost frightening ease.

Right now, the shadowhand twisted and dropped as the wall loomed up, so Daunt couldn't put his weight behind the meeting with the wall without cracking his own skull. And if he dropped with the shadowhand, that would put him down and vulnerable, just as the second shadowhand arrived.

He dropped anyway, shoving as hard as he could against the wall and driving his knees into the shadowhand sagging under him.

Which was when fate, or the gods—in the form of the Keeper of the Vaults—intervened. By flinging his door wide and demanding to know, "What's going *on* out here?"

His answer came in the form of the door, which opened out into the wide hallway, thudding into two struggling men and sending them rolling over helplessly—right into the ankles of a third, fast-charging man, who tripped over them and toppled just as helplessly into a face-first meeting with the door.

Boom.

Which didn't just daze that second shadowhand as it broke his nose, it drove the door half-closed again on the arm of the Keeper of the Vaults. Who cursed as he staggered sideways, then regained his balance—and then in anger shoved the door open again, hard.

Causing a second impact with the second shadowhand that wrenched his neck and struck him senseless, so his limp weight sagged atop Daunt and the first shadowhand. A pommel of a sheathed dagger strapped to the second shadowhand struck Daunt bruisingly on the forehead, and he responded by plucking it from its sheath and driving it down into the shadowhand beneath him, hard. One, twice—and thrice.

That man stopped struggling with a queer sobbing gasp, and Daunt rolled and kicked his way free, found his feet, and raced around both sprawled shadowhands to confront the man glaring at him around the opened door.

"Are you the Keeper of the Vaults?" Daunt asked.

The man eyed this hard-breathing stranger, and drew himself up, visibly swelling with importance. "I am, but if you've any complaint or concern, kindly come back during daylight hours and request an appointment. As you can see, I'm a very busy man—*uuuuurrrkh!*"

"Not any more," Daunt said dryly, sidestepping to avoid the blood from the Keeper's just-slit throat, and letting the man reel and then topple onto his pompous face on the Palace passage floor so Daunt could lean in and make certain of the demises of the two shadowhands with the same handy dagger.

Which he liked the feel and balance of, and had decided he'd keep. Right now, though, having made sure of his two recent assailants, he glanced up and down the hallway and determined that no one had seen or apparently heard this little encounter. Accordingly, he laid the dagger quietly down on the glossy hall floor and devoted himself to dragging dead men through the Keeper's doorway.

Where in the pleasant, lamplit chamber he could see a tablecloth within easy reach, on a table that also sported a decanter, a bowl of nuts, and a lurid painting still swathed in wrappings that had been partly opened.

Daunt glanced at the painted scene, and lifted an eyebrow. My, my. The Keeper was obviously a collector of rare taste.

Thankfully rare taste.

But aesthetic concerns could wait; right now, that tablecloth would serve to wipe the passage floor clean of blood, and then do the same to his new favourite dagger. Daunt performed those cleanups, then scooped up the nuts to munch on, quietly closed the door on the bodies of the Keeper and the two shadowhands, and set off down the passage in search of his second target: the Seneschal of Riverfleet Palace.

He was leaving the hardest to reach target, the Chamberlain, a great lazy bear of a man who rarely stirred from his heavily-guarded and document-crammed chambers, for last.

Though the hour was late and the seneschal might be abed, his office was the likeliest of his three targets to be called upon, given the violent events of the day just ended, to consult with the King or to carry out planning ordered by the King. Which meant he might not be in his rooms, or might be there but awake and dressed and working, almost certainly attended by clerks and pages to convey messages and bodyguards. A rather large muster for one little dagger.

Daunt glanced down at where his own pair of daggers rode hidden, sheathed on the insides of his high boots. All right, *three* little daggers.

But still...

"Halt! You, there! Halt, in the name of the King!"

The voice wasn't raised in a full shout, given what time it was and the exalted ranks of those whose bedchambers were in this part of the Palace, but it was sharp, and close, and was clearly directed at him.

"Who're you, and what are you doing here?"

"I'm the Seneschal's naughty painting procurer," Daunt replied calmly, "and I'm headed to him right now, to take his next order. If you *don't* mind."

"*What?* His *what?* Come here, where I can get a good look at you!"

The night had just become interesting.

And quite possibly fatal.

#

The three burly men in dark cloaks paced through the night with care, counting under their breaths, and came to a halt at a particular point along the great curve of the Palace walls.

Where the tallest of the trio reached out to stone after stone, running his gloved hands over them like a caressing lover—and suddenly there came a faint grating sound as that stone moved inward.

Opening into a dank diagonal passage with a faint smell of mildew. It was a tight fit; they edged along it in pitch darkness until they reached its unseen end and had to feel around until there came another movement of stone, and they could see night-gloom, and a courtyard between two wings of the Palace, where lamps glimmered through window-curtains.

In unspoken accord, the last of the three turned back, to close the outer end of the secret passage, while the second man opened his cloak to remove a sash from around his waist. That he held ready for when the last man reappeared. When he emerged to join them in the Palace courtyard, the tallest of the three started fondling stones again—and when he found the right one and the inside door of the passage started to swing shut, the man with the sash cast one end of it into the closing gap to be trapped, so the end he still held could be left dangling, as a marker.

And then, still in silence, they turned as one and strode boldly across the courtyard, in search of the door they'd been told about.

That was the nice thing about Ath Cliath. Sufficient gold could outbid any loyalty to the One-Eyed King—if such a thing even existed. They'd not found any evidence of it yet.

That was the danger of taxing so highly, and bringing so much wealth to one place, and luring those who wanted to grow rich. In the end, it didn't matter who sat on the throne; the true ruler was gold.

The three men advanced in calm, purposeful silence, for they did not serve their king for gold. Yet by his command, it was gold they had come here to seize.

Not so much to beggar the One-Eyed King, for three men couldn't carry a hundredth that much. More to rile him. For there were times when one king wants to unsettle another, and this was such a time.

They found the door, and it was unlocked, and they drew swords in careful silence, and stepped inside.

It was time to annoy a king.

#

"*What?* His *what?* Come here, where I can get a good look at you!" As he snapped this, the duty guard was already reaching for his weapon.

Daunt gave him a smile, and spread empty hands. "And who are *you*, and what are *you* doing here?"

"I'm the duty guard for this, the *private* wing of the Palace, tonight, and no one passes me except by prearrangement—no surprises, see?"

The guard's sword flashed as its point was raised, to dance under Daunt's nose. "And you're a surprise; *no one* is cleared to pass me tonight."

"I see. Dear, dear. I doubt the Seneschal is going to be pleased to learn, in the cold light of tomorrow when his time will be taken up with, ah, security precautions in light of the, ah, *unpleasantnesses* of today, that you prevented him from seeing me at the time he so carefully and specifically arranged with me. If passing you is forbidden, could you perhaps go and inform him that I'm here? While I await here?"

"Er, *no*. No, I can't be leaving you unattended in the private wing of the Palace at this time of night! You could do *anything!*"

"I often do. So that's wise thinking on your part. Could you perhaps be even wiser, and solve our mutual little problem by *not* leaving me unattended, but instead allowing me to accompany you to the Seneschal?"

"I—no. No, I don't think so."

"Do you know any other decisions aside from 'no'?"

"Uh, not right now, no."

"Oh, dear. The Seneschal is going to be *very* annoyed. I wonder what decision *he* will make? About you?"

"Why should he—"

"Help! Aid! *Helllp!*" That voice came from far back down the passage. And belonged to someone horrified, who had just swung open a door and seen something to horrify them.

A door that was probably the door of the office of the Keeper of the Vault.

"Come *quickly!*"

The duty guard shot Daunt a look, then snapped, "Come with me!"

And then set off at a trot in the direction of the horrified servant, who was now enthusiastic waving and calling.

Daunt hurried to catch up with the guard. Who gave him another glance, then devoted himself to hurrying.

Daunt hurried, too. Just enough to catch up with the man again, and hurriedly drive his new dagger into the man's throat, then spin him around against the passage wall, face first and with Daunt behind him, so that the dying man shielded Daunt from the worst of the blood.

"Little tasks," Daunt muttered to himself, springing away from the guard—who was busily sliding down the wall—and striding back the way he'd come.

Behind him, in the distance, the horrified servant went on being loudly horrified.

Which meant it was time to find that cross-corridor and depart the Palace, before the whole place was roused. Only one of his three targets taken, but then again, an exit now meant he might live to try again.

The question now was: would the Seneschal emerge in answer to the discovery of the slain Keeper of the Vaults? And if so, would he be surrounded by a ring of bodyguards?

A moment later, Daunt had both of those answers: yes, and yes.

Calmly he kept on walking towards them. He had to get to the cross-corridor, just *there*, before they did. Luckily, they weren't running yet. Just looking irritated, and talking amongst themselves.

Perhaps his luck would—

No.

"Ho! You there! What's the trouble?"

"Servant back there off his head about something," Daunt replied. "None of my affair."

"Oh?"

"I," Daunt replied with dignity, turning into the cross-corridor, "concern myself only with pleasing my clients."

"And who *are* you?"

"The King's long-lost brother. Risen from the dead by the grace of the White God."

"*What?*"

"Do any of you in this Palace know any other words besides 'what' and 'no'?" Daunt drawled that back over his shoulder as he found the side-passage he was seeking, turned down it—and started to sprint, as fast as he could.

He thought he heard one set of heavy-booted footfalls coming after him, no more. Good. There was still a chance he'd survive this, then.

A slim chance.

This door. Daunt wrenched it open, flung himself across the door-lined room beyond, and clawed open the end door, in the far corner—then hurled himself through it as lantern-light flooded the room behind him, coming from another just-opened door. The lantern was in the hands of a man he knew by sight and fell reputation: Mael the Sharp.

Who flung down the lantern—it exploded on the stone floor with a wild flash of flame and shattering glass—and raced after Daunt.

Slimmer chance.

Daunt burst through the door and out into another long, glossy-floored, empty Palace passage, long and straight and—and he hoped he had wind and speed enough to stay ahead of the King's head shadowhand.

Being as his life depended on it, just now.

He ran, faster than he'd ever run in his life before, whooping for breath and windmilling his arms and racing on, on, his shoulderblades a-crawl with the anticipation of feeling a hurled dagger sprouting between them at any moment…but he dared not lose any ground zigging or zagging to try to avoid a thrown blade, when he *had* to stay ahead of the deadliest slayer in Ath Cliath, if not the world.

His lungs were burning, his feet were starting to feel heavy, he was flagging, fading…

And just then, three burly men suddenly strode out of a cross-passage ahead, turned in his direction, and advanced. Forming a living wall across the passage…

Neven Daunt's heart sank, but he kept right on running, because it was all he could do.

They loomed up fast, this trio, faces unreadable and unfamiliar. They had the look of seasoned warriors, and he was sure they were armed under those cloaks, by the way the cloth hung over what had to be sword-scabbards, but they were making no move to draw blades, merely watching him calmly as he gasped and panted his way towards a hard collision with them.

At the last instant they parted to let him plunge between two of them, and he saw the third man pluck a dagger from somewhere under his cloak, and hurl it. Down the passage.

Daunt risked turning his head, though it might mean a crashing fall, because he *had* to see what that dagger had been thrown at.

And was in time to see it bounce just in front of the running feet of Mael the Sharp, and skitter on the polished floor, and go under those hastening boots.

Then the King's senior shadowhand was falling, crashing heavily to the floor, and sliding along it to a stop.

As the three burly men advanced on him steadily, still distant from him but apparently unimpressed by the man they'd felled.

Daunt wondered if they knew what danger they faced, but for him it meant the salvation of an escape from nigh-certain death.

He took it, thankfully and speedily.

The way this night had unfolded, he doubted he'd be handed another chance.

#

The patrol's lanterns bobbed to a stop right below. Brandr resisted the urge to peer over the roof-edge at them, because that would mean showing himself.

"Just *what* is so interesting, Julfr, about a dead gull? Is your larder at home empty?"

"What's interesting, Baltr, *if* you can leave off being insulting for a moment, is that its neck has been wrung. Which means it's dead because a human killed it. A human who likely tossed it down from up…*there*."

Brandr kept very still in the brief silence that followed.

"I can't see anyone."

"There probably isn't anyone, by now, but it seems to me that if we walk about six shopfronts farther on, and look back, we should be able to see the front slope of that roof."

"You're starved for entertainment, aren't you?"

"Romundr, some of us earn our pay, and some of us don't even know how to spell the word 'diligence.' Now, being as that's the way we have to walk anyway, why don't you all humour me, hmmm?"

"All right. Do we pick up the gull, as evidence? Because if so, *you* pick it up. *I* still stink

142

from the time you wanted all those dead rats collected."

"No, leave it for now. But let's go and take a look at that roof."

Oh, for the love of all the Tuatha De Danann...

Brandr clambered up the roof as quickly as he could while taking care not to slip or make a sound. He might even have succeeded had there not been a patch of loose slates that sent him sliding helplessly back down for just long enough, ere he dug his fingers frantically into now-exposed boards and pegs, to send two slates tumbling over the edge to shatter deafeningly on the street-cobbles below.

Oh, dung dung dung dung dung dung *DUNG*.

Julfr started rapping out orders as fast as his tongue could wag, and heavy-booted goldhelms started trotting obediently into position. Brandr abandoned all stealth in his haste to get up the roof and over its peak to where he could get a look at possible leaps to adjacent roofs before the building he was perched on got surrounded...

And that was when the smoke-gray night clouds parted, and the moon merrily bathed all of the rooftops as far as Brandr could see in pearly-white light.

"Curse you, Odin," the Flower of House Fylan hissed aloud, and hastily sank down low, draping himself over the roof-peak ridge.

He kept his eyes busy, though, measuring distances and deciding...

That roof. Underhanging the one he was on, which meant that all he had to do was race down this one, and leap, and he couldn't help but land well up on that one. Which was shallow-pitched, and of old, well-worn wooden shakes; if he sprang with daggers in both hands, he should be able to drive them in deep enough to serve as handholds.

Right. Do it. Now.

He rose, evoking an excited yell from a soldier below, drew daggers, and launched himself down the slates at a brisk run that of course in two paces was a helpless headlong rush.

Just before he ran out of roof he bent his knees and leaped, far and fast, daggers ready, and—

Crashed down hard, winding himself, bouncing once amid much moss-dust and hurtling wet-rotten soft splinters, and—

Down again, plummeting through the rotten roof and into waiting darkness beneath, an attic or some such full of things that wouldn't budge, and were very, very hard.

Brandr Fylan slammed into several too many of them, and the world went away in a whirling instant.

chapter 26

Baltr came pounding up to Julfr, panting from his exertion. "Surrounded, and he didn't manage to get to another roof or out the back door and away without us seeing. There're just the two doors—and the hole in the roof where he fell though. He's still inside."

"Good," Julfr snapped. "Any windows he could burst out of?"

"Seven, but only three are low enough that falling out of them wouldn't end in him being maimed; these two you here, and one around back. Flanking the doors, all of them."

"Good. Keep watch. Romundr? You lead Erlendr and the rest in pounding on the front door. If we can't rouse whoever lives here, we break it down. If we meet with resistance, Baltr, you break down the back door. Take everyone inside alive, for questioning, if at all possible."

"As you command!"

"Wait! Before you rush off again, do any of you know who lives here?"

Julfr saw Romundr's face change, and snapped, "Out with it! Tell me what you know!"

"Er, Gloa the Golden. I think."

"The, ah, *infamous* lady of many pleasures?"

Romundr nodded unhappily, his unlovely face going a deep red in the moonlight.

"And how is it that an honest, upstanding soldier of the King knows where Gloa the Golden rests her, ah, *head* of nights?"

"Patrolled these streets since King Sitric took the throne, and saw who came and went. Nothing more!"

"Glad to hear it, *loyal* Romundr. Right then, awaken the lady—*if* she's home. If not, rouse her servants. And if she has none, she's going to find her front door chopped to the threshold when she does get home. Worry not about making noise; roused neighbours may well be annoyed enough to have tongues that'll wag."

The hole in the roof could be seen plainly enough in this silver sea of moonlight from five fronts westwards along the street, and they'd all heard the crash and seen the splintered remnants of a few rotten shakes tumble to the cobbles. The fugitive fleeing from them along the rooftops had fallen through the roof of this rather shabby old house, tall and narrow and right beside the house where he'd been hiding on the roof when they'd come along on patrol. The shutters were drawn and there were no lights showing on either house.

That changed when Romundr and his six fellow goldhelms started kicking and beating their fists and thumping the butts of their spears on Gloa the Golden's old but stout front door; it boomed loudly under their assault, and lamps were kindled—or unhooded, and shutters thrown open—up and down the street as they shouted. "Open up! In the name of the King, open!"

Julfr was standing well back, watching from across the street, from a position where he could see the lone soldier stationed at the next corner, to relay any signals to and from Baltr's men at the back of the house. With grim amusement he watched lights glimmering into life up and down the street.

Though not in the house of Gloa the Golden. That remained dark and silent.

After a long, loud time of battering at her front door, Romundr trudged rather unhappily across the street to report. "No sound from within; no reaction. Belike no one's home."

"Except whoever fled from us, and fell through the roof," Julfr reminded him crisply. "He won't be evading the King's justice *that* easily. Break the door down."

The door was stout, and the doorframe massive; axes were required, and time, and a lot of noise. Ere the door fell with a crash, to reveal only darkness.

As the lanterns were unhooded, Romundr drew his sword and looked a question back at

Julfr, who commanded briskly, "*In.*"

Swords flashed out, and Romundr led the heavy-booted rush.

Silence fell.

And stretched.

Finally the sentinel at the corner waved his lantern in a query; Julfr stepped out into the full moonlight to signal 'Maintain Position,' and watched the lantern bob in an affirmative.

A moment later, Romundr was trudging out of the house and across the street to report: "Furnished, and with food in the larder and half-eaten on a platter. The hearthfire's hot but banked, and two lamps have just been extinguished. Someone's living there, and is likely hiding from us up in the attic—because the door at the top of its stairs is closed to us. There's a low cellar, and we've searched it. No one hiding anywhere but aloft—and no hidden passages or the like."

"Right. Go and open the back door, and let Baltr and those with him in. Then axes to the fore, with spearmen ready to defend the axe-wielders when the door gives way, and let's get up into that attic. With luck we can have this miscreant out and back at the Palace for questioning before the lady gets home."

"It will be done," Romundr promised, and it was.

And so Julfr had his own sword drawn, and was flanked by lantern-bearers, when the attic door gave way and his patrol surged up into the attic.

To find themselves facing a man sitting behind a mended-leg table on a backless chair—a table upon which sprawled a face-down, senseless man.

The seated man did not look pleased to see them. "Is this how soldiers of Ath Cliath treat law-abiding citizens—and their doors?" he asked.

"*I'll* ask the questions here," Julfr barked. "Who are you, and who is that on the table—and what have you done to the woman known as Gloa the Golden?"

"Hallvardr Thorolfsson is my name, carter by trade, and I've done nothing to Gloa but buy this house from her. She's moving up in the world; bought herself a grander house, in better repair, and was good enough to sell me this one. Which was adequate enough, until this dolt—a stranger to me—fell through my roof, and *you* dolts broke down my doors! Which you'll be replacing, *right now*, with your abject apologies!"

"I think not," Julfr snapped. "You're coming with us!"

"*I think not*," the carter snarled right back at him. "Get out of my house, all of you! I'll be complaining to the King in the morning, and—"

"Oh, enough of this!" Julfr barked. "*Take him!*"

Hallvardr Thorolfsson glared at him with eyes that burned with sudden fire, and drew something in the air before him with a forefinger, an intricate rune that blazed like fire in midair for a long and coiling moment as it hung, growing larger and brighter, as Hallvardr spoke words that thundered and echoed, beating on Julfr's ears like strokes of a forge hammer striking red-hot work on an anvil.

"He's a galdr!" Romundr shouted fearfully—in the instant before he and every other soldier in the attic and down the stairs erupted in madness.

Gibbering, shrieking, and roaring in a wild cacophony of hacking at everyone and everything in reach, they fell upon each other, and Julfr might have died among their wild hewing and slashing had he not hurled himself headlong down the stair, flattening Baltr and two others in the process, and fleeing wildly out into the night.

As it was, he reached the cobbles dazed and bleeding, having crashed into three or four score sharp, unyielding, and very hard things on his unremembered way. All he could recall was the carter Thorolfsson extinguishing every lantern within reach, behind him, and the raw dying screams of his men as they sliced and chopped *and tore* each other apart.

He heard footfalls approaching behind him—someone who'd come out of the house, for sure—and in a fresh wild surge of rising terror clawed his way to his feet and fled down the street, howling.

And in pursuit, close behind him, someone pounded the cobbles who was barking and baying like a vargr on the hunt.

Up ahead, in the distance, Julfr saw lanterns bobbing, and lanternlight reflecting off spear heads and gilded helms. He made for them, weeping, and when their first shouts of challenge reached him, he barked and bayed and shrieked in grateful response—and scarcely noticed when they clubbed him to the ground, and the world went away in a rain of blows and fearful curses.

#

It had rained just before dawn, leaving the city wet and glistening, the cobbles slick underfoot. Neven Daunt bought smoked and salted herring from a lad just wheeling his cart out into the street for a day's sales, and gobbled it hastily on the way to the disused warehouse where a certain wall awaited.

Nevertheless…

"You're late," the voice from the far side of the wall said coldly.

"*Almost* the late Neven Daunt," Daunt replied, "but no. On time, and alive—while the Keeper of Vaults is not."

"As to that, anyone can *claim* to have slain targets. If you expect to get paid, you should tender severed ears, as proof."

"That wasn't our deal," Daunt said calmly.

"You're not in a strong bargaining position, Neven Daunt," said the voice through the wall.

"Neither are you, Stigr Helgason," Daunt replied, and a chill silence fell.

"It is unfortunate for you that you know that name," the voice said at last.

"And it's unfortunate for you that the One-Eyed King already knows who the traitors in his Palace are," Daunt returned. "We both know I'm expendable, but *you're* the one he's watching. You need me to be your killing hand. I want gold, but frankly there are far safer ways to get it. I undertook your 'little task' because I wanted to see some of Sitric's most pompous courtiers dead, and him given something to mend rather than continued leisure to think up mischief to make things worse for his citizens. So can we dispense with the menacing threats and get back to work? Sitric could tire of watching to see who you'll betray to him, and order Mael to execute you—painfully, I'm sure—at any time. So you might want to devote yourself to thinking of how you'll escape Ath Cliath alive, and get back to working with me to accomplish your desired executions."

"There…is a certain accuracy in what you say."

"Indeed. Restore your dignity any way you like, but pay me for the Keeper. I'll try for the others again tonight."

"And why did you not eliminate them last night?"

"The private wing of the Palace was rather populated at the time; there were at least three other intruders, besides me."

"Oh? And they were?"

"Outlanders. Soldiers, by their bearing—and far better in training and battle-calm than Sitric's goldhelms. And before you ask, I've no idea how they got in, what they were after, or how

146

their intrusion fared."

"How do you know they weren't there by invitation?"

"Their habit of hurling daggers at Mael the Sharp, for one thing. And advancing to calmly do battle with him, for another."

"Blood of Odin! Who won?"

"I saw not. I was busy making my escape—before the shrieks of a particularly persistent servant succeeded in bringing every goldhelm on duty running right into my lap."

"Very well. You shall be paid for the Keeper. And tonight, you shall end the lives of the Seneschal of Riverfleet Palace, and the Chamberlain of Ath Cliath. I don't need to see any ears."

"I'll do my best."

"Best or worst, I care not, so long as they're dead. And if Mael the Sharp is still alive, and comes within your reach, I'll pay as much for the ending of his life as for all three courtiers put together."

"I'll bear that in mind. He will take thrice the killing, I'm thinking."

"Our thoughts run together in this regard. Now I must go. We'll talk again tomorrow morning."

#

"I've boarded up the windows as best I could," Mist told Teaghan. "The one Oswin burst in through more securely, because it's the only one a sane man would try to reach. That shadowhand must have been part vulture, or part spider, to get in that high a window."

Her aunt thanked her with a smile, her face pale and drawn with pain. Oswin offered her the same decanter she'd given him to drink from, earlier, but she shook her head with a weak chuckle.

"I'm not sure priests should be trying to get vulnerable women drunk," she reproved him.

Oswin shrugged. "I've done worse. As well you both know."

"That," Mist said firmly, "was not worse, but better. You saved our lives. And if you're wise enough to stay shut up in here with us, you can go on saving them. I've a feeling the next few days in Ath Cliath are going to be...interesting."

#

"Last night was rather more *interesting* than I like things to be in the Palace," Mael said grimly. "Violence and tumult are supposed to happen out there, in the streets, at times and places of our choosing. Not brought here to our feet and laps, by the foes of the King."

"Did you recognize any of these intruders?" Stigr asked, leaning forward eagerly.

The head of the shadowhands frowned and shook his head. "The one I was chasing had a gait that made me think I've seen him in Ath Cliath before, but I could put no face nor name to him, no. The three who took me down I *know* I've never seen before. Yet I'm sure they're veteran warriors. Not in our service, so in whose? And why were they here? *How* did they get into the very heart of Riverfleet Palace?"

"Are the secret ways in becoming too well known? To courtiers or outsiders who can be coerced or bribed to share them?"

Mael nodded. "Likely. But although the how is our larger concern in days to come, the why is what I'd most dearly like to know. Who is sending warriors—*good* warriors, senior men of the sort not easily thrown away, because not at all easily replaced—into our midst? To do what, exactly?"

"There's no trace of them in the Palace now?"

Mael shook his head. "I'm having every last cloak-closet and back alcove searched, and the roofs and cellars too, but so far—"

There came a tentative but insistent knocking on the door. Mael and Stigr exchanged glances, and those looks told Stigr enough to rise in smooth haste and unlock the door.

A breathless young servant almost fell into the room, nodded thanks to Stigr, looked to Mael, and blurted out, "Three thousand gold rods are missing from the vaults!"

"The Underkeeper is certain, I suppose?"

The servant nodded emphatically.

"And the King has been informed?"

"The Underkeeper is doing so right now."

"Good. Go and find yourself something to drink."

"I—sorry?"

"*Leave us.*"

The servant went pale, nodded so violently it seemed his head might fall from his shoulders, and backed out, whimpering in fear.

Stigr closed the door on him and relocked it. "Well, there's your answer to why those three were here. Strong men; they could carry a thousand rods each."

Mael nodded, frowning. "It's so little as to not even be an annoyance, but as a message—a warning; see what we can do to you?—it's effective enough. It's no mere theft."

"I agree. They were showing us what they can do. Whenever they please."

"The King will not be pleased with us. Our job is to know about covert threats, and block them, before they can reach into the Palace. As they please."

"So cowering would be a mistake. We should be out there hunting these three thieves, so when the King sends for us, we'll be *doing* something."

"If I had the faintest idea where to start hunting," Mael said coldly, "do you think I'd be sitting here talking to you?"

#

"I am the Seneschal of Riverfleet Palace," the handsome man said coldly, across a desk littered not just with papers, but with a large and ornate goblet, and a domed gold platter from which steam was lazily escaping, "and am not accustomed to receiving reports from city street patrols. Still less from soldiers who look like they spent the night brawling in a tavern. Make this *good.*"

"*Yes*, sir," Julfr said unhappily, forcing himself not to stammer in haste to get the words out. "We are the last two survivors of the patrol under my command. The others slew each other in the grip of madness—magically-induced madness. We managed to flee, though it affected us, too. We believe it represents a threat to the city you should know about, sir."

"And how do you know this madness was magically induced?"

"We saw and heard the rune cast, sir. By a carter whose home we entered, because he was harbouring a man who was hiding on rooftops by night. When we confronted him—he'd shut himself up in his attic, sir—he used a rune spell on us. He's a powerful galdr, sir."

The Seneschal frowned. "A carter, you say?"

"Yes. One Hallvardr Thorolfsson by name."

The frown deepened. "He's won several Palace contracts, to shift furniture and provisions as we rebuilt and expanded the Palace. Amiable, rugged, able to lift and heft heavy

148

pieces...and you tell me he's secretly a *galdr?*"

Julfr spread his hands. "I...saw what I saw, sir." Baltr nodded confirmation, but said not a word.

The Seneschal looked from one soldier to the other, then rose, drained the goblet in one long pull that left him gasping and holding into the desk for support, and said curtly, "Come with me. Tell your tale to the King. And if you're lying, Odin save you."

#

Brandr looked around, groggily. Broad stone pillars marched away in all directions, through prevailing gloom. He could smell mildew, and hear water dripping in the distance, slowly but steadily.

"I know this place," he said slowly, fixing his eyes on the scowling man bending over him, "but who are you?"

"A man who had to throw his comfortable life in Ath Cliath away last night because *you* fell through his roof," came the growled reply, "and if you'd done your moonlit walk twelve nights from now, I'd've had the roof repaired, and none of this would have happened."

"So did you bring me here to kill me?"

"*What?* Who do you think I am?"

"A man who had to throw his life away because of something I did, who is enraged at having to do so," Brandr replied, trying to sit up—and failing.

The man's glower became a lopsided smile, and a shrug. "Fair enough, lad. No, we're here because I need to hide us both. And need advice, too."

"Advice? Whose advice?"

"Ah," said a lilting feminine voice Brandr Fylan knew, from somewhere behind him, "I rather fear it would be *my* advice. And I shall be the means of hiding, too. I hope your magic is stronger than Sitric's, Hallvardr, or it'll mean all our deaths, and soon. Or do you just want me to get you both out of the city faster than the King can hunt you down? Are clan Uterni ready to defeat an army from Ath Cliath?"

Brandr groaned. "Can someone just drop me through another roof or two? Wouldn't that be easier?"

The Lady Lecora O'Hart's burst of laughter was a high, merry, somehow silvery peal.

chapter 27

Julfr and Baltr went to their knees in bruising unison. "Hear us, O King."

The man on the throne stood up, tall and terrible. Like a living temple spire he loomed, in a sweeping dark robe with upswept horned shoulders, wearing a high-spired crown that added the height of two heads to his real one. Eyepatch a-gleam with jewels, face dark and displeased.

He sighed and waved dismissal to the Seneschal, who bowed and withdrew hastily, seeming relieved to be departing.

"Dispense with formality," commanded the One-Eyed King. "Just tell me what the Seneschal thinks I need to hear from you."

The two men fought to stop cowering and start speaking. Sitric set his jaw and gave them time. He was already in a rage—his Palace invaded by night, gold stolen from his treasury, his Keeper of the Vaults slain and several shadowhands dead, one of them in these halls, three intruders who if Mael could be believed were warriors serving some other king, and his next most senior shadowhand turned traitor, seduced by a rival king whose identity he did not yet know, so he must needs leave the traitor alive for now to try to find out who that king was—it would have given him great satisfaction to take these two terrified idiots by their throats and break their necks.

Yet one did not retain a throne by giving in to whims and rages.

And behold, the one he'd thought would find tongue first was speaking.

He listened. And learned.

By the ravens, what *else* would Odin send, to make this handful of dark days complete?

So it seemed there was a galdr to rival Sitric Cuaran dwelling in Ath Cliath. And likely had been since he'd conquered the city. All that time, keeping rune mastery hidden.

And who was to say there weren't more?

He'd built a city of wealth, and wealth lured power and those who wanted it.

And some would come who already had power, seeking patrons. And victims. And cover, amid all the dealings, for their own darker deeds.

Three such, he knew all too well. Three who'd heeded not the warning he'd sent them, by slaying the fourth.

Lecora, who'd he'd once been so fond of. Cairbre Dathaill. And Torloch Dargan.

Sitric sighed.

"*Enough*," he told the two kneeling soldiers. "Up, and begone. Your city thanks you, and your King thanks you. Return to your quarters, on full pay, until you receive new assignments."

He ignored their clumsy thanks and leavetakings, except to notice when the silence of solitude had returned to the room.

Whereupon he went to a bell-pull, that would bring a servant running whom he could send to summon Volundr the Voice to him. It was time to command the attendance of that self-styled 'lady' and her friends the two 'lords' into his presence, for some heavier warnings. Or outright punishments, if they gave him any defiance.

Time to summon them *again*.

They were behind some of these setbacks and insolences. He was cure of it.

His memories of Lecora had made him too lenient on them. That must end. Now.

\#

"Nice of you to be so prompt," Falki," Grimkell the Throat rasped.

"I was followed," Falki snapped. "Do you *want* to be arrested for treason?"

"Not this month," the skald replied calmly. "Being as I haven't managed much of it yet. So, have any of you hatched any *useful* ideas of how to harm or hamper the King since we last met?"

"I've released my rats into the Palace," Falki said proudly.

The others around the table all gaped at him.

"You *what?*"

"Odin smite me dead!"

"Don't *say* that, fool! He *does* listen, you know!"

"Longbeak, I thought you were just flapping your jaws about the rats! You *meant* it?"

"Tell us more," Grimkell growled, cutting through the expressions of disbelief. "*How* did you get your rats into the Palace? Can we use this means to get some *saner* royal peril in there?"

"I got myself hired to deliver timbers for refurbishing the vaulting of the underpantry. It wasn't hard; I just reduced my price to near no profit, but didn't have to take a loss, and they pounced on it. Six glaring soldiers climbed all over my first wagonload, half-heartedly peered at the second, and left me alone after that. The rats were in a cage in the fourth load; by then, even the watchguards by the loading doors had wandered off in boredom. They're too complacent by half in the Palace, you know; too convinced the One-Eyed King is so deeply feared by all to think anyone would dare do anything. So they've stopped being half as vigilant as they need to be."

"So you let how many rats out into the Palace?"

"Two score and six."

The skald shook his head. "A mighty blow struck, Falki. So, I ask again: have any of you come up with anything *useful* to harm Sitric or his rule since we last met?"

"Poisoned wine," Eylir muttered. "It seems an evil and underhanded means, but..."

"But our King is as evil and underhanded as they come," Forkundr Redbeard put in.

"Is he, though?" Grimkell growled. "Feared and with good reason, yes, but he's far more forebearing and less a brute than many kings, if we can believe the sagas spun by skalds in the past. Here's the thing about poisoned wine: it may slay many, and sicken many more, but they're highly likely to be courtiers, and to succumb before any drop of tainted wine reaches the King."

"Besides, poisoned wine can be traced," Borekr told his drinking-jack. "And I know there are poisons that remain deadly when mixed with wine, but I don't know how to make or get them. Nor do I know which ones don't betray their presence by taste, or murkiness, or changing the hue of the wine, or some such. Nor yet how to afford them, or find a buyer within reach who won't betray us to Sitric One-Eye for all the gold Sitric can lavish on him, compared to the paltry skatt we can muster."

"Well, now," said the Redbeard, "if you're going to be practical, we'll *never* get anything done."

"Har har," Borekr replied. "A thought strikes me: Falki, are all of those timbers delivered?"

"They are. Why?"

"Well, get yourself hired to deliver something else to the Palace. Right inside, that is. After all, they trust you a little now, don't they?"

"Oh, I'd not go that far, but say on. What am I going to be delivering after the first few wagonloads of just what they expect?"

"Desperate slaves, handed weapons and told they'll win their freedom by slaying anyone they meet. Three score of them, or more, ought to cut quite a few gaps through the ranks of the goldhelms."

"Sitric will just hire more. He certainly has the gold to do it."

"Yes, but what price loyalty? Men he merely buys may be bought by someone else a day later, and turn on him; he needs soldiers he can *trust*. And where's he going to get them?"

"Us," Eylir said suddenly. "When he's fought off slaves marauding in his Palace, and poisoned wine in the drinking-jacks of his goldhelms when they're out drinking in the city has thinned their ranks still more, here we'll turn up at the Palace gates, vowing our loyalty to our King in his time of need."

Silence fell.

Then Grimkell shook his head. "An idea to make us all think, to be sure, but you forget that Sitric Cuaran is a galdr. He can use his magic to make certain of our loyalty—and our deaths, very swiftly, when he finds out what we're truly thinking. No, we dare not come to his attention, if we would go on living."

"You think we haven't already? *I* think we're still alive only because he has far bigger foes to watch and be ready to fight."

"Well, *that's* a cheering thought, Fork. Pass the wine, you bold morale-booster."

"What if we set the Palace afire?" Falki asked suddenly.

"What, and cook your rats? Seriously, man, how does that help? Besides, it's so much stone and so little timber; there'd be no rush to get away, and so run right onto our waiting swords, if that was your plan."

"What if we doused haybales in the river, then set them with a few dry ones, that we torch? Smoke the courtiers out—and the King with them—to run onto waiting spears, held by goldhelms, who will be us wearing the helms and armour of a patrol we ambush, kill, and take the gear of?"

"Oh, don't be such a ridicu...wait, now. That just might work. *After* the slaves running amok and all."

"Regardless of how we get at the King, I like the idea of surrounding, trapping, and slaying entire patrols. But we have to get them all, every last man, and it must be quick and quiet. So they haven't time to warn or summon another patrol, and so there're no witnesses."

"Again," Grimkell rasped, "I remind you that Sitric is a powerful galdr. He may be able to find out what happened to a patrol that just vanishes."

"So we get or goad others into doing the surrounding and slaying, not us."

"Wise of you—so how? A *contest?*"

"A bribe? This *is* Ath Cliath!"

"Get a tavern-full drunk?"

"Reeling drunks may not be able to *entertain* a patrol, to say nothing of butchering them."

"You're being *practical* again."

"*I* know! We'll invite Sitric to one of these little traitors' gatherings, and *talk* him to death!"

Grimkell the Throat closed his eyes, shook his head, then reached for all the wine that was left, and drained it all.

An impressed silence fell.

Until he belched and then staggered to his feet and growled, "None of this is getting rid of our unwanted King. Go, all of you, and let's *really* start thinking. Unless you want to wait for old age to take Sitric Cuaran off the Riverfleet Throne. Because the way we're going, passing years will likely claim most of us before they take him anywhere."

#

"Ah, Stigr, I have a task for you." Sitric's voice was almost a purr. "It's time to settle scores. A *lot* of scores. And high time to reduce the number of *traitors* in Ath Cliath. Accordingly, you will go to the home of the woman Mor, and exterminate everyone you find within its walls. Take however many agents you feel you need—but lead them personally. If you do not find Mor, Agata, and Embla there, hunt them until they are dead, wherever they may be within the city. Then report back to me without delay."

Stigr nodded, meeting the royal gaze steadily for a long moment. "This shall be done," he said calmly, and withdrew.

The One-Eyed King smiled at the door that had closed behind Stigr. "And now you certainly know I'm aware of your treason, Stigr Helgason, if you did not before. Yet it is too late for you to run. You will die in the house of Mor and I'll be rid of you, but it is just possible that you may do me some service by taking down Mor or some of her women. And if you do somehow survive, I have other tasks just as perilous."

There came a tentative rap upon the door.

"Enter," Sitric ordered, and the door swung wide to reveal Volundr the Voice.

"You sent for me, O Dread King?"

"I did indeed," Sitric reply, turning the sigh he felt like making into a sour smile. "I have a task for you that will seem familiar..."

#

"Well?" Mael asked.

It was one of the junior shadowhands, a dour woman by the name of Alvilda. "I bring word from Fjalarr, in Alba. It seems King Constantine sent three of his most trusted warriors here, a month back. They came to our city one by one, as traders, and have just sent a report back that Fjalarr's spy claims was thus: 'First success. Gained entrance to the Palace.'"

Mael nodded. "This is good to know. Go to Fjalarr yourself to impress on him that we need to know everything that spy learns of these three, as swiftly as possible. Half a day, or less, matters; he is to use all haste."

Alvilda nodded and went out, hiding a smile of satisfaction.

Mael nodded. She'd earned that much, and more. So, from Constantine of Alba. Who'd also communicated with Stigr...

But where *were* these three, now? They seemed to have vanished from the city without trace. And thanks to the debacle at the slave market, the King wouldn't let him use all the shadowhands save Stigr to hunt Constantine's three wolves down; they were needed for too many other urgent duties.

Bah. Pounce hard on one problem, make sure it was no longer a problem and would not be again for a long time, if ever, then turn to the next one. This trying to dance with a dozen problems was foolheadness.

Sometimes, having to obey a king was a royal nuisance.

"Ha ha," he said aloud, feeling no mirth at all.

#

None of the three miscreant merchants were at their homes, curse them. He might have known. Typical of his luck, typical.

And typical of them, the utter, traitor *bastards*.

He desperately wanted a rest, to be soaking his feet in warm scented water and pouring good wine down his throat, but the King's orders had been quite specific: the summons must be delivered in person, and without delay, just as soon as Volundr could find Lecora O'Hart, Cairbre Dathaill, and Torloch Dargan. Even if it took him half the night or more.

Or more, Odin take them all.

He'd trudged from one end of the city after all, and was now being openly sneered at by doorwardens at the clubs he sought the three in, thanks to his exhausted bedragglement.

He stumbled out of Valgerd's Valiant Valkyrie, lurching right past its splendid full-height gilded entry mirror without pause, despite the fine carved wooden warrior-maidens flanking it. He might otherwise have stopped to admire his reflection, contemplating the full sartorial magnificence of Volundr the Voice between two fawning handmaidens of Valhalla, but right now, he was just too weary, sweat-soaked, and trudging to care. Or to have the slightest interest in seeing the wreck of his dignity.

Trailing a string of curses, he set off down the street in search of places a high and mighty merchant might have gone.

In Ath Cliath, there were a dire-dancing-draugar *lot* of such places.

#

"Ignore it," Teagan said wearily, "and perhaps—just perhaps—it'll go away." It was a forlorn hope, and they all knew it.

The insistent rapping on the doors of Teagan's house, front and back, had been going on for some time, increasing in insistent speed and apparent anger, and was now at the boomingly-shaking-the-doorframes stage.

And as they all exchanged grim glances, they heard the first axe land, and wood splinter beneath its blade.

"The doors won't hold under *that*," Oswin said unnecessarily, and Teagan, yellow-white under her bandages, nodded grimly.

"We'll have to answer," she said reluctantly. And looked at Mist. "*You'll* have to answer. From the front bedchamber window; that's high enough that no one can reach it. We'll have to hope they have no bows ready. Warn whoever it is that this is a house of sickness, and that's why we haven't been answering."

"And if they insist on entry?"

"Tell them we have the plague. Do *not* tell them Oswin Silverlock is under this roof. We're two sick women."

So Mist went and did that, but when she thrust open the squealing shutters, she beheld five royal soldiers in full armor, and commanding them a man in nondescript smoky-gray leathers who almost had to be a shadowhand. When she told him, "This is a house of sickness," he sneered.

"Is it now? Dear, dear."

"Who are you, to mock two sick women?"

"We are the firm reaching hand of the King, who is determined to gather all traitors and enemies to face his justice. That includes *you*, Mist Damhain. And Oswin Silverlock, who we know is in there with you."

"My, but you seem to know a lot of things," Mist said wearily.

"The eyes of the King," the shadowhand quoted the city saying merrily, "are *everywhere*."

And he waved to the soldiers who had axes.

There were three of them, and in unspoken accord they fell into a rhythm of landing chopping blows on Teagan's front door, nigh its hinges.

By the way it gave under that assault, Mist knew it wouldn't last long.

So she closed the shutters and went back and told Teagan so.

"Go and get all of my perfumes, to hurl into their eyes," her aunt said grimly. "And the pantry table, to wedge across the forehall and buy us some time. Priest, gather all the kitchen knives and cleavers. And the slops bucket; we'll fill it with the doorstop-stones and rig it on a chain."

Oswin shook his head gloomily, but went for the knives. Teagan did not have to say "Doomed last stand" for them to all know that's what this was.

They'd managed to wedge two tables and the bucket on its chain, and be up on the first landing, before the front door finally yielded, falling in with a mighty crash.

And the soldiers charged in with enthusiastic yells.

Mist popped up from behind the table to dash perfume into the eyes of two of them ere they learned prudence and retreated; one was foolish enough to hurl his axe at her, so she retreated from the table with their defensive arsenal bolstered by one axe.

The shadowhand ordered the youngest and most agile soldier over the barricade of tables—so he was the first to die, his face crushed by the swinging bucket in mid-scramble.

As he fell down on top of two of his cursing fellows, the shadowhand purred, "Ah, now, you're making this almost *interesting*."

And Mist found herself shivering.

ChAPTER 28

It took the soldiers longer to destroy Teaghan's barricade of tables than anyone expected, because the second one, balanced on edge atop the first, thundered straight down when they reduced the first to kindling, wedging itself across the bottom of the stairs amid the wreckage of the hewn-apart table so thoroughly that the soldiers ran out of curses—and then out of wind entirely, as they hacked and chopped.

Oswin almost got them with the bucket a time or two, and when one goldhelm was foolish enough to try to catch hold of it and ride it over the barricade on its backswing, Mist sprang up from behind the surviving table and had Teagan's longest kitchen knife into his throat before he even had time to wave his own blade.

So that left but three soldiers for the shadowhand to command, with all their smiles and clever comments quite gone.

As they destroyed the table she was sheltering behind, Mist got in some practise at bobbing up to hurl this small, not-much-use-in-a-fray kitchen knife, and then that one. Most merely annoyed the goldhelms as they bounced off helms or hastily-raised forearms, but they forced the soldiers to keep their helms on, so they sweated all the more, and glared at her through their matted hair.

And when at last the table was nigh gone, and Mist spun around and fled up the stairs headlong, the boldest surviving soldier stumbled after her—but failed to notice she was scampering only up the left-most edge of the steps. The rest of the steps, under his boots, were carpeted with all manner of kitchen implements, from forks to sharpening steels to ladles.

He managed only three steps before he fell on his face on the hard stairs, with some very hard and sharp things beneath him, and Mist whirled and drove the knife still in her hand into the side of his neck, half-shearing off an ear. His clumsy, bleeding retreat down the stairs, accompanied by shouts of pain, drove his fellows back down to the bottom with him, almost pinning the shadowhand to the doorframe behind.

Whereupon the invading King's forces all cursed each other with feeling. When they ran out of harsh words, they discovered the stairs before them were now quite deserted.

The shadowhand then had some difficulty in persuading the soldiers to advance up to the next floor, but a combination of vicious threats and promises of reward accomplished it in the end, though the advance was wary, with swords and axes out and ready.

On the landing, the soldiers discovered the hard way that a floor-coating of fresh honey makes boots slick and slipping and falling not just easy, but frequent and painful. On the second flight, they were running out of curses again, though they managed to avoid being killed by the redeployed bucket, which succeeded only in bruising armoured arms and shoulders.

There was a curtain across the head of the stairs where the flight reached the floor above, but the foremost soldier sneered at that, and thrust deep and repeatedly into it in blind search of any defender who might be behind it.

His flashing steel met with nothing but curtain and air beyond. Twice, thrice, and then a fourth and fifth time, as he worked his way across the stair-head in rising, snarling fury.

His last thrust still met with nothing, but evoked a brief feminine shriek, so he charged that way, blundering into and through the curtain in time to see a bandaged Teaghan flee around a corner. He charged after her, hacking at the air in her wake—to find no sign of her, but an open door straight ahead where the passage turned.

He had just time to realize it opened into a closet or some other small confined space with a wall close ahead when someone slammed into him from behind, running hard. He was shoved into the space and falling before he could even start to twist around or slow down.

Falling because the closet lacked a floor, and was in fact Teaghan's kitchen refuse disposal: a shaft dropping down into darkness and–*plosh*–very cold river water.

He came up gasping, heard the man who'd pushed him in stammering out prayers for him from above–and then something hard and smelling of fried onions hit him very hard on the side of the head, and the world went away forever, lost above him as he sank senseless under the cold, cold water...

Back at the top of that shaft, the second soldier had seen Oswin Silverlock burst out of hiding to shove the first soldier. That goldhelm now came boiling up the last few steps to try to sword the priest from behind. But as he burst through the swinging halves of the curtain, Mist pounced on him, wrapping a generous fold of curtain around his head and beating at that round knob of cloth with a fireplace poker.

Roaring in muffled pain, the soldier tried to turn on his heels and hack blindly at her with sword and axe, and she hung back, mindful of her peril–and, a moment later, even more mindful of the last soldier and the axe he'd just thrown at her head from the stairs below, as it slammed off a wall right beside her head, and almost took off her nose in its ricocheting tumble.

Oswin spun around on the lip of the closet, tugged on the curtains to haul the soldier in a helpless stumble past him, then slammed the goldhelm against the nearest wall, sending the man's sword clattering. The goldhelm hacked at him with his remaining axe as the curtains came off his head, but Oswin kicked him in the stomach, sending him helplessly backwards–and down the floorless closet shaft, to join his fellow in the water below.

Where Teagan applied her kitchen skillet to his head, and let the water do the rest.

Just as Oswin's luck ran out. The last soldier came up the stair in time enough to run him through from behind, and as he shrieked in startled agony, the shadowhand charged past soldier and dying priest to get at Mist. Who retreated in the face of his sneering grin and flourished pair of wicked-sharp daggers. With catlike, crouching tread and great care, he advanced, weaving a deadly pattern of sharp blades in the air to wall her in, backing her into a corner, where he thrust low, then high, then past her desperately-swung but slow and heavy poker to slice her high on one arm.

She was wise enough not to clutch at her wound in pain, but to keep both hands on the poker to parry his next thrust, an up-from-the-knees gutting attack that almost found the lower edge of her chin. Mist twisted back and away, knowing he was advancing like a striking snake to press his advantage and end her life painfully there and then, and also knowing there was precious little she could do about it, and–

The shadowhand grunted in startled pain and fell forward heavily onto all fours, punched hard in the backs of both knees.

Mist saw who'd felled him sagging to the floor dying behind him: Oswin, grinning at her through the blood spewing from his mouth. Even as she watched, the light in his eyes went out and he pitched to the floor staring at nothing, revealing the soldier behind him whose bloody blade the priest had dragged himself off to strike the shadowhand from behind.

Mist stomped hard on both of the royal agent's hands, jumping up and down and *hearing* fingers break under her weight. Then she kicked away his daggers, one of them skittering somewhere beyond the fray, and the other back into her reach.

She bent and swept it up in a vicious thrust that almost took the shadowhand's throat out but in the end sliced its way up the side of his head as he turned and hurled himself away–so she settled for flinging the poker in her other hand into the face of the soldier who'd slain Oswin.

Sending him reeling back into the clutches of Teagan, who brained him with her skillet, then dropped it on his foot and, as he howled and hopped, wrapped an arm around his neck from behind, bent him over backwards, and cut his throat as she swung him around and flung him down the water-shaft.

By then the shadowhand was gone from between them, scuttling on all fours like a spider to get clear and then racing back down the stairs.

Mist launched herself after him. If he reached the Palace, to report...

As she hurtled past, she caught a brief glimpse of Teagan throwing something past her with one hand, reaching for Oswin with the other, and bursting into tears, and then she was down a flight and seeing the beautiful slim dagger her aunt had hurled, quivering in the stair-rail awaiting her.

She plucked it free and took it with her, not slowing a whit, and slammed down the stairs with a dagger in either hand, just as the shadowhand had been armed, earlier.

She was no match for him, and this would probably mean her death, so she was trembling with fear, but...but it was beyond time to stand up and be the Mist Damhain she had planned to be when she'd agreed to come to Ath Cliath in the first place.

This city hardened you, it did, and you either took the blows of the smith's forge-hammer and the hissing pain of tempering, or you broke and died and were forgotten like so many before you. Mist burst out of her aunt's house with the shadowhand twenty paces or so ahead and running like a gale in a hurry, and fancied she heard a faint splash behind her that was probably Oswin Silverlock following all the dead soldiers to the bottom of the shaft, and she set her teeth and lowered her head and ran like she'd never run before, daggers flashing in both hands and not caring who saw them.

She was going to catch the royal agent ahead of her, she *had* to catch him. And in the fray that followed, she was going to prevail.

For if she didn't, Teagan was doomed.

#

Unless in his hard-sighing exhaustion he was mistaken, this was the very last of Ath Cliath's clubs. And like all the rest, there was no sign of any of the three self-styled merchant lords he sought, even in the private back rooms he'd taken so much abuse from the house guards to ascertain they were not, in fact, hiding in. Volundr the Voice turned on the last step, utterly dejected. Where to search *now?*

Well, there was always the chance that they'd been merrily promenading from one club to the next an elegantly-booted stride or two ahead of him, and were now relaxing at home. As he so longed to be. Besides, he didn't know where else to search. So although he'd doubtless be sneered and jeered at by the servants and doorwardens at those grand mansions, he had to go back—for his third visit to each on this foray—and ask again. The high house of "Lord" Cairbre Dathaill was closest, so Volundr set himself to plodding in that direction.

He was too tired, he discovered after half a block, to even think of curses to gasp out. Not that even he would have been listening.

#

She was close behind him now, she was gaining on him, he was more wounded than she'd thought...

And he could only turn to the right and keep up his speed, for three old crones in cowls and old patched robes had just tottered out of an alley-mouth to fill the street to the left, tottering on walking-sticks that looked as old and weathered as they did. He could crash through them, to be sure, but not without being slowed, and then Mist would be upon him.

They were now exclaiming in loud and quavering fear at the man racing right at them, their voices rough and high-pitched, and somehow—gleeful?

Perhaps they viewed all excitement as entertainment that was all too scarce, and so, precious...

But now the shadowhand was dodging to the right to keep clear of them, and Mist was pounding along right behind him, lungs searing and feet getting heavy but as fiercely determined as ever to run the man down and—

And he sidestepped with a grace that didn't seem fitting for a wounded man at all, and spun around to confront her, with a sneer that told her he had no doubt at all how any fray between them would end. Speedily.

There was yet another dagger gleaming in his hand—and then in both hands, as he drew one more steel fang from one of the many, many sheaths he wore all over his dark body-harness.

As he strode to meet her wearing confidence as if it was full battle-armour.

"So, little rabbit," he chuckled, "so eager to die? *Well*, then..." He waved his daggers with a flourish, and came on.

Mist turned her headlong run into an awkward hop to keep from running right onto the points of his daggers, then sidestepped to get out of his reach, planted herself, and—

Gaped in astonishment as two swords burst through the shadowhand from behind, sliding out at different angles amid his gore. He struggled, eyes bulging in astonishment and pain, to run forward off of them, and succeeded, almost falling as he whirled to see his slayers.

And beheld the three crones, swords now in their hands and masks plucked away from beneath cowls to reveal younger male faces that held no mercy, but a calm ruthlessness.

As the one whose sword wasn't yet bloodied cut at him, and when the shadowhand lurched and staggered away, pursued him, hacking with deft precision.

Mist watched open-mouthed as a dagger spun away into the air as the hand that held it flopped, hacked half-off. Another swift rush and another slash, and the other hand lost its dagger—and then all connection to the arm it had adorned for so many years.

The shadowhand mewed in pain and turned to flee, and the warrior who was no crone hamstrung him with a slash across the back of one knee, watched him hop and fall, then finished severing his hands with the almost jovial question, "Your name?"

The shadowhand stared at him, then mumbled something around a great spew of dark blood, and the warrior smiled, nodded, stepped back to ground his blade on the cobbles, and leaned on it to bring a long strip of parchment into view.

"Ah, yes, here you are. Not all that far down the list."

He smiled broadly at the shadowhand's expression, and added, "Oh, yes, Stigr gave us the entire roster of Sitric's sneak-thieves. We'll have you all, in the end. Probably soon."

"Who...who..." the shadowhand tried to ask, but the crone who was not a crone had already turned away to settle his mask back into place, then his cowl, retrieve his walking-stick, and rejoin his fellows in melting back into their alley.

Leaving Mist Damhain standing over the dying shadowhand, with citizens gathering to stare from a safe distance.

A distance large enough that it seemed they did not deem her anything akin to 'safe.' Or perhaps it was just long-reinforced fear of being too close to any shadowhand.

Blood was oozing rather than pumping from the stumps of the dying man's arms now, as his dulling eyes fixed on her. He tried to snarl at her around the bubbling gore, so Mist leaned close and hissed, "I am come to kill the King" into his face.

That brought on a look of horror, so that was what he was wearing when he died.

Mist turned away, feeling sick rather than elated.

She needed Teagan's comforting arms and advice, not more bloodshed.

"Why, yes, Lord Dathaill *is* at home," the splendidly-garbed servant said pleasantly from the top step, for all the world as if Volundr was an unfamiliar but very welcome guest, not a man he'd had two previous and unpleasant encounters with, neither very long ago. "And whom shall I say is calling upon him?"

"A messenger from the King," Volundr said, managing with an effort not to snarl, though his smile would have fooled no blind men, "who brings urgent word from Sitric Cuaran, Lord of Ath Cliath. For your lord's ears alone."

"I shall ascertain if Lord Dathaill's ears are available," the servant replied smoothly, and withdrew, two implacable doorwardens drawing together to form a human wall in the wake of his disappearance to bar Volundr's way to the grand double front doors. Their heavily-armed stances were a silent "Wait here" more curt than any verbal one could have been.

Volundr found himself too tired to take the slightest offense.

#

"Welcoming, isn't it?" Sirnir murmured to Stigr as they stood in the street gazing up at the rising stone magnificence of Mor's mansion. The sculptor of the pack of guardian vargr adorning the stone blocks at the foot of the curving flight of entry steps had designed their stony glares to intersect right where the nine shadowhands were standing.

Uneasily, because although they feared nothing and no one in Ath Cliath save Mael the Sharp and the King above him, they were used to skulking and dark-hours work, not striding along openly in public, being stared at with curious hostility.

And although the sun was lowering, it was still broad daylight, not yet sunset, as they stood before the rising spires of the house of Mor.

"Cheap intimidation," Stigr snorted. "Intended to make up for the fact that, so far as I know, there are but three women inside the place, one of them elderly and bedridden."

As if in response to his scorn, the front door opened, and a tall woman in a dark gown strode out. She looked not at them, but up at the beautiful black lantern that hung, tall and ornate, in the stone archway above her.

Her gaze might have held dragon fire, for the lantern promptly kindled, untouched and otherwise unbidden, into bright flame.

Only then did the woman drop her gaze to favour them all with an unfriendly look.

"I know why you've come," she said calmly. "So we may as well get started."

CHAPTER 29

"It is my pleasure and my duty," Volundr said, drawing himself up to full tiptoe height and throwing out his chest in his usual fashion, "to deliver unto you the words of the King: you, Cairbre Dathaill, are hereby summoned into the royal presence, at the Riverfleet Palace, and expected to attend the King in person, sending no envoy nor other representative in thy place, as expeditiously as humanly possible on your part. You are to communicate with no other persons beyond your personal servants, and send no word to any other individual by any means, of this royal summons. Delay not, but present yourself before the King. Who, I may add, was far less than pleased at your departure, the last time he summoned you to the Palace."

"Meaning, don't do it again?" Cairbre asked, obviously amused.

"I mean just that," Volundr said severely.

"I hear and understand," the merchant lord drawled. "You have my leave to depart, Voice of the King, so you can hasten and inform Lecora and Torloch of the same summons. For you want all three of us as usual, hmm?"

"Er, yes," Volundr replied, bowing and backing away. "I don't think it's betraying any royal confidence to confirm that."

"Good, being as it's blot-bleeding obvious," Cairbre responded, reaching for a decanter. "I'll just freshen my throat. Walking across this city is thirsty work for any purpose or at any time or in any mood, I've discovered."

"Indeed," Volundr said dryly, bowing his way back through the door.

Cairbre waved him a mocking farewell as two carefully expressionless doorwardens drew that door closed, and waved the King's envoy along the way out as if he was a stranger to this mansion and the city beyond it.

Strangely, Volundr found his spirits raised by the mocking gesture.

#

The shadowhand beside Stigr drew his favourite knife and threw it in one lightning-swift motion, but the woman under the lantern was faster. She ducked, the knife sailed into the entry hall over her shoulder—

and the front door slammed.

Stigr gave the knife-hurler an amused glance.

"I'll get it back," he snapped.

Stigr nodded, and looked to the most distant of his nine. "Leidulfr?"

"Harekr just gave the signal," Leidulfr called back, not bothering with stealth. Stigr nodded. That meant the three shadowhands sent behind the mansion, to make sure no one escaped out the back door, were in position and ready.

So...twelve shadowhands, and Stigr himself, against three women. One bedridden, but all of them poisoners and wielders of some sort of magic.

So why were his thoughts so dark?

He shrugged, and made the hand-signal that meant the assault on Mor's mansion should begin.

In response, his nine eyed the walls and upper windows of the grand old house, paying the front door and lower windows no attention, as they were the likeliest to be trapped. Then, one by one, they chose their spots and started to climb.

The walls were old and of well-fitted stone, but the shadowhands were veterans, and scaled the blocks with deft ease, as swiftly as a tiler or painter might climb a good steady ladder. Heading for the upper windows, three and four floors up. And once there, they clung and waited, so as to be ready to attack the shutters—drawn shut, every pair—in unison. Two mobile women, no matter how swift, can't be everywhere at once.

Now.

Stigr made a cluck-clucking sound, and nine belt-chisels struck nine pairs of shutters at once. Trying for speed, not stealth, shattering the wood and tearing the fragments aside to shower down, to smash through the windows beyond and inside.

Seven shutters gave way readily, and seven men plunged inside.

Only to come hurtling back out and plunging to the cobbles below.

Two of them, necks broken or faces crushed, never moved again. A third and fourth struggled to rise feebly, but failed, groaning, limbs broken. Three got up, bruised and wincing.

The two whose shutters had offered more resistance faltered and then froze, looking down at the carnage and then at Stigr for orders.

"*What,*" Stigr demanded, waving that pair back down to the ground, "just happened?"

"Effigies awaiting us," one of the fallen but still mobile shadowhands answered tersely. "Stone warriors covered with runes. We went in, at speed—and they punched us right back out again."

"So which one of the women is the galdr?" one shadowhand panted to another, who shrugged.

"It matters little, here and now. Time enough for speculating on that when we're taking the old woman's head back to show the King."

"You've got to get a head in this world," Leidulfr muttered darkly, and started climbing the mansion walls again.

#

"You've got to get a head in this world," Volundr the Voice snarled aloud, as he lurched down yet another street. "And I for one will be glad when these three merchant lords lose theirs. They rush around this city like gulls racing after dropped fish. If they'd just *stay put*, Odin take them!"

"Odin," growled an old man striding the other way shoving a heavily-laden handcart, "takes us all, soon enough."

"Hel takes us all," Volundr corrected him. "Odin wants us all to flourish and triumph. Just like King Sitric."

"Hunh," the old man shot back over his shoulder. "That'd be why the one of them gave us Fimbulwinter, and the other one beggars us with taxes so he can live high and proud, hey?"

And Volundr trudged on, unable to think of any crushing answer to that.

A block away, he uttered a hearty "Bah!" but it offered no comfort. He eyed some squawking gulls on a nearby rooftop and thought gloomily of how much wind and footsore weariness he'd save if he somehow learned to fly.

#

"Handaxes," Stigr ordered curtly. "Traps or no traps, front door it is. Unless all of you have learned to fly in these last few moments."

The shadowhands nodded. Save for Leidulfr, halfway up the walls again, who called,

162

"Roof hatch?"

Stigr indicated the various roofs of the mansion with a flourish. "Go see."

In silence, hefting their handaxes—actually short-handled pickaxes, with stout curving spikes protruding from the back of the axe-heads—he and the rest of the shadowhands watched Leidulfr climb the walls to a flat part of the mansion roof that had a railing around it.

And watched his axe crash down, twice and thrice, and heard wood splinter.

And then saw his body jump convulsively into the air, driven up by three crossbow bolts thudding up into his gut, to reel and stagger backwards and over the railing. Leidulfr crashed off an impressive number of roof-edges and balcony railings as limply as a child's rag doll ere finally slamming into the street cobbles with more splatter than thud.

"Front door it is," Stigr repeated laconically, into the silence that followed, and the remaining pair of still-mobile shadowhands moved forward as one. Reluctantly.

#

Volundr eyed the ornate front door of Torloch Dargan's mansion with distaste, then reluctantly mounted the flight of six broad steps that led up to it—for the fourth time since he'd left the Palace to deliver this latest royal summons—and bypassed the large knocker, this time, in favour of pulling the bell-cord.

His reward was a deep, muffled tolling from within that was grand and ponderous enough to belong to the Palace, and not a mere private residence.

Volundr glared sourly at the closed and glossy-polished black front door. It was past time the King humbled these three merchant lords. Or better yet, executed them. That would show Ath Cliath that its King was not to be crossed.

The door swung open in well-oiled silence, and an elegantly black-clad steward stepped out.

"I am the King's senior royal envoy," Volundr announced, as if he and this servant had never seen each other before, rather than having enjoyed two previous confrontations earlier this day and half a dozen previously, "and the King has sent me here to speak with Torloch Dargan *without delay.*"

"Ah," the steward exclaimed pleasantly. "And whom shall I say is calling?"

When Volundr gave the man his best stony glare, the steward added mildly, "I presume you have a name?"

"I do, and it hasn't changed since the last time I tendered it," Volundr told him flatly. "So kindly dispense with the unnecessary verbal fencing, which merely demeans you, and go and tell Torloch I have to deliver the King's commands to him. *If* he wants to avoid the fate of Ardgal Loughnane."

"We *are* testy today, aren't we?" the steward observed reprovingly, shaking his head, and withdrew, slamming the door so it boomed shut in Volundr's face.

The envoy demonstrated that he was indeed testy by spewing a rapid sequence of the most heartfelt and colourful oaths that came into his mind.

They lasted almost until the front door opened again.

#

Stigr didn't even have time to shout a warning ere one of the two shadowhands hewing at the door was pinned to it by a heavy war-quarrel between his shoulderblades; the narrow window it had been fired from was already banging shut again.

He was a long time dying, but by then Stigr had sent his surviving fellow shadowhand around the mansion to bring back Harekr and the two shadowhands under his command. They dragged the two maimed shadowhands down the street until its curve and therefore the intervening walls of buildings rendered them safely out of bowshot.

When Stigr ordered them to attack the front door again, Harekr pointed out that the back door he'd been guarding wasn't overlooked by any windows that would allow a defender a good vantage point for archery or hurling refuse or any sort of attack, so with a sigh of exasperated acceptance, Stigr waved them around the house to the back door.

And were there, or were there not, some titters of mirth from behind slightly-ajar shutters in neighbouring houses, as the shadowhands abandoned their frontal assault?

#

"Beard of Odin!" exclaimed Torloch Dargan heartily, "if it isn't my old friend Volundr the Voice, faithful warhorn of my King! And how does Fimbulwinter find you this morning, hmm?"

"*Executing* my royal duty with my usual right good will," Volundr snapped. "Wherefore, know you, that it is my pleasure and my duty to deliver unto you the words of the King: you, Torloch Dargan, are hereby summoned into the royal presence, at the Riverfleet Palace, and expected to attend the King in person, sending no envoy nor other representative in thy place, as expeditiously as humanly possible on your part. You are to communicate with no other persons beyond your personal servants, and send no word to any other individual by any means, of this royal summons. Delay not, but present yourself before the King forthwith, in all haste."

"My, my," Dargan replied. "Me alone, or have you already delivered the same summons to Lecora and Cairbre?"

"All three of you are summoned to attend the King," Volundr replied curtly, spun on his heel, and started trudging away.

"In a hurry to get off duty and rest your feet?" came the mocking question from behind him, but the King's envoy did not bother to reply, or even turn his head. He might not even have energy or wind enough to get back to the Palace, and he still had to find and deliver the King's words to Lecora O'Hart. Whose various rudenesses somehow always stung him far more than the levity of the two male lords.

The two *remaining* male *self-styled* lords, he reminded himself spitefully, and let himself gloat for the seven strides the glee that thought brought him lasted.

"The Lady O'Hart's house, as I recall, lies in *that* direction," the steward said helpfully, pointing.

Volundr limped past the man without a word or glance. Odin smite him *down*.

He waited for a groan or thud as he went down the steps, but in vain. It seemed Odin was hard of hearing just now.

#

"You will go," Mor said firmly, "and you will *not* tarry to try any nastiness against the King or his shadowhands, but will leave the city just as fast as you can get onto Runa's boat. The people of Hibernia will need aid in this deepening winter, and whatever comes after it, long after Norse kings are gone from Ath Cliath and everywhere else. I have lived a long and full life; do not turn its ending into ashes by forgoing the rest of the long and full life you were born to live."

Embla glared back at her, but then dropped her gaze and bowed her head in obedience. "I hate this, but I will do it. You are wise, and right. You have *always* been right. Doesn't that weary

164

you, sometimes?"

"Child," Mor replied, "you have *no* idea just how much it wearies me. Someday you will. But by then I trust Sitric Cuaran will be long in his grave, and many more Norse fools besides. Entertain yourself by helping to put your share of them there. Now *go*. These underhanded King's slayers are bumbling dolts, but they won't take forever. You should be gone."

Embla stepped forward, kissed her mother fiercely, then whirled away and was gone through the door and down the tunnel beyond. Mor closed the door, then the door in front of that door, and then drew the tapestry that concealed that outer door back into place.

And walked back to meet her doom. Calmly.

#

The back door of Mor's mansion yielded readily enough, opening into an apparently deserted passage. The shadowhands were half-astonished to find neither defenders nor traps, and raced up the servants' stair when they found it, Stigr at the rear.

They were fast and deft men of action, and so struck aside the various darts that came hissing at them from the darkness above. Poisoned, no doubt, but harmless when they found not their targets.

Harekr took rearguard, and Stigr kept ahead of him, and three lower-ranking shadowhands took great wary care.

And so their unseen attacker was forced to retreat before them as they advanced like prowling cats, gaining ground room by room and floor by floor. They were six floors up, by Stigr's reckoning, when they turned a dogleg corner and found themselves—so far as they could see in the unlit gloom—in a long, straight, narrow passage.

"I mislike the look of this," one of the shadowhands muttered. Yet silence reigned, and no attack came, as they cautiously advanced.

"Light the lantern," Stigr ordered another, "but keep it hooded. I want our careers as targets to be short." This was done, and they continued on in the endless listening silence, wondering when the attack would come.

Which was when Harekr heard a small sound far behind. A thump, as if something solid had butted into something else solid. There followed a click; something metallic fastening.

He hurried back, and found the straight passage now ended in a wall that hadn't been there before.

By the time he'd hastened back to Stigr to whisper what he'd discovered, the rest of Stigr's force had heard another thump and click. And found the passage ahead ended in a wall.

About then, there came a squealing sound from the wall to their left.

That went on for some time. It sounded like a wheel or capstan that rarely turned was now turning.

"Unhood the lantern," Stigr ordered. And went to the wall and put the toe of his boot against it.

And promptly felt the wall shoving against him.

He drew a dagger, set it down where floor and wall met, and stepped back. In the lamplight they watched it move, thrust sideways by the advancing wall.

The five men traded glances. Not a word did they need to waste for all of them to know that they were caught in a trap that would pin and then crush them.

"The ceiling," Stigr said. "Harekr, you be the bench. The rest of you, take turns standing on his back and using your picks on the ceiling, right at the wall ahead of us. Stop and say if you lay bare solid stone."

The shadowhands scrambled, for their lives now depended on haste.

And as Stigr had hoped, the picks on the backs of their axeheads shattered plaster and brought it down, then the stretched hide and lath above it, laying bare beams with boards above them. Beams spaced widely enough that a man turning himself could fit his shoulders through them.

Reversing their axes and working in swift shifts ere they tired, they attacked the boards. Wood shrieked and thundered, and splinters flew.

The first shadowhand to break through was boosted up in a rush that didn't save him, for Agata was ready with a long, slender blade and ran him through.

But he twisted on it, snarling, as he died, and so dragged it from her grasp—and when he fell, two of his fellow agents swarmed up into the room above the deadly passage.

Poisoned darts found their faces and necks right away, but they kept their feet as the poison burned through their veins, and rushed her, one old woman with daggers in both hands.

One shadowhand tossed something to the other, who caught it and veered away, pulling taut a wire that sliced through Agata's wrists and sent her daggers clattering to the floor. Before she could get away or even begin to shriek the shadowhands charged—and the wire sliced her head from her shoulders, sending it bouncing and rolling amid much gore.

The headless women was still toppling as Stigr and Harekr clawed their ways up and past her, lantern swaying.

There was an archway beyond, and another a little way beyond that, and light coming from a chamber farther on.

They went there, and found themselves in a dim, lofty-ceilinged room hung with a labyrinth of tapestries. There was an old smell.

With dagger and sword the four shadowhands advanced, slicing aside tapestry after tapestry, going slowly as they looked up at the ceiling above and down at the floor below for traps at every wary step.

They found no such perils as they cut their way along, tunneling through hanging after hanging until quite suddenly the latest one to sigh away under their sharp steel was the last, and they found themselves facing an old crone, black-gowned and regal, sitting on a bed as if it was a throne. Her eyes were black as night, and as sharp as the points of two drawn daggers.

"You are the woman called Mor?" Stigr asked.

"I've been waiting for you," came the calm, fearless reply.

"*You are Mor?*" Stigr snapped sharply. "Answer me, in the name of the King!"

Wrinkled old lips twisted into a smile. In a shrunken, almost hairless head that looked like a skull.

"This, fool who serves an evil king, is how you win victory, but discover you have found defeat after all," the old woman told Stigr, and blew him a kiss.

And fire flared in her dark eyes—an instant before the world vanished in roaring flames.

ChAPTER 30

The Palace bells tolled; they were closing the gates. At what would have been nightfall, ere the coming of Fimbulwinter.

A footsore and winded Volundr the Voice turned to face where the sun should have been setting.

And sighed.

The King's orders had been very clear: he was to keep at the task of finding the three merchants until he could deliver the royal summons, face to face, to all three of them. Just as soon as possible.

Which was why, weary as he was, he had just turned his back on the mansion of Lecora O'Hart, where an oh-so-kindly servant had directed him to a club where she *might* be. Halfway across the city.

Cursing mightily, he trudged off in search of it.

Three blocks along, he came upon some excitement that might have interested him if he hadn't been so Odin-bedamned *tired*.

First came a blast that rocked the cobbles under his feet and left him blinking, as shattered tiles rained down everywhere, shards clacking off walls and roofs and the stones of the street.

Then patrols of goldhelms rushed past him, heading for a fiery glow that was climbing into the dark sky ahead with frightening speed.

Around the next corner, he saw the conflagration directly. He was gazing at the towering flames of a raging fire, with a stone building at its heart. A mansion of some size was burning— and no one was getting out of that inferno alive.

The heat beat at his face, but Volundr gave it all only a brief glance as he trudged on. Fires, no matter how spectacular, didn't find him Lady Lecora O'Harts.

Two corpses were lying in the street ahead, broken arms and legs splayed grotesquely. Volundr kept walking.

Two men, dressed like shadowhands—yes, there were the sheathed daggers all over them, belts crisscrossing their dark leathers.

With a start, he realized they hadn't perished of their broken limbs; they'd died because someone had slit their throats.

Droplets of blood on the cobbles trailed away in the direction of several nearby houses.

Had *multiple* people had cut their throats?

And with another start, Volundr realized he knew them both: senior shadowhands of the King.

So just who among Ath Cliath's citizens was formidable enough to defeat veteran royal agents?

Worse than that, who among the folk of the city would dare?

#

The Palace bells tolled; they were closing the gates. At what would have been nightfall, ere the coming of Fimbulwinter.

Neven smiled sourly and stepped out of the dark doorway he'd been waiting in. Stigr had no doubt arranged a trap, ahead in the Palace, to have a certain Neven Daunt killed.

So he'd not try for the two remaining targets tonight, but use the secret way in and then just lurk and watch, to see what befell.

He went to the Palace wall, put his back to it to gaze all around in the gloom in search of the man—or men—he *knew* were following him, but saw no sign of them.

Not that he'd really expected to; they'd be shadowhands, and good ones.

But they'd not be expecting him to do what he was going to do the moment he got through the secret passage, so this just might work.

He went into the passage with daggers drawn, but doubted any attack or trap would be waiting in that tiny dark way; it was too busy a route, and too useful as a royal secret, to have any alarm or fuss associated with it. There were probably standing orders about doing nothing too near it.

Through it without incident, swift and keeping low, because he had to reach cover before his tail traversed it behind him.

He managed it, going belly down under a garden planting nigh some dark windows across the Palace yard in the opposite direction from the door he should have been trying for. And lying still, to watch and wait.

And sure enough, he'd barely drawn his third silent-as-he-could manage breath when a dark figure stepped silently out of the passage and headed for the door.

Neven Daunt bided right where he was until a good six breaths after the man who'd been stalking him had vanished inside the Palace a good.

And it was as well he did, because here came *another* visitation via the secret way through the wall: six men, skulking like excited lads on a lark. At the fore was a man Neven knew: Lord Cairbre Dathaill.

So, undercover agents of the King, or here to do the King ill?

Very likely the latter. Hmm. *Very* interesting. What if he relocated to just beside the secret passage, to await who came back out?

Then he could slip back into the surrounding city just head of whoever it turned out to be, or lie in wait in the pitch-black confines of the passage itself to slice them. Depending on who they were. He'd not mind murdering a few shadowhands; violent death was a fitting fate for every last one of them—though he probably couldn't make it as painful and slow as they truly deserved.

Neven Daunt smiled, and rose from the garden with vengeful blade drawn.

#

"Just don't waste any," Cairbre had warned, "as I can't get any more soon—and I doubt we'll get a second chance."

His men—loyal servants, all—had nodded in silent unison. Now, though, the nearest one leaned close to whisper in his lord's ear, "Kill the shadowhand?"

"No, let him go. We're here to poison the royal wine, not butcher royal agents. Their turn will come soon enough. I fear we'll run out of time before we can find it all; our King can put it away like a berserker thrice his size, and doesn't like to run short."

Cairbre's fears proved well founded; they went from room to room and wine cellar to known wine cellar, patiently squirting exotic venoms from their little hand-bladders into a seemingly endless array of decanters, kegs, and casks.

Until the moment came when they rounded a corner to face the sudden blinding light of an unhooded lantern, and above it the cruel smile of the Seneschal, surrounded by a dozen soldiers in half-armour.

"Surrender," he sneered, "*and* die."

Cairbre Dathaill's response was a wordless charge at him—but when soldiers stepped in front of the Seneschal to defend him, he darted aside and past, sword slashing back to hamstring the nearest goldhelm.

In the silent moments of dancing and lunging that followed, the merchant lord and his bladesmen seemed to be everywhere, and soldier after soldier died fervently wishing they were in full armour, with gorgets and all.

In a seeming trice the Seneschal was backing away from them, pale with fear. Alone, with all of the soldiers he'd commanded sprawled dead before him.

"How—? Mercy!" he gasped. "I—*urrkh!*"

In the flickering light of the lantern clutched in his trembling hand, he stared down in disbelief at the sword, dark and slick with his own blood, that had sprouted out of his belly. From behind.

"He didn't even see Anlon slip around behind him," one of Cairbre's men said in disbelief, as the Seneschal sank to his knees and slid off the sword that had slain him, choking and gurgling on his own blood.

Cairbre shrugged. "He's wont to see nothing but the nose on his own face. When he's preening in front of his mirror, every few hours. That's the trouble with a King who hands out Court offices as rewards. Now let's get the rest of this venom put where it'll do some good."

They hastened to do that, but might have tainted wine with less calmness had they known that the Seneschal had alerted on-duty shadowhands to prepare a deadly farewell for Cairbre and his men in the secret passage through the Palace wall.

In the end, no such reception awaited at their departure, though the secret passage was sticky with blood underfoot—for the shadowhands hastening to be that trap never saw Neven Daunt awaiting them in the darkness, with drawn steel that he fed each of them as they set foot in the secret passage, one by one.

#

"This is good cheese," Brandr murmured, as Ath Cliath receded behind them, and the chill of the river rose on all sides.

"And better ale," Hallvardr Thorolfsson replied, passing the hand-keg over. The bread was gone already, and much of the haunch, too.

Brandr looked around; they seemed to have the river to themselves. Theirs was the last in a string of empty barges being towed downriver to fetch firewood to take back to hearths all over the city. The silent rowers in the ship at the head of the string worked for the Lady; ship and barges were both owned by the Lady Lecora O'Hart, and enriched her at every firewood-fetching upriver trip.

Where the string docked, that ship would pick up not just small mountains of cut and split wood, but the infamous Gloa the Golden, who'd been downriver on a buying trip.

Brandr and Hallvardr, however, were to remain downriver until Lecora sends word to them to return aboard the barge on a later trip.

"It may be six days or twelve, or more," she'd warned them. "It all depends on what the One-Eyed King does with what we're about to dump into his lap."

However, a senior tax collector awaited them, whom they could question thoroughly—using Hallvardr's galdr rune spells as a threat, if need be—to get him to tell them all he knew of Sitric Cuaran's money flows, so Brandr could render a useful report back to the Uterni.

"There's a boat following us," Brandr said suddenly, pointing. "No lights."

Hallvardr squinted. "Not following," he grunted. "Overtaking. Not interested in the likes of us. Runa's running someone out of Ath Cliath who wants to leave quick and quiet, seen by none—the King's spies least of all."

"This Runa does that a lot?"

Hallvardr grinned. "You'd be surprised. Now pass back that ale."

#

It was well after the triple bell that signalled the opening of the Palace gates when a reeling, dog-tired Volundr the Voice finally found the Lady Lecora O'Hart—who looked as fresh and rested as if she'd been at home abed all night, and half the day before that.

He delivered the King's summons in more of a croak than his usual full-blown pomposity, then lurched away yawning uncontrollably.

His nose led him to one of the sailor's taverns by the docks, where meat was sizzling. His stomach promptly rumbled like an angry bull, so he appeased it with a huge breakfast, then plodded three thresholds down to a nondescript old door he pounded on ruthlessly until a sleepy old seithkona he knew answered, her hair a wild rook's nest and her eyes only half open.

He left her beaming with the amount of gold he'd emptied into her hands, in return for a potion that could rouse the weary.

And it worked, too.

Fortified and invigorated, heart racing but all fatigue gone, Volundr the Voice swaggered back in the direction of the Palace, gleefully triumphant.

Next time, he'd be properly sneering and high-handed to whoever the King sent him to deliver a message to. That was, after all, what made the job fun.

Now, though, after working all the night through wearing down his boot-leather and getting his finery soaked with sweat, he was more than due for a celebratory drink.

Ah, but not that swill at the Palace—the King kept the good stuff for himself.

Besides, Sitric Cuaran and most of his courtiers preferred fiery-strong, sourer drinks than the King's best and most senior envoy, who liked the sweeter fruit wines now flooding into Ath Cliath.

Which meant he'd head for home, and his own cellar.

Yes!

Grandly he hailed the next patrol of goldhelms he saw, and commanded them to hasten to the Palace to inform the King that the three merchant lords had all personally received their summons. Then, dusting his hands in satisfaction, Volundr the Voice headed for his own home.

A modest enough domicile as yet, being as the tastefully-rearing stone lyngormyr carvings he'd ordered hadn't yet arrived to flank his front door, but he liked it, and when he finished acquiring and razing the houses on either side to expand his place into the fitting mansion it should be, he'd have a cellar as large as his current feasting hall.

And servants, to boot. Right now, the place was dark and lonely.

Yet his familiar chair and lamp were comfortable enough, and he'd put half a horn of his favourite wine inside him when there came a knock upon his door.

Someone using the knocker hesitantly but repeatedly. But who, at this time of a morning?

Volundr frowned and made for the door, ire rising in him.

By the time he flung the door wide and drew breath for a snarl of profanity, rage was dark in him. He caught it between his teeth when he saw it was a Palace servant, and a woman, too; for it might be word from the King.

Confusion dampened his anger when he saw tears in her eyes.

"Oh, Volundr," she said, and anger soared in him again at such familiarity. Where was her use of his title, her deference, her groveling?

"It's Muirenn. You recall the storm that so ravaged the city? She was caught out in it, rounding up her cows. Lightning struck her. She's dead, Volundr."

Muirenn *dead?* Volundr stared at the servant in disbelief, shaking his head, but she was nodding, weeping openly now.

He dropped the drinking horn, his favourite wine suddenly tasting like filth in his mouth, and staggered unseeingly away.

#

"It's a passable forgery, no more," Torloch warned. "I paid well, and the woman has some skill, but she had only three samples of Cuaran's fist to work from."

Lecora shrugged. "A passable forgery is all it has to be. We can't use it unless Sitric is too dead to object."

"True enough," Cairbre agreed. They strode on, and the gates of the Palace loomed up before them.

The forgery they'd been discussing, neatly folded, rode beneath the insole of Torloch's left boot: a writ of abdication formerly turning the Riverfleet Throne over to a council of merchant lords, that was also a suicide note. They hoped to find the King dead of drinking poisoned wine, so they could put it with his body.

Sitric was known to drink wine with every meal, and more besides—and Cairbre had poisoned all the wine in the Palace he could find.

Which was all the wine in the Palace, they hoped.

Their very lives might depend on that hope.

Yet nothing seemed amiss as courtiers smoothly guided them into one of the inner, more private audience chambers.

A room lined with tapestries, two of whom parted within moments of their arrival, to reveal King Sitric Cuaran, very much alive.

Tall and at ease and somehow terrible, he smiled at them and silently downed horn after horn of wine, raising each as if in a toast to them.

He knows.

And then the One-Eyed King poured them each a goblet, setting the golden cups, brim-full, on a table before them.

"Lords and Lady," he purred, "will you not drink to the burgeoning health of our fair city?"

They hesitated, then took up the goblets.

After all, he was drinking and taking no harm...but was some galdr magic or other protecting him?

"You *worms*," the King sneered. As masked and hooded shadowhands rushed out from behind tapestries all around the room to seize hold of the three merchants.

Stripping them with brutal, hard hands, tearing their clothing off them and searching them thoroughly. In Lecora's case, Mael made very sure she was hiding nothing, anywhere about her person, and by his smile, she knew very well who he was, despite the mask.

The writ was found in Torloch's boot and brought to the King, who read it expressionlessly. Then looked up at the three merchants with a cold smile and said, "You see, I know all about your plan. As anyone can be bought."

As the trio eyed each other with dawning suspicion, Sitric Cuaran drawled, "Nonetheless, I will spare you. *This* time. For Ath Cliath is home to all, and will enrich all, and ensure the survival of as many as possible in this deepening Fimbulwinter."

They stared at him mutely, shadowhand daggers at their throats.

"Oh, yes. For now, I need you alive and well, but obedient to my rule."

He was gloating openly now, strolling back and forth in front of the three naked merchants.

"My shadowhands," he commanded, "escort these good *and loyal* citizens of Ath Cliath back to their homes. Now that they've seen the error of their ways."

Lecora bent back helpless over his arm, Mael jerked his head in silent direction, and the shadowhands holding Cairbre hustled him towards the door.

Then Mael looked to Torloch's captors, and they forced their lord after Cairbre.

Whereupon Mael collapsed, Lecora twisting free of him as he fell.

"Mael?" The King demanded sharply, but Mael lay in an unmoving heap on the floor.

"Take her!" Sitric Cuaran commanded to the other shadowhands with Mael, pointing at Lecora—but one by one, as they strode towards her, they fell on their faces, too.

Cairbre's escort had similarly collapsed—and as Sitric stared, those gripping Torloch fell, one after another.

Leaving the One-Eyed King facing the three naked merchants. Alone.

They advanced on him, plucking up daggers from the fallen shadowhands as they came, and Sitric hastily retreated, fear rising onto his face. And backed into the table where he'd set the goblets of wine, upsetting it onto the floor.

Hastily he recovered himself. Yet they made no move to rush him.

Lecora met his eyes. Her gaze held him like a snare.

"Remember, O King," she said, soft menace in her voice, "that we *loyal* subjects spared you. When we could have been rid of you at last. Rule well. Oh, I warn you: rule well."

#

It was the quietest, most private corner of the House of The Hanged Man, though the entire tavern was brighter and cleaner than it had been in its earlier, lowlier incarnation as the Skald's Beard.

So Grimkell was trying to speak quietly, and to keep his fellow conspirators muttering in low tones, too. Yet the drink was having its usual effects, and the volume level had been rising for some time.

"Fork, that'll *never* work."

"Well, Eylir, why don't you think of something brilliant, then? After all he's only *one* king! We have him outnumbered!"

"Sshhh! *Idiot!* You *want* to die on the end of some shadowhand's dagger?"

"Borekr, *shut it.* Now, what about..." Falki leaned forward over the table to whisper.

"No, no, that'll never work," Grimkell the Throat growled.

"Ah, but what if we...no, no, that won't work either."

They were interrupted, then, by a sudden, grief-ridden outburst of song, tuneless but heartfelt.

The Hanged Man fell silent as Volundr the Voice, thoroughly drunk, raised his voice in lament, one of the old, old songs for the departed.

He couldn't carry a tune, only remembered about half of the words, and his voice was raw and harsh with grief—but the din is arresting, and all chatter fell silent in the tavern.

Even passersby in the street outside paused to listen, as the Voice of the King rose, quavered on one last, flat note, then ended with a despairing shout, "Gone! *Gone!* What is there to live for *now?*"

THE END

When the voice of the One-Eyed King is heard in the house of the hanged man, life will finally take a change for the brighter.

Fate of the Norns: Ragnarok
SAGA - FAFNIR'S TREASURE

Fate of the Norns: Ragnarok
CORE RULEBOOK

CHILDREN OF ERIU

Fate of the Norns: Ragnarok
LORDS OF THE ASH

PENDELHAVEN PUBLISHING